THE RENEGADE BILLIONAIRE

HAPPINESS EVER AFTER

AVERY MAXWELL

That's What She Said Publishing, Inc.

THE Renegade BILLIONAIRE

ISBN: 979-8-88643-960-1 (ebook)

ISBN: 979-8-88643-961-8 (paperback)

averymaxwellbooks.com

012025

PLAYLIST

Music is usually a very important part of my process. I spend days curating a playlist that fits the vibe of the story I think I'm about to write. With this story, my characters liked to go off script sometimes, so I'd write in silence for a few days while I got them back on track.

But for Braxton and Madi, some of my favorite moments in their story are set to music...I just had to get in the weeds and feel it as they would.

And once I did, the small fictional town of Happiness, Georgia came to life in the most vibrant of ways.

I hope you enjoy the soundtrack to their story. You can download it here:

https://geni.us/TRBPlaylist

AUTHOR NOTE

My stories are created the way I see life—big, messy, and full of love. In real life, love stories are not created in a bubble that only includes the hero and the heroine. They happen in the relationships that make love amazing—the family with opinions, the protective friends, the chaos-inducing side characters that bring us all together.

And you get them all in my books.

The meddling family, the sidekicks, the tension breakers, the friends who are more like family, they are what make my love stories feel so very real.

I hope you enjoy them all.

Braxton and Madi both grew up fighting for love that should have been given freely, and it shaped who they became in adulthood. Braxton grew up as an overachiever, fighting his parents' belief system every chance he got, while Madison's goals for herself were very different. She wasn't looking for a big, grandiose life; she simply wanted safety, security, and peace as so many of us do.

In The Renegade Billionaire, pregnancy is discussed in all its scary, amazing facets. It also explores the emotions and feelings of what happens when you're scared to want something but also terrified of not getting it.

You also see alcoholism through the eyes of an innocent casualty of the disease—Madison.

If you or anyone you know is struggling with addiction, please reach out for help.

https://www.usa.gov/substance-abuse

Love, like life, is complicated.

Xoxo,

Avery

BRAXTON

LAUGHTER IS INAPPROPRIATE. I WILL NOT LAUGH AT THE reading of this will.

If I keep saying it in my head while staring straight ahead, perhaps I'll keep myself in check.

"That's the biggest hourglass I've ever seen," my childhood best friend, Greyson, whispers out the side of his mouth, and I quietly cough to hide my smile.

Smiling at a will reading isn't acceptable either, especially in these circles.

"I'm certain that's Ace's doing." It definitely aligns with my grandfather's sense of humor. This was the first attorney's office I'd ever been in, when I moved in with Ace and he brought me along to meet with his lawyer. Mr. Coop hasn't changed a damn thing in all those years.

The hourglass stands close to six feet high and takes up a good portion of the book-lined wall—it must be four feet wide.

Greyson glances at his watch. "Think they'll show up on time?"

"Money is involved. They'll be here." I lean into his

space and lower my voice. "I bet when my grandfather adopted you and Sage all those years ago, you never thought you'd end up staring at an hourglass big enough to pass for a center lineman—let alone one engraved with two men sitting cross-legged facing each other on it."

It sends us over the edge, and laughter erupts from us both. If others find that offensive...well, truly, I really don't give a shit, because the reality is, this is fucking ridiculous. And Ace would've loved it, so I have no doubt he's the reason this particular monstrosity is sitting in here now.

"Trust me," Grey says under his breath, "had we not moved in with you and Ace when we did, we'd be looking at something else equally disturbing, but without the stable mental health to deal with it."

My family is messed up, but so is Grey's. He and his nephew came to live with us after his sister, Violet, died giving birth to Sage when she was seventeen years old.

Unfortunately, Grey's childhood has left scars that may never heal. His mother passed away when he was seven, and their entire family fell apart. My family didn't want me but wouldn't give up their parental rights, but Grey's dad—well —he's a monster of another kind.

When his dad found out about Violet's pregnancy, he made choices that landed him in prison—we were twelve the day everything changed.

With no other living relatives, custody of Grey and Sage was awarded to Ace. And my parents had already left me on my grandfather's doorstep years before, only checking in when it suited my mother or when my father, Alistair, wanted to throw his weight around.

I think they'd have done anything not to see me every day. It's why we vowed to protect Sage—and we took owner-ship of his care the day he was born.

From the ashes, we created our own family.

A family my parents can never compare to.

Mr. Coop enters the office with his suit buttoned up as though he weren't at our home a few hours ago, clinking glasses to honor the life of an amazing man.

"They didn't show up for the wake. Do we really think they'll show up here?" Grey asks bitterly. He has even more reason to hate my family than I do.

Where they had indifference for me, they flat-out loathed him because Ace treated him as his own grandson.

"I made it perfectly clear that all accounts are frozen until the stipulations of the will have been met." Mr. Coop's voice wobbles with age but also with sadness. He was a close friend and confidant of my grandfather for longer than I've been alive.

"They'll be here," Grey and I say in unison.

"Nothing's more important to them than money." The words burn the back of my throat.

"What's with the hourglass?" Grey asks Mr. Coop while attempting to cover the twitch of his lips with the back of his hand.

"Another way to fuck with us, I'm sure." Alistair, my sperm donor of a father, mutters as he strides into the room with false confidence that the world cowers before him.

And in some situations, people do. But I haven't been that man in ten years.

My mother, Amara, and siblings follow him into the room and stand behind him, forming the familiar A-frame I was always excluded from.

"A still stands for asshole," Grey whispers. Alistair, Amara, Anastasia, and Archie.

I peel my gaze away from my family. I spent years attempting to gain approval from them, but they were never going to accept me. Alistair made sure of that by naming me Braxton and giving me my grandfather's surname. I was the oops baby left to be raised by my grandfather.

A selfish act made by selfish people, but it's one I'll always be grateful for. I am who I am today because of Ace.

"I don't have all day, Peter," Alistair barks, causing the older man to startle in his seat.

Reaching over the desk, I place my palm on his stack of papers while directing my glare at Alistair. "Take your time, Mr. Coop. No one is rushing you."

"Don't you—"

"Enough." The threat steeling my tone has all the A-holes turning in my direction.

"Don't forget your place, Reyes." Alistair hisses it out as an insult—he always has—but his words stopped cutting me open when I learned what kind of man he truly is.

"Oh, don't worry, *father*. That will never happen. My place, as Braxton Reyes, Ace's grandson, is right here. Don't *you* forget *that*."

"Can we get on with this?" My mother speaks up for the first time. "Anastasia and I have a yacht to catch."

Disgust has me snorting in her direction. "Of course you do." Sometimes I wonder how my siblings would have turned out had they also been raised by Ace.

"He was my father." She sniffs. "I'll mourn how I see fit."

"Seems as though your mourning won't be any different than any other day," Grey mutters.

"You stay out of this, you freeloading piece of trash." Archie's hatred of Grey has never been a secret, and at least now he's being honest about it.

I don't bother explaining to them that Greyson is better family than they'll ever be, or that he's already made more money for Omni-Reyes than my father has made in a lifetime.

They're blinded by their own jealousy. They'll never hear the truth because they're too dependent on the lies that they've built their lives on.

"I said, that's enough," I snap.

Everyone spins to face me, and I relish their expressions of shock and confusion. I haven't had a relationship with these people in years. I'll abide by my grandfather's wishes for his company, but I will not stand for their blatant disrespect any longer.

I roll my hand toward the elderly attorney. "Mr. Coop, when you're ready, please."

He nods with a kind smile for me. When he turns to my family, he plasters on an agreeable but blank expression.

"This will take some time. If you'd please take seats."

"We're fine." Alistair throws his shoulders back. It's a move he believes holds power, but all it does is make his giant belly more pronounced.

"All right." Mr. Coop opens the folder and lays out Ace's final wishes—the inheritances, the requirements to receive them, and the delays that mean no one is getting anything today...or even this month.

The room throbs in complete silence.

My father is the first to find his voice. "Let me get this straight, his—" He points in Grey's direction. "That bastard's nephew gets an inheritance?"

"Say that again and you won't be able to walk out of here, you feel me?" Grey snarls. He doesn't use unnecessary words with outsiders, preferring to be the silent one in the shadows, but nothing makes him jump out of his own head faster than someone insulting our nephew.

"And he, Greyson, who isn't even family, is to run Omni-

Reyes for six months, and then he gets a fucking inheritance?" Alistair continues.

"That's correct," Mr. Coop agrees blandly. "However, Greyson is, legally, family."

"But his blood relatives, Ace's real *family*, even me, we're the ones who have to jump through goddamn hoops just to hear his will six fucking months from now?"

"Greyson will abide by the same stipulations as the rest of you. It's all laid out very clearly in your paperwork. Sage, I'll remind you, was also legally adopted by Ace, and graduated high school at age fourteen. Therefore he will gain access to his inheritance when he turns eighteen and start-up money at twenty." I might be mistaken, but Mr. Coop appears to be enjoying this back-and-forth.

My head throbs as tension creeps up my shoulder blades, through my neck, and settles around my temples.

"This is something he'd do," Grey whispers. Unlike Alistair, we were expecting to be thrown a curveball.

"I know," I say, while my sister sobs and my brother throws a book across the room. He's forty-four years old and still hasn't grown out of his toddler stage.

Ignoring them all, I ask Mr. Coop, "What is it he wants us to do, exactly?"

The fine lines of a happy life crease his features as he relaxes into his chair. "The objective is the same for all six of you, but the locations and situations are all different." He stands and hands each of us a manila folder.

I open mine and angle my shoulder so Grey can read along with me, and he does the same with his.

Dear Braxton,

If you're reading this, my time has ended, and the games are about to begin. Always remember that riddles make the world go round—or something like that.

I'm sure you're questioning why I'm asking you to do something so wild and out of character. And that is precisely why I want you to do this. You've always done what you thought you should do. I fear, my dear boy, that you're at Omni-Reyes because you believe you owe me something. I've always worried that you are there because you think that's what's expected of you, not because that's where your heart is.

But what I want, more than anything in this world, is for you to find your place.

Find your happy, Braxton Reyes. Find what makes you smile and want to jump out of bed in the morning.

"I have to go to Montana, live in the cold for six months, and work in squalor?" My sister's whiny tone rises to dolphin-like decibels, dragging my attention away from my grandfather's letter.

My hands are clenched around my folder so tightly the corners crinkle, so I drop it back into my lap.

"It's a school in an economically depressed rural town," Mr. Coop corrects. "Teaching is what you went to college for, Anastasia." How is he keeping his tone so neutral? I would be howling with laughter at their expressions. It's why I've kept my head down.

"For what?" she screeches. "He wants us all to do good deeds for six months to get our inheritance?"

"That's correct." Mr. Coop pushes his glasses higher on his nose using his pointer finger.

"Be thankful." Archie scowls. "I'm going to fucking Maine. Toilwood, Maine to—to work at a farm because when I was seven years old, I said some bullshit about wanting to have my own cow? This—we'll fight this. Right?"

I lift my gaze to my parents.

"Quietvale?" my mother squeaks, staring at the sheet of paper in her trembling hands. "Where the hell is Quietvale?"

"Just outside of Detroit," Mr. Coop says. Okay, his tone is slightly cheerful now.

"Detroit? Oh my God. Detroit?" My mother might be on the verge of hyperventilating. "Is that safe? My own father wants me to work with homeless women for—for perspective. Dear Lord, I think I might faint."

Alistair's expression is irate, and spittle has settled in the corners of his lips.

"Where did he even find these towns?" Grey shrugs next to me, but he's looking a little pale. Glancing down at his letter, I see Ace basically told him the same thing—find your place, find your happiness—except his is centered around trusting himself to become the leader Ace knows him to be.

"Honey, what does yours say?" my mother asks Alistair. When he doesn't answer, she takes the folder from his hands. "Truth or Consequences, New Mexico." She laughs, a completely unhinged, shrill sound. "That's a joke, right? It's a joke? You can't be a companion at a nursing home. It's as if he didn't know any of us at all."

"It's your father's gallows humor at play again, dear," Alistair says through clenched teeth. He doesn't raise his voice, but it hits with deadly accuracy, and the hairs on the back of my neck stand at attention. He turns his dark, lifeless gaze my way. "And where is he sending the golden boy?"

I'm no longer terrified of my father, but sometimes my body doesn't quite get the memo. Fortunately for me, I've had a lifetime of hiding my emotions from these people, so when I speak, my voice is clear and confident. "Georgia."

An inn in Happiness fucking Georgia.

"To do what?" Alistair growls.

I quickly scan the rest of the document. "To rebuild a town." That's not exactly what it says, but it's the gist of it. Ace wants me to find the heart and soul of the town and fix it.

"No pressure or anything," Grey whispers.

No shit. How the hell does someone find what's broken with the heart and soul of a freaking town they've never even heard of before?

The silence that descends on the room could be heard all across California. The tension in the room is suffocating.

Mr. Coop takes a deep breath. "Yes, well, different towns, same rules."

"And what are those?" my sister cries.

"You are to inhabit these towns for six months. Make a difference in your specified area. Be the good Ace wanted to see in the world. But you do it without funding from Omni-Reyes."

The outcry from my family could wake the dead, and it takes over five minutes for Mr. Coop to regain control enough to explain.

"Simply put, your assets connected to Omni-Reyes are frozen, but all personal accounts, meaning anything you've earned on your own, is, of course, yours to use as you see fit." Mr. Coop doesn't contain his smile then.

Surely Grey and I aren't the only ones who have earned money, invested it, and diversified. Are we?

Grey nudges me with his elbow, and I know he's thinking the same thing.

Is my family really so fucking dumb that they've never tried to stand on their own?

"And if we don't have any money that isn't in our trusts?"

My brother's finally showing an emotion that's not rage. But fear doesn't look any better on him.

"You were all given start-up money in college, or in your case, Alistair, when you married Amara. Ace was very clear that you should attempt to make a name for yourself. Did you not do that?" Mr. Coop's jaw drops as he glances around the room. "Are Braxton and Grey the only ones who followed directions?"

"Montgomery Media is my company," Alistair says with an arrogant laugh.

"Actually," Mr. Coop interjects, "you took over Reyes-Veritas and rebranded it as Montgomery Media with Ace's blessing and connections. As you will find in your contracts from that transaction, upon Ace's death, the entity reverts to the Omni-Reyes umbrella." The attorney takes a step back, rightfully putting more distance between himself and Alistair.

"That's bullshit." The veins in Alistair's neck strain against his skin as he jabs his finger toward Mr. Coop. "I will fight this."

"Yes, Ace was sure that you would, but as a courtesy, I'll advise you, he had twenty-two of the top attorneys in the country from twenty different firms working on his will for the last five years to ensure his wishes couldn't be overturned."

"And to make sure that twenty of the top law firms in the country would immediately have conflicts of interest." Grey taps his chin while he thinks out loud.

"That too," Mr. Coop says quietly, but the twitch above his left eye makes me believe this was probably his idea.

I nod in appreciation, and the sparkle in his eyes proves me right.

"Conflict— I—I've worked there for forty years," Alistair bellows.

"And you have the chance to continue working there. But there are procedures to follow."

"Procedures? You mean wild goose chases across the country. This is unacceptable," my mother says. "Alistair, do something."

He glances from my mother to me with unadulterated loathing.

Chaos breaks out then as Archie and Anastasia begin to yell over each other. The raised voices alert the office's security team, and within minutes, Grey and I are left alone with Mr. Coop, who turns over the giant hourglass.

I lean forward as a new image comes into view. On this side of the hourglass are two etchings. The one dropping the sands of time has a man flipping us his middle finger. But it's the two at the bottom, collecting the sand, that has my attention...because it's us—me and Grey.

Well, twelve-year-old versions of us. The image is clear as day. If only the message were too.

"I know Ace enjoyed his puzzles, Mr. Coop, but what exactly am I looking for in Georgia?"

The older man sighs and falls into the chair beside me. "I spent over fifty years trying to keep up with that guy, son. I never could do it. But I know he wanted you all to make a difference in the world. But with you, I think he wanted you to figure out what it is you truly want out of life."

"And he thinks I'll find that in some town called Happiness?"

Mischief sparkles in his tired expression. "I think he wanted you to find happiness, however that looks for you, Braxton."

"How, exactly is this all going to work? What will determine if I've made a difference?"

Mr. Coop lays his hand on top of mine, his aging skin paper thin. "Ace always had a plan, but know this—to him, making a difference wasn't always what could be done with your bank account. Sometimes it's your time and attention that leaves an impact on the world around you."

"'Time will always be more valuable than gold.'" It's the phrase I heard Ace say a million times, and the ache of missing him rears up at knowing I'll never hear his voice again.

"That's it." Mr. Coop pats my hand one more time before standing. "Invest your time and your heart, Braxton. Those are two commodities you've kept close to your chest for too many years now. I believe that Ace thought it was time for you to share the best parts of your soul."

"Make a difference by giving my time," I mutter. Turning to Grey, I see the worry etched all over his face—it's an emotion he rarely shows.

We've been running Omni-Reyes together since college. First with Ace's help, then on our own for the last five years. Failing Ace is his biggest fear.

"You've got this, Grey. You know that, right?"

He nods and rolls his lucky coin between his fingers as he stares at the floor.

"The rules say you have to be in Georgia, Braxton," Mr. Coop says. "But they don't say you can't have help or help others. Ultimately, Grey does have to make the tough decisions for Omni-Reyes while he's in charge, but the two of you have always put thought before action—you've discussed and collaborated. You've grown Omni-Reyes into something far exceeding anything Ace could've ever imagined, so he was very careful with his wording."

Using my thumb, I press into the ache that feels hollow in my chest. "Grey is to be the face for six months, but we can still work together to ensure we're making the right decisions?"

That's where my value for Omni-Reyes lies anyway—being able to pull the ideas from Greyson's mind and then drafting the plan that he executes.

We are truly the perfect team.

Mr. Coop nods, and Greyson pitches forward in relief beside me. "Greyson isn't required to travel like the rest of you, but that doesn't mean he can't travel."

Grey drops his head into his hands.

"I'll give you boys a few minutes to talk privately." Mr. Coop stands, but confusion must show on my face because he nods toward the stack of papers in my hands. "You leave tonight, Braxton. And I'll give you a word of advice—I've known your father since before you were born. When he fails, and he almost certainly will, he will try to sabotage you. Don't make it too easy for him to trace you. It was a very smart move not saying the name of your town, but Georgia is only so big."

We're silent as he leaves, then Grey turns to me with his shoulders pulled back in determination.

"You need a break, man," he says. "You've been going twenty hours a day for six months. When's the last time you even slept in a bed and not cat-napped in your office?"

I shrug, but exhaustion and sadness do feel heavier today than they have in months. "You're one to talk. We have a goal, and if we want to undo all the years of abuse Alistair's choreographed under the guise of freedom of speech, I had to get everything in place to oust him at our first opportunity. Montgomery Media reverting to Omni-Reyes is our opportunity, and now we're prepared."

"You know I'm still on board with our plan—the world needs a bipartisan source of information—but that doesn't have to be your whole life. Alistair made choices, but they're not yours to correct. Where the hell would I be if I had to undo all my father's corruption?" He swallows hard.

"You okay?"

"It's no secret that I was born a Wells, Brax. Ace spent his entire life building a brand that people could trust, and they trusted it because of him. The Wells name...when it comes out that I'm the acting CEO." He grips his hair in frustration. "Nothing good happens when a Wells is attached to anything."

I know what it cost him to admit that. He never talks about his family.

"Then it's a good thing you're not a Wells, Grey. You're a Reyes, and you are not your father either." Grey is a better brother than Archie has ever been, and Ace made sure that we were family the way it should be, with unconditional love and acceptance. "What the fuck am I going to do in Happiness, Georgia?"

His smirk shows just how funny he finds my predicament, but his fear is etched into his face like a tattoo. "Make it an adventure. Do what Ace said and figure out what it is you love to do instead of doing what your loved ones needed you to do. Ace is sending you there for a reason—he always said there was healing to be done in happiness."

I snort, and my shoulders bounce until my laughter escapes, then I pull out the postcard of the place Ace is sending me to.

"I just don't understand what could be waiting for me at an inn in Happiness, Georgia that's so important he never bothered to mention it until he was dead."

"No idea, man." He takes the folder from my lap and

starts sifting through it. When he holds up a credit card I recognize, I pinch the bridge of my nose. "I guess he knew about the DDD after all."

He hands me the folder, and I place my car keys in his open palm. Our nephew will love it.

"Tell Sage to be careful with it."

"Come on," he groans. "You remember that he's only seventeen, right? Giving him a hundred-thousand-dollar car is ridiculous."

My lips curl up at the corners. "I know. It'll secure my crown as the fun uncle."

His laughter rings loudly in the stuffy room.

I can still hear it as I shut the door and walk away.

For better or worse, Happiness, here I come.

2

MADISON

THE BIRDS ARE TOO LOUD.

It's not even light outside yet, and I've had this dang pillow over my head for close to an hour. I swear little miss robin chooses the same spot year after year just to mess with me. Is her internal clock broken? At least pretend to be a rooster, miss robin. This before-daylight crap is making me grumpy before I even get out of bed.

Eventually I toss my pillow aside, push myself to standing, and turn on the light. It instantly blinds me, and I scowl at the offending light fixture.

It's not natural to be up this early, but I couldn't say no to the football team—they need options for their study sessions, and that means less sleep for me. It's for the greater good though. If I keep reminding myself, it will become my truth.

Tiptoeing to the bathroom across the hall, I avoid the creaky floorboards with years of practice so I don't wake up Pops.

Done in the bathroom, I creep down the stairs, skipping the fourth and eighth ones because they could wake the entire town when the slightest weight is applied to them, then I stumble to the kitchen to start the coffee.

I won't make it through the day without a constant stream of caffeine.

What is today? Monday? No, it just feels that way. Today is Wednesday—I think. That means I have all day at the Chugaloo, and my mood instantly improves.

Every night this week, I've been there editing and producing podcasts in my sound booth until the early morning hours because while the Chug is profitable every month, this place is not.

As much as it pains me to admit, seeing the number of renovations the inn needs upsets my stomach. Someday I'll get to them. I will.

My chest tightens, a not-so-subtle reminder of what I've lost. Maisie's Hideaway Inn was named after my grand-mother, and I'm doing everything I can to save it, but I'm terrified it won't be enough—that I won't be enough.

Ever since Pops turned the Chug over to me, I've raised the coworking membership twice, but even that's not enough to cover repairs at the inn.

Shaking my head, I cross the cool wood floors, refusing to mope around in my despair any longer. I'll make it work. I always do. And to do that, I can't be a Debbie Downer. "Suck it up, buttercup."

I grab the carafe from the new coffee machine Clover gifted me last Christmas and shimmy in place—this thing is better than sex...mostly. I seriously have the best friends.

They're more my family than my parents ever were, but I suppose it's hard to feel connected to your parents when they ship you off to live anywhere that's not with them because parenting was an inconvenience—not that they ever tried very hard.

The old grandfather clock in the entry way chimes five times, hurling me into motion. Crap. I'm going to be late, and I really need to finish the audio I was proofing before I open the doors for everyone. I hustle over to the sink to fill the pot with water and nearly drown myself as water hits me in the face with the power of a firehose, spraying in every direction.

What the heck?

"Argh, what's happening?" I splutter into the empty room while attempting to turn off the faucet, but the dang thing breaks off in my hands.

No, no, no. Not today. Please, not today.

When I drop the broken piece into the sink, the clatter of metal on metal rings loudly in the room, but I'm too focused on containing the water with both hands to worry about it, and when that doesn't work, I add my right foot to the tap. Yup, I have two hands and a foot in the kitchen sink and water is still spraying every available surface.

This isn't happening. I can't afford this.

The creaky swinging door behind me squeals on its hinges, and I drop my foot back to the floor. Oh, thank God.

"Pops! I need help. Shut off the valve under the sink," I shriek while water sprays into my mouth and nose. I'm attempting to point all the water on me or in the sink, and failing miserably, but every time I remove my hands, water douses the whole room.

Control the damage, Madison. Dang, my inner voice has all the advice but fails miserably on implementation. But it's okay. I'll dry, water stains on the walls will just be one more giant bill to add to my mile-high list.

"Pops, let's move it. The wrench is already under there from yesterday."

The floorboards creak, and goosebumps explode all over

my exposed skin, which would make sense if the water were cold, but it's not. The water is actually warm, nearing hot.

When I feel my grandfather behind me, I attempt to move to the side, but that changes my hands and the trajectory of the water.

"You'll have to climb under me," I splutter into a spray and instantly choke on it.

"Well now, this is an invitation I've never had before."

It takes more than a moment for my brain to react. The voice is deep and gravelly, and certainly not my seventy-year-old grandfather. It's another long minute before I get my neck to work and my chin drops to my chest to find a stranger, *a stranger*, lying on the floor on his back and wedging himself between my legs.

"Who the heck are you?" I shout into the spray of water. It goes up my nose, and I sneeze—it's a horrible sound that pierces my eardrums.

Sneezing is never cute, but especially when I do it.

His eyes crinkle at the corners just before his head is fully ensconced in the cabinet.

"I'm Braxton," he says casually. "Brax."

"That means nothing to me. Why are you here?" I splutter, sneezing again. Is that snot running down my chin?

"Pops checked me in late last night. He said you were working and that I'd meet you this morning. This..." He pauses, and I pull back an inch to get a good look at him.

I shouldn't have done that—who has a body with that many dips and grooves and zero cellulite? Who is this guy?

"This is quite the introduction." His chuckle sends prickles rolling across my skin.

The water slows to a trickle before shutting off completely, and my handsome rescuer slides out from the cabinet enough for me to see his face.

Pops checked in a very handsome stranger and didn't think to tell me or even leave a note. We're going to have a conversation about communication as soon as possible.

"This is a first I'll never forget," he says with a crooked smile that has my stomach skydiving without a parachute.

Brax, what kind of name is Brax anyway? Like Braxit? Or is that Brexit? Do I even know what Braxit is? Braxit or Brexit? Gah, I'm spiraling!

He slides out a few more inches, his broad shoulders rubbing against the inside of my shins as he stares up at me. It's only now that I realize I'm dripping water all over his chest. And that I'm nearly naked because Pops never gets up this early and we weren't supposed to have any guests.

Finally, my brain shouts, *move, Madi, move*, and I attempt to step over him but slip in the water.

Then everything happens in painfully slow motion.

My eyes fly open. His hands raise to protect himself while my arms windmill and reach for something—anything—to hold onto.

And then I fall spread-eagle on his chest, his hands catching my thighs and absorbing some of my weight, but he still lets out a low *oomph*.

My wet, nearly naked vagina claps her hands as though this is her lucky day. Why, God, why did I choose today to wear the white boy shorts with bright pink kissy lips all over them?

Talk about mortifying on an entirely new level.

He smiles. I frown. We both freeze. Then he shows even more glossy white teeth while my lips open and close with no words.

"If I didn't know better, I'd think you were trying to live out a Heartmark movie here."

His words snap my mouth closed, and my face heats to

shades of red I'm positive are a precursor to lung failure because I cannot breathe.

"I, ah, I'm so sorry." I scramble to my feet and shiver when his hands slowly fall away from my thighs. "No. No. I'm sorry," I say wagging my finger the way my kindergarten teacher used to do every time my parents forgot to pick me up. "No Heartmark films here. I'm off men. Really, really off them. I mean, I was on you, but not *on you* on you."

He raises an eyebrow, and it makes him even sexier.

"I mean, I'm not dating. At all. Ever again. Man, woman, or alien, they're all off limits." *Holy crap, shut up, Madi.* "This is not a Heartmark movie, and I am absolutely not looking for any type of relationship, ever, with anyone. Ever."

Oh my God. When did I lose control of my mouth?

"Ah," he says knowingly. "Bad breakup?"

My entire body flinches as he lifts himself to sitting, and I finally put my pointer finger away.

"Something like that," I mutter. "Only worse."

Both brows raise while he stares at me. Then his gaze roams lower and lower until his heat has touched every inch of my body.

"I'm so sorry about this. We're...ah...renovating. Sort of. The sink doesn't usually go this wonky though. If you want to give me your clothes, I'll get them cleaned for you right away."

"You want...my clothes?" he asks with a devilish grin that is definitely not suitable for a Heartmark movie. This man would make millions by simply smiling at women all day on some X-rated website for smile kinks.

When he stands then grips his shirt at the back of his neck, I spin to face the wall.

"No." My voice cracks, and I purse my lips. *Get a handle on yourself, Madison.* "Not right this second. Just, change and leave them in the hallway. I'll get them going as soon as I dry off and start breakfast for you."

"It's fine." His voice is smooth as silk and covers me like a hug.

This is dangerous.

"Turn around." The command in his tone heats my skin even more. "Please," he adds. It's the please that bends me to his will.

Slowly, I spin to find he's wearing the same easy expression. "I'm Brax," he repeats.

"You said that."

"I did." There's a casual confidence in the way he carries himself that sets off mild alarm bells. Not enough to make me run, but enough that my ovaries scream *warning, warning, proceed with caution.* "It's customary for you to introduce yourself as well though, and you didn't."

I slap my forehead with my open palm. "I'm so sorry. I don't normally start my day assaulting guests."

Holy crap, Madi. What's wrong with you?

"That's a shame." He chuckles. Why. Why does that sound worm its way under my skin?

Ignore the flirting. Ignore. It. "My name's Madison. My friends call me Madi. How long will you be staying with us?"

Be professional. That's the name of this game. Professionals do not react with their vaginas.

He folds his arms over his chest looking even more amused—cocky, but amused. "I'm not sure yet."

"No wife or girlfriend. A dog, a job, a Bob. Anyone waiting for you wherever you hail from?" Where in the heck did my filter run off to?

"Nope." He rocks back on his heels. Is it possible for that grin to get any freaking bigger? And why does he have to have dimples? I love dimples. "I'm completely single, unless you count my best friend, Greyson, or our nephew. No one else even knows where to find me." He frowns for half a second. "It's shocking how happy that makes me."

"You're hiding?"

"I'd call myself a principled explorer."

"You're running away?" I surmise.

The way he stares at me makes my insides do a funny little dance that has me backing up a step. "Maybe I'm a renegade."

I shouldn't be enjoying this interaction so much, but I can't seem to walk away either.

"So," I drag out the word, biting my lip as I attempt to focus. "You're a traitor."

He playfully clutches his chest. Playful Braxton is even more dangerous than handsome Braxton.

"Never," he says in a silvery voice. "I'm simply changing my priorities."

"From what?" Water drips down my face, and I wipe it away. It's then I remember I sneezed earlier, and I surreptitiously take a swipe at my chin.

He smirks, but his gaze has me in a chokehold. "The kind of responsibilities I didn't get to choose?" With a shrug, he drops his gaze. "My family, I guess. They're...not aligning with who I want to be."

Lord, do I know how that feels. I've spent the last sixteen years trying to be better than my parents, not that they set the bar all that high.

"Huh," is what I say as I grab a hand towel and hand it to him. "I...can understand that."

And that's as personal as I can get with this handsome stranger.

"Well, I should get dried off. I'll have breakfast ready in thirty minutes."

Crap. Crap. Crap. I wasn't anticipating making breakfast for anyone but me and Pops this morning, so frozen waffles are out of the picture. If I hurry, I can get something made and only be fifteen minutes behind. Possibly.

"Anything I can do to help?" he asks, his voice pitching higher as though his own question startled him. Then he frowns while glancing around the kitchen—it's as if he's truly seeing it for the first time.

I know what he finds as he scans the space. The floorboards in desperate need of sanding. The old cabinets that date the house. The tired wallpaper curling at the edges. What he doesn't see is all the love and life that's happened here.

And no one may ever see that again.

Swallowing around the lump permanently lodged in my throat, I offer something that probably looks closer to a grimace. "No, but thank you. You're the guest, just give me a few minutes."

His gaze returns to mine, and there's something in his expression I can't read—understanding, or maybe sadness he's trying to hide. But it doesn't matter. I cannot afford to get caught up in whatever mess he's running from.

I've got my own problems to solve—starting and ending with saving the inn.

"It looks as though this was a great place to grow up. There's a lot of love in these walls." His voice is sandpaper rough, as if he isn't used to speaking so gently.

The ball in my throat grows spikes—that's the last thing I expected him to say.

"What... Why do you say that?"

"It's the way you look at it, as if it holds all the stories of your life." His jaw tightens, and he runs a hand through his thick dark hair. "Sorry, I didn't mean to overstep. I'm— It's been a rough couple of days."

How did he go from soft and tender to stone-cold in the span of a sentence?

The sun is starting to rise now, and the glint of amber in his stare is intense. No, scratch that, I have a feeling he's intense all over. I need to check the book and see how long he rented a room for. The sooner he leaves, the better.

"Did you know amber eyes are one of the rarest colors?" Instantly, I slap a hand over my mouth.

Those dang amber irises my mouth appreciated so much sparkle when the corners crinkle, gentling his features.

"I did not know that, but I do love a good fun fact."

He stands there, staring, smiling, taking me in for longer than is comfortable.

"Sorry," he mutters, dragging his gaze away from me and back to the sink. "I'm not quite myself. It's— There's been a lot of change for me in the last couple of months, but I'll, ah, get out of your hair."

Before I can tell him that he can stay, he's gone. The old swinging door sings its age behind him.

It isn't until I'm alone in my room that I realize my shirt is completely see-through and not once did he perv out and leer at me.

I LEFT BREAKFAST FOR THE NOT-HANDSOME GUEST IN THE kitchen, then ran back upstairs to get my stuff together for the day. So when I step out onto the porch, the last thing I'm expecting to find is Braxton with a stack of pancakes in one hand and his phone in the other.

Glancing around, I don't see a car in the parking area other than mine. I bite my tongue, hard. I do not offer strangers rides. Even if said stranger is sleeping in the room next to mine for who knows how long. Leave it to my grandfather to not include a check-out date.

"Do you need a ride somewhere?" Stupid people-pleasing curse.

His gaze jumps to mine, and for the first time, I get the full experience that is his face in the sunlight—because it is an experience.

Oh, crap. He's more than handsome. He's freaking devastatingly beautiful. And then he goes and smiles again. Why the heck is he so happy?

"No thanks, Madison. I've got it covered."

I'm thankful and perturbed that he didn't accept my ride, but I walk down the steps to my car with a generic expression saved for strangers and police officers.

"Okay. Have a good day. I'll be back to make dinner around six."

He nods and waves as I back out of the driveway, feeling more unsettled than I have in a very long time.

3

BRAXTON

The scent of dirt permeates everything.

"Are you all right? You haven't answered your phone for three fucking hours," Greyson mutters.

I glance up at the sky and instantly regret it. It's so damn hot that when I tilt my head, sweat rolls down the back of my neck. Even in the fall, it's hot as balls here, a swampy heat I don't believe I'd ever get used to.

"I spoke to you when I landed last night, *Dad*. I was exhausted and..." Images from my encounter this morning flash across my mind. "Sleeping. Then I spent the morning acclimating to Happiness, otherwise known as the devil's asshole. Do you know that it takes two point five seconds before you sweat so much you need another shower? Two point five seconds outside. That's it. I timed it this morning."

His chuckle is comforting. "And where are you now?" he asks.

"Is that Braxton? Put him on the phone," my mother demands. He must already be at the office because she hasn't set foot in Ace's home—our home—for years.

"No, it's my food delivery order," Grey says flatly. "I told you, I haven't heard from Braxton since he followed the rules of the will and took off immediately."

This makes me chuckle. Only Grey would dare speak to my mother that way, and it's only because he knows a lot of dirt on her. He has an uncanny ability to learn and retain gossip.

"So." He drags out the word, and I know he's speaking to me again, then I hear the click of a door and his voice echoes as though he's locked himself in a restroom.

"I used the Discreet Daily Deeds credit card and checked into the inn using my middle name. Braxton *Mitchell* slept like the dead, by the way, then I woke up to an interesting show, and stupidly walked three miles in armpit-sweaty air and ended up..." I glance around at my surroundings. "Here." The air is so thick, I think I can taste the dirt. A faint breeze kicks up a dust storm that gets lodged in my nostrils and throat.

"And where is that?" He's full on laughing now. "Do you even know?"

The sign over the falling-down garage says Blinky's Used Car Sales. When I googled the closest car dealership, this wasn't exactly what I had in mind, but it was within walking distance of the inn and the rideshare app had shown no available drivers for my area.

My thoughts immediately splinter, visions of the inn owner's granddaughter filling my mind, and now I'm blinking as I imagine Blinky would do. There's not even any dust to blame.

"Some place called Blinky's." I swipe at the sweat on my neck with my free hand.

I hear Grey clicking away on his phone, and then all falls silent. Even though it's mid-morning, the lampposts shaded by a huge tree are flickering. It's eerie as fuck out here and feels like we're in the middle of nowhere—the chain-link fence trapping me in doesn't help either.

The closest I've come to roughing it was with what my sister called glamping during her outdoorsy phase, when she thought she'd become a famous travel influencer, before I found out they were all running out of their trust funds but expecting me to support them. It was the only reason I'd been invited in the first place—to pay.

Familial manipulation is a special kind of hell.

"You're..." Grey trails off, his voice sounding tinny and far away. "That's a used car dealership. Did you know Happiness has less than five thousand occupants?" he whispers. "When the hell would Ace have been there?"

"No idea."

"What's it like?"

Madison's face interrupts my train of thought. "Different."

He laughs. "Well, that tracks." He continues typing on his phone, and the click, click, click is oddly comforting. "Blinky's is...something else. That's where you're going to buy a car? The place doesn't even have a website."

"If you saw it in person, you'd understand why, but I need to blend in for a while and figure out why the hell Ace wanted me here. Do you think my family will be able to trace the DDD account?"

"They would break every law if it meant they could keep the money train going, but no, the DDD isn't something they'd ever think of, and we're the only ones with access— well, and apparently Ace. Are you really going to purchase a used car?"

Glancing at the options, I frown. "No, I'm going to purchase a truck."

More laughter has my fingers itching to hang up on him.

"Greyson," I grumble.

"Fine, fine. No, I promise you they can't trace it. But you should know, the gossip mill is salivating. Your family found out we've already removed Alistair from the board of Montgomery Media, and they're threatening to plaster your face all over the internet if you don't fix it." Alistair is a fucking snake. "Oh, and he put out a story this morning calling you the renegade billionaire. All the other gossip sites picked it up in minutes. He has a source on the inside because our guys never would have approved that."

Fuck me. I just had to go and call myself a renegade to Madison this morning.

It's unusual for someone in my position to have near-complete anonymity—it's one of the few things I can actually thank my parents for, even if they did it for self-serving reasons.

They've never missed an opportunity to let me know I wasn't wanted, and when they learn that Grey and I don't intend on supplementing their trust funds beyond what Ace put in his will, they'll do whatever's necessary to take me down.

Running my knuckles over my heart, I close my eyes and count to ten. Just long enough to hear a bell chime and a door slam shut.

"I hate to say it, but Happiness might be the perfect place for you to lay low for a while." Grey chuckles. He's having way too much fun with this.

"We'll see. I have to go buy a—a something. Maisie's Hideaway Inn isn't so bad, but I don't need to draw unnecessary attention to myself either."

Madison standing in the kitchen with a foot in the sink flickers to life in my mind, and I couldn't stop my smile if I tried.

"Ace truly was a mastermind," Grey says, dragging my attention away from the inappropriate thoughts. "Your father will never look for you at a run-down inn. Do you know he already tried to bill a ten-thousand-dollar-a-month rental to the company? When that didn't work, he hired a helicopter to take him from El Paso every day, but I don't know where that money came from yet."

I grunt in response just as a man far too young to be as bald as he is saunters up with his thumbs hooked into the loops of his dirty-kneed jeans.

Ending the call, I hold out a hand that he stares at with barely contained disgust. Well, that's a new one for me. I drop my hand.

"Name's Harry Terdsley, how can I help you today? Sir." The "sir" drips with condescension.

Okay, he's not a fan. Got it.

"Brax R—Mitchell." I'd better get used to using my middle name really quickly. "Braxton Mitchell. I'd like to purchase a... Honestly—" I look past him to the heaps of metal that surround us. "What's the most reliable vehicle you have on the lot?"

This man snorts in my face. "We sell used cars, Mr. Mitchell. Walk around and take your pick. How do you plan to pay? We don't finance out-of-towners."

"That's fine. I'll pay for it outright if we can get it done today."

He makes a show of looking at his watchless wrist and whistles.

"Well, ya better choose quick then. We close for lunch soon." Harry Terdsley spins on his heel and leans against the building, watching as I scan the small lot.

Some of the trucks are rusted, and some look to be in good condition, but if my instincts on Harry are correct, I'll be spending a lot of time at an auto repair shop either way. Considering I know next to nothing about cars, I'm guessing I'm about to get screwed, but this is my only option for now.

My phone dings with an incoming text.

> Grey: I looked up the inn. It's owned by M. Ryan and Madison Ryan. It's pretty run-down.

> Me: It's perfect.

> Me: And it has stellar reviews.

> Grey: All from locals. But whatever, maybe that's what you're supposed to fix. Regardless, it's truly the last place they'll look for you.

That's true. I can hear my mother's voice now. "A Montgomery in a small-town inn in the middle of nowhere? How dare you?"

Except I'm not now, nor have I ever been, a Montgomery, regardless of my Montgomery DNA.

> Grey: FYI, I just got a notification from Whisperloop.

My shoulders hitch up around my ears. The Whisperloop is Alistair's baby. A so-called news site that reports, and I use that term loosely, all gossip all the time with little care about unveiling the actual truth.

He gets away with it by using tiny unreadable letters that say *allegedly* that no one ever sees or pays attention to. He does whatever's necessary to grab clicks, regardless of who he hurts along the way.

It's why Grey and I started full-time at Omni-Reyes in

college. One exposé and I never looked at my father the same way again.

Me: What now?

Grey: Screenshot sent.

Grey: My guess is that Alistair's planning his attack early.

I zoom in on the screenshot. The image says: *Where have all the Montgomerys gone?*

Me: Fuck. I don't have the energy for this.

Grey: I'll stay on top of it. You go buy a heap of metal and hope it makes it back to the inn.

He'll never believe me if he doesn't see it for himself, so I take a quick photo of my options and send it to him.

Chuckling, I thank my lucky stars for Greyson Reyes and pocket my phone, but I swear I hear the slimy excuse for a salesman clicking his tongue as if he were a second hand on a clock somewhere behind me.

I hurry through the next few rows and stop when I see a polished, but old, Chevy pickup with a large blue stripe down both sides. It's something straight out of the old eighties movies I had to watch in my film and entertainment course in college.

And I love it.

Tearing the tag from the window, I walk back to Harry Terdsley. What a fucking name. He acts like a high school quarterback who's still living in his past.

Am I judgmental? Yes. Am I wrong? Not generally.

"I'll take this one," I say, handing him the tag.

He stares at me as though I'm handing him a bag of dog shit, and am I imagining it, or are his lips already curling into a snarl?

"Why that one?" he asks. Everything in his tone is confrontational.

Shrugging my shoulders, I feign indifference. "It's the one that caught my attention. Is there a problem?"

"No problem," an older gentleman says as he shuffles around the building. "That truck belonged to his high school sweetheart's grandfather. And this jackass ruined that relationship spectacularly, twice."

"Dad!" Harry clenches his fists as he snarls at his father.

"It's true," his father says with an annoyed shrug. There's no mistaking the disappointment in his features. "Come along, son. I'll get you going on your paperwork."

"But, Dad, I'm gonna buy that truck."

The older man glares, yes, glares at his son. "With what? The money you're borrowing from me every month? It's over, Harry. I'm selling it."

My gaze ping-pongs between the two men before me, then I dutifully follow the older Terdsley into the run-down building.

"It's a good rig. It'll last you a long time. And don't pay no mind to Harry out there. He runs his mouth all over Georgia, but not here. I don't run a dirty shop, and he knows it. If he wasn't the only one his grandmama remembered, I'd'a pushed him outta here a long time ago."

"Ah, well, I'm glad to hear the truck will last."

The older man glances out the window with such sadness I feel bad for him. "Harry wasn't always this way, ya know." He chokes out a cough, obviously upset he let that slip. "How you payin'?"

I keep my gaze lowered—something tells me he needs a minute to collect himself. Removing my wallet from my front pocket, I sort through the credit cards until I find the one I'm searching for.

"You lookin' to make a deposit?"

"No, sir. I'll pay in full."

His gaze narrows, scanning my face as though he doesn't know if he should trust me or not.

"Well, son. We don't get many of your kind around here. Are you planning to stay a while?"

I don't get the sense he's gossiping or that he has any idea who I am, so I lower my guard a little.

"I'm thinking about it."

"Word of advice then?"

I wait while he runs my card for $4200.

"You'll want to hit up the Walmart on Main Street and buy some regular clothes. Walking around as some sort of fancy pants is the fastest way to get the gossipers circling for your story."

Walmart. Right. I've seen their commercials—I've just never actually been in one.

"Thank you. I'm trying to keep a low profile."

He laughs a thick smoker's laugh that tugs at my sadness. Ace used to laugh that way.

"Good luck with that around here." He hands me a stack of papers to sign. "You ever lived in a small town before?"

"No, sir," I say while reading the contracts.

"Well, you ever need some advice, you come see me. This town will eat you up and spit you out, but they'll also be first to pick you up when you stumble—after you've proved yourself loyal."

"That's quite the oxymoron."

"You got no idea," he says. The nametag sewn into his

overalls says Roger, and it suits him. "Let me get you the keys. And ignore my son—he has a fairy tale planned around that truck that ain't never gonna happen."

Great, making enemies on my first day in town. Not exactly the way to fix a broken heart and soul now, is it?

Roger returns and walks me to the truck, presumably to keep Harry from picking a fight. But he's right about one thing, I'm going to need some new clothes—I wasn't exactly thinking when I packed a suitcase yesterday. Somehow, I don't think I'll be needing many suits around here.

"Good luck." He knocks on the side of the door and walks away. Glancing around at the interior, I'm thankful for my minor obsession with sports cars in my early twenties, and even more grateful I was determined to learn to drive a stick, or I'd have just bought a truck I can't drive.

I open the map app on my phone before I start the truck, then press down on the clutch and gas as I shift into first. There's a violent lurch that has me reaching for my seat belt as the engine stalls.

Well, shit.

I try again, and this time manage to get out of the parking lot, but in the four-mile drive to Walmart, I stall six more times.

Exhaustion slaps me across the face, but I force myself into the store. I only hope I can recover from the loss of Ace and figure out what he wanted me to do here before the Montgomerys attempt to destroy everything I've ever worked for.

4

MADISON

"Oh my gosh, guys. I'm so sorry I'm late," I say while rushing up the front steps of the Chugaloo. "Things got, well... It was a messy morning, and then I had to turn around because I forgot Pops had a doctor's appointment, and then he was hungry, again, so I made him a snack, and before I realized it, I was later than I thought."

"No worries, Miss Madi. You're always worrying about other people, but we haven't been here long. Practice ran late 'cause Coach was all shades of mad at the D-line this morning," Ethan says in his thick Southern drawl.

He's a hometown kid so I've known him since he was little, and now he's a superstar on the local college football team.

"Yeah, my body's gonna hurt tomorrow," Trevon says. He's the starting defensive end this season, and he's worked hard to make that happen.

"Oh no, Coach B. is at it again?" I ask as I unlock the door.

"I'm surprised you didn't hear him yelling over at the Hideaway," Trevon grumbles.

"Sorry, kid. You've got this though." I enter the building first and turn on all the lights. "Blissy will be here soon, and I'm sure she's got something in her cart for you."

Blissy's real name is Brenda, and she hates it, but she's been called Blissy the entire time I've known her. She's an older woman with kind eyes who owns Blissful Beans & Leaves, the popup caffeine shop here at the Chugaloo, and she knows every piece of gossip that passes through these walls.

The heavily debated war in town over what's better, coffee or tea, keeps me from calling it a coffee shop because I prefer peace to war. If you ever need to change the subject though, you just ask anyone in town "coffee or tea?" and then watch the fireworks.

The residents of Happiness, Georgia are serious about their choices.

"You have midterms coming up, right?" Bending down, I plug in Blissy's equipment for her. Thursdays are the only day she doesn't get in earlier than me. Then I turn on the lights in the sound booth for the high school club that'll be here after school.

"Yes, ma'am," they say in unison.

Reaching into the quiet room, I turn up the AC then shut the door. Even at the tail end of September, Georgia's sticky air lingers. "Are you both ready?"

Groans give me my answer.

"Trig is brutal, but I'm doing all the study packets," Ethan says.

"My sociology midterm is a twenty-page paper, and it's killing me," Trevon says.

"I could help you with that," says a deep voice I recognize.

I spin around so fast, I get dizzy.

Braxton.

"Ah…" Okay, I can no longer form sentences.

Braxton moves away from the doorway and shuts it behind him. "I was a journalism major with a minor in marketing and business management. I'm pretty good with a red pen," he grumbles, the timbre of his voice scorching my insides.

"Um," Trevon says, his gaze bouncing between us.

"Trevon, this is Mr. Braxton, Braxton, this is Trevon. Trevon's very important to all of us around here because he's a starting defensive end. You'll quickly learn that we take college football very seriously in Happiness."

I swear, Trevon blushes.

"It's nice to meet you both." Braxton turns to Ethan. "Sorry, I'm not much help with trigonometry. I failed that in college."

Something about him admitting he failed at something makes him seem less godlike, but I have a hard time imagining him failing at anything. Everything I've seen so far screams that he's the kind of guy who gets what he wants.

"Ah, that's okay. I have a study session with a tutor tomorrow." Ethan is trying not to stare, but he was born and raised here. New blood doesn't happen often unless they're part of the university, and the professionals who move here are hardly ever this young.

Wait, does he work for the university? My professors certainly never look like Braxton Mitchell.

"That's good." Braxton scans the space. "I'd never be able to teach." Turning back to Trevon, he says, "But if you need a proofreader, I can do that in my sleep."

But he also answered my earlier thought…he's not working for the university, so what the heck is he doing here?

Trevon stares at him skeptically, but finally nods. "That would be great, thank you, sir." He sounds so hesitant I almost laugh.

I take a closer look at Braxton and realize he's changed his clothes. And they look...new. In fact, his jeans still have the clear size sticker on the leg.

"Ah, you've got something...right here," I say, pointing to the back of my thigh.

I've never found a man blushing to be so freaking sexy before, but color me excited.

"Thanks." He's holding a MacBook still in the box in one hand and a Walmart bag in his other. It's too far to walk from the Hideaway into town. Did he call Moe's Taxi for a ride?

Why hadn't he let me drop him off?

Braxton turns away from us to scan the Chug.

"Was there something I can help you with?" I ask.

"I was just driving back to the inn—"

"The Hideaway," Ethan interrupts. "The locals call it the Hideaway."

That makes Braxton smirk, and it shouldn't be so sexy. So when he does it, why the heck do my panties throw a party?

"The Hideaway, huh?" He chuckles, and I suppress a shiver. I need to talk to my friends because I'm not acting right around this guy. He can't be so hot that he turns my brain to goo, it's just not natural. "Then I definitely picked the right place," he says, melting away my mental spiral.

Braxton's stare sees right through me. "I was passing by and saw the sign for a coworking space." He gestures with the brand-new laptop. "I'm loving the...Hideaway, but the Wi-Fi was a little spotty out there. I figured this would be a good place for me to spend the day."

"What?" I choke out far too quickly. "What do you do?" I amend.

He averts his gaze. "Marketing," he says, then rolls his shoulders back.

"Huh." Come on, Madi. You can do better than that.

"Do you work here too?" Before I can answer, Blissy walks in.

She stares at the four of us, then gives me a troubling click of her tongue. "I heard we had a new friend in town. I'm Blissy. I'll get your caffeine fix here in a minute, but think long and hard about what you choose. There are enemies on both sides."

His brow furrows, and I even like this expression. Does he do anything that's not attractive?

"I'm Brax."

"Half the town thinks coffee is the best way to wake up, and the other half thinks it's tea. It's started all-out wars before," Ethan says.

Braxton's lips curl at the corners. "Wars, huh?"

"He's not kidding," I whisper.

The sparkle in his gaze dances with glee. "And you work here too?" he asks again.

"Pops has owned the train station since before I was born. A few years ago, he let me turn it into a coworking space."

"And now it's the heart of the town, right along with the Hideaway." Blissy is full of maternal pride I don't deserve. "It is," she says when she catches my eye roll. "Madi here has given all of Happiness a place to belong. She's the town treasure, that one."

"Is that...right." Braxton's voice hitches strangely, almost as though he's just learned a secret, but my biggest secret is that I can't say no to anyone, ever—and it's not exactly a secret to begin with—so that can't be right.

Great, now I'm filling in his blanks with all kinds of made-up crap about myself.

"Okay." I clap my hands a little too loudly. "So, let's get you set up with an account, and then I'll give you a tour."

"Do you not take compliments easily, or is it that one in particular that makes you uncomfortable?" Braxton's voice is pitched low, so I think he intends for only me to hear, but he'll learn quickly that every wall in this town has ears.

"She can't take a compliment to save her life," Blissy huffs. The sound of coffee beans grinding drowns out any response I was going to make, so instead, I walk on wobbly knees to the desk hidden away in the corner.

"You can buy one session, a pack of ten, or a monthly unlimited pass." At least those words manage to sound professional.

"How often are you here?" he asks to a chorus of *oohs* and *ahs* from my favorite football players.

I lower myself to the chair and drop my forehead to the desk. "You realize the entire town will think we're dating by the end of the day, right?"

He snorts. "Because I asked you how often you'll be here?"

"Because we want her happy," Blissy calls out over the rattle of jars as she takes down tea leaves for the day.

"Blissy," I hiss.

"Sorry, Mads. Happiness means well, but we're a bunch of talkers. Don't ever say anything out loud that you don't want repeated." Blissy is either blissfully unaware of my embarrassment or she just doesn't care.

"Truth," Trevon mutters. Internally I cringe over his own history with the grapevine. His first week here, he let slip that he sometimes watched *Bluey* because it reminded him of his little brother.

Within the hour, the entire town knew, and he heard about it from the stadium stands all season, poor kid.

"S-so," I slur the word like an idiot. "What are you looking for today?"

The way Braxton traps me in his orbit with only his gaze makes me dream up all kinds of inappropriate answers that he would never, ever say.

Maybe the stress of life has finally gotten to me.

After what I deem to be an eternity, he winks. Freaking winks. Who winks anymore but creepers and peepers and dirty old men? Well, apparently this late-twenties/early-thirties too-handsome-to-be-real man does.

When's the last time I had sex? That's the only explanation for my wandering thoughts. It's been so long I can't even remember. Maybe we'll have to girls' trip it to Charleston soon.

But that will cost money, my inner voice sing-songs.

"Madison?" he says, and then I notice everyone in the Chugaloo is staring at me as if I missed the question more than once.

I bolt upright. "Sorry, what did you say? So, so busy today," I ramble. "I guess my mind wandered to a to-do task."

That full, plump lip of his hitches on the right side. "That doesn't say much about me if I've already bored you into a to-do list."

Humor is written all over his face. It's a joke. I know it's a joke, but my cheeks burn as hot as the pits of hell while a flush engulfs my entire body.

"I'm playing with you, Madison."

"Madi," I correct.

"Does everyone call you Madi?"

I nod.

"Right. Okay, well, I'll take the membership please, *Madison*." He says my name in a silvery tone that has even Blissy fanning herself behind him.

Good Lord. He's going to cause me nothing but trouble.

"A membership?" I squeak. "How long are you staying?"

He shrugs one massive shoulder. I'd known he was a large man, probably six foot four, and built, but when he stands here in a straining T-shirt with a red soda can on it and jeans that shouldn't look that good on him, there's no denying this man is more than a snack—he's the whole dang meal.

"As long as it takes," he says breezily.

"As long as what takes?" I purposefully don't look at him while typing his name into the computer.

"To find my happy."

My fingers freeze on the keyboard, and my gaze is laser-focused on the floor six feet in front of me.

He's looking for his happy.

For heaven's sake. This handsome stranger is going to seriously turn my town upside down. And if I'm not careful, I might forget why I've sworn off all romantic relationships forever.

"He's looking for his happy?" Savvy asks for the third time. She's the most practical of my friends, which was why I was so shocked when she and Clover followed me home after my life was turned upside down at the end of our freshman year of college. "Was that some kind of a pick-up line or something?" Her bluntness is sharper when she's concerned.

I press a button on my phone to expand the FaceTime images of my friends.

"He's handsome, isn't he?" Clover asks in that wispy voice of hers.

"Yes." My answer came far too quickly.

"And he's staying at the Hideaway?" Elle asks. We've been friends since I came to live with Pops when I was young. She was the town sweetheart who grew up to marry her high school love.

At least that worked out for one of us.

"And the handsome stranger is at the Chug right now?" Clover will probably call him *handsome stranger* in her head for the rest of her life. For a thriller writer who routinely scares the crap out of herself, she truly has a romantic soul. I've been trying to convince her to try romance for years, but she says she needs the fear to feel.

My friend is a complicated soul with a heart so big it contains oceans full of love.

"Yes," I whisper-shout. "He bought a monthly unlimited membership for an entire year, but he says he has no idea how long he'll be staying. It's probably a waste of money."

"Or he's smitten." Elle makes googly eyes at the camera as only she can.

"We'll be right there," Savvy announces. "Elle, tell your bodyguard to stand down. I'll be there to get you in five minutes. Clover, meet me at my car. And Madi, don't move a muscle."

"I have to. I'm hiding in a closet on the second floor, and it's so hot in here I have boob sweat."

"That's impressive with your B-cup." Savvy has more snark than the rest of us combined.

"That's why I said it. I'll meet you guys downstairs. Come quick. I can't tell if he's just trying to fit in, or if he's going to kill me in my sleep."

"That's a real concern in dating these days," Clover says sagely. "You can never be too careful."

"Clover," Savvy and Elle say together.

"Right, sorry, they're not dating. We'll be right over. Love you, Madi."

"Love you. See you soon."

With the knowledge that backup is on the way, I ease out of the closet, shake out my shirt to encourage the air to dry my boob sweat, then head down the rickety stairs to find Ethan and Braxton sitting side by side, taping Ethan's laptop back together again.

Why does the handsome stranger have to be so dang helpful?

5

BRAXTON

The space is cozy and inviting. It's so far removed from my sterile office at Omni-Reyes, and I'm honestly not sure why I never changed the office after I moved in.

Or you could have taken Ace's office, the voice in my head taunts.

Madison's Chugaloo is much more my speed. Or what it would have been had I not been hardened by learning of Alistair's choices the last few years.

I told Madison I was searching for my happy. Who the fuck says that? It just...happened.

I want you to find your happy, Braxton. Find your purpose and reason for getting up in the morning. Ace's letter has been messing with my mind since I read it.

And don't get me started on why I offered the football player help. I must be bored—that's it. My body's used to working eighty hours a week. It's all I've done for the last six months.

Rolling my neck and enjoying the crackle of the stretch, I open my new laptop. I need to focus on something other than Madison Ryan.

Which should have been easy because she's spent a good part of the last hour hiding, something I know courtesy of Blissy. The older woman filled me in on a little of the Chugaloo's history while Madison's been MIA.

She told me enough to know that Madison has dumped her blood, sweat, and tears into this place, and it shows in every piece of local artwork on the walls, in the comfy chairs she chose for the quiet room, and in the relaxed expressions of every person who enters.

I've been here for a couple of hours, and before she went into hiding, the woman hadn't stopped once. She's the fucking Energizer Bunny for the entire town. So far today, I've seen her help Blissy with the trash, work with the football players on a time management plan, and then she helped a group of high schoolers from the local high school sign up for time in the sound booth to record their own podcasts for a class they're taking.

Does she ever do anything for herself?

Now she's sitting with her back to me with who I assume are her close friends because the second they walked in, they grabbed her by the arms, dragged her to the table farthest from me, put their heads together, and all I've heard are hissing sounds ever since.

Every once in a while, one of them will lift their head to look around, but their gazes always land on me. I know because I haven't been able to stop staring at them.

When did I turn into a stalker?

When the assertive-looking one with brown hair pulled into a severely high ponytail glares at me, I know it's time to distract myself.

Opening up the messaging app on my new MacBook, I type out a quick message.

Me: Can you find an address for a college football player at Happiness State University named Ethan—he grew up in Happiness— and then send him a new MacBook so it doesn't come from Georgia?

Me: Say he won it in a competition or something.

Grey: Is there a reason we're gifting a $2000 machine to a kid you don't even know the last name of?

He chooses now to call me out?

Me: I'm sorry, aren't you the one who encouraged me to do this shit in the first place?

My gaze darts around the room as though I'm about to get caught robbing a bank. When I don't find any police or Blissy holding a broom to my throat, I go back to typing out another message.

Me: He needs it. And he's a good kid.

Me: I helped him tape his laptop back together again.

Me: He said he only needed his to last two more years until he graduates and gets a job to afford a new one.

Me: He donated the one the football team gave him to a freshman who needed it more.

Jesus. I just had texting diarrhea.

Grey: Huh.

Me: Huh what?

Grey: An act of kindness.

I groan because I know exactly where this is heading.

Me: You told me to do this shit. And this is exactly why we started the DDD in college. It's the only way for me to give back without my mother turning it into a PR stunt for herself, which meant I could no longer attend.

Or it was.

If feels different helping now.

When the Montgomerys donate money, they give it to whatever charity will offer them the most recognition, and they never volunteer unless there's a camera crew following them. The DDD, Discreet Daily Deeds, is something we started after my parents stepped so far over the line that I knew I would never be like them.

That was the year Greyson and I both got our start-up money from Ace and pooled it together. Half of it we invested—luckily Grey is a savant with investments—and the other half we used to buy into an early-stage online commerce website.

Later that year, we left college for good.

We've funded our lives, Sage's, and the DDD ever since. I don't even remember the last time I touched my trust fund.

Me: I forgot how much I enjoy helping just because I can without someone taking over and manipulating the situation to make it feel promotional.

Doing good deeds anonymously also keeps the risk of being used to a minimum. If no one knows I'm doing it, then no one can try to get shit from me.

> Grey: I didn't say anything. It's just been a while, and I was worried you wouldn't remember who you are.

> Grey: And FYI, you're not the asshole CEO you've been hiding behind. So can I assume that Happiness, Georgia is living up to its name?

> Me: I've been here less than twenty-four hours.

> Grey: And here you are, making a difference for a kid you met once, but not wanting anyone to know it came from you.

> Me: He mows Madison's lawn for her.

As soon as I hit send, I know I've just sunk myself. My phone rings. Thankfully it's on silent, and I ignore it.

> Grey: Madison, the inn owner?

> Me: And the owner of the coworking space I'm currently sitting in.

> Grey: Fine, you like the old lady, I get it.

I frown at my screen, then reread our messages. I guess I can see why he'd assume Madison is older, and for my own sake, I continue to let him believe that.

Grey: I'll get the computer sent out in a week or two so it doesn't look too suspicious.

Me: Make sure it can't be traced back to me.

Grey: Secret acts of kindness from the renegade billionaire, done.

I groan so loudly it has heads turning my way. Madison lifts a brow.

"Everything all right over there?" she asks.

"Sorry, yes. Just a meeting with someone who annoys me."

Her smile is soft but tired, and it makes me want to fix that too. She returns to her friends who've raised their voices to normal volume now. I guess they're done discussing me and my reactions to Madison.

I came on too strong today, but when I saw her shimmying in the kitchen as water sprayed all over her, something snapped in my chest, and I haven't been able to think straight since.

For some reason, I'm drawn to Madison Ryan, and luckily, I have all the time in the world to find out why.

By three in the afternoon, I can no longer sit and stare at Madison, whom Blissy has informed me is the town sweetheart—something that stays with her until marriage, and then they announce a new one.

It was also the first time I saw Madison appear truly upset as Blissy off-handedly mentioned this bit of news. Her agitation was clear in the way she plucked at the elastic on her wrist, but it made me want to know all her whys and what-ifs.

I didn't want to make her any more uncomfortable though, so I grabbed a coffee—and a tea because I haven't chosen sides yet—and I'm trying not to spill them as I pull into the Hideaway's driveway.

Holding the cardboard tray in one hand, I exit the truck that I didn't stall once, thank you very much.

"Nice truck," Pops says from the porch swing.

I shut the door and instantly feel my shoulders relax. There's something about this old man that I really connect with.

"Bought it today." Why do I sound so proud? I've bought cars worth forty times what this cost.

"Looks good. Let's go." The older man stands from the swing and walks with his left arm out as though he's feeling his way around, but I saw him reading the paper this morning, so it catches me off guard.

"Everything okay?" I ask, hurrying to the stairs in case he falls.

"Just peachy. I got some errands to run. Whatcha got in there?" He points to the tray I'm still holding in the air.

"Coffee and a tea."

His laugh is a comfort I didn't know I needed.

"Ya weren't ready to pick a side, huh? Smart. I'll take the coffee." Pops sticks his nose into the cup closest to him, takes it from the holder, then runs his free hand along the hood of the truck and climbs in.

"Should we let Madison know we're heading out?" The driver's door creaks as I open it.

"I'm not her ward, boy. Back her up and head toward town."

Suppressing my laughter, I buckle my seatbelt, put the tea I have no intention of drinking into the cup holder, and follow his directions to town.

"So, what kind of errands are we doing this afternoon?"

"Gotta run to Huckabees. I've got some fixin' to do, and now I've got a helper, so we're doing it together."

"Oh yeah? Who's your helper?" Looking both ways, I turn left at the four-way intersection.

"This here is called Compassion Corner. If you keep going straight, it'd take you to Bitter Creek."

My lips tilt up at the corners. "So the town really stuck with its emotional theme, huh?"

"Damn straight, boy. Happiness folk ain't afraid of crying."

"Good to know. What other areas should I be aware of?"

"Joy Junction's where the movie theater is. Bitter Creek has the best swimming hole in all of Georgia. Envy's Edge is a beauty at night—y'all never seen so many stars. Oh, and Pride Peak is where all you young folk go hiking. Turn right up here."

I do as he says, and a few moments later, we're parking in front of Huckabees Hardware Store.

"This is a good truck, boy. You did good." Pops, who still hasn't given me his real name, waltzes into the store with me trailing behind.

"Afternoon, Marty," Pops says to the man behind the counter.

"Pops, what are you doing in here today? Is Madi with you?"

Does everyone call him Pops?

"Nah, she's over doing her thing at the Chug. I've got some shutters to hang and some drywall to patch up." Pops turns to me. "Grab a cart, boy."

Dutifully, I obey.

"Ah, Pops." Marty groans, then tosses his hands into the air. "Don't get me in trouble with Madi again. You know she doesn't want you working on the inn right now."

"Don't you worry about it," Pops says with a thread of defiance in his tone. "I've got a helper. Marty, meet Brax. Brax, meet Marty."

My head snaps up. "I'm the helper?"

Marty chuckles, and Pops keeps on moseying down the aisle.

"Pops, you know I can't let you charge stuff to your account. Madi said things were tough—"

"I know what Madi said, Marty. But we gotta fix some shit."

Pops moves farther into the store, and Marty scratches the side of his head. I could tell the Hideaway had seen better days, but is it because they're not able to afford the repairs?

One look into Marty's conflicted expression tells me everything.

"Hey, ah, Marty?"

"Yeah, kid?"

I slip him my credit card. "Whatever Pops gets today, put it on my card, okay?"

He stares at it as if it's going to bite him. His big arms cross over his chest, and everything from the line between his eyes to his rigid posture indicates he's put up his guard. "Why would you do that?"

I shrug. Why am I doing it? I have no explanation other than I have the same feeling I got when I had Grey order Ethan's laptop—it makes my bitter ass feel better.

And it's what Ace would've done.

"Just helping out," I say, then walk away to find Pops.

He's already in the back of the store, talking to a man about my age.

"There you are," he says to me. "Didn't take you for a slacker though. Braxton, this is Hunter. He dated Madi in the eighth grade."

I'm not sure who blushes harder, Hunter or me.

"That's a bit of history you probably didn't need to know," Hunter says with an easy drawl. "Nice to meet you. Glad Pops has some help over at the Hideaway. Sure would be a shame to see it shut down."

"Shut down?" The back of my neck itches.

"Oh, you run your gossip somewhere else. Boy, grab three of these sheetrock slabs and stick 'em in the truck for me."

I glance between Hunter and Pops, then do as I was asked, stopping by the counter first so Marty can see what I'm taking.

By the time I find Pops, he's got an entire cart full of supplies and is heading toward the checkout.

"I should probably tell you, Pops, I've never fixed anything before."

"Pfft," he grumbles. "Ya shut the water off this morning, didn't ya?"

"Well, yeah, but Madi gave me instructions."

"So will I. Marty, you got all this?"

Marty looks from Pops to me, and I give my best "don't tell him I'm paying" look. Marty nods, peers into the cart, and rings us up while Pops struts—yes, struts—toward the door. It's the only way to describe the way he saunters out to the truck.

"Thanks for that. If you don't mind, I'd appreciate it if we kept this between you and me."

Marty stares at me for a long moment before his face relaxes. "You've never lived in a small town, have you, son?"

How the hell does everyone know that?

"No, sir."

"Well, I'll keep your secret, but those two over there have probably already told half the town. The other half will know by suppertime."

I look to where he's pointing and find two older gentlemen whispering to a third who's staring at me.

"Great," I say as my spine locks up like a zipper. "Thanks, Marty." As I walk away, I'm assaulted by the gossip of strangers. Their hushed words peck at my skin, picking away at the confidence doing good deeds had awarded me.

At the truck, Pops is talking to a young couple who stand arm in arm. It's like he knows every person in town.

"Braxton, this is Jenny and Peter Cowles. Peter dated Madi in, what? Was that the seventh grade, Jenny?"

What the hell is happening right now?

"Yup," the woman says as if it doesn't bother her in the slightest. "Then again after...you know."

"Yes, but before Mark down at the station," Peter says with a laugh.

"It's really not as strange as it sounds," Jenny says quietly. "It's a small town. Everyone has dated someone else's ex at one point or another."

"That's...interesting," I mutter, still unsure why I'm irrationally upset by this conversation.

"Half the time, Madi's simply matchmaking, but Pops insists they're dates. It's what she does, she's the very best matchmaker I know. Pops just wants her to be happy," Jenny says.

"The first week she came to live with us, she had a pet wedding between a neighbor boy's rabbit and Mrs. Cracken's cat, Louie." Pops voice fades as he speaks. When he blinks hard three times, he chuckles. "She's gotten a hell of a lot better since then."

"She sure has. We're living proof. Nice to meet you, Braxton." Peter takes Jenny's hand and guides her back to the sidewalk while I put all the supplies in the bed of the truck and Pops sits up front.

"Where to next?" I grumble, climbing into the driver's seat.

Pops pulls out three sheets of paper. "I've got a list," he says.

"I see that." Giving him the side-eye, I wonder just how wily this old man is. "How'd you know I didn't have to work or something?"

"Ya said you didn't know how long you were staying. You didn't come with much luggage, and you don't seem to be in a hurry to go nowhere. Figure if you've got the time, might as well make an honest man out of ya."

My spine slowly curves in, releasing my shoulders from my ears in the process, because now it's my turn to laugh. Pops doesn't sugarcoat anything, and you have to appreciate that about a man. "All right, Pops. Where to next?"

His expression is something I'd expect to see on a naughty little boy, and I have the distinct impression that we're both going to be on Madison's shit list by the time we make it home.

It might even be worth it.

6

———

MADISON

"That was fabulous," Derek, my producer, says as I exit the small recording studio at the Chugaloo. "People are going to flip for this week's podcast. Absolutely flip. Do you think you can prep six more by next week?"

Next week! Has he lost his mind? No. The answer is no, Derek. I can't do that and fix the inn, and run the Chug, *and* keep Pops out of trouble, make sure the football team is on track with their grades, get the donations at the church sorted for Betty, and produce Clover and Savvy's podcasts all by next week.

"Sure thing" is what I actually say.

"This is what I wanted. I wanted people to rely on me, and I wanted to be needed," I mutter to myself as we walk down the hall.

When I was in high school, I started a podcast called *The Matchmaker Manual*, and it took off faster than I could keep up. It's always been my little slice of happiness. I learned early on what love shouldn't look like from my parents, and living with my grandparents showed me everything I'd been missing out on.

I became obsessed with finding true love for everyone in my orbit at a very early age. By the time I was in college, I had syndication offers.

Well, until it all came crashing down and I scrambled to modify every plan I had ever created for myself because what kind of matchmaker could I be if I can't even find love myself?

But for the last couple of years, with encouragement from my friends, I've been building it back up. Somewhere along the way, I'd lost who I was, but matchmaking is in my soul—it's in my blood.

Thankfully, my loyal listeners came back in droves. Last month I was offered a new syndication deal, but I've been dragging my feet on accepting it. After The Ones We Don't Name left a bad taste in my mouth, I find it hard to trust anyone in a suit with an offer that sounds too good to be true.

Derek stops my stroll through memory lane with a hand on my forearm when we reach the main room.

"Thanks, Derek. Sorry I'm a little behind. We've got an unexpected guest at the Hideaway, so I'm shifting some stuff around this week."

"Oh, don't you worry. I've heard all about Mr. Braxton Mitchell. They're calling him the hometown hottie."

My mind freezes as though I'm stuck in the Matrix.

"They're what? He's not even from here. He's just passing through." Can Derek hear the fear in my tone?

"Well, Jasper was in the hardware store earlier," Blissy says smugly. "He told Jesse who told Mrs. Cromley who told me that he saw Braxton with Pops, buying up all the things. That doesn't sound like someone just passing through."

Panic flares in my chest. What the heck did Pops buy?

We can't afford a hardware store run right now. We can barely even afford groceries for our guest.

"What do you mean? Pops isn't supposed to leave the house until we get his depth perception figured out."

Blissy shrugs but doesn't bother hiding her grin.

"Oh my God. This is a disaster. Blissy, can you close up tonight? The high school kids will be done by seven. If not—"

"Go, Madi. I've got you."

I give the older woman a quick hug, causing the navy handkerchief she wears covering her hair to shift.

She quickly reties it while I give Derek a hug too.

"Thanks, you guys. I appreciate you." As soon as the door shuts behind me, I scowl and nearly stomp my foot in frustration.

What the heck is Braxton thinking, taking Pops out? And why is Pops spending money he knows we don't have?

Once I'm in my little VW Jetta, I blast the AC and take a deep breath. I'm sure there's a reasonable explanation. I just have to go home to see what it is.

I PULL MY CAR INTO THE DRIVEWAY, AND I'M PRETTY SURE I'M hallucinating. Why is Pops' old truck here?

He agreed to sell it. He knows driving isn't safe with his condition.

"Against the hallway," Pops yells, spurring me into motion.

Stepping out of the car, I come face-to-face with Braxton.

"What the heck is going on?" I ask.

Braxton's gaze darts from me to Pops, and when he faces

me again, he scratches the center of his chest and flashes the best puppy dog eyes the world has ever seen.

"Don't puppy dog face me, Braxton Mitchell," I say, poking him in the chest and immediately regretting the contact. Sparks shoot up my arm, and his gaze flames with amber fire that has me jumping back a step. "Taking Pops out is dangerous. He could have been seriously injured."

"Bull hickey," Pops mutters from his porch swing.

Spinning on my grandfather, I point my finger at him. "Don't you start, old man. You and I had a deal, and I know you. Somehow you tricked Braxton into being your sidekick. And what the heck is your old truck doing here?" My voice loses some of its fire. "We talked about this, Pops."

"Ah," Braxton interrupts.

I suck in a deep breath and count to three before I turn to face him again.

"It's actually my truck. I bought it today from Terd—"

I lurch forward, reach up on my tiptoes, and close my palm over his mouth, startling us both. My chest presses into his rib cage, and adrenaline rushes through my veins. It's unnatural, to have these types of reactions to a stranger —it must be.

"Do. Not. Say. That. Name. Ever. Understand?"

He nods beneath my hand, and I release him. With some space between us, the unnerving sensation rattling through my bloodstream falls away.

"So, I bought it from the Turd. I didn't know it was Po—" He stops mid-sentence and stares at me.

"What?" I may have just growled at him.

"Harry Turd said... Oh my God." He turns to Pops. "You're the grandfather who owned the truck. And that makes you—" His gaze drops to mine, and so many emotions swirl in his irises as he stares. "That makes you the one who got away," he says so quietly I practically lean in to hear him.

"The one who got away?" I snarl. "Is that what he said?"

"Harry Turd is a pissant," Pops grumbles.

"Harry...Harry Turd?" I don't want to laugh, but hearing Pops call my lying, manipulative ex a Harry Turd cracks me wide open. It's so childish, immature to the nth degree, but it also takes some of the vitriol I carry for my ex and turns it into something I can laugh about.

That hasn't happened, ever. Not until Braxton Mitchell.

I've completely lost my mind. I'm doubled over with my hands on my knees, laughing so hard my stomach cramps. But then Braxton's hand lands on my back, rubbing small, soothing circles.

It sobers me quickly enough that I stand upright to face him again, this time with tears of laughter spilling down my cheeks. I quickly brush them away.

"I don't mean to pry—"

"Then don't," I interrupt.

"I just mean...the Turd-o-nator is kind of..."

"Sleazy," Pops fills in.

Braxton scratches at a spot on his chest. "Ah, yeah. That's it." He chuckles. "And he's not very—"

"Attractive. Guys lost his damn mind right along with his hair. Madi dodged a real bullet there." Pops whistles to the sky as the swing carries him back and forth.

"Okay, Pops. That's enough." When I turn back to Braxton, he's studying me—it twists me up like a Rubik's cube. "My ex...he wasn't always this way. He used to be—"

"Sober," Pops blurts.

I purse my lips and drop my gaze to the ground. "Alcohol has changed him."

Braxton slides both hands into his front pockets just as

Savvy's car pulls up in front of the house. Good Lord, save me from this night.

"You bought Pops' truck?" I'm desperate to change the subject.

"Yeah," he says, pulling on his neck with one hand.

Closing my eyes, I nod three times.

"I'm going to make dinner now." Lifting my lashes a fraction of an inch, I still get lost in the pull of him. "Ah, and I'll apologize in advance for my friends. They're more than friends, actually, they're our family, and they feel the need to join us for dinner tonight to make sure you're not a body-snatching murderer looking to make a skinsuit."

"A skinsuit, huh?" He rubs his jaw with his thumb, and why is that the sexiest move ever? "I promise you, I'm not a skinsuit murderer."

I shrug. "Isn't that exactly what you'd say if you were?"

His dang crooked smile makes my limbs tingle. "I suppose it is."

"Listen, it's not me you have to convince. It's them." I hook a thumb in the direction of Savvy's car just as she, Clover, and a very pregnant Elle step out.

"I'm going to need some wine," I mutter, then make my escape to the house. "Pops, you and I are going to have a little chat about your shopping trip today, and then we're going to go over, again, why it's not safe for you to be out without someone helping you."

He waves me off with a shooing motion while watching the girls as they march past Braxton. Clover makes an "I'm watching you" motion with her fingers to her eyes, and Pops hoots with laughter.

I'm never going to survive this night.

"Anything I can do to help?" Braxton asks, poking his head into the kitchen.

"Where are you from?" Savvy asks before I can open my mouth.

"West Coast," he replies vaguely.

"What do you do?" Clover continues their line of questions.

"Ladies." I attempt to interrupt, but Savvy speaks over me.

"How long are you staying?" she asks.

Braxton enters the kitchen, and the door swings shut behind him. I watch out of the corner of my eye as he sticks both hands in his pockets and rocks back on his heels.

"I'm not sure yet. I'm kind of on a…sabbatical."

"How can you 'kind of be on a sabbatical'?" Clover asks, but she's more curious than anything. She can't keep the edge to her voice in the same way Savvy can—she wasn't built for it.

"You can do what you want when you own the company." I can feel Braxton watching me. It's not a completely unwelcome sensation, just…different. "Madison, can I help with anything?"

Instead of raising my head, I pretend to be focused on my pie crust and just shake my head.

"Good luck getting her to agree to help," Savvy mutters.

I love the girl, but seriously, sometimes she is a giant pain. "No," I say gently. "But thank you. Everything will be done in about ten minutes. If you want to tell Pops to get ready, that would be fine."

"So, if you own the company, you can afford to take time off and stay here…indefinitely?" Savvy is so damn persistent.

"It wouldn't be prudent of me to take off if I didn't have

my company and my finances under control, now would it?" He doesn't seem the least bit bothered by my friends.

"Hmm," Savvy hums.

"So, you could pay for a month's stay in advance and still be comfortable?" Elle asks shyly, then stuffs a giant piece of chocolate into her mouth with an apologetic shrug.

"Elle," I snap. I know where she's going with this, and I don't like it one bit.

Braxton seems to be taking us all in, as well as the kitchen and now the big boards of sheetrock laying against the back door.

"I'm happy to do that," he finally says. "I'll go settle up with Pops now." The way his eyes crinkle at the corners makes me think he's kind—a gentle soul maybe, but there's an edge to him too that I haven't figured out.

No one can give a command that makes my body melt the way he did and not have extra layers to him.

"You really don't have to do that," I blurt, but he's already halfway out the door.

"No problem at all, Madison," he says, waving over his shoulder.

"It's Madi—"

The door squeaks shut, cutting me off.

"Elle," I say, spinning on my friend.

"Don't 'Elle' her," Savvy says, bumping me out of the way. "If you roll out this crust any more it's going to be too thin to use. And you know if he pays up front, that would help a hell of a lot around here, and since you aren't sure how long he'll be staying, this gives you a little security that he won't up and leave while stiffing you on the bill."

"I don't think he's someone who would skip out on a bill, Sav."

"You never know," Elle says.

The doorbell rings, and we all stare at the closed door.

"Did you invite someone over?" Clover asks.

"No," I say, then groan when I hear Pops welcoming someone in. "But I bet Pops did during his little escape into town this afternoon."

Savvy laughs. "He must be so happy to have his social butterfly wings back now that he's got Brax carting him all over town."

Wiping my hands on my apron, I bite my tongue because it's the situation I'm frustrated with, not my friends. It wouldn't be fair of me to take it all out on them.

"Let's go see what kind of mess Pops has made now."

Clover is sitting closest to the door, so she pushes it open slowly—just enough for us to peer out into the hallway that opens up at the foyer.

"Pops wanted a party," Clover whispers.

"Or an inquisition," Savvy snickers.

Pops' oldest friends, Moose and Chief, stand in the entryway, while Pops is behind the desk with Braxton.

Moose opens the front door, and Cian walks in with Shep and Beau Collins.

"What are they doing here?" I whisper above Elle's head.

"No idea, but Cian's going to be pissed I didn't invite him myself." Elle snickers.

Braxton must hear us because he turns just in time to see all our heads stacked in a row—my head on top of Elle's, Clover's on mine, and Savvy on top of Clover. Elle jumps back when she sees him smirking at us, and we tumble to the floor in a heap of tangled limbs that twist and turn, trying to keep our weight off Elle.

The four of us lie there in shock and only move when Braxton pokes his head inside again. When he sees us, I swear the light reflects off his bright white teeth.

"You spend a lot of time on the kitchen floor, Madison?" He enters and offers Elle a hand, since she's the first one he reaches, and she's super pregnant.

"Only since you arrived," I grumble.

"Good to know." He chuckles, then offers me and Clover a hand. He pulls us to standing with zero effort as Savvy stands on her own. "I just wanted you to know I was only around for the invite to Chief—is it true that he's retired but refuses to give up his badge?" My friends laugh, and someone must say yes while I'm here trying to get my words to work. "Anyway, the other five, I'm not sure when they happened, but I'm happy to help if you haven't made enough for dinner. I can order something or—"

"Madi cooks for an army of fifty every time. She can't help herself," Savvy says, then waggles her brows at me.

"Mads?" Pops finally enters the kitchen, looking far too pleased with himself. "Oh, good. Girls, ya mind setting the table for me?"

"We've got it, Pops," Clover says, patting his arm. "You're in a lot of trouble." She whispers, but it sounds as though it echoes in the open space.

Pops laughs, but otherwise ignores her. "We got any beer, Mads?"

"I wasn't expecting a full house, Pops. We don't really have the..." I cut myself off when I remember that Braxton's hovering nearby.

"I can run to the store. What kind do you want, Pops?" He's always so stinking accommodating.

There must be something wrong with him.

"No—"

"Anything from Briar Patch Brewing is good. It's local, ya know," Pops says so proudly you'd think he owned the dang brewery.

"You need anything else, Madison?" The way Braxton's voice dips when he says my name makes my stomach turn over. He genuinely wants to help, and I'm not sure how I feel about that. It would be easier if all he wanted was to get in my panties.

My chest thumps wildly at the thought, but my shoulders slump as I give in to another mess created by my grandfather. "No. I appreciate you asking though."

"Sauvignon Blanc is her favorite, you know, if you're feeling generous." Savvy's not so helpful.

I love how Braxton's lips twitch at the corners. "Thanks for the tip. I'll be back." Instead of leaving, he walks over to the refrigerator where I have a notepad and pen hanging, and my jaw falls slack as he scribbles something down. When he looks up, his gaze pins me to my spot. "My number," he says. Why is he so smiley all the time? "In case you think of anything while I'm out."

"Smooth, real smooth." Pops chuckles.

"Pops, please," I plead. "Just stop. Braxton, if you give me a minute, I'll give you some cash for the beer."

If I can find some.

"My treat," he says as he walks out the door, and I immediately spin on my grandfather.

"Pops. What are you thinking? You know we can't afford all this stuff." I point to the sheetrock. "And I need a warning before you invite the town over. We can't afford to be the local pub right now either. Why did you invite the Collins brothers, your poker pals, *and* Cian over for dinner?"

Instead of answering, he pulls me in for a hug. We stand there for a long moment, enough that my racing heart slows, and the anger or anxiety that was tightening my muscles relaxes. Then he kisses the side of my head before releasing me.

As he's walking back out to his friends, he drops the next bomb on me. "We're all right, Mads. That boy just paid for a six-month stay. In full."

The girls and I all spin to face each other. I can see Savvy working the numbers in her head, while Clover is most likely evaluating the emotional toll it will take on me having him in my space for—for six months. Elle has found a bag of cookies and sits at the island, downing two at a time while crumbs land on her belly.

"That's...thirty-one thousand dollars, Madi. Thirty-one thousand." Savvy's voice rises along with my blood pressure.

"Thirty-six even," Pops corrects. "He insisted on two hundred a night because we're including meals." When the kitchen door snaps shut behind him, I return my shocked and bewildered gaze to my girls.

"Something is definitely wrong with him," Savvy mutters.

"You could put a down payment on a condo or something for that amount. Well, almost." Clover sounds as confused as I am.

"Who pays thirty-six thousand dollars to stay in a run-down inn in the middle of nowhere, Georgia?" I ask.

"Someone with a lot of secrets, that's who." I can almost see Clover's mind twisting this into a new thriller novel in her mind.

"Well, if he's got them, we'll find them," Elle vows through a mouthful of chocolate chips. Where the hell did those come from?

"Let's Google him." Savvy's already pulling out her phone.

"Sav, you know how I feel about that." I groan. When you've been the victim of cyberbullying, you try your hardest not to engage in any kind of snooping or clickbait.

But when my friends hover around Elle, staring at Savvy's phone, I watch their expressions go from suspicious and curious to confused and back to suspicious.

"There's not much about him online," Savvy says with her face turned down into a frown. "He doesn't even really have a current social media presence. It's all from high school and college. Who doesn't have social media these days?" she mutters. Her frown deepens the more she scrolls.

"I'm sure there's an explanation," Elle says cheerily. "There's no such thing as secrets in Happiness. He'll find that out one way or another. Come on, Mads. Let's finish this up. The sooner we serve it, the sooner the night will end."

"Maybe." Clover is wearing her thinking expression, with her brows furrowed and her bottom lip pinched between her thumb and forefinger. "What?" she asks when she finds us staring at her. "Brax is getting beer and wine, and Pops hasn't had a guy's night in months. This could be a long night."

I groan because she's one hundred percent correct. "Please pour me a glass of Sunny's." It's the cheapest wine in town, and I don't even care about the headache it'll bring me tomorrow. Anything to get me through the next couple of hours.

But even as I place the pies in the oven, my mind is screaming *thirty-six thousand dollars.*

Who can afford to do that?

And why is he spending it here?

7

BRAXTON

Never in all my life have I experienced a beer run that was so unrelated to beer. I'm sitting in Madison's driveway now, trying to process it before I go inside.

I need a few damn minutes to figure out what the hell happened.

My head is still in my palms when there's a light knock on the truck window.

I'm not sure I have enough energy to meet more new people, but reluctantly, I lift my head. Nope, scratch that—I'm up for anything.

Madison stands on the other side of the glass. She's wearing an uneasy smile, but there's something in her worried expression and pinched brows that has me wanting to know...everything.

She makes a rolling motion with her hand, and internally I groan while I do as she asks. It only took me an embarrassing few seconds to realize that it is, in fact, an actual crank to roll the window down.

"That bad, huh?" she asks, resting her folded arms on the door. The truck is so high, or she's so small that she's able to rest her chin on her forearms without bending much. She pats the inside of the door. "Old Fender here is still pretty loud. I heard you pull in, and everyone's been watching you for the last fifteen minutes."

Leaning over the steering wheel, I see no less than six heads that immediately duck when they notice I've caught them staring.

"Fender?" I ask, choosing to focus on that and not my embarrassment about hiding in my truck.

"Yup." She laughs. "Pops taught me to drive in this thing, but I could hardly see over the wheel. I had a homemade booster seat, but I still left my mark all over town. The locals started calling him Fender Bender, and they cleared the streets when I got my license."

Madison's expression lightens.

"That's a great story," I admit. "My mother hired someone to teach me after my grandfather pressured her to spend time with me."

She scans my face as if she'll find what she's looking for if she only searches hard enough.

"Is that how you grew up? Raised by other people?" There's no judgment in her tone—if anything, there's understanding there.

I shrug, feeling hot under the collar. "Pretty much. I was an oops baby, and my parents really couldn't be bothered with me."

I shouldn't be telling her this. My whole reason for being here is to accomplish Ace's mission and get home, but she's too easy to talk to.

"I know how that feels." Her words are soft and full of understanding. "So, you ready for dinner? I should've warned you that Pops was probably setting you up. The entire town is on Braxton watch. I'm sure the trip to the packy was interesting."

"The packy?"

"The package store. Where you bought the beer."

"Oh, yeah." I drop my hand to my lap when I notice I'm scratching at my chest. It's a tell of mine that I've never been able to shake. "Is it normal to have your height measured in a liquor store? Or—or asked your blood type? What my intentions are? Why I paid for a six-month stay? How did they even know that one? It hadn't even been an hour."

She opens my door. "We will discuss that, by the way. You seriously overpaid, and I won't accept it. And to answer your question, yes, it's normal around here. This town loves hard. They protect even harder. For newbies, they put you through your paces before you're accepted. And those of us who have been here a while, well, we always know we're safe. Come on inside."

"Is that what this is tonight?" I point to the window, where all the spying eyes once again duck away, while pointedly ignoring her comment on money because I'm not budging on that.

"Pops likes you more than most. I'm sure this is his hazing plan to get it all out in one go so you two can be friends." She nervously tugs on the elastic around her wrist.

"Hazing? I thought that was illegal now." I laugh as I exit the truck, dragging the box of beer and wine with me.

"You'd be surprised what you can get away with here in the South."

"Why don't you have an accent?" The question comes out of nowhere, but now that I think about it, her friends don't either.

"I didn't move here until I was ten. I lived with my

parents before that in New York, Maine, and Massachusetts. I guess I missed my chance for a Southern drawl."

I heft the box, and she shuts my door. "And your friends?"

She pauses on the porch steps. "I met Savvy and Clover in college. They both followed me home when...when I transferred home for my sophomore year, and you haven't spent enough time with Elle because she's as Southern as they come."

"Huh." There's more to that sophomore-year transfer, but I'm not going to push her for details.

"Dinner will be an inquisition for sure. Just take everything in stride, and you'll be all right. If it gets too out of control, I'll hit the breaker in the basement to cut the power. That'll be enough to get people moving."

She opens the door but pauses and smiles at me—and the impact is like being shot out of a cannon. "Just remember, Pops likes you."

"Should I be nervous?"

"I guess that depends on how honest you are."

I trip over the threshold. I can be honest about everything except who I really am—that ruins everything. It always has.

"Should be easy then."

If she hears the crack in my voice, she doesn't comment on it. Either that, or the noise coming from the dining room drowned me out. It could go either way right now.

"He's home." Pops' voice carries over the crowd. "Come on in here, boy. Let's see what you got."

Carrying the box into the dining room where everyone is still rushing to be seated, I lower it when I reach him so he can peer inside.

He nods as he inspects the bottles. When he lifts his

gaze to mine, I see for the first time that this man has my number. I don't know what he knows, but I'm sure he sees something in me I wasn't ready to divulge.

"You did good, boy. Pass 'em around, then come sit."

I do as he asks and walk around the table while everyone grabs a beer. When I get to Savvy, she pulls out a bottle of wine and raises a brow in my direction.

"Most expensive bottle at the packy? Good to know you're aware that our girl is worth it."

Heat creeps up my neck, and I'm one thousand percent sure everyone in this room is witness to my blushing.

"Savvy," Madison reprimands her with one word. Savvy shrugs and sets the bottle on the table while I make a quick retreat to the kitchen to put the rest of the beer and wine away.

By the time I return to the table, there's only one chair available—directly to Madison's left and dead center in the middle of everyone.

What's the worst that can happen, right? They've all been nice so far. So I take a seat next to Madison and let the games begin.

My ass isn't even in the chair before Pops speaks.

"Boy, meet Shep. He dated Madi after college."

Poor Shep chokes on his beer.

"Ah, I wouldn't call it dating." Beau chuckles.

Madison lifts her wine glass to her lips and tips it back, swallowing three times before she sets it back on the table.

Clover, who sits to my left, leans in close. "Don't worry about Pops. He's just messing with you, it means he likes you."

"And then Beau tried to date her for a time." Pops is sitting at the head of the table and completely in his element.

"That wasn't dating either," Shep says. "Madi's a matchmaker, remember? Just because she goes out to dinner with someone doesn't mean it's a date for herself."

"Clover and Madi dated this nitwit," the man introduced as Chief says. "Madi only dated this one in middle school."

"Ah, Uncle. I can feel the love from here," Beau says.

"Why are you giving my dating history at dinner, Pops?" Madison asks.

"What's the big deal?" Beau asks. "Newbie over there might as well know if he's going to date one of us, he's dating all of us. That's how it works around here."

"That's disgusting, Beau." Savvy throws a roll at him. Turning to me, she shrugs. "The dating pool is abysmal in town, so sometimes you date your friend's ex. It's not as incestual as they make it out to be."

Now it's my turn to chug my beer, and when I do, I make eye contact with the giant named Cian who hasn't said two words. He blinks as though he's bored, and I focus on my beer.

"Who said he was here to date anyone?" Clover asks. Is she coming to my defense? She might be my favorite of Madison's friends.

"Have you seen the way he looks at Madi?" the second-biggest man in the room says. There's no denying that he lives up to the nickname Moose.

Once again, my face is on fire.

"He's blushing. Leave the boy alone," Pops says.

"Pops," Madison scoffs. "You're the one who started it."

He shrugs her off, picks up a casserole dish, puts a scoop on his plate, and passes it to the right.

Everyone else takes that as a cue to do the same, and before I know what's happening, dishes of all shapes and colors are making their way around the table.

"What are you doing here for six months?" one of Pops' friends asks, but I'm not sure who. Everyone is running together at this point.

"I'm on sabbatical. Just regrouping and figuring out what direction I want to take my company in going forward."

"What kind of business?" Savvy asks, and all heads turn in my direction. Didn't she already ask me what I do? They don't mess around with their inquisitions.

"Um, marketing mostly. That's where my heart is." It's only a partial lie. I do have an entire marketing department, but the last thing I need anyone knowing is just how much money I come from or that I'm one of *those* Montgomerys.

"What does that—"

"Guys," Madison interrupts. "Let's eat before it gets cold, okay?"

Blessed silence falls over the table for thirty whole seconds.

"Was this your destination, or did you just land here?"

"What do you plan to do for six months?"

"Can you afford to just sit on your ass all day?"

"Did you max out your credit card to pay for a six-month stay?"

And those are the easy questions. My mind is spinning in a way even the most seasoned of public relations personnel wouldn't have been able to control.

Maybe I am in over my head here, because I think I just got my ass handed to me by three old men and three guys I think have all dated the woman to my right.

And the only part of it that I care about is who's dated Madison.

"Just so you know, Pops is messing with you to see how you'll react," Madison whispers. I inch closer to her, drawn in by her heat, her kindness, her. "Savvy dated Beau. Then, years later, I had dinner with him to help him plan a proposal that never happened, and Pops counts that as a date." She's a mind reader. "He's probably also told you I've dated everyone I ever went to the movies with, sat next to, or talked to on the phone. It's all to see how you'll react so he'll know what to watch for. He's done this since I came to live with him."

"Why?"

"He's hellbent on marrying me off before he dies."

I spin to face her. "Is he ill?"

She laughs and tucks her hair behind her ear. Even her fucking neck is delicate, and why I'm noticing this shit is freaking me out a little. "He's going blind in one eye—that's why his depth perception is off—but otherwise he's as healthy as he's ever been. He'll probably be here for another twenty years."

"Huh," I say as I mull over her words. "So, are you saying he thinks I'm a potential suitor?"

She covers her mouth to hide a laugh. "Suitor? How old are you?"

"Thirty. So, does he?"

She sighs and glances around the table. "If Pops has anything to say about it, every eligible bachelor is a suitor."

"And what about you? What do you want?"

She turns her gaze on me, and I swear to Christ, all the noise of our tablemates becomes muted.

"I don't know anymore." The sadness in those four words makes my chest ache.

Before I can respond, she stands. "Ready for dessert?" she asks no one and everyone.

A chorus of yeses goes up. I start to rise, but Clover pats my arm. "Sit. We'll help her."

My ass hits the chair again as Madison and her three

friends hurry to the kitchen, carrying dirty dishes. So many questions are floating around in my head that I don't even know where to start.

The swinging door to the kitchen is still swaying gently when laughter cuts through my focus. I turn back to find Pops watching me with a suspiciously smug expression and a smile that makes me think he's all too happy to play matchmaker himself.

It's hours before the last guest leaves. After the initial rapid-fire questions session, things settled down, and by the time dessert was over, I found I was enjoying myself.

I never checked my phone to see if my family had caused any more headaches for me yet. In fact, I'm not even sure where it is at the moment, and I don't care. Instead, I head to the kitchen because I know that's where I'll find Madison.

The door swings open with a nerve-grating sound. There must be some kind of oil or something for that. I'll have to remember to ask Pops in the morning. Three beers for the old man, and he was in bed before his friends even left.

Madison spins around to face me. The bottom half of her shirt is soaking wet, and she's wearing hideous lime green rubber gloves.

"Did the faucet break again?" I ask.

Confusion makes her brows pinch together as she looks from me to the sink and back again. "No, why?"

I move closer and point to her T-shirt. She glances down and laughs. "I'm guessing you've never hand-washed dishes before?"

Shame burns in my face. I've lived a life of privilege even if my parents made sure I knew I was a burden to them.

"Once or twice in college, but my fraternity house had a chef and a house cleaner on staff."

"I didn't peg you for a frat boy." Once again, there's no judgment there. It makes me wonder if she ever judges anyone.

I shrug. "I did whatever I could to avoid my parents." Even living with my grandfather, they still found ways to make my life a living hell because they also refused to hand over guardianship of me—it was Alistair's way of maintaining control.

She's biting her bottom lip as she listens. Then she returns to face the sink. "I'm sorry your family didn't see your worth. I hope you've found people who do."

Those words slice through my armor. She truly cares if I have people to depend on, and she doesn't even know me. It makes me want to care for her in ways I've never even considered caring for another person before.

It's as though her kindness is weaved with magic meant only for me, and I'm not going to lie, it's kind of terrifying the fuck out of me.

"Grey is like a brother to me," I say, then cautiously move to stand next to her at the sink. Picking up the towel on the counter, I wait for her to hand me a wet dish.

She's hesitant to let me help again, and she holds the plate between us before finally relenting and handing it to me.

"You really don't need to help," she says, her voice a whisper.

"Do you ever allow anyone to help you, or do you always do it yourself?"

"It's just easier to do things myself sometimes."

"Ah," I say. "You're a people pleaser. Do you ever put yourself first and say no?"

Her body stiffens next to me. "I take the path of least resistance."

"You avoid conflict."

She huffs and places one dripping gloved fist on her hip. "You're a paying guest, and someone Pops duped into overpaying."

"Not true," I say, taking another dish from her soapy hand. "That was my choice. If I had to eat out for breakfast and dinner, I'd be paying a lot more. If anything, I'd say you're undervaluing your service."

We fall into companionable silence as she washes and I dry. It's not until we're down to the last casserole pan that she responds.

"We can't charge more until this place is restored."

"How's the restoration going?" I think I know the answer, but I want to see how honest she'll be with me.

A twinge of guilt sours my stomach. I'm asking for honesty when I haven't been truthful from the start.

"It's not. Pops was a carpenter by trade, but his vision has made it impossible to do the work himself. I'm really not sure why he bought all this sheetrock and stuff. He knows we can't afford it, but he's probably in denial about not being able to do the work anymore."

I think about that for a moment and then reflect on our outing today. From the hardware store to the diner, he introduced me to everyone as though I was a friend helping out —as though I were someone who would be here for a long time. Maybe he thinks I can do something with this place.

Why does that idea excite me? I've never built or painted anything, or even so much as swung a hammer in my life, but the concept of actually fixing something instead of what my father has done for the last ten years excites me as nothing else ever has.

"Maybe I can help," I say.

Madison stares at me curiously, then reaches onto her tiptoes to put a dish on a top shelf she has no way of reaching.

Stepping behind her to take the dish from her hand is an immediate mistake. She smells like summer—light, fresh, with a hint of citrus that reminds me of sunny days at the ocean.

The second my hand touches hers, she steps back into my body, and it's as though we're the chemical bond of two atoms. We just fit.

She gasps at the connection, and I take the large bowl from her hand before it slips even as my pulse gallops in my chest. "I've got it." My words are quiet and low, but they convey an attraction I shouldn't be feeling after only a day.

Madison tilts her head back then up, her baby-blue irises glowing in the dim overhead lighting as she stares at me. For the first time I can remember, I have the urge to kiss a complete stranger.

"Thank you." Her voice is throaty and so damn sexy I can't look away from her as she turns to face me.

"Happy to help." My body inches closer, needing the sizzle of her skin to jolt me back to life.

Time slows as our bodies press together, eyes locked. Even our breathing syncs.

She licks her lips and I lean in, attracted to the shimmering moisture her tongue leaves behind. A kiss from her might ruin me for all others. The pull between us is inescapable, irrefutable, and terrifying as fucking hell.

"It, um, goes on the top shelf," she says, barely above a whisper.

I slip the bowl onto the shelf without looking. "All set."

Madison nods, and so do I.

I'm going to kiss her. She opens her mouth to say something, but we're interrupted by a loud whoosh and then a crash.

We jump apart with electricity still zinging between us and turn toward the sound.

She holds a hand to her heart. "Oh my God. It's the dang sheetrock."

I peer around her. Two of the three sheets I had leaned against the door are on the floor, cracked in half.

"They're broken," she chokes out. "No matter what Pops says to you tomorrow, you cannot let him buy more. We can't afford it. I know I shouldn't admit that to you, but it's the truth, and I know how pushy that old man can be."

"I promise. I won't let him buy anything else."

"Thank you," she says quietly. "Thank you for your help. I, ah, have an early morning so I should get to bed. Do you need anything before I go?"

"No, I'm good. Thank you for letting me help. I've never felt...useful before. It's a new experience for me, and I don't hate it." My lips pull into a smile that she reciprocates. "That is truly embarrassing to admit."

"Not embarrassing, it's honest. I appreciate that. And I'm very happy to be at your service. So I'll see you tomorrow?"

"See you tomorrow," I say as I follow her out of the kitchen and up the stairs. It isn't until she opens a door that I realize we share a wall.

Madison stands at her door while I walk past her to mine. Our gazes collide with that magnetic pulse that thrives when we're close.

"Goodnight, Braxton." Her words are soft and gentle. They make me want to hold her tight.

"Goodnight, Madison."

She opens her mouth, probably to tell me to call her Madi again, but I open my door and walk through it before I do something monumentally stupid and drag her into my room.

But I won't call her Madi—that's a name for everyone else. Madison feels like a secret just for me, and I want that sensation much more than I should.

8

MADISON

I'M STANDING IN FRONT OF THE MIRROR IN THE UPSTAIRS bathroom with a towel wrapped around my head and another around my body when a loud knock startles me enough that I stub my toe on the lower cabinet.

Dang, that hurts.

"Madison?"

My heart rate accelerates, but I ignore it. The longer he's here, the harder it is to do though. Steeling myself, I open the door a crack and peek outside to find Braxton standing in the hallway with his hands in his hair, crap all over his T-shirt that clings to his sculpted muscles like a second skin, and sweatpants that ride dangerously low on his hips.

Come on, Braxton. I'm not going to survive sweatpants season.

Thankfully, I'm an adult and I'm able to keep my focus on his troubled expression that has worry lines forming between his brows.

"What's wrong?" I ask.

"Ah, Pops and I tried to help." He fidgets nervously, and

my stomach plummets. Pops means well, he always has, but it also always ends in disaster.

I open the door more, and his eyes flash with amber heat before he stares at the ceiling.

"Help with what?" I sniff the air, but I don't smell fire or hear Pops shouting in agony, so it can't be too bad.

But when Braxton winces, I feel the blood drain from my head.

"We thought we'd make you breakfast for a change."

"Braxton, I don't know if you're aware, but A, you're a guest here, and B, my grandmother forbade my grandfather from even making a peanut butter and jelly sandwich on his own over fifty years ago."

This time, his entire body flinches.

Stepping back, I shut the door and hurry into my robe, then meet him in the hallway. He's only been here a couple of weeks, and already he fits into the fabric of our daily lives.

"What did you do?" I ask, as we practically run down the stairs.

"You might ban me from your kitchen too."

This has me stopping short and him barreling into my back. His hands drop to my hips to keep me from falling forward, and even though there's a thick layer of terrycloth between his skin and mine, my body tingles where he squeezes before he steps back and releases me.

"I'm sorry." He sounds truly defeated. "I was following the recipe, but Pops had a different tactic and, well, it's best if you just see for yourself."

Biting my tongue, I push through the kitchen door, for once not hearing the squeaky hinges because what's before me is something straight out of a prank show.

"What is that?" My hand shakes as I point to the giant

blob pushing the oven door open. Yes, a blob. Every square inch of the inside is filled with a bright yellow goo.

"I wanted them fluffy." Pops frowns and stares at the floor—as petulant as ever.

"The recipe called for a teaspoon of baking powder, but we could only find baking soda," Braxton explains.

"And." My tone is sharp as I move past Pops to turn off the oven.

"And now Google is telling me that baking soda mixed with lemon juice might cause a reaction."

Using my pointer fingers, I press hard circles into my temples and count to ten.

"And I wanted them fluffy." This time Pops doubles down on his words by crossing his arms.

"What did you do?" Remain calm, Madi. Remain calm.

"I dumped the box in." Pops kicks at the floor with the toe of his boot. Is this what Grams dealt with for all those years, or is old age making him more stubborn?

"An entire box of baking soda?"

"And lemon juice," he mutters. "I like lemon."

I count silently in my head until I'm sure I can control my tone. "Okay, what was it supposed to be?"

Braxton hands me his phone, and I read through the recipe for a lemon breakfast soufflé.

"We thought if we doubled it, we'd have leftovers for tomorrow. But then doubling it didn't really work out, so we doubled it again." Braxton is freaking out. His voice pitches higher each time he speaks, and he's pacing the small space behind me.

Rubbing my temples, I nod. "Okay, new rule. No one is to make a soufflé in this kitchen ever again."

"Of course. How can I clean this up? It just keeps...growing." The man's eyes are practically bugging out of his head as he surveys the scene before us.

"You know what would be really helpful?"

"What? I'll do anything," he says in a rush. "I feel terrible. I was trying to help because you've been working so late and this...this is the exact opposite of helping."

"I appreciate that, I do. Pops is...creative. So, if you could take him over to the diner for breakfast, I'll get this cleaned up and then hopefully I won't be late getting to the Chugaloo."

"Sure. Yeah, I can do that." He's rubbing his knuckles along his chest, and I almost feel bad for him.

"Thank you. Pops, behave yourself."

Pops kisses my cheek and walks with a swagger I haven't seen in a very long time.

Braxton leans close when Pops is out of earshot. "I truly am sorry about this."

"I know. A little word of caution, though. Pops means well, but trouble follows him around when he's left to his own devices. It always has. I have no idea how Grams kept him in check for so many years. But please, keep that in mind if he tricks you into any other...excursions, okay?"

Braxton nods aggressively while tugging on the back of his neck. "Yeah, shit. I feel like a complete asshole. I'll buy you a new stove if we've ruined this one."

"Thank you, Braxton. That's not necessary." *I hope.* I try to keep my tone light, but he must see the despair I attempt to mask because his shoulders slump and regret is written all over his face.

"I'll, ah, just take Pops to breakfast then. And again, I'm so sorry about"—he waves his hand around the kitchen—"all of this."

"It's okay, I appreciate the effort." And I do. I don't remember the last time a man tried to do something nice for me. I need to get out more. I match up couples on-air, for crying out loud. My own dating life should not be so disastrous.

He swallows hard, then leaves me alone with the abominable blob crawling down the oven door.

"WHOA, ARE YOU ALL RIGHT, MISS MADI?" TREVON ASKS AS I push through the Chugaloo doors over an hour late.

I'm not sure if Braxton and Pops put marshmallows in their concoction, but that's the consistency I was working with while attempting to clean out the oven this morning. After an hour, I gave up.

"Just a tough morning. It's all good." I give him a too-bright smile.

"Tough?" Blissy scoffs. "Betty told me your boys came into the diner this morning looking glum as roadkill."

Telling her they're not, well, that *Braxton* is not "my boy" will get me nowhere, so I ignore it.

"They were trying to be helpful."

"Was it really overflowing so much it opened the oven door while cooking?" one of our regulars in the coworking space asks.

"It was a mess, but it's the thought that counts. So, what did I miss here this morning?"

"Just the morning caffeine rush. You don't have anything on the books until two." Blissy hands me a much-needed extra-large coffee. The scent of vanilla and cinnamon hit my nose first, and my body finally relaxes. This is my idea of heaven—the perfect coffee and my little business in my quiet little town with all the people I love.

"Thanks, Blissy."

"You've got it, kid. Word is your boys hit up Happi's Hot House and filled the back of the truck with new plants."

I press my lips together so I don't say anything rude. Braxton promised me after dinner that first night that he wouldn't let Pops keep spending money, and for the last couple of weeks, I think he's kept a leash on Pops.

"Then they went to the Senior Center and played shuffleboard with some of Pops' old friends before hitting up the high school."

"What were they doing at the high school?"

"You got me. No idea with that one, but I heard that Pops was beaming at every stop."

Guilt makes my palms sweaty. Pops is practically the mayor around here, but I've had to work so much lately so we don't lose the inn that I haven't been able to take him to all his favorite places. Perhaps Braxton's stay is a blessing in disguise—if I can just get him to stop allowing Pops to spend money we don't have.

"Okay." I sigh. "The meditation group will be in the quiet room this afternoon, so I'm going to set it up for them. Let me know if you need anything."

Trevon crosses the room and wraps me in a giant hug. He's a huge teddy bear of a man who treats me and my friends like the big sisters he never had.

"You're doing good, Miss Madi. Just remember that."

I pat his back. "Thanks, Trevon. I'm fine, really. It was an unexpected morning, that's all."

He doesn't believe me, but he goes back to his corner where he always does his homework. Happiness has been truly blessed with the best football players around—and they all have such big hearts.

Without another word to anyone, I enter the quiet room

and begin moving furniture around for the class coming in later.

Once that's finished, I check the snack order the football team placed for their mandatory study hall. Fall classes are in full swing, and Coach B. requires his boys to be in here at least ten hours a week during the season doing homework or studying plays.

By the time I sit in the back row of coworking spaces and attempt to plan my next three podcasts, I'm already exhausted—all the late nights are finally catching up with me. However, as soon as I start, I'm immediately lost in my work. I only wish it paid enough to take away my always-present financial anxiety.

Is it too much to ask for a quiet, stable life? Some people dream of exotic vacations and designer clothing, but not me. I just want to finally feel safe and at peace—it's probably the only thing I've ever wanted.

An hour later, the meditation class filters out of the quiet room and gathers around Blissy's caffeine stand. I scan the space and notice Braxton is sitting a chair away from me.

How long has he been there? There are several work-spaces free, and he could've sat anywhere, but he chose to sit right here, close to me.

When I give him my full attention, he hands me a paper bag that smells like heaven.

"You didn't," I say, taking the bag and greedily inhaling the scent of cinnamon. I groan and lick my lips.

He shrugs. "Pops told me it was your favorite."

Once the bag is open, I practically stick my entire face inside it. I would sell my kidney for Moravian sugar cakes from the Ravenels' farm on Hickory Lane.

"Oh my God. I didn't know they were selling these at the farm stand yet."

"Ah." He scratches at his chest, causing a smile to tip the corners of my lips. "Pops can be very convincing."

"And where is my meddlesome grandfather?"

"Taking a nap. He said *I* wore *him* out." The sheepish expression he flashes melts some of my irritation from earlier.

"I'm sorry if he's commandeering your time. I'll speak to him."

"No," he blurts, then swallows hard and looks away. "It's okay, really. We've sort of worked out a schedule."

I groan. "Please don't feel guilty about saying no to that old man. He can take it."

Braxton's laughter has everyone watching us, not that they weren't before, but now they aren't even attempting to hide it.

"It's fine, I promise."

Just then, Clover and Savvy walk in and sit at my table with matching curiosity gleaming in their eyes. Braxton not only returns his attention to his laptop, but he gets up and moves a few chairs down.

Huh.

"So, tough day?" Savvy asks, drawing my attention away from my mercurial houseguest. Her expression is wily—she already knows every gory detail, probably with some embellishments thrown in too.

"You could say—"

"Miss Madi! Miss Clover! Miss Savvy! Where's Miss Elle?" Ethan barrels toward us in a way that makes me worry he won't be able to stop. "This is too much, too, too much."

"Ah, what's up, Ethan?" Clover asks while simultaneously backing her chair away.

He holds up a brand-new MacBook Pro in one hand and

the box in the other. "Thank you. I—I can't accept this, but the fact that you would even think to do it—well—it means the world to me."

The big teddy bear is tearing up, and I have no freaking clue what he's talking about. The girls and I trade confused glances.

"I'm not sure what you're talking about, Ethan." I look from him to Braxton, who's watching us with a scowl.

Ethan pauses and looks down at the card in his hand. "It's from the DDDs."

The three of us share an embarrassed chuckle. "Um, but..."

"I thought the logo looked different than the one on your wine night glasses, but it's the DDD for sure," he says happily.

"Can I see the card, Ethan?" Savvy asks, and he hands it right over.

She places it on the table in front of us.

Dear Ethan,

The DDD wishes to congratulate you on all your accomplishments and award you with this gift. Your compassion, work ethic, and community outreach make you our DDD.

Keep up the good work.

Sincerely,

DDD

I spin the card toward me and look at the logo. There's no mistaking the three Ds, but it's not our font, and it's not our signatures. Then something catches my eye, and I notice that the ring around the Ds actually says something. Pulling it closer, I read it out loud, "Discreet Daily Deeds."

"What the heck is that?" Clover asks, snagging the card away from me.

Farther down the table, Braxton is hard at work, his fingers flying over his keyboard.

Savvy is focused on her phone. "The website says Discreet Daily Deeds is a nonprofit organization doling out daily good deeds. It was founded ten years ago, and the corporate office is in Seattle. How the hell..."

"Sorry, Ethan." Clover leans in and whispers, "This didn't come from The Darlings of Disastrous Dating. It came from Discreet Daily Deeds."

Braxton's fingers stop their frantic typing and hover over his keyboard.

"I told you it was a dumb idea to give us a club name," I tell the girls. "We're too old for that, and it sounds ridiculous out loud."

"But it was the best idea we've ever had after three bottles of wine." Savvy rolls her shoulders back. "I'm proud of our club."

I drop my head onto the table in front of me.

"We're all disasters, Madi. Don't worry about it. Well, Elle's not, but we couldn't exclude her." Clover will forever see things through Clover-colored glasses.

"Thanks, Clover." She's not the matchmaker who can't find her own match though, so that probably makes me the queen of disasters by default.

"But if it wasn't the darlings, then who, exactly, is behind the Discreet Daily Deeds?" Savvy asks with her gaze laser-focused on Braxton. Maybe she noticed him conspicuously ignoring us also.

I nudge Savvy with my foot and shake my head. "He's been with Pops twenty-four seven."

"Isn't it a little strange that he was in here helping the

kid tape up his computer and then a new one mysteriously appears a few weeks later?" Savvy hisses.

"Perhaps it was just his lucky day," Braxton says from his chair. "Seems as though he could use some luck, don't you think?"

"Braxton, did you—"

"I don't even know his last name." He shrugs but doesn't make eye contact with anyone. "But I'm happy for you, Ethan. You seemed to have a good head on your shoulders when I was talking with you. I've got some stuff to do. I'll see you back at the Hideaway later, Madison. Good to see you ladies again."

Braxton's chair scrapes against the hardwood floor, gaining the attention of everyone at the Chug. He quickly packs up his stuff and storms out the door without so much as a backward glance.

"He didn't really answer you," Savvy points out.

"I... It's been a real crappy day, Sav. Can we table this for now? I still have to make a grocery run tonight."

She pats my right hand while Clover does the same to my left.

"We've got you, lady." Clover bumps my shoulder with hers, and some of the day's tension leaves my shoulders.

"Ditto," I say.

"Now, exactly how bad was your kitchen this morning?" Savvy waggles her brows, and the last thread holding my sanity together snaps. I laugh. I laugh so hard I cry while my friends join in and heal my soul like the magical little friend fairies they are.

9
____

BRAXTON

I'M HALFWAY BACK TO THE HIDEAWAY WHEN I PULL THE TRUCK over and rage-text Grey.

> Me: Really, Grey? Really?

> Me: I didn't want it traced back to me. The card was over the top.

> Grey: Calm down.

I almost chuck my phone out the window.

> Grey: It's a shell company no one can trace. I made sure of that when we started it.

> Grey: It's also a tax write-off for us.

> Grey: After everything that happened back then, you spent ten million dollars doing good deeds.

> Grey: That money can't just go missing.

Grey: Now it's an actual 501(c)(3) company that cannot be traced to either of us.

Me: There's another DDD in town. The Darlings of Disastrous Dating.

Grey: (Laughing emoji sent)

Me: I'm serious. The kid thought it was them, but they knew it wasn't.

Grey: Okay. What does it matter? No one can trace it to you.

Me: I'm going to need you to come out here and stay at the inn.

Oh, fuck. Why did I say that? My only explanation is that when shit goes south, we stick together.

My phone rings in my hand.

"What the hell do you need me in Georgia for?" Typical Grey, he doesn't waste words with a greeting.

"Because I can't just rent you a room for five months and not have you here."

"Five months? Have you lost your fucking mind? What the hell am I going to do in Georgia?"

"Help me keep my head on straight. I've been here for what? Almost a month? And I'm already losing my damn mind. Plus..." I glance out the window. There's a calmness here, but it makes my skin so itchy I could actually be allergic to it. "The inn owners need the cash. They're good people, but Madison can't keep up with the bills by herself right now and I think I ruined their oven this morning."

Grey is quiet for a beat, then another. "How do you know all of this?"

"I don't know, I connected with Pops. We picked up his mail this morning, and I accidentally saw an old bill about taxes they're behind on, and I'm not sure Madison knows."

"You really have a soft spot for this old couple, huh?" Greyson's tone lightens. Neither of us come from very happy homes, but at least we got to experience it with my grandfather, and I know we're both feeling the hole he left in our hearts.

"I do." Grey will find out that Madison isn't old soon enough, but I don't need to deal with his inquisition right now. "You don't have to be here the entire time, just make them think you will be."

He sighs. "Okay. When do you want me?"

"Tomorrow."

"Tomorrow, Brax? Are you shitting me?"

"No. I'll rent you a room, and I'll rent another room to be your office. You won't really need a suit here, so pack casually. Sage already takes most of his college courses online anyway, so he can go back and forth with you."

Grey's muttering under his breath, and I hear him moving about whatever room he's in.

"Five months, Brax? Are you really going to drop money for two extra rooms that no one will be in?"

"Maybe." My hand clenches around the steering wheel. "It's not like we would ever miss that money, and it's a way to help them out. Ace wanted me here for a reason, Grey. Plus, there really isn't anything tying us to California anymore. We can live and work anywhere."

"You. He wanted you there. Jesus, Braxton. You can't just up and move a billion-dollar company on a whim. We have employees, people who count on us."

"I'm not firing anyone. At least not yet. Some with ties to my father will have to go, and I didn't say anything about moving the company here." Though it does make me think. Would moving such a large company here be a way to help fix the heart of Happiness?

"Braxton." Grey mutters my name as though he's said it a few times.

"You can just fly back and forth until I figure out what I'm supposed to do here, and while you're here, we'll come up with a plan to deal with my family."

"I hope you know what you're doing." He sounds frustrated, but also concerned. "I'll take my plane so your parents can't trace me."

"You don't have to do that. Mr. Coop said we're all restricted from Omni assets. Everyone has been given instructions to bar them on sight—even in the hangers."

"It's fine." His heavy sigh says otherwise. "It's just sitting there anyway."

Greyson Wells was the only heir named to the Wells Diamond Emporium even though he has a nephew, but since his family was even more corrupt than my own, I suppose nothing really surprises me anymore.

Taking Ace's surname was the first thing he did when he came to live with us. That and ensure Sage was also a Reyes. But he's refused to touch a dime of his inheritance even after selling off the company piece by piece. He tried to split it between me and Sage, but we both refused it, so it all just sits in a bank earning money on money.

"It's your call. I'll see you soon."

He blows out a frustrated breath. "Yeah, I'll let you know my flight information once I've got a plan. We also need to discuss your mother."

A tension headache connects with a right hook to my skull. "What now?"

"She was escorted out of the shelter for refusing to

engage with a woman in need of a shower and a bed. She's on probation and can return next week...with restrictions. She'll probably be put on kitchen or cleaning duty now."

Freaking hell. Why are they all so fucking selfish? "Okay, does Mr. Coop know?"

"He does. He was about to call you when I called him for some paperwork. I said I'd relay the message."

"Thanks, Grey."

"It's you and me against the world, right? What else am I going to do?"

Grey and I made a pact when we were eleven years old —brothers first and always.

"Always."

"See you tomorrow, Brax."

"Bye."

He hangs up, and now the panic sets in. What's Madison going to say about this?

She's going to find it shady as hell, because it is.

I don't have an explanation for my behavior. I'm out of control, and it's a feeling I haven't had since...well, since the last time I ran away and tried to blow through my parents' money to spite them.

That was different.

Last time, I went on a bender doing good deeds up and down the West Coast because my parents didn't deserve what they had. This time, I'm using my own money but the sentiment is the same—I'm trying to correct shitty behavior by anonymously throwing money at people who deserve the good things in life.

My therapist would have a field day with me.

Madison Ryan won't accept a handout, but will she turn away paying guests?

Probably.

I can see her stubborn streak a mile away, but she'll have to get used to a helping hand because I'm incapable of walking away—not when the dark circles smudge her eyes every day. And not when my grandfather's final wish was for me to find happiness here.

Hopefully, my help won't end up as it did this morning ever again, though.

Tossing my phone onto the bench seat of the truck, I hurry back to the Hideaway to square things away with Pops before Madison can say no.

I just need to make a quick stop at the high school first.

"George said he'd be here in about an hour to upgrade the wiffee for you," Pops says. I stop taking the bed apart and look up at him.

What the hell is wiffee?

"Isn't that what you said you needed for those TV calls? I don't understand why business ain't done in person anymore."

Wi-Fi. I chuckle and go back to unscrewing the headboard from the frame. We can only fit a twin bed in here if I'm going to convert it into an office. If Grey and Sage end up staying for any real amount of time, I'll have to make some sort of a deal with Madison because I already know she won't let me pay for another room.

Maybe I should've just rented four to begin with.

"Wi-Fi, Pops. It's an internet connection. Grey is handling a lot of accounts for us right now. This will help him be able to do that."

He takes a seat in the desk chair I picked up at Walmart. "And why's he gotta be here again?"

I shrug and look away. I hate lying to his face. "It's our company. We work best as a team, so it's better if he's with me, and I don't want to be out west right now. This seems like the perfect solution. I want a slower pace, but we still have a company to run, so this is a win-win."

"Are you in trouble with the law, boy?"

His question has me tumbling back on my ass with a laugh. "I've never been and hopefully never will be in trouble with the law. You have my word."

"Yeah," he mutters. "I believe you."

"What the heck is happening in here?" Madison's voice sets off a bundle of nerves I knew were coming but I'm still not prepared for.

"We rented two more rooms," Pops says proudly.

"To whom? For how long? And won't they need a bed?" She drops her oversized bag on the floor and enters the room.

At first, I think she's going to take the screwdriver from my hands, but instead, she holds the longboard that connects the headboard to the footboard, and suddenly it's a hell of a lot easier to unscrew the damn thing.

"Nope. They're using this one as a home office with a twin bed for when his nephew visits." Pops is as carefree as ever. If anything, he's looking a little too smug for my liking —Madison's going to be pissed.

"They? This isn't a home or an office building, Pops. This is an inn." She turns those dangerous blue eyes on me. "This is you, isn't it?"

Swallowing hard, I duck my head, pretending the screw is more difficult than it is.

"My acting CEO, Grey—"

"Your best friend."

I look up and nod. "Glad to see you were listening. Yes,

my acting CEO and best friend is coming to stay, and since I'm on sabbatical, he'll need a private office to take virtual meetings in."

"This...none of this makes sense. For how long? How long is he going to be here?"

Once again, I look away, and Pops answers before I can.

"They booked two more rooms for five months." He flashes a wide, toothy grin.

"F—five months? Why wouldn't you rent a house or an Airbnb?"

This time, I look her square in the eye. "Because I like it here, and I don't have a lot of places where I can just be... me. So I wanted to stay here."

Her face scrunches up in the cutest way. "You feel like you fit here? With us?"

I nod.

"And you can afford to...holy crap. Ninety thousand dollars, Braxton? Did you pay ninety thousand more dollars?" She swats at my arms with both of her little hands. "I don't even know if I could get that much selling the place. What the heck is wrong with you?"

"With Grey here, it'll be a business expense. I'm not paying for it, the company is."

"Your company, Braxton. Your. Company. But." She's searching the room as though it'll give her some answers. When her gaze finally meets mine, hers is watery and fragile. "There's that much money in marketing?"

She shakes her head and holds up a hand. "Sorry, don't answer that. It was an incredibly rude thing to ask. But this with the amount you've already paid, it's just too much. Take it back."

My shoulders shake with laughter I hold in. If I outright laugh in her face, she might try to kill me.

"I'm at a point in my life where I need to make some changes. I'm comfortable in this town, Madison, and that doesn't happen often."

"That's not true. You've liked everything and everyone since the day you showed up here."

My cheek twitches with the beginnings of a smile. "Here, yes. But with the way I'm making changes to my company, I'm not sure I'm very well-liked at home. I'm...different here, I guess."

"Different." The cute little line between her brows deepens. "What makes you behave differently here?"

You, I almost say. Instead, I remove the final screw in the bed before answering her. "I'm not sure. Maybe it's the sense of community, or that there's no city traffic clogging up the streets. I like that everyone cares about you and Pops. I could do without the constant interrogation, but I get that people do it because they're protecting their community. I don't know where I'll end up, so while I'm on sabbatical, I want to be where I'm happy, and what better place for that than Happiness?"

"That's...you like an awful lot of things, Braxton."

"Miss Madi, Miss Madi!" A young female voice filters up the stairs.

"Jessa?" Madison calls out. "We're upstairs." She turns her frown my way. "We're not done with this conversation. There's no way you're paying $100,000. That's highway robbery."

Footsteps crash against each stair, and then the doorway is filled by a teenage girl wearing a basketball uniform.

Damn it. Does every good deed have to be shared with Madison Ryan?

"We did it. The fundraiser you helped me set up. We did it. We'll be able to fund a team this year and refurbish the gym floor during Christmas break." The girl jumps up and down.

Madison releases the board she was holding with a loud thud, and the girl crashes into her for a hug.

"Thank you so much, Miss Madi. I might have a shot at a scholarship now. Coaches will be able to come see me play. It's no cap amazing."

Jesus, the teen-speak is the same here as it was in California. I'll never understand why no cap means no lie or why they can't just say no lie.

The chair Pops is sitting in squeaks as he turns toward the window and begins to whistle.

Well, that doesn't look guilty at all.

Madison directs her gaze in my direction, every question she wants to ask playing across her features.

"Jessa, that's great, honey. But, how? The projection we came up with was for next season."

The girl shrieks and claps her hands and I almost cover my ears. "I know. Isn't it amazing? Coach said we got a ton of online donations. A few big ones, and a lot of the hundred-dollar levels. I think my TikTok must have worked faster than we thought it would."

"Your...TikTok." I might be the only one hearing the skepticism in Madison's tone because this girl is too happy to pay attention.

"Now that's something to celebrate," Pops says cheerily. "I guess your wiffee really does work like magic."

"Wi-Fi," Madison and I correct in unison.

"I'm so happy for you, Jessa." Madison is still frowning at me. "Coach has confirmed all the donations?"

"Yup. It's all in the account we set up. Thank you. Thank you. Thank you. Thank you." The girl's knuckles turn white as she wraps herself around Madison again.

Madison's curious gaze hasn't left mine though, and heat creeps down my spine. Doing anonymous good deeds shouldn't be this difficult.

"I really didn't do anything, Jessa. I just helped you set it up. You have to thank the donors."

"How? How should I do that?"

"Well, if you think the donations came from TikTok, I'd start there with a heartfelt thank-you video, and anyone you have contact info for should get a personalized thank-you card."

"Okay. I can do that. Can you believe it, Miss Madi? This is the luckiest day of my whole entire life."

Madison's gaze on me is like a physical weight, so I keep staring at the bed that's nearly disassembled.

"Yup." Madison pops the P with an exaggerated sound. "Seems to be a lot of luck flying around here lately."

"Okay, I wanted you to know first. I'm going to start the thank-you stuff. Thanks again, Miss Madi. You changed my life."

"Ah, kiddo. You did that all on your own. I'll see you tomorrow at the Chug."

"Yes. I'll be there early to help you set up."

"That would be great. Come on, I'll walk you out." She turns what I'm sure she thinks is a glare my way. "And we will finish this conversation, Braxton. I'm serious."

I simply watch her retreating form, feeling really fucking good because I have no doubt she'll try.

As soon as I hear them on the stairs, I turn to Pops. "Madison really cares about everyone in town, doesn't she?"

"She has since the day she moved in. She spent a lot of time on the outside, and once her life had some stability, she made sure no one felt as she had." His shoulders droop, and he clasps his hands on his knees. "Sometimes I think that's why she works so hard making love matches. She doesn't ever want anyone to feel like she did with her parents. A loveless life isn't a life at all."

"She's pretty incredible," I admit.

"She's been crowned Happiness Sweetheart for a reason, and it's not just because she plans the best festivals, even if she does. She's the sweetheart 'cause she deserves the love she shares so freely."

"Yeah." My throat is thick with emotion that sits like hot embers on the tip of my tongue.

"Well, you finish up in here. I'll go see about dinner."

"No," I shout. "I'll help Madison in a minute. Why don't you go see if that show you were talking about is on?"

"*Dumpster Diving*. This program is going to change your life," he says as he slowly rises from the chair. "I'll have Madi record it so we can watch it together."

I smile at this old man. His heart is always in the right place, but I have a feeling Madison's assessment is spot-on and trouble follows him everywhere.

"Sounds good."

He's standing in the hallway when he says, "Real good luck over at that high school, huh?"

I swallow hard. "Sure is. There's a reason all the big companies are advertising on TikTok now. If you hit it right, it can change everything."

"Mm-hmm," he hums. "Come on down when you're done here. We can make a list for what your guy will need."

I nod and go back to work, feeling an odd mix of satisfaction and regret. Seeing the faces of two good deeds is something I'll always remember, but the guilt over lying to Madison about it sits as spiky as a thorn in my chest.

My innkeeper, Madison.

Maybe my friend Madison?

My phone buzzes in my pocket with a text.

Grey: Touchdown at 8 p.m. tomorrow.

Me: Great. See you then.

Me: Madison's getting suspicious of my good deeds.

Grey: Then I suggest you don't drop $200K in less than 24 hours.

Grey: Spread that shit out, dude. I'm not surprised she's suspicious.

Me: Right. I've got to be more careful.

Grey: Or you could take credit for being a good guy.

I stare at his words for a long moment.

Grey: Not everyone will take advantage of your kindness, Brax.

Grey: Eventually you'll have to trust again.

Me: Right. See you tomorrow.

He doesn't respond, and that's just fine. I have a lot of deeds to deliver, and now I have to figure out how to do them all without relying on the DDD.

10

MADISON

"Okay, so he rented out two more rooms, and then something at work kept his friend from coming for over a week?" Savvy leans forward. This girl loves gossip more than anyone I know.

It's our monthly DDD meeting. The Darlings of Disastrous Dating normally meet at the Chugaloo, but we're in the den at the inn because I have to keep an eye on Pops and Braxton.

Every time I leave, they start a new project I haven't been able to get to.

So far, they've patched holes in walls, stripped the wallpaper in the kitchen, installed new hardware in the sink, and I don't even want to know what they were doing in the attic when I came home this afternoon.

"Yes, and the rooms just sat empty for two stinking weeks." Taking a sip of the wine Braxton bought, I suppress a moan. It's so good. "Apparently his dad went to some of Braxton's VIP people at his company and told them that Braxton ran out on all his obligations, leaving the company dangling. So Greyson's had to take meetings with everyone from board members to investors cleaning up the mess."

"Jesus, are there any good parents left in this world?" Savvy mutters.

"Obviously there are." I drag my finger through a line of condensation on my glass. "But we do seem to collect friends with crappy childhoods."

"Maybe we should have named our group the Crappy Childhood Coalition, the CCCs, instead of the DDDs." Elle giggles.

"And he wouldn't allow you to refund the unused days?" Clover sits crisscross in an oversized chair with a giant fluffy blanket around her—the poor thing is perpetually cold.

"No, he said he's taking up the room for an office and wants the other one available for his friend whenever he does show up. Trust me, it's been an argument every time I bring it up."

"Huh," Savvy says, tapping her chin. "You know, I looked him up again."

"Sav," I groan. "You know how much I hate cyberstalking. It's an invasion of privacy. Remember—remember what it did to me?"

If I could avoid the internet for the rest of my life, I would. I hate giving my past any power at all, but deep down, I know it's part of the reason I'm so conflict-averse and maybe why I'm still single.

The frown line between Savvy's brows slowly disappears. "I wasn't doing it like that, Mads. I promise."

"What did you find?" Elle asks.

"Elle!" I scold. She's usually on my side when it comes to these things, but lately, she's all over the place. If I asked her, she'd blame pregnancy hormones for it.

She shrugs and sits in front of the old air conditioning

unit. Pregnancy is making her run so hot that her husband, Cian, bought her a bunch of personal-sized fans that she always forgets in her car. "It might not be a bad idea to make sure he isn't a serial killer."

"He's not a serial killer."

All of my friends stare at me with blank expressions.

"He's not, okay? He's...nice."

"They thought Ted Bundy was too," Clover says before taking a sip of her wine. "This is really, really good."

"I didn't find anything to suggest he's a Bundy in hiding." Savvy pulls out her phone. "There's a lot of pictures from college. Some random life updates about a job in marketing right out of college, but no company name, then a lot of him volunteering at a dog shelter. Nothing about his family, but there are a lot of pictures of that Greyson guy and a little boy. And by the way, Greyson has an even smaller social media footprint, and none of them show a last name anywhere. Have you even asked him the name of his company?"

"No," I admit. "It seems like a sensitive subject, and I don't want to pry. And so what if they don't have social media? They're probably trust fund kids who prefer to keep a low profile." Though something about that excuse doesn't sit right with me. Braxton isn't like any trust fund kid I've ever heard of.

"Maybe," Savvy mutters.

Clover sets her empty glass back on the coffee table. "We should go dancing." Her cheeks are the shade of pink that only happens when she's had one too many glasses of wine. And by one too many, I mean one glass. She's our lightweight, and I love her dearly. It's because of her I've been saved from making a fool of myself more than once.

"I don't think..."

"Madison?" Braxton asks with a soft knock on the pocket doors closing off the den.

"Come in," Clover says, jumping to her feet.

The door slowly slides open to reveal the crooked smile that makes my entire body run hot. Braxton Mitchell is too handsome, too kind, too...everything.

"Ah, hey?" he says shyly, waving uncomfortably in the air at my friends. "Pops said you ladies need a ride to the Firefly."

"Yes," Clover says as Savvy grumbles something about eavesdropping that has Braxton's face turning all shades of red.

"We don't really—"

"If we've got a designated driver, we might as well take advantage. Plus, when's the last time you let everything go and just danced for a little while?" Elle levels me with a mischievous smirk. "Brax, did you know Madi loves to dance? Especially at bonfire parties. The hometown sweetheart can shake her ass like no other."

"Just shoot me now. Seriously, right now would be great." Groaning, I drop my face into my hands. "I'm not the hometown sweetheart, I can't even match myself, for crying out loud."

"Perhaps you just haven't found the right partner." Braxton's tone drops to that dangerous level I've only heard directed at me, and it sets fire to the alcohol coursing through my system until I'm buzzing from head to toe. "But the dancing? Now that's something I'd be happy to see."

"Give us ten minutes to get dressed and we'll meet you outside." Savvy pulls me to standing and then drags me toward the stairs behind Elle, who waddles faster than I've seen her move in a while.

"You really don't have to do this," I tell him on my way by.

"Oh, Madison. I'm really looking forward to it. Trust me." His gaze seems to drink me in, and I shiver.

"This is a mistake," I hiss in Savvy's ear.

"Why, because you'll have fun? Because a very hot stranger is already giving you come-fuck-me eyes? Or because you know both of those things are true?"

Why don't I just say no? It's as though I'm allergic to that one little word, but I know I'm going dancing because I don't want to disappoint my friends.

"Geez, Sav." Clover slips into my room behind us. "You don't have to put her on the spot. Let's just go dancing and see what happens." She hiccups, and it turns into a giggle fit that I adore.

Clover doesn't laugh very often, and it always makes me sad—escaping a cult at fourteen and losing her best friend in the process broke her in ways I'm not sure she'll ever recover from.

My friends raid my closet, not that anything I have will fit them. Elle has perfected the baby bump, and Cian made sure she had every outfit she would ever need. Savvy is tall and slender, where Clover and I are on the petite side.

Well, Clover's too thin. The word frail has been used to describe her more than once. It's as though all the weight she's carried on her shoulders has taken her strength and she has nothing left for herself.

No matter how hard we try, we've never been able to get to the demons at her core. I fear there's only one person who will ever be able to get through to her, and that's her childhood friend, Valen. The one she sends letters to every week. And the one whose responses are seriously lacking.

"Put this on," Savvy says, tossing me my favorite denim skirt with a pretty yellow flowy top.

In the corner, Clover is picking up my favorite sparkly cowgirl boots.

"I'm fine going in this." I protest, pointing to my leggings and oversized T-shirt.

"No. Get dressed, and then we'll do your hair." Savvy's using her *do not mess with me* tone, but I've had a full glass of wine and feel the rumble of my stubborn streak as it flares.

I'm about to ask what they're going to wear when I realize that they're all dressed as though the plan had been to hit up the Firefly all along.

"Am I the only one who missed the memo that we were going out tonight?" I lift my T-shirt over my head and replace it with the shirt Savvy threw at me.

"It's Friday night," Elle says with a shrug. "And it's Cole Swindell night."

"Plus, you've been wound so tight we're afraid you'll snap. Nothing settles your mind like dancing, so that's what we're doing." Savvy makes one last sweep of my closet, and when she's sure she's picked the right outfit, she spins, lifts her sweatshirt over her head, and crosses her arms. She's wearing a beautiful red tube top with cutoff shorts that make her legs look impossibly long.

Clover removes the blanket but tugs her cardigan close while buttoning it up to the top. Her skinny jeans stop at the ankles, and she's wearing cute little tennis shoes. Elle sits on my bed, rubbing her belly through her tank top with one hand and waving a wrapper in the other.

"Where the heck did you find a Pop-Tart?" Her pregnancy is enough to make me hungry.

Elle smirks and holds up her bag. "Cian filled it up for me before I left."

I'm pulling off my leggings when Clover grabs a front section of my hair and quickly twists it into a French braid that sits across the top of my head and disappears into the hair behind my ear. It's her go-to style for me, and I love it.

Savvy squeezes my cheeks so hard my lips pucker, and she adds some gloss that I hate. I'll have eaten it all off before we're even to the Firefly, but if I know her, she'll be chasing me down all night to reapply.

A quick coat of mascara and they're ushering me out of my room, down the stairs, and out the front door. Pops is sitting on his porch swing, staring at Braxton.

"Don't keep her out too late." My grandfather chuckles.

"Pops, I'm a grown woman. I don't need a keeper."

He shrugs and looks up to the sky. He sits out here a lot when he's missing my Grams.

"Are you okay, Pops?"

"Never been better, kiddo. Boy?" I have no idea why he doesn't use Braxton's name, but Braxton always answers.

"Yes, sir?"

"Don't let that Harry Turd anywhere near our girl. You got it?"

"Our girl?" Savvy whispers while Clover and Elle pretend to swoon. Did Clover have more than one glass when I wasn't looking?

"Pops, knock it off." Turning to Braxton, I should be unnerved to find he's already watching me—it's become a stalkerish habit of his—but I can't deny that I like the attention. "You really don't have to do this. The high school runs a car service on a buddy system for locals on the weekends. It's a way for the teenagers to make a little cash, and it keeps most people from drinking and driving."

"Madison," he drawls as though he were born and raised in the South.

"What?" I snap. I don't like how he makes me feel sometimes.

Liar, liar, Madi. You don't want to like how he makes you feel.

Ugh, that girl who sits inside my head urging me into bad decisions is seriously the worst.

While I've been playing mental gymnastics with myself, Braxton's inched closer and the girls have entered the truck. Clover and Savvy sit in the back, and Elle is in the passenger seat.

"Get in the truck, Madison."

Why don't I despise that commanding tone of his?

"Why?" My voice cracks as I crane my neck to meet his intense gaze.

He smiles down at me with his dimples on full display and his hair falling messily over his forehead.

"Because if I don't take you to the Firefly, Pops is going to have me sanding floors." He holds up his right hand, then turns it to show me the back. His knuckles are all cut up with scabs forming.

"What in the...?" I spin on Pops, but Braxton catches my elbow and turns me back to him as if we're already on the dance floor. My palms sprawl flat against his chest, and I gasp.

"Don't yell at Pops. I enjoy spending time with him, and he's teaching me stuff I'd never learn anywhere else. But my knuckles are sore as fuck, so I'd much rather watch you and your friends and make sure you get home safely than do anything else on his list tonight."

"W-why are you doing all this?" My voice is a shadow of itself. It's fear. Fear that I might catch feelings for this man. Fear that Pops already has. Fear that my heart pitter-patters in a way it hasn't since I was a teenager whenever he touches me.

His left hand presses into my back, keeping me tightly against him, and he uses the finger of his right hand to trace the headband braid. "This looks nice," he says quietly.

Then his gaze falls to mine, and my mind screams at me to pull away. We have an audience, for crying out loud, yet I don't move. I'm stuck in his sphere, and I'm pretty sure if I stopped lying to myself, I might even love it.

Braxton chuckles before stepping back, as though he just realized the peanut gallery is taking us in.

I take a deep, cleansing breath.

"I'm doing it because I've never felt needed before," Braxton says. "And apparently, helping is my superpower. I promise he isn't getting me to do anything I'm not willing to do. Especially tonight."

Helping might be his superpower, but so is his ability to get me to lose myself.

He opens the door, takes my hand, and helps me up into the cab, waiting patiently until I slide over the bench seat with my legs straddling the gearshift.

It's the same as it was when I was a kid, except instead of Pops driving and Grams in the passenger side, it's an enigma of a man and my pregnant best friend.

His door shuts with a crack in the night, and I jump. Pops waves as Braxton reaches over my thigh and shifts into reverse.

Our eyes catch for a flash of a moment when his forearm rests on my knee, and when I don't pull away, he relaxes into the position and follows Elle's directions to the only bar in town.

God help me and the rumor mill that's about to tear up my life—again.

THE SCENT OF STALE BEER AND FRENCH FRIES IS ODDLY comforting when Savvy, Clover, Elle, and I enter the Firefly as we always do—arm in arm. But this time, it's our shadow that has all the attention focused our way.

Braxton's body heat warms me from behind, and because I barely reach his shoulders, I know everyone sees him standing guard over me.

"You ready for this, big guy?" Savvy taunts over her shoulder.

"You'll soon find that very little rattles me anymore, Savvy." His words hit the top of my head, and I swear his scent engulfs me.

"That so?"

"Savvy," I hiss. "Leave him alone."

My eyes close when I feel his warm lips at my ear. "You don't have to protect me, sweetheart. I've got this."

He steps back, and I blink wide. Dang it. What is it about this man that makes me lose all control of my body?

"Well, let's see how you do tonight." Savvy points to the bar along the back wall that faces the dance floor. "Why don't you go take a seat and get us a round of Southern Mules?"

Braxton's hand skims my lower back. "That good with you?" I swear he whispers the words to me, but that can't be true—the music is already at full volume. I nod in answer, and he removes his hand. I almost fall back as though it were his touch holding me up.

I stand there for a long moment, watching his retreating back, and when I break whatever spell he has me under, I find my friends staring at me with impish grins.

Just then, the door behind them opens. My heart plummets when Harry enters, head down and avoiding eye contact as he makes his way to the corner.

If only he would use the shame he's feeling now to make a change for the better instead of washing it away with copious amounts of alcohol, as I'm sure he's about to do.

If he'd get sober, he could be so much better than he allows himself to be. The version of him I loved all those years ago, the boy who carried my backpack, the athlete who waited for me after practice to tell me I was doing great.

Somewhere along his path, he lost himself, but it's no longer my job to fix him. He's made his mess, and only he can fix it, so I do what I've trained myself to do over the last year—I turn my back on him.

"Let's go, ladies." Clover shimmies to a Cole Swindell song, completely oblivious to the internal war happening in my chest for a boy I once loved and the man I can no longer stand.

Savvy grabs my hand, which sets off a chain reaction as I grab ahold of Clover who grabs onto Elle, and we slide through the crowd to take up a spot in the center of the dance floor as all the patrons separate into four lines.

As soon as my boots hit the dance floor, my shoulders unwind and I get lost in the music—in the dances I've known for as long as I can remember.

With my arms swaying above me, my body falls in step with the music, and I let myself go. My worries get pushed out of my mind as I sway and twist and stomp and twirl.

At some point, I catch Braxton sandwiched between Clover and Elle at the bar. Elle sits in front of Cian, who has his giant arms wrapped around her middle, happiness swirling around them like a giant aura of love.

Braxton's gaze follows my every move.

That knowledge turns a key deep in my chest that I thought I'd thrown away, and I move with a confidence I've been missing. It's as if I'm dancing just for him, and something about that allows me to break free from the chains that have been holding me prisoner in my own life.

I trip over my feet, thankful when the woman next to me holds out an arm to keep me steady so I don't fall on my face.

There's something about Braxton Mitchell that opens me up, and I don't know how I feel about that.

Dance, Madi, just dance. Deep thoughts on half a bottle of wine are never a good idea, so I dance.

The next time I make eye contact with him, Savvy is dancing in her chair next to Clover. They're laughing and chatting, but Braxton's oblivious to it all because his gaze is directed at me. Has he been staring at me this entire time? At least ten songs have played since the last time I looked his way.

He's wearing a lazy smile on his face, but his expression is so intense, so heated, I swear I can feel the burn along my exposed skin.

This time when the song changes, I don't look away. My body moves as if it's laced with the song, but now I show him that I'm dancing for him, getting lost in how he reacts to me. It's addicting. And it's why I know the instant something's wrong.

His face falls into hard lines, and his jaw clenches as he stands so suddenly, he nearly knocks Clover off her stool.

Then I feel the body behind me. The scent of old-man cologne makes me gag as my history threatens to invade the one night of freedom I've had in ages.

"Baby, you know what your moves do to me." Harry's wet, raspy words cause an involuntary shudder. Gone is the ashamed shell of a man who walked in here, and in his place is a man controlled by his demons.

I blink away tears that form from the reminder of his

betrayal any time he gets this close, but I'm frozen to the spot, stuck in a memory that never fully releases me. Then Braxton is parting the sea of people and coming for me faster than a runaway train.

He reaches me just as Harry places a hand on my hip. Braxton's gaze narrows with a possessiveness I've never experienced before. Has anyone ever looked at me the way he does?

"Harry," he says as a curse. "Thanks for the truck."

Before Harry can respond, Braxton's arm slides around my back and he drags my body flush with his.

"May I have this dance?" he whispers against my neck, and my knees buckle, but I don't fall—I have a feeling he'd never allow me to either.

"Hey," Harry slurs. "Get your fucking hands off my girl."

Braxton's body stiffens beneath my fingers.

"It's okay," I whisper. "Just ignore him."

"Is this how it is, Mads?" Harry slurs. "What are you going to do when he gets bored of this place, huh?"

I turn my head to glare at him, but all I can muster is sadness—sadness that I wasted so many years on this jerk. I hate that he can still make me freeze up and revert to that nineteen-year-old girl who hid from her life because of him, his choices, and the people he brought to my doorstep. He reaches for me, but Braxton is faster and moves me out of his reach.

"No, Harry, you're not doing this to her tonight," Braxton growls. With his hand cradling the back of my head, he holds my face to his chest while he angles his body away from my ex.

His heartbeat is strong and fast. I can't see his expression, but I know he's glaring at Harry. In my periphery, I see

Savvy holding a beer bottle as though it's a weapon at Harry's side, and my entire body tenses.

My stomach waffles, swishing around all the alcohol, and I feel sick. I need to get out of here before Harry causes another scene.

Then Braxton's palm slides down to my cheek and he tilts my face up, up, up until my gaze meets his. "Savvy has it handled. Whatever that jackass did to you, it's in the past. He can't hurt you now unless you allow him to. Stay here, with me, in this dance. That's all that matters right now."

When Braxton Mitchell stares at me this way, the rest of the world falls away, and I have no doubt I'm heading toward a heartbreak I may never recover from. Because as much as Harry hurt me, I never felt as safe with him as I do with this near stranger.

And I don't think there's enough Kevlar in the world to safeguard my heart—not when it starts beating after such a long hibernation the second I'm held in Braxton's strong arms as though I matter.

11

———

BRAXTON

I saw the change in her as soon as she recognized the scumbag who waltzed up behind her as if he had every right to be there—to touch her.

The worry lines that mar her beautiful face on a daily basis had finally disappeared. She looked free, and happy, and so fucking perfect my chest actually ached.

Then that Harry Turd slithered his way up against her and everything changed. Her expression nearly gutted me. In an instant, I saw that the pain, fear, and betrayal she carries is bone-deep, and I have no doubt that fucker was the one to cause it.

Savvy saw him before I did, but my body was propelled toward Madison as if by magic. And now that she's in my arms, I wonder how I'll ever let her go.

Me, the guy who has only ever trusted his best friend.

Me, the man who didn't know what he was missing out on until she fell into his lap.

This can't be healthy, the obsession I have over my innkeeper, but the longer I spend in Happiness, the more the parts of my life that I've felt drowning me loosen their grip.

"We all have a past, Madison. It's okay to leave him there."

She stares at me with watery eyes, and when a tear slips free, I catch it with my thumb. The drop melts into my skin, filling me with a desire to make sure she never cries again.

Jesus, maybe Savvy drugged me. That would make more sense than the shit flying through my mind.

Madison nods, sending an electric shock through my unsteady pulse. What did he do to her that turns my strong, stubborn woman into a meek, sad girl?

The song ends and a new one begins with a slower beat that has her relaxing into my hold. But when she rests her head against my chest, I think I might explode because nothing, and I mean nothing, has ever felt this right.

"Do you know how to dance?" she asks. When she tilts her head back to look up at me, my heart melts. Those goddamn lessons my mother made me take in high school might actually come in handy.

"I'm a fast learner."

The smile she graces me with breaks the rest of the tension her ex caused.

She raises her brow and nods toward everyone else on the dance floor. People have partnered up and are moving in a circle to a song that it seems they all know.

"It's 'I'll Be Your Small Town,'" she says as I sweep her into the circle of people.

Holding her hand, I spin her so her arms are outstretched until she gasps, then I pull her back into my chest and watch as the light reenters her face.

"I accept," I say, using my hand pressed into her back to guide her around the dance floor.

I dip her low, with our faces only inches apart.

"You accept what?" She laughs.

"You can be my small town. I accept."

Madison's laughter rings out over the music, and I can't be sure, but I'm willing to bet that every person in this bar is praying to hear that sound again.

Scooping her into my arms, I hold her close, loving how our bodies fit together.

"I meant that's the name of the song." The light, tinkling sound of her voice as she laughs at me is a drug, and I'm already searching for my next hit.

My hands fall to her hips, and I lift her into the air, so we're face-to-face. "I know what you meant, and I meant what I said." I slowly lower her to the floor and love that her face flushes red as I do.

The pulse in her throat explodes, and it hits me then —I'm happy. Not the kind of happy my parents expected of me. Not the kind of happy I thought I was when fulfilling my role as the heir to my grandfather's fortune, but the kind of happy that is so pure nothing can taint it.

The song changes again, the beat faster, and everyone steps into lines as they hop and jump into a dance.

"You're a fast learner, huh?" Madison laughs.

I take a moment to watch as she taps the toe of her boot behind her, stomps on the floorboards, hops twice, swings her hips in time with her hand in the air, and then spins to face the other wall.

I wait until she spins again so she can see me next to her, and I jump right into the line dance.

I'm terrible. Truly and embarrassingly horrid, but I throw my entire body into it just to hear her laugh.

The guy on my other side taps my shoulder, and when I

face him, he's laughing too. "Follow the person in front of you. It's four steps. You'll get it."

Knowing that people are staring at me is something that would have sent me into hiding anywhere else, but here, I let go and laugh right along with them if for no other reason than I'm standing by Madison's side.

Just when I get the dance down, the damn song changes, and so do the moves, but I stay by Madison's side, dancing like an idiot until I'm a sweaty mess, and she's so carefree you'd think I had harnessed all the shooting stars to make her wishes come true.

"I need a drink," she says, falling into my side when the music slows and people pair off again.

"One more dance." I capture her hand. "Then I'll get you whatever you want. I promise."

Her smile falters so briefly I would have missed it if I wasn't so focused on learning every inch of her face. But then she nods and steps into my space, places her cheek against my chest, and rocks in time with me as if this is the only place she's meant to be.

I have no idea how long we've been dancing, but now that we're barely moving, I notice that the crowd has thinned out. Clover and Savvy sit happily at the bar giggling with each other while Elle leans against Cian O'Brien, who I saw again at the hardware store on my fourth time in there.

Others have taken up tables in corners. But straight ahead, puffed as a peacock with his arms crossed over his disgusting beer belly, is Harry Turd, glaring at me as though he's plotting my murder.

I raise my brow when I catch him staring on our second spin, and though his curses don't reach our ears, I can tell by the spittle flying that he's going to be a problem—for me. I'll do whatever I can to keep that fucker away from Madison.

My Madison.

"Let's get you that drink," I say when Turd takes a step in our direction. The sooner I can get her to the bar with her friends, the easier it'll be to protect her if he turns out to be a bigger prick than I expect.

When Madison Ryan slips her hand into mine and allows me to lead her through the bar, I know I'm going to fall for her.

We reach her friends, and I can tell by Savvy's expression that we're being followed. With one hand at Madison's back, I usher her to the bar in between her two friends who immediately angle their legs to box her in.

The only person who has ever protected me that way is Grey. Madison has an army at her side. I'm not jealous—envious maybe, because the love these people have for each other is something I haven't seen much of in my life.

Out of the corner of my eye, I recognize a couple of guys heading in my direction. On my other side, a group of football players, including Ethan and Trevon, are closing in too.

Fuck me. Are they all about to beat my ass for dancing with Madison?

"I don't have time for this." I groan to the ceiling, then square my shoulders and turn toward Turd.

Within seconds, I'm flanked on either side as a human wall of protection is formed.

"We've got you, Mr. Brax," Ethan murmurs.

On my other side, Cian rumbles something deep in his chest. He's about my age but a mountain of a man who makes my 6'4' frame seem small.

"We haven't seen Madi this happy in years. You hurt her, and we'll gut you faster than a fish and feed you to the pigs," he growls.

I chuckle until I realize he isn't joking. "I'm glad she has all of you."

"He's an oxygen thief who can't take a hint." Cian nods in the direction of Madison's ex.

Turd stops a few steps away, and both Ethan and Cian nudge me forward with their elbows.

Well, I guess this is my fight now. At least they know I'm better than this asshole.

I rest my hands on my hips and wait. I'm not a fighter, but I can hold my own and I know how to handle egos like this—I've been doing it my entire life. If I give him enough time, he'll stick his foot in his mouth before I have to do anything.

"You going to say anything?" he snarls.

I shrug. "I'm not the one with the problem." Making a show of glancing left, then right, I ask, "Any of you have a problem?"

About ten heads shake no.

"Only with that gobshite." Cian's voice booms over the music that slowly lowers to a whisper.

Remind me to never get on his bad side.

"Fuck off, Cian. You taking this dipshit's side shows what a traitor you really are. And you boys, I'm your fucking coach. Show some respect."

"Respectfully, Mr. Harry, you're our ball boy," Trevon deadpans. "You haven't been able to...coach in years."

"I'm on the fucking coaching staff," Turd bellows.

My side sizzles when a tiny hand lands there, then pushes me aside.

Madison barrels in between me and Cian. I reach out for her and only manage to fist the waistband of her skirt, but it's enough to slow her down so I can step in line with her.

Unfortunately, it does nothing to calm down her ex.

"What are you doing with him, Mads? I told ya I came back for you. We can work this out." He's so drunk he sways in place, and when he attempts to reach out for her, I tug her back by her belt loops.

It is probably all kinds of inappropriate for me to be fisting the top of her skirt like a caveman, but it's also keeping me from swinging at a man for the first time in my life, so I don't worry too much about it.

With her left hand, Madison reaches around and covers my fist with her own until I'm calm enough to release it, then she steps forward again and pokes her ex in the chest with her other hand.

I've been here long enough to know that Madison never sticks up for herself. She's a people pleaser to her core, so she's either had one too many cocktails or something has given her the confidence to fight back tonight.

It's incredibly arrogant to think that I may have something to do with it, but it doesn't stop me from hoping.

"You came back after six months, Harry. Six freaking months, only to return with excuses and not a single apology. And let's not even discuss the lies you told, the damage you caused, or the fact that you skipped town so you wouldn't have to face the repercussions of your actions—both times."

"Mads—"

"Don't," she growls. "Don't you Mads me. You see this?" She points to the line of men and women who have closed ranks around her. "They're doing this, protecting me, because every person in this town knows you're a liar, a cheat, and a miserable excuse for a human being. They were the ones here protecting me. Picking me up off the bathroom floor when I was convulsing from crying and being too scared to leave my house. They're here for me because you've burned all these bridges one too many times. Even Cian stayed with you for a week to help get you sober, and he can't stand you. And how did you repay him?"

"Fucking oxygen thief locked me in a bedroom so he could get beer," Cian grinds out. His entire body appears to be made from stone. "You really are a twat. Move along, Harry. She's not your girl anymore."

"And she's his?" the oxygen thief slurs.

Pulling Madison to my side, I step right up to this drunk bully. "Madison is her own woman. She doesn't belong to anyone but herself. And while I'd love nothing more than to sit here and watch her berate you for another twenty minutes, you're drunk, and we're trying to have a good time, so why don't you do us all a favor and head home."

I barely get the last word out when he swings wildly. My entire focus shifts to tugging Madison out of the way, which means I allow his fist to connect with the right side of my face to ensure her safety. As soon as I know Trevon has her, I block the next hit—thank you, Ace, for making Greyson and I take so many years of self-defense courses.

Before I can hit back, all hell breaks loose. Savvy grunts like an animal as she attempts to knee Turd in the balls while Cian is holding him by his arms and dragging him toward the front door.

"Sav. Knock it off." Cian chuckles. "Call the sheriff instead."

The noise in the bar escalates until I can't hear a word Madison is saying, even when I hitch at the waist and put my ear to her lips.

As the beast of a man drags out the belligerent jerk, people spin in their chairs and curse him out. There doesn't seem to be one person in this place on his side.

My instinct is to feel bad for the guy, but I know that

whatever he did to garner this kind of reaction in his hometown had to have been much worse than anything I can currently dream up.

"Braxton." I barely catch my name but focus my attention on the woman before me.

"Are you okay?" I ask, thankful that with Cian outside, the angry voices are dying out. Slowly, the music filters back into my conscience.

"Me?" She scrunches up her nose and stares at me as though I'm not making any sense. I've never seen Madison pissed off. Not really. But the fire in her expression now could burn a man. "You're the one who got punched in the face. Are you okay?"

"Mads?" the bartender calls.

She turns toward the voice and then catches a bag of ice out of midair with one hand.

"Come on, we're leaving." Madison takes my hand and leads me through the crowd.

Am I imagining it, or are people smirking and giving me not-so-subtle thumbs up as we pass them?

"Oh, for Pete's sake, Charlie. Grow up," she says to a younger man who is definitely flashing two thumbs up in our direction. "Braxton, give me your keys."

"Madison."

She doesn't listen and simply continues toward the door.

I glance behind us to see Savvy and Clover shimming in place and shooing me along.

"Don't the girls need a ride home?" I ask.

"No, Cian doesn't drink. He'll drive them."

"An Irishman who doesn't drink?"

She stops at the door and lowers her chin to her chest. I can't tell if she's laughing or crying, so I usher her into a corner, then lift her face to mine.

I still have no idea if she's laughing or crying. Her expression is...lost.

"Keys," she demands again.

"Sweetheart, you've had at least two drinks. You can't drive tonight."

She stomps her foot and frowns. It's so fucking cute I want to kiss every inch of her pouty face.

"Shoot," she mutters. "I forgot. Freaking Harry—"

"Hush. We don't say that name around here." The right corner of my lip twitches when she looks up at me. "It's Harry Turd or oxygen thief from here on out."

Madison's face lights up our tiny corner of the bar when she smiles brightly. "That's been Cian's favorite insult since high school."

"It's a good one. It's definitely been entered into my vernacular."

"He'll be so proud. Seriously, though. Are you okay?" she asks, holding up the bag of ice.

My jaw is swelling, and my cheek is on fire, but I don't tell her that.

"I'm fine. It's you I'm worried about."

Flashing red and blue lights roll through the windows of the bar, and she groans.

"Does this happen a lot?" I ask.

"He's...he doesn't like to lose."

"How long has he been bothering you?"

Madison shrugs, then takes my hand in hers again and tugs me outside where we find Cian sitting on Turd's back while the officer cuffs him.

I stop to stare at him and laugh out loud. "Cian's having a good time."

"You have no idea how much pleasure this brings him," she says quietly. "Cian was a late bloomer when he moved here in high school. This is him getting revenge on his high school rival."

"Nice." I chuckle.

We stand against the brick wall of the bar as another officer approaches. "You who he hit?"

I nod.

"You want to press charges?"

I look to Madison, who shrugs. "It's up to you. I don't think it'll make a difference either way."

"Can I think about it? I want to get her home."

The older woman closes her notebook with a snap. "You're a good egg. Take care of our girl. If you decide to press charges, just come down to the station." She hands me a card, and I slip it into my back pocket.

"Thanks," I say. "Madison? You ready?"

She nods. "Cian, can you get the girls home safely?"

He gives her a two-finger salute as if he isn't sitting on top of a pissed-off donkey.

He and I should get along just fine.

12

MADISON

THE BAG OF ICE IS FREEZING MY FINGERS, BUT I DON'T PUT IT down when Braxton slides into the truck.

His massive thigh presses against mine because I'm sitting in the middle again, straddling the gearshift, even though there's plenty of space.

I still don't move.

"Do you want to talk about it?" he asks at the same time I say, "Are you okay?"

He turns his body a fraction of an inch, pressing closer into my side, and butterflies take flight in my belly. How does he do that? Just suck all the tension from my body with an innocent touch.

Even in the dark, his jaw seems swollen. Leaning into him, I press the bag of ice to his skin and hold it there. He hisses on contact.

"You can tell me if it hurts, you know? I won't think any less of you. The jerk sucker punched you when you were... when you were..."

"Getting you out of harm's way, which is exactly what he should've been thinking about too."

"I was never his priority," I admit quietly, readjusting the bag of ice on his face. "Not when it mattered. I'm certain he's so drunk tonight that he had no idea how close he was to me, but I honestly don't think even if he'd been sober, I would've factored into his train of thought. For him, it isn't even about winning, it's about not coming in last."

His hand snakes around my wrist, and my pulse hammers beneath my skin.

I swallow hard before lifting my gaze to his. He's staring down through thick lashes I'd die for, but there's a storm brewing behind his eyes, and a pull ignites between us that's explosive and exciting.

"You're not an object to lose, Madison. And if he thinks you're a game, then he's a fucking idiot. You should have always been his first, last, and only priority." Braxton's voice rumbles in the silence of the truck. It bounces off metal and glass, reverberating through my body and heating my core.

"I don't need saving, Braxton."

Painfully slowly, he tilts his head, pressing more firmly into my hand. Our gazes are fused together, each of us locked onto the other, and I know I have zero chance of breaking our connection first.

"No, Madison. You're a strong, independent, incredibly amazing woman. You don't need saving—you need to be savored. There's a difference."

A full-body tremble starts at my neck and works down my body. Savoring? Holy hell, now I can't stop imagining what being savored entails.

Braxton takes the bag of ice from my hand and tosses it to the floor of the passenger side, then presses my palm to his face in its place. It keeps us close enough to share air.

"Do you want to talk about it?" he asks again.

I purse my lips tight, too afraid that if I speak, if I open up to him now, I'll never be able to stop.

"I don't know what's happening here," I whisper.

His lips part as though he's tasting my words, and a flame of desire spreads faster than wildfire through my veins.

He blinks, and his lips curl up at the corners. Lips I want to lick.

"I don't know anything about you." My words barely touch the air. "Not really. Nothing important, but I feel like —like…"

"Like you've known me for years?" He lifts a brow while he waits for a response.

"Yeah, but that's silly. Right?"

His hand tightens on my wrist. Not painfully, just the slightest pressure to seal us together, and then his thumb strokes back and forth across the inside of my wrist and every thought in my head vanishes into thin air.

"There are very few people in my life that I have a connection with, Madison. In fact, besides Grey and our nephew Sage, I work very hard to keep everyone out." The sadness in his tone tells me he's being honest. "But here, with you and Pops? It's as if someone rewrote my life and dropped me into a new story. One where I belong just for being me. One that has me working harder than I've ever worked in my life, smiling more than I knew possible, and dreaming of a girl who might still poison my breakfast just to get me to move along if I'm not careful."

I gasp and jerk back, but he doesn't release my wrist, so my fingers twitch against the scruff of his jaw.

"I would never poison anyone." I gasp haughtily.

His teeth shine in the moonlight. "No, you wouldn't." He

says it as if he knows me, understands me. He says it as if there's not a doubt in his mind that he can trust me.

My gaze drops to his lips, those perfectly pillowy lips, and my heartbeat hammers in my ears. Have I ever wanted to kiss someone as much as I want to kiss Braxton Mitchell?

I snort a laugh, and his entire face dances with amusement.

"What were you thinking just now?" he asks, peeling my fingers away from his jaw and holding my hand in his lap.

Gosh dang. How long have we been sitting so...so intimately?

"It's probably better if I don't say." I've never been so thankful for the cover of darkness as I am right now because heat travels at warp speed across my cheeks, down my neck, all the way to the tips of my aching nipples.

Never. Not once in my life have I ever thought the words *aching nipples* in relation to my own breasts. I guess it's another thing we can chalk up to this handsome housemate of mine.

I giggle to myself again, but he doesn't press. He watches me with a mix of amusement and lust. It's the lust that sobers me quickly.

"Your skin is so soft," he whispers. I stare at where his thumb swipes over my pulse point.

"I like lotion. It makes everything slippery." Oh my God. Did I seriously just say slippery? Slippery Madison? "Soft. I said soft."

His rumble of laughter is a balm to my burning skin. "Slippery, huh?" he asks while running the thumb of his free hand along his bottom lip.

"Soft. And I bet your lips are soft." Did I just moan that out loud?

Okay, Madison Melissa Ryan, I know you only had a couple of drinks tonight so get it together.

"Madison," he rumbles in warning. "As much as I'd love to show you just what I can do with my lips, we need to get you home. You've been drinking, and I'm not that guy."

"You're not?"

His grip on my wrist sends an electric shock throughout my body when he squeezes—it's a tease of what he could do to me without any clothes on.

"Oh, God. I think I'm drunk."

Braxton throws his head back and laughs, and even though I know he's laughing at me, I can't help but savor the sound—he's infectious.

He leans in so our foreheads are nearly touching. "Did you have fun?"

When I nod, our noses touch.

"That's all I wanted. You deserve to have fun, Madison. Fun and so much more."

"Do you have to go home?"

The muscles in his body bunch next to mine. "Home in general, or home right now?"

Both, but I want to play pretend for a little bit longer—pretend that he is actually the hometown hottie. "Right now."

He scans my face, but I have no idea what he's searching for.

"I have somewhere I want to show you, and it's still warm enough out to do it. Another month or so and it'll be too cold, at least for me." My voice quivers in anticipation. "It's my favorite place in all of Happiness."

The energy in the cab of this truck is incandescent. Even the windows are beginning to fog up, casting the streetlamps in a twinkling haze, but finally, he lets go of my wrist and tucks a piece of hair behind my ear.

"I think I'd very much like to see all your favorite places, sunshine."

"Sunshine, huh? I shudder to think what you'll call me when my clouds roll in."

He puts the truck into reverse but leaves his arm resting on my thigh and his hand on my knee.

"Does that happen often?"

I don't want to talk about my fears—and that's all that seems to roll around in my mind these days, so I deliver directions instead. "Head toward the hardware store and take the second right."

"Yes, ma'am." He squeezes my knee, and then his thumb taps against my skin in time with the song on the radio as if he and I are the most natural thing in the world.

And sitting here, this way, with him, we just might be.

BRAXTON TURNS HIS HEAD TO SMIRK AT ME. "THIS IS WHERE you wanted to take me?"

I glance through the windshield to the vast emptiness below us and shrug. There's only one other vehicle up here, and I know their mamas would flip out.

"Madison, is this where the locals go to make out?" he asks in mock outrage. At least I hope it's mock, because if he's truly unhappy, I'm going to feign a horrible, debilitating illness until he leaves.

I scoff as if he didn't just call me out. "If you're sixteen, maybe. But I come here for the stars. There's no light pollution up here. We can see everything, so back this truck up and let's go."

"Back it up?"

I nod, feeling lighter than air. "Yes, we have to get in the bed of the truck to look up at them, obviously."

His wide, uninhibited grin should make the cover for the sexiest man alive. "Obviously," he teases, then performs a perfect three-point turn until the tailgate is a few feet from the safety wall the mayor installed years ago.

Braxton turns off the truck and removes the keys.

"Come on, get out. You're going to love it." I playfully nudge his side with my elbow. Not that I moved him even an inch. The guy is a wall of muscle. I bet he doesn't even have an ounce of body fat. Jerk.

With raised brows, he opens his door, climbs out, and offers me a hand. It was never a question that I'd follow him out his side.

"Now what?" he asks, closing the door behind me.

My back is pressed to the truck, and he hovers over me, so close our thighs are touching. I lift a hand to his chest and press. He backs up at my unspoken request, and I turn to peer into his back seat.

"Oh, Braxton," I chide. "Old Fender here hasn't been outfitted for small-town life yet."

He presses into my back, cups his hands around his face, and peers through the glass over my head.

"What am I supposed to have back there?"

"A blanket, first aid kit, snacks. You always carry snacks. If nothing else, you can toss them to a black bear and make a run for it."

I turn slowly, but his hands stay pressed to the truck on either side of me. "You get a lot of black bears around here?"

His voice is low, controlled, hungry.

I nod despite being full of crap. "We could. They're in

the mountains, and even Google says they could be in southeast Georgia."

Braxton leans down, his words hot against my ear. "Have you seen any?"

"N-no," I stammer. I'm pretty dang sure he just inhaled my hair. "But that doesn't mean they're not here."

He pulls back enough to study my face. If he stuck a piece of paper between our mouths, our mingling breaths would surely turn it to wet mush in seconds.

"Well, Madison. You've got me here, and I'm apparently woefully unprepared. What *are* you going to do with me?"

Dear God, if I make a fool out of myself right now, please don't let me remember this tomorrow.

Before I can talk myself out of it, I lift up onto my tiptoes and seal my lips over his. My eyes are wide open—the shock of my actions registering too late, and my surprise is reflected in his matching expression. One second. Two. Three. Then his mouth curves into a smile against mine, and my lashes flutter closed in relief when his arm bands around my waist and hauls me to him.

Our bodies press together from my breasts to my knees, and my entire being melts as I sag into him.

His lips are so dang soft and gentle but firm as he angles his mouth over mine, deepening the kiss, and yup, I open to him with a low moan, the sound seeming to urge him on.

"Braxton," I gasp, when he fists my hair. Holy Hades. It's not even painful, but the illusion of how he could control my body has my stomach doing somersaults and my thighs clenching.

He nips my neck, just once, before resting his forehead against mine. "Just a taste," he whispers. "You had fun tonight." He sighs. "A lot of fun. And as much as I'd love to continue with this kind of fun..."

My mouth drops open when I register his hardened length pressing into my belly. That's not a cock, that's a weapon of mass destruction, and I'm ready to be its target.

"Oh, God," I groan, my head tipping back. He kisses my chin, then pulls his body away from mine.

"As much as it's killing me, tonight is not our night."

"Does that mean we'll have a night?" I snap my mouth shut. "I didn't mean that. I..."

He takes my hand in his. "I hope you did, actually. But we'll talk about it another time. What's our plan here, sunshine?"

Embarrassment is a real drain on liquid courage because suddenly, I have no idea what to do.

"Madison," he says gently.

"Um. Just a sec," I say, then slip out from under his arms, march over to MJ's truck, then bang on the window. Thankfully, they're too busy to have noticed what was happening on the other side of the parking lot. Hopefully.

The two teens jump apart, and Marty Jr. rolls down the window. "Miss Madi? What—"

I hold up a hand to stop him. "I know your mama thinks you're at the youth group campout right now."

The kid's face pales, and the tiniest fissure of guilt sneaks up my spine.

"I won't tell if you head back there with no stops."

"Yes, okay. Of course, Miss Madi." His voice cracks, and that guilt kicks me in the ribs. Haven't we all snuck out of youth group at one point or another?

"One more thing," I say before I turn around. "Can I borrow your kit?"

His brows raise, then he squints, trying to make out who is leaning against Pops' old truck.

"Sure thing, Miss Madi. Are you sure you're okay up here?"

This is what I love about small towns. Even scrawny little sixteen-year-olds watch your back.

"I'm fine. Mr. Braxton's a city boy. He's never seen our Georgia moonlight before."

Marty Jr. hands me the bag from the back seat of his truck.

"Thanks, MJ. I'll get this back to you tomorrow."

He nods, spares one more questioning glance Braxton's way, then starts his truck. I don't move until his taillights have long faded.

"Is scaring away teenagers one of your many talents?" Braxton asks. He hasn't moved from where he's leaning against his truck, but his voice carries to me on the breeze.

"You have no idea what kind of talents I possess, Mr. Mitchell."

He winces at the same time a sound rumbles out of his mouth that has the effect of a magical incantation because my body floats to him on its waves.

When I reach him, he takes the bag from my hand, opens it, removes the blanket, and holds it in the air. "Your move, Madison. Show me what I've been missing."

I press my lips together almost as tightly as my thighs. *Stand down, vagina, he means the stars. He means the stars!*

13

———

BRAXTON

"Did you see that one?" Madison shrieks with delight—it's such a departure from the woman who tries so hard to be everything to everyone that she forgets to allow her own joy to shine through sometimes.

She's pressed up against me, under my arm, and the hand she's pointing to the sky with falls back to my chest when she shifts up to search my face.

"I saw it," I fib. The truth is, I haven't seen one damn shooting star because I can't take my gaze off her.

Who could with a woman like her in their arms?

The line forms between her brows as she scans my face. "Did you really?"

I couldn't wipe the grin she causes from my face if I tried, but I nod.

"Which way did it shoot?" That feisty side I've seen glimpses of is returning.

I lift my brow and feel the laughter bubbling in my chest. "Down?"

"Ugh," she scoffs, and slaps my stomach playfully, but

she also returns her head to my chest, and all feels right with the world when we're connected.

I have no idea what time it is, if Pops will be waiting up for her to return home, or if we are actually in danger of a bear attack. At this moment, the only thing I care about is how good her body feels snuggled into mine.

This, with her, in the bed of this old Chevy truck on a blanket borrowed under questionable circumstances, is exactly where I'm meant to be.

"Isn't it beautiful?" Her voice is wispy with wonder. She's probably been up here a hundred times and still manages to sound so in awe, it could very well be her first time.

"It is."

"What did you want to be when you were a kid?"

Such a simple question, but it stumps me, and I shrug. "I'm not sure I was ever given a choice."

Her shoulders droop under my arm. "What do you mean? That's so...sad. Didn't you have dreams as a kid? An astronaut or a firefighter? A ballerina clown in a circus?"

It's so damn easy to laugh with this woman. "You have a very active imagination."

"So, no ballerina clowns, I take it?"

"No," I chuckle. "No ballerina clowns. I didn't exactly have a normal childhood."

"What is normal anyway? Did anyone *really* have normal?" Her voice carries an edge of sadness to it that I feel deep in my bones.

"No, I guess not. We're all weird in our own way."

We're quiet for a long moment, her watching the sky, me watching her. Very quickly, this woman has become my favorite obsession.

"I guess, at one time, I thought I'd play football with

Greyson." The admission twists something long forgotten in my chest.

She instantly rises onto an elbow, and I cover her other hand where it's splayed on my chest so she can't move it. I like it there—it fits.

"Hold up a minute. You played football?"

"You don't have to sound so surprised." I laugh, only slightly offended.

"I just, you, when you helped Ethan tape his laptop back together, you never mentioned anything."

"No," I agree. "I didn't. It wasn't a great time in my life." *Have there been many good times?* "Plus, Grey was the athlete. I just worked my ass off so he didn't leave me behind. Not that he would've ever done that."

"He's been a good friend to you."

"The best," I agree. "Greyson's my family."

"What about the rest of your family?" She slowly lowers herself back into position next to me, and I don't waste a second before I'm pulling her in closer to my side.

But a familiar pang clogs my throat, and the sigh that escapes ruffles the flyaway hairs on Madison's head. "My parents and siblings aren't good people, Madison. They only ever saw me as a problem to pawn off on someone else."

She swallows and tucks her head against my ribs. Is she hiding?

My hand skates down her back in what I hope is a soothing motion that's probably more for my benefit than hers.

"My grandparents were amazing, though. Did you ever watch reruns of *Mister Rogers' Neighborhood?*" I ask.

"No," she says quietly. "I was more of a *Sesame Street* kid."

I nod, allowing my hand on her back to calm my racing thoughts.

"Well, my Nana loved it, and so did I. When I was six years old, I told my dad I wanted to be a helper when I grew up." Madison's chest stops rising in the calming rhythm I was taking strength from—she's holding her breath.

"What did he say?" she whispers.

My jaw clenches at the memory, and I'm thankful she can't see it. "That helping anyone but myself was a sign of weakness, and it was more proof that I was a mistake."

"He's a jerk." She slides her chin up my side to look at me. "Sorry, but your dad is horrible. He doesn't deserve you."

Emotion rumbles deep in my chest—she's defending me. But before I can comment on it, she nuzzles into my side and hides her eyes.

We lie in comfortable silence, and I finally watch for the shooting stars that make her so happy.

"My parents sent me to live with Pops because I caused too much trouble."

Something like acid crawls across my skin.

"I guess I was a lot like Pops as a kid, but my parents never tried very hard. I think when I came to live in Happiness, I buried that side of me. I became the perfect kid so someone would love me. I also became obsessed with love." She laughs, but it's a hollow sound. "Why did some people get love but others didn't? I wanted everyone to experience it, even our pets. I started having pet weddings when I was eleven. In middle school, I was setting up friends with the best boyfriends I could find. By high school, I was actually good at it...well, for everyone but myself. I'm still working on deserving that love, I guess."

"Hey." Without thinking it through, I drag her up to straddle me and cup her face. A single tear slides down her cheek and over my thumb. It's a magical thread that weaves around my heart and connects my spirit to hers.

She lowers her chin but leans into my touch.

"That's why I hate being called the small-town sweetheart. It makes me feel like a fraud." Her words are so damn sad that my stomach clenches. "I know it's terrible because they all mean well and want what's best for me. What I'm saying is, sometimes parents suck."

I nod, too angry and wound up to say anything useful. Instead, I pull her down to rest against my chest. She settles on top of me, and I wrap my arms tightly around her back.

Have I ever grown close to anyone else this quickly? Even Greyson had to follow me around the playground for two months before I agreed to be his friend, and our grandfathers were the best of friends. If our fathers hadn't been bitter rivals, things probably would've been different. But holding Madison intimately is the most natural thing in my life.

"I'm sorry your parents made you believe you didn't deserve love. But they're wrong, so fucking wrong, sweetheart. You deserve love more than anyone I've ever met." It's not enough. Not nearly enough, but when I think about what I would've wanted someone to say to me every time my parents told me I was a mistake, I decide to go with honesty. "If I've learned anything from my shitty family, it's that I am not their mistake. I choose who I want to be, how I want to be, and who I'll be in the future. So do you, Madison."

Her body sags into mine, and I rub her back. Eventually she relaxes even more and emits the most delicate snore I've ever heard. I press a kiss to the top of her head, then allow my head to fall back to the bed of the truck with a dull thud.

That's when I see it—my first falling star under the Georgia moon.

Closing my eyes, I wish upon a star—I wish for happiness.

THE INKY NIGHT SKY BEGINS TO GLOW, ANNOUNCING THE SUN'S imminent arrival. The air is frosty, but luckily, I run hot, and Madison's burrowed into me, soaking up my body heat. I glance down at her and smile. She's left a small patch of drool on my shirt, but the beauty of her relaxed face is worth it and the backache I'm sure to have later.

I should've woken her up. Driven us home.

But I didn't.

Instead, I chose to hold her all night long, watching the stars and conceding that she was right. There is nothing in the world that can compare to her Georgia nightscape.

A soft groan has the corners of my lips twitching. She wasn't that drunk last night, but having seen her in action for the last few weeks, I know she doesn't drink all that often. How will she feel today?

Her open palm slaps against the bed of the truck to my left, then my right.

"What in the heavens?" She cracks one eye open, then squeezes them both shut. A moment later, her hands lift to my shoulders, then my face, patting as she goes as if she's reading my body with her fingertips. "Oh, God."

I chuckle. "How do you feel, sunshine?"

"Not like sunshine, I can tell you that. Why am I passed out on your chest?"

"Take a deep breath. All we did was talk last night. Well, you did kiss me, and I'm pretty sure you got me drunk off the fumes of that kiss, but that's all."

Her head lolls side to side against my chest, and then she begins to sit up. "I'm such an idiot."

I grip her hips and press her body back into mine until she gasps adorably. I love all her sounds.

"Explain." I don't intend to be a demanding prick, but there's something about her talking down to herself that irritates the hell out of me.

"Seriously?" she grumbles. Her head pops up and her chin digs into my chest. It's not painful, just a pressure point that tells me she's real.

"Seriously. Please explain how you're an idiot because maybe I am too, but I had a great time last night."

Her brows furrow, and even in the early morning darkness, I can tell she's blushing.

This time when she struggles to sit up, I let her go. She slips to the side and rests on her knees facing me, then raises one finger into the air.

"One, I passed out on top of you. Two," she lifts another finger. "I have a sneaking suspicion that not only did I kiss you, but you kissed me back. Three." My grin grows wider as she thrusts three fingers toward my face. "I said some really embarrassing crap that I don't talk about ever, with anyone. Four—"

I snatch her hand before she can continue and hold it to my chest. "Four," I say, "I'm thankful for every conversation we had last night because I can't tell most people about the shitty people I grew up with. Well, I could, I suppose, but who the hell wants to hear that? Five, I can't dance to save my life, but I'd cut off my own hand if it meant I got to dance with you again. Six—"

"Braxton," she whispers.

"Six, I've never dated, but if I were to describe my perfect date, last night would've been it, so please don't say you regret it." The thought of that burns. "Please."

"You've never been on a date?"

"I spill all my secrets, and that's what you focus on?"

"But…" She frowns. Does she not believe me? "But how is that possible?"

"It didn't take me long to figure out that most people were more interested in what my family could do for them than they were in me. Never knowing if people want you for you or for what they think they can get from you, that motivates you to put up walls pretty quickly."

She huffs and mutters something that sounds like "assholes,' but I'm not sure I've heard Madison swear before.

"Madison." I wait until she lifts her gaze to meet mine. "My family is…"

She lunges forward and covers my mouth with her hand.

"I don't give a crap about your family, Braxton. In fact, I'm sorry to say this, but I already know more than I need to. I have no desire to know anything about your family unless they do anything else to hurt you in the future."

"They don't hurt me, Madison." The words are a mumbled mess against her palm, so she releases me. "I'd have to care about them for them to hurt me."

"I know firsthand that families can infect faster than cancer, even when we've taken all the steps to cut them out. What I'm saying is that unless you're asking for support, the only thing I want to know about is Braxton Mitchell."

Fuck. I need to tell her my real last name.

"Is that so?" I ask with a bravado I don't feel at the moment.

"Yes." She crosses her arms over her chest and frowns,

but the sunshine radiating from her still heats my body against the cool morning air.

"Well," I spread my arms wide. "What do you want to know?"

"Have you really never been on a date?"

"That was quick." Leaning side to side, I stretch out my achy back. "Don't get me wrong, I go out with Grey, and have occasionally..." Shit, this makes me sound like a dick. "I haven't been celibate, but I guess I never met anyone that made me want to try for...more."

Until now.

Her cheeks plump up as her lips curl at the edges. "What is it you want, Mr. Mitchell?"

I lift a brow and fight the ever-present chubby I have in her presence. "I want a lot of things, Madison."

"So greedy." Her gaze dances with mirth in the early morning sun. Fuck me, do I love it when she flirts with me. "What would you like from me? Right now?"

A groan of desire starts in my gut, then rumbles and rolls through my chest. Did she intend for that to sound so sexual?

"Braxton." Her tone carries a warning, a light flashing orange. She isn't telling me to stop, but I haven't earned the green light yet either.

"A dance," I say, standing and fishing the phone out of my pocket.

"A dance? Now? Here?" Her words follow my back as I jump down off the back of the truck, then spin to face her.

"Right here, right now." I scroll on my phone until I find the song I'm searching for, then press play and hold out my hand to her.

"What song is this?" she asks but stands and places her palm in mine. When she reaches the tailgate, I wrap my arms around her thighs and let her slide down my body slowly. It's the best kind of torture.

I make a point of staring at the brightening sky. "It's called 'Stargazing' by Myles Smith."

Madison throws her head back and laughs.

Her arms wrap around my neck as I guide her in a slow dance that doesn't fit the song. "I had a really great time last night," I tell her honestly.

"Yeah?" Why does it always sound as though she doesn't believe me?

"Madison, I don't say things I don't mean. Any man would die happy if they got to watch the sunrise with you every morning." Her cheeks tinge pink, and it sets fire to desires I'm struggling to control.

"Any man, or you?"

"I should be so lucky," I say gently. It's a tone I've come to equate with Madison.

"I think you've been wasting your talents by not dating," she mutters. "You're a natural charmer."

"You think so?" I laugh. "I think I've just been waiting to find someone worth charming."

"Smooth, Braxton. Real smooth."

My face hurts from smiling so much. It's definitely a first.

"Too cheesy?" I use my hand at the small of her back to press her closer.

"Maybe a little. To be fair, I haven't had many opportunities to be charmed, so you could be nailing it and I have no idea."

The song ends, but we continue to sway to a beat that vibrates between us.

"That needs correcting. I'll have to talk to Pops about charming and wooing you. Something tells me he isn't going to let last night slide without a discussion."

She laughs so hard, tears dot the tips of her lashes. "He really likes you, Braxton."

"And you?" I drawl. "How do you feel about me?"

Her cheeks are a delicate pink that reminds me of cotton candy.

"I think I'm worried that you're some kind of mirage. You know, too good to be true."

"Ah," I say. "Were you always a pessimist, or is this lingering fear from whatever Turd did to you?"

It was the wrong thing to say. She shrugs and attempts to pull away. "That wasn't a dig, sunshine. That was me, asking you to show me your skeletons so I'll know how to bury the memories."

"Braxton, you don't even know me. What if my skeletons have already filled the cemetery?"

Hitching at the waist, I bring my nose in line with hers. "Then I'll cremate the fuckers and spread the ashes wherever you ask me to." As soon as I say it, I know I mean it more than anything else I've ever said.

Ace always talked about how love struck him with the precision of a whip the first time he saw my grandmother. I don't even know if I believe in love at first sight, but whatever this connection is with Madison, it definitely feels as though I'm headed in that direction.

"That's pretty intense for a man who's never even been on a date before."

I shrug and stand upright. "Not true. That was pretty intense for a man who went on the best date of his life last night and hasn't made it home yet."

She scoffs. "This wasn't a date, Braxton."

Holding up one finger, I correct her. "One, I've been called worse things than intense. Two, we had drinks."

"*I.* I had a drink. You didn't."

"Three," I tap her nose with my fingers. "We danced. A lot."

Madison rolls her eyes, and I have a momentary vision of tugging her over my lap and spanking her bare ass for the infraction. I've never had a spanking kink.

This woman is bringing out all kinds of interesting shit in me.

"Four, I fought for your honor."

"My ex was being an epic twatapossamus. That's not fighting for my honor."

I tap my jaw where a light bruise has formed. "Five, we talked about our shitty childhoods. Six, we snuggled—all night long while watching for shooting stars. Seven, we're dancing to the sunrise. I know I'm not an expert—yet—but I've seen enough movies to know that this could rival any Heartmark first date."

"You have a strange obsession with Heartmark, Mr. Mitchell. Plus, you weren't even watching, so *you* didn't see any shooting stars."

She loves to bicker with me.

With a hand pressing into her back, I dip her low and allow my body to follow so our mouths nearly touch. "Au contraire, mon amour. I did see a shooting star, and my wish already came true."

She searches my expression for the truth.

"You wished on a shooting star, and it already came true?"

"I did, and it did."

Who knew that my happiness looked like Madison Ryan?

Unable to stop myself, I press the gentlest of kisses to her soft lips. When she gasps for air, I lift her upright.

She exhales. "We missed the sunrise."

"I guess we'll need a do-over then." I lead her to the driver's side door and help her into the cab, then wait until she slides to the middle. "I'll see what I can do for date number two."

"This was not a date, Braxton." The exasperation she was going for isn't quite packing the punch she intended. "A date requires you to ask me if I want to go."

"I did. I asked if you wanted a ride last night. And this morning, I'm taking you home," I smirk.

She drops her head to the back of the seat. "I swear you're doing this on purpose. The entire town probably thinks we spent the night together."

Now it's my turn to groan. "I don't give a shit what the town thinks, Madison. But when we do spend the night together..." I bite my lip until she looks at me.

"What?"

"When we do spend the night together, you won't be going home carrying all this...frustration, I can promise you that."

She gapes at me. "Pretty confident in yourself for someone who doesn't date."

"Baby, dating has never had anything to do with it...until now."

When her mouth falls open and her face darkens to the pretty shade of red I'm starting to believe only happens for me, I put the truck in drive, more confident than ever that my shooting star wish is Madison Ryan.

14

MADISON

"'Bout time," Pops says with a chuckle, catching me off guard.

Why did I ever think we'd be able to sneak in this morning?

"Pops, why are you waiting in the dark?" I turn on the foyer light, and he's sitting in his recliner, wearing pajamas covered in turkeys with his hands clasped over his belly and a smile so broad his cheeks smoosh up like Santa Claus.

"Why are y'all sneaking in at six in the morning?"

"Ah," Braxton's voice cracks. "That was my fault. Uh..." He cuts a nervous glance my way then flashes Pops an uneasy shrug. "We had a flat tire?"

I groan, but Pops throws his head back and laughs while swinging his feet back and forth on the footrest of his recliner.

"Try again, boy. I didn't let Madi get her license until she knew how to check her oil and change a tire."

"Ran out of gas?" Braxton tries again, not even bothering to hide the humor in his tone this time.

"Gas station ain't open yet." If I didn't know better, I'd say Pops is enjoying this just as much as Braxton.

"A bear was blocking the road." Braxton crosses the room to sit on the sofa closest to Pops.

"What color bear?"

Braxton turns a cheeky grin my way. "Black bear."

"She's still telling folks there's bears around here?"

"Pops," I huff. He's supposed to be on my side.

"Chin's not lookin' as bad as I thought it would," Pops says, eyeing Braxton's face.

"Not bad at all." As if to prove his point, Braxton works his jaw side to side.

"How'd he get the jump on ya? That jackalope hasn't been sober since he crawled home again."

Braxton leans back into the sofa and crosses his arms behind his head. How can he look so...just...at home here? "I had more important things to protect than my ugly mug, Pops."

My grandfather harrumphs in victory. "That's right. And don't you forget it. This staying out all night ain't good for her reputation though. Whatcha going to do about that?"

Swinging my arms wildly in the air, I step in front of them both.

"I swear to all things holy, Pops. I'm not a teenager, and this is not the 1950s. The only one who should be worrying about my reputation is me. I'm going to start breakfast."

Halfway to the kitchen, I spin back around and point a finger at my grandfather.

"What are your plans today, old man?" I narrow my gaze at the oldest child Happiness, Georgia has ever seen.

Pops tries to move me along with a flick of his hand. "I'm not your child, Madi. Don't you go worrying about me."

"Pops!"

"Fine." He huffs. "The boy and I have a lunch date at the diner, and then we're gonna check out the Chug. Haven't been there in a while, and I want to catch up on things."

My shoulders inch toward my ears with guilt, and the sass I'd been wielding escapes on a wheeze. "I know I haven't had as much free time to take you to all your activities, but we really do have a budget to stick to."

He ignores me as he always does when I attempt to talk about our finances.

"Patty's fundraiser at the barn is tomorrow night," he says. "Moose is takin' me, but the boy here, he's going to help us get set up today."

Braxton doesn't even flinch. It's as though he couldn't care less that he's become my grandfather's gopher. In fact, he nods as if he's enjoying every second of it.

"Pops, Braxton's knuckles are all cut up from whatever the heck you had him helping with yesterday. He isn't your handyman or your rideshare driver. He has actual work he needs to do." Turning to him, I frown. "Don't you?"

"I have some phone calls to make today, but I've got time to be Pops' steward."

"You're not helping," I groan.

"He is. Now, do you want to talk about why you were out all night with the boy, or do you want to get on with our day?"

"Pops, it's not like that," Braxton says gently.

"Like what?" I ask, spinning on him. Why is it so easy to confront this man when I can't even tell my lifelong best friends that I don't want to go out for a stinking drink?

What am I doing? I'm losing my dang mind, *that's* what I'm doing.

Braxton's jaw jumps, and whatever he's thinking has his irises shifting to a darker shade of amber.

"I didn't do anything to disrespect her honor, Pops. I swear to you." He's speaking to my grandfather, but his gaze is saying something completely different to me. Something like, *I didn't disrespect her honor, but I sure as hell wanted to.*

He raises a brow in my direction, and my cheeks get hot and tingly.

"Madison showed me the Georgia moon, and she fell asleep trying to get me to count shooting stars. She's been working so hard I didn't have the heart to wake her."

"Mm-hmm," Pops says noncommittally. "And I s'pose you were watching for bears too."

"Yes, sir."

"Ugh." The urge to stomp my feet in frustration is only dimmed when Braxton pulls his phone out of his pocket, and I see his face fall.

"It's three in the morning in California. I'm sorry, I have to…" He answers the call. "Grey? What's wrong?"

Pops and I exchange a worried expression. I don't know how much Braxton has shared with Pops about his life in California—in fact, I still don't know much, but I do know that Grey is his family, and judging by the way Pops sits his chair upright and leans forward, resting his forearms on his thighs, he knows it too.

"When? Is Sage okay?" Braxton's gaze darts to mine, and my pulse rages in my ears.

Sage? He's said that name before, but I can't place it.

"Of course," Braxton puts his elbows on his knees, and his shoulders tighten, but his stare never leaves me, and it secures me to the floor. His fear carries to me as though he's the flame and I'm the gasoline. "I'll figure it out before you get here." He nods, but I see the pain in his expression. "Whatever it takes. Keep me posted, and I'll have everything situated before you guys arrive. Love you too."

He drops the phone into his lap, his hands flex, and his breath escapes in short bursts of air through his nose like a trapped animal.

"Braxton?" My voice is unsteady, and he swallows hard, but his gaze darts back and forth as if he's trying to come up with a solution to an unsolvable equation.

"Son?" Pops asks. This time, Braxton blinks, and determination covers his features.

"That was Greyson." His voice is vibrating as if he's trying to control himself. "He'll be here in a couple of days."

Pops and I share a look and nod.

"Any chance you're willing to take on an extended stay for one more?" he asks. "If not, I understand. The hotel probably has openings, I never bothered to check, but they'll no longer be commuting between coasts. They'll need to be here, with me, for...a while."

"Is everything okay?" I ask. Pops is already lifting himself from the recliner and waving me over toward Braxton.

We both take a seat on either side of our guest who has quickly become a friend.

"What do you need, Braxton?" My head snaps up to my grandfather. It might be the first time I've heard him say Braxton's name. "Besides another room."

Braxton lifts his gaze to mine, and I understand his pain without knowing the details. It's the same way I'd feel if Clover, Savvy, or Elle were in trouble.

"Are they okay?" My throat is tight, expecting the worst.

He lifts his hand to his chest and scratches a one-inch space above his heart, then nods. "My parents—and maybe my siblings—aren't happy they've been cut off financially. They went after Sage—my nephew—to prove a point."

Cut off? Just how much money does this guy have?

"Did they hurt him?" Are we safe? I spare a glance at Pops, but he's not at all fazed.

"Not physically. Sage is, he's—he hasn't had the easiest life." He drops his gaze to the floor. "His mother died in... childbirth, but he's such a good kid. My father had him arrested for stealing my car." His face hardens, the angle of his jaw more pronounced. "A car that I left for him. It's hitting the papers this morning and painting Ace, Greyson, and me as shitty role models."

"But why? Why?" It's all I can think to say. My body is growing itchy, and my lungs clam up as though they've been caught in a bear trap.

The media and I have a dark history.

"Because when my grandfather passed away, he placed six-month contingencies on everyone's inheritance, but my father refuses to play by the rules. He's never thought they apply to him. I'm sure in his mind, doing shit like this will scare Greyson into forfeiting his inheritance. He'll probably come after all of us instead of doing what he's supposed to."

"You're safe here, son. This town will take care of ya," Pops says with certainty in his tone.

"He'll do all of this over a—a marketing company? What kind of things do you market?" I ask cautiously. The itchiness crawls across my skin at the thought of an innocent child being hounded by reporters. It triggers the worst time in my life.

Braxton takes my hand in his. Pink creeps across his cheeks, and his fingertips turn white where he's digging them into his chest.

Is he embarrassed to tell me?

"It's, ah, a worldwide, um, corporation. My great-grandfather started it so he could publish my great grandmother's articles. It was just a small-town monthly periodical that became a beloved magazine in northern California. Then my grandmother was more interested in movies and television, so when my grandfather took over the company, he expanded it so she could follow her dreams."

"Why do you sound embarrassed by that?"

He shrugs and drops his gaze to the floor. "I'm not. It's not my great-grandparents or my grandparents I'm embarrassed by either. They led our company with love and compassion. It's my parents who attempted to ruin it. I never thought of it as my passion, but I took over by default because my parents had no moral compass. My grandfather supported me and Grey learning the ins and outs of the company in college so we'd be ready. I didn't earn my place there, but I spend every day trying to maintain the legacy it was meant to be."

"I knew there was good in ya, boy. We've got plenty of room. Don't you worry about that." Pops pats Braxton's knee with the fondness of a grandfather.

I swear dollar signs are lighting up behind his eyes though. "Pops, we are not taking any more money from him, do you hear me? We have the room at the end of the hall, and he's already overpaid. I won't—"

"I'll make a deal with you," Braxton says, and I purse my lips together. As much as I innately trust this man, he has a sneaky way of getting me to agree to things I wouldn't if he were anyone else.

"What kind of deal?"

"I'll help Pops fix up whatever needs fixing around here in exchange for room and board for Sage." I open my mouth, but he squeezes my hand. Freaking hell. I'd forgotten he was still holding it. "If they stay longer than a few weeks, we'll renegotiate."

"That's a very generous offer, Braxton. But I know my

grandfather. Fixing up the inn is going to cost more than a few weeks' stay."

He shrugs. "Then it's a deal you shouldn't refuse."

It takes effort, but I remove my hand from his. "I don't understand why you'd do this. I love Happiness, don't get me wrong, but people don't just drop thousands of dollars to stay in a run-down inn. They don't make these kinds of deals. It doesn't make any sense, so forgive me if I'm a little suspicious."

Braxton's Adam's apple bobs as he swallows. "I feel as though I have purpose here, Madison. For the first time in my life, I'm doing what I want to do. I'm making a difference. I'm making friends—" He drops his chin to his chest. When he meets my gaze again, I see the truth in his words. "At least, I hope I'm making friends. You asked me what I wanted to be when I grew up, well maybe this is it. Maybe it's finally time I get to be the helper."

Fist, meet stomach. It's an emotional sucker punch, but how can I deny him that? He wants to be a freaking helper, and all I want to know is how this kindhearted man ended up in my inn, spreading kindness like he's some kind of stinking fairy.

"Do you have any idea what you're signing up for here? In case you haven't noticed, my grandfather doesn't exactly believe in boundaries."

Pops harrumphs from his spot on the sofa.

"I promise I won't do anything I don't want to do, and I'll make sure we stay on a budget too."

I stare at a spot on the wall that used to hold a picture of me and my parents at the lake. We removed it when I moved in because it made me spiral, but there's something about that empty spot now that has my insides trembling. The picture hook it hung on is still in the drywall, and the longer

I stare at it, the heavier and more out of sync my heartbeat grows.

I haven't had this sensation in years. Not since before my parents threw me away—when I thought I knew what love felt like.

It's as though some hidden piece of myself is nudging me to trust Braxton, or at least to give it a try, and it's so overwhelming. I nod and stand quickly.

My guest is not teaching me how to love again. He's just not.

"Fine. That sounds fine. How do we claim that on taxes, and what will it do to the insurance and house evaluation? Would we acknowledge it as a gift? Or a grant? Are there scholarships for renovations?"

It's so off-topic and so far removed from the spiraling happening in my mind, I choke on a laugh. It's something Pops would do to ease the tension.

Gah. I cover my entire face with both palms. "What's wrong with me?"

Braxton chuckles too, but it's subdued. I'm probably freaking him out, and he has enough to worry about, so I lower my hands to my lap.

"I'm not sure how you'd claim it, but I promise to find out," he says with kind eyes that shatter my reserves.

"Great. Breakfast."

I spin so quickly, only one foot touches the floor before I'm nearly sprinting for the kitchen.

"I signed us up for the peanut butter cream cheese brownies for tomorrow," Pops calls through the swinging door, and I drop my forehead to the cold metal of the refrigerator.

"You're the only one who eats those, Pops," I shout back.

"The boy'll eat them too."

The boy. In what world is a grown freaking man okay with being called *boy* all day long?

My world, apparently. Or the wonderland I've fallen into, anyway. Because there's not a dang thing about Braxton Mitchell that makes sense except that he makes my body sizzle in ways I've only ever read about. But if my brain doesn't get on board soon, I'll end up right back where I was all those years ago.

And there isn't a man alive who I'll allow to break me again. It's a good reminder for me. Braxton Mitchell is a guest, a passerby, a town visitor. I cannot get my heart involved.

Braxton's rich laughter booms from the family room, followed by Pops' voice working a new scheme, and my body sings with familiarity. No matter how much I deny it, that man in there makes me feel safe.

Maybe it's too late. Maybe my heart is already involved, and I don't know if there's anything I can do to stop it.

15

BRAXTON

"Wʜᴀᴛ ᴀᴍ I ʟᴏᴏᴋɪɴɢ ꜰᴏʀ ᴜᴘ ʜᴇʀᴇ?" I ᴅᴇsᴘɪsᴇ ᴛʜᴇ ᴡᴀʏ ᴍʏ voice quivers as I lay on my belly on the damn roof because I'm too fucking scared to stand up.

Six weeks. That's all it took for this old man to get me to climb onto the roof. Imagine what he could do if he used his powers for the good of the world. Jesus, he's a tricky son of a bitch.

"Count the rotting pieces. How bad does it look?" Pops is shielding his eyes from the sun with both hands, and I swear the old man just might be dancing down there too.

Climbing up onto the roof was not what we had planned to do today. But after we cruised through town yesterday, we went to lunch with his friends where everyone in the place had ideas for the Hideaway.

Apparently before we prioritize projects, we have to know what we're dealing with. Unfortunately for Pops, I don't know a shingle from a gutter shield, something Moose had a field day with at lunch.

I stare at the black-and-gray rectangles in front of me. "I don't know, Pops. It looks old, and it's saggy in some places."

"What the hell are you doing up there?" a loud baritone voice booms to the sky louder than a Fourth of July firework.

Scrabbling around on my belly so my head hangs over the edge of the roof instead of my toes, I find Cian glowering in my direction.

Just what I need.

"Are you trying to kill yourself?"

"We're working here," Pops shouts back, though it sounds a little petulant, even from three stories in the air.

"And I told you that when you were ready, I'd come over and do it for you." Perhaps Cian isn't yelling. I'm beginning to think that his giant frame only comes with one volume—loud and aggressive. "Brax, get the feck down here, will ya, before you break yer neck and Madi skins my hide."

His Irish brogue is thicker toward the end of his sentence. He's pissed.

Army-crawling back around, I feel with my feet for the rungs of the ladder.

"Are ya taking the piss out, Braxton?"

I peer over my shoulder and see Cian sprinting toward the house.

"This is the ladder you used? You can't place a ladder on a porch roof. You're really going to kill yerself."

"My ladder didn't reach the roof," Pops explains while I creep forward a few inches and cling to the hot pieces of sandpaper I now know are roof shingles.

"All the more reason to come get me, ya old fool. Braxton, so help me, St. Monica. Do not move from that spot. I'll be right back with the proper tools, ya bunch of bubbletwits."

"Did he just call us bubbletwits?" I call down to Pops,

who's stuffing his hands into his pockets and whistling to the sky.

Why does everything feel like a trick with this guy?

Moments later, Cian's muttering as he stomps up the driveway, hauling a giant ladder as if it weighs as much as a jump rope.

"If one of ya gets hurt, that's going to hurt Madi, and when Madi's hurting, so is Elle, and Elle is very, very pregnant. If one of you makes Elle sad, I'll bury you in the back-yard and build a dog park over you."

"A dog park?" It's so very...specific. I bet up close he's a scary motherfucker right now.

"Pops hates when dogs piss on his lawn. Imagine how he'll feel being pissed on day in and day out."

Pops grunts his disapproval, but I laugh so hard my belly shakes, and an involuntary yelp escapes when I slide two inches.

Cian returns to cursing while propping the biggest ladder I've ever seen against the house. He does something with it to brace it against the wood slats, then holds it steady from below.

"Get down," he growls.

"No arguments from me." I'm already crawling closer to him.

I've never been afraid of heights, but if I never climb onto a roof again, I'll be a happy man.

Once my feet are securely and safely back on the ground, Cian rolls his eyes.

"Betty told me at the diner you fools were making plans over here. I didn't think you'd be idiot enough to go at it without any professional help," he says evenly. But his massive arms are crossed over his chest with bulging veins from his balled-up fists, so I know he's still upset.

"Why pay you to do it when me and the boy can do it for free?" Pops rummages through the set of tools Cian dropped on the ground when he ran to get the ladder.

"I've told you a hundred times, I'm not going to charge you, Pops. Elle and I have our dream home thanks to you. Let me help."

Pops mutters, but he's also fully engrossed in inspecting everything Cian brought over—he's a kid in a candy store.

I frown at Pops. He's assumed I'll help and has bossed me around for six weeks now, so why is he hesitant with Cian?

"It's that easy to tell I have no idea what I'm doing, huh?" I laugh a little desperately, and Cian curses under his breath. I don't care what Pops says though, I'll gladly take Cian's help.

"Look at this drywall saw, boy. We've gotta try this out."

Before Cian or I can stop him, Pops heads into the house, carrying a red and black tool I have no idea how to use.

"Feck," Cian curses. "Let's get in there before he has holes in every wall and the ceiling too."

He moves quickly for such a big guy, and I follow.

"To answer your question, yes. While it's nice of you to help out, you don't look like someone who's ever worn a toolbelt."

Feeling slightly defensive, I stand taller. "Maybe not, but I'm a fast learner."

Cian stops in the foyer and stares at me for so long, I nearly take a step back. I'm really not trying to get a black eye to match my sore jaw.

"You'd better be a fast learner, Brax. I've got about a month before my baby's due, and Elle says I'm driving her nutty, so she sent me over here. If we're going to get the big stuff done in that time, you'll have to pull your weight."

"No problem." In my head, I panic though. This might be a problem—a big problem because Cian's right. I don't even own a hammer, let alone know how to swing one.

A buzzing sound interrupts my internal struggle as we take off for the kitchen, Pops stands in the center of the room, wearing a toolbelt and safety goggles.

"We can use this to cut a hole in the ceiling to fix the leak," he announces while holding up the power tool in his right hand—his own personal trophy.

"Slow your roll, big guy." Cian steps forward and Pops reluctantly releases the tool, but not without a little tug of war with Cian first. "Let's see this list I heard you were making at the diner, and we'll go from there." His Irish accent is less pronounced when he isn't attempting to save people from rooftops.

Pops pulls out a folded-up sheet of paper and slaps it down on the island. Cian cuts a look my way, but not only am I in over my head, I'm so deep I can't see sunlight any longer.

The big guy pulls out a stool, and I do the same while Pops leans against the sink. Somehow the old man manages to have the look of a preteen who knows he's about to get into trouble, but when he winks, he proves that he doesn't give a shit.

What must that be like? To go through life not caring what other people think of you?

"I'm going to need all the fecking saints here," Cian mutters. "Christ on a turdloaf. You told me you had half of this fixed already." The guy certainly is colorful with his insults.

Pops drops his gaze, but not before I see something close

to embarrassment in his downturned expression. "Some...ah...investments didn't pan out as I thought they would."

Cian stiffens next to me. "What...investments, Pops?"

The old man kicks at the wood floor with the toe of his boot. There's something so youthful about him, and I can fully imagine the hell he raised before settling down with Madi's grandmother.

"I did it before." Pops lifts his gaze to mine and quickly cuts to Cian. "Before we found out."

My hackles are officially raised.

"How much did he lose, Pops?"

"Who are we talking about?" I ask.

The tension in the room is stifling.

"I'm a smart man." Pops' voice is almost fragile, something I've never heard from him before. "I...I thought I was doing the right thing."

"It's not your fault. Harry's a conman, Pops."

That name, again. My fists clench until my knuckles are white. Why is it every time something goes wrong in this family it's because of him?

"I gotta know, though, Pops. How much did you lose?" Cian gives me the side-eye. "And does Madi know?"

"I'm not bad with money," Pops says defensively, and I wonder if he's saying that for my benefit. "We should've been okay. I even had enough to leave Madi a little nest egg when I'm gone."

"How much, Pops?" Cian asks again.

"All of it," he admits gruffly. "I didn't know until I went to make a withdrawal for the taxes two years ago. He said to give his partner time and that it was normal. I never trusted Turd, but his partner, he seemed like a real smart guy. When all that went down last year, I realized everything was gone."

"What's going on?" I finally ask. I hate seeing Pops so...

broken. This isn't the meddlesome, interfering man I've befriended. This is someone else.

"Fucking Harry started running schemes after his...accident, but he had a friend who came to town a few years ago. He was..." Cian looks me up and down. "He was kind of like you. Rich, nice to everyone, and smart. Harry talked a lot of people into letting this guy, Sam, manage investments for them, and at the time, most of us were still trying to help Harry get back on his feet. Hell, I even gave the guy some money. Sam appeared to have all the credentials and he said all the right things. Not only that, but he also spent time in town getting to know everyone. Now we know it was just a long con."

Cian stands and paces the kitchen. "We told you not to give him everything, Pops. What happened?"

Pops shrugs. "I wanted Madi to have a good life. I wanted her to stop working all hours of the day. I wanted to give her the security her parents took away, so when he showed me the return on my first investment and suggested I go bigger, I did." He's so dejected, I feel sick to my stomach.

"Sam and Harry preyed mostly on the elderly," Cian informs me. "But we all got swindled." He stands in front of Pops. "What's going on with the taxes?"

Pops waves at us to follow him, then leads us outside to the shed where he pulls out an old toolbox. Inside are a couple of envelopes from the IRS.

"I don't know what the hell this means," Cian says, handing half of the stack to me.

As soon as I open an envelope, a heavy, old-fashioned key tied with a blue ribbon falls into my palms. The ribbon says The Hideaway on it. I turn the key over in my hands, then read the papers it was tucked into.

What the fuck? "Madi doesn't know about this?"

Pops grunts, then lowers his head. They were close to foreclosure due to back taxes right up until seven months ago.

The weight these papers carry sits heavily on my chest. My knees are about to buckle, so I lean against the old wooden structure. "How did you know my grandfather?"

Pops shrugs. "Ace was a good man. We played poker a few times, kept in touch over the years." His answer is vague as hell, but I'm still trying to work out why my name is on the deed to the inn.

"This doesn't make any sense, Pops."

"What's it say?" Cian steps closer to peer over my shoulder.

"They were close to foreclosure, then seven months ago, Pops sold a portion of the inn."

"Feck me, Pops. You sold it? Why didn't you tell Madi? Criminy Joseph, this is going to break her. Who'd ya sell to?"

My chest tightens, and sweat forms on my brow.

Pops throws his shoulders back and lifts his head, his pity party for one apparently over. "I did what I had to do. I'm working with the police to get my money back, but this sale ensured we wouldn't lose her."

"It can take years, and that's if they can find Sam and if the cases are found to be fraudulent. That's a lot of ifs, Pops. It's more likely that money is gone," I say absently.

How the hell do I own part of Madison's inn?

"This place is falling apart. You should have come to me, Pops. What if the other owner wants to sell?" Fear and sadness mingle with Cian's words.

"He won't." I peer up at Pops.

"But how do you know? You aren't exactly turning a profit lately."

Pops turns his hangdog look my way—he must have perfected that expression sixty years ago.

Pinching the bridge of my nose, I hold up the key in my hand. "Apparently, I'm the owner."

"Wait, what? How? Ace." Cian says the four words in staccato. "Ace, you said Ace."

I nod. "He was my grandfather."

"He came to Happiness a few times a year for about ten years now, I think. He always stayed at the inn."

My head snaps up, and Pops looks slightly guilty.

"He did," Pops says. "And we became friends. He wanted you to be happy, boy."

"So, he bought stake in an inn and put the deed in my name? What the hell sense does that make?"

"This is going to devastate Madi. Jesus, Joseph, and Mary. Elle's going cry." The desperation in the big man's voice would be comical if the situation weren't so dire. "Anything else I should know?"

I quickly scan the files, and guilt swamps me faster than a heatwave in July.

"Mitchell is my middle name." I can't make eye contact with him. "My last name is Reyes, just like Ace. And this says I'm on the hook for all the repairs. I can't even think about selling or gifting the inn back to Madison until all the repairs are made and the inn turns a profit." I lift my gaze to Pops. "That's why you were buying all those supplies from Huckabees."

"Well, *I* didn't buy them, now did I?" This guy should have been a salesman.

"You know, I came here to get away from people who were using me, Pops. This is some kind of bullshit right here," I say, waving the papers in front of me.

"Mm-hmm." Pops rocks back on his heels, but he's not

whistling this time. Instead, he stares at the floor of the shed. It's how Sage would stand when he was younger and knew he was in trouble.

Somehow this betrayal doesn't feel as hurtful as the shit my parents have pulled, but I have no idea why.

"Ace asked me not to. He wanted you to fall in love in Happiness before we tied you to it."

"You should have told me, Pops," I say gently, choosing to ignore how he said 'fall in love *in* Happiness,' not fall in love *with* Happiness. "And you absolutely should have told Madison. She has a right to know."

He nods, and his neck bobs as though he's having difficulty swallowing.

Pinching the back of my neck, I run through different scenarios, but the only solution I can come up with is to tell Madison the truth.

"What are you going to do? Help them." Cian doesn't end his sentence in a question. He tells me, but I'd already planned to.

"I—helping isn't the problem." I grip the key tightly in my palm.

"Like you helped Jessa over at the high school?" Cian smirks.

"Or the tip you left at the diner after you heard Betty's grandson needed physical therapy?" The humor in Pops' tone is frustrating.

"I didn't..."

Cian chortles, which is a funny sound coming from someone his size. "Come on, Brax. You blow into town and suddenly good deeds are popping up wherever you go? It wasn't hard to figure out."

Dammit.

"No one knows it's you, boy. They just got their suspicions is all." At least Pops has the sparkle back in his eyes.

"Yeah, but what's with the DDD? That's fecking weird."

"No, it's not." I tug on the collar of my shirt. "It's...listen. I don't know what I'm doing here. After my grandfather passed away, his attorney handed me a postcard of the inn. On the back, he'd told me to go find my happy, and I'm trying, but it's also the first time people don't treat me as though I'm the bank. Does that make any sense at all?"

Pops pats me on the back. "You're a good kid, boy."

Freaking *boy*. "Pops, do you know that I'm thirty years old? I haven't been a boy in years."

"You're a boy until you prove your salt. But your secret is safe with us, right, Cian?"

Cian nods but doesn't look happy about it. "What are you going to tell Madi? You haven't exactly been sly around here, you know. People don't just drop the kind of money you have to stay at the Hideaway."

The deed in my hand weighs me down much more than a piece of paper should. "I did that before I knew I owned the damn place."

"I'm still trying to figure out why you did. What did you think you were getting from any of this? Because I have to tell ya, if you hurt Madi, I will fecking skin ya alive, you hear me?"

"Yeah, I got it. And I wish I knew. But I don't know what to tell you other than I feel alive when I'm here. I don't have to hide or pretend to be someone I'm not. I've never had that before."

Cian nods, then raises his brows and gestures at the deed.

"So, what are we going to do?" he asks.

"Easy, we're going to tell Madi she has a new business

partner." Pops says it so fucking merrily that a stranger looking in would think this was his plan all along.

"You're what?" Cian chokes on his words. "Just like that? You're going to drop this on her? This is her dream, Pops. Her life."

"It ain't like the boy's a stranger—not really. Madi and I owned the inn fifty-fifty. I only sold Ace forty percent, that way she maintains control of all the decisions."

Holding up my hands in surrender, I inch closer to the door. "I'm going to gift it back to her."

"Nope, ya can't do that. It's all in the contract Ace's lawyer drew up. Ya have to get the inn back to fighting shape, then it has to turn a profit for three full years before you can even think about dumping it."

My chin drops to my chest. "What were you two trouble-makers scheming up here, Pops? That's not a sound business deal in any way you look at it."

"Well, you already made a deal to dump a shit ton of money into the place. I guess it would go over better if you were an owner. A silent owner," Cian's tone leaves no room for argument, but I meant what I said—I'm not looking to take Madison's inn away from her.

"All settled then," Pops says, edging past me toward the shed door. "Now all you got to do is tell Madi."

The tension in my neck crawls up into my forehead. "Me? Why do I have to tell her?"

Cian belly laughs at my side, then claps my shoulder a little too forcefully, and I hitch forward. "That man has nine lives and then some. If you thought for a minute he was going to face Madi's wrath over this, well, then you've still got some learning to do here in Happiness."

I snap my mouth shut, but not before a grin pokes through.

"I don't know why Pops has taken such a liking to you, Brax, and it's not my place to question it, but what is my place is protecting Madi. She's been like a sister to me for half my life, and she doesn't deserve the shit she's been dealt. So I'm going to tell you now not to hurt her. And listen when I say that, because if you do hurt her, you'll never see me coming."

"I'm not going to hurt her."

He stops and scans me head to toe, but when he meets my gaze, I find a kindred spirit who is ruled by his protective instincts. "I hope not, Brax. I don't hate ya, so it would be a real bitch to have to kill you." He starts walking again, then calls over his shoulder, "Oh, and a piece of advice?"

"What's that?"

"If you're going to spread good deeds in town and want to stay anonymous, stop dropping off twenty-thousand-dollar checks with your signature on them, you fecking boob."

A bark of laughter rips through me. The neighboring town was having a fundraiser for girls in STEM, and I drove over there yesterday to drop off a check since they didn't have any way to submit donations online. "I didn't think anyone would be able to read my signature."

"Oh, you're making a name for yourself here, Brax. Don't worry about that. But if you truly want your anonymity, then come to me and I'll help you out."

I stop on the grass. "You will?"

He nods. "I may not understand you, but I get what you're doing. Being the good you want to see in the world is noble. I'm just sorry you have to be so secretive to do nice things. People will like you for you around here no matter what your bank balance is. Remember that."

Cian stomps off in the direction of his truck.

"Will you be at the fundraiser tomorrow night?" I call to his back.

"Have you met my wife?" he replies over his shoulder. "She won't miss a social event even if I tied her to our bed."

"Kinky."

He chuckles and waves as he walks away.

As I glance up at the inn, the calm that surrounds me here is replaced with worry. Madison isn't going to like anything I have to tell her, but there doesn't seem to be any other way around it.

16

MADISON

WHAT THE HECK IS HE DOING NOW? LADDERS ON ROOFS WILL never be a good sign—especially not when Pops thinks he has Braxton at his beck and call.

I park my car and am emptying the trunk when I hear heavy footsteps on the porch. I know they're Braxton's before I turn around.

"Need help?" Two words that cause goosebumps to race down my arms. It's not the words themselves, it's the deep baritone he speaks in—it's the way the timbre of his voice makes my heart race. He feels safe, and that scares the hell out of me.

"Ah, yeah, sure. Thanks. I ran to Walmart for a few new sets of sheets for your family."

"Madison." It's a low rumble, a plea, a warning all rolled into my name. His arm brushes mine as he leans into the trunk, and my stomach flips over. Why does one innocent touch from this man tangle up my insides like a pot of spaghetti?

"You don't have to go to any trouble for them." He steps closer, and the heat of his thigh sends tingles down my hip.

"They're very laid-back and are just happy to be away from the West Coast for a bit."

A fissure of unease has me squaring my shoulders. Business is business, and I really need to get my bodily reactions under control. "But they're also guests, Braxton. I know this is—well, I don't even know what this is to you, but this is my livelihood."

"His too." Pops chuckles, then plops down on his porch swing.

"Pops." Braxton's warning is surprisingly sharp, and I search his expression.

"Come on." He hip-checks me out of the way. "We've got some stuff to talk to you about."

Pursing my lips, I glare at Pops. What the heck could he have done in just a few hours? I know, I know, dumb question. Pops can get up to all sorts of trouble in minutes, let alone hours.

Braxton closes my trunk with his elbow and marches inside. With no other options, I follow him into the house and down the basement steps to the washing machine.

"How did you know this was down here?"

"Pops and I were down here looking at pipes earlier."

I stand on the bottom step as he opens the first two sets of sheets, stuffs them into the washing machine, adds soap, and then starts it.

The sound of rushing water hits my ears, and I remember to close my mouth.

"What are you doing?"

"I'm helping, Madison. I realize it's not something you get a lot of, but you might as well get used to it. I'm going to be here a while."

"Why?"

"I'm comfortable here, remember?"

The lone swinging light bulb flickers above his head, a metaphor for my energy that is suddenly zapped dry. Sinking to the stairs, I place my elbows on my thighs and stare at him.

He raises a hand to draw small circles on his chest and I smile. It's nice knowing one of his little tells.

"What's on your mind, Braxton?"

The muscles in his forearms bunch when he lifts himself to sit on top of the dryer. "You're not going to like it."

I instantly drop my head into my hands and practice breathing exercises that never work, but I keep doing them anyway.

"What did he do now?" Of course whatever he's about to tell me has something to do with my grandfather.

"Can you promise me something?"

"What? You want me to promise not to get mad? Not to have a complete and utter breakdown that he's putting us deeper into debt without any true understanding of what it will take me to repay?"

"No. Promise me that you'll keep an open mind."

"I'd really rather you just spit it out." Freaking stress makes me so stinking sweaty. Gathering all my hair, I twist it up into a messy bun to cool my neck.

"The inn was in trouble."

Somehow, that's the very last thing I expected this man to say.

"He told you about the taxes?"

Braxton's jaw drops to his chest and his brows nearly reach his hairline. "How..."

I snort out a defeated chuckle. "When Sam disappeared, I had a feeling he was leaving everyone in a bad way. I started pulling all the files I could get my hands on."

"But Pops has all the documents—"

"In the shed. It's where he hides everything. Listen, I appreciate you looking out for him, but I'm raising the money to repay the loan he took out from his friend. I'm almost there, that's why all the improvements have been put on hold. But now that you've paid a king's ransom to stay here, we should be fine."

"A loan?" The words squeak past his lips. "And how are you saving that much money?"

"I took on a bunch of new clients. I produce audiobooks for indie authors and sometimes do sound engineering for podcasters. I do them at night when no one else is in the studio so I can rent that space out as much as possible. We'll be on our feet soon enough. His friend, Ace, sadly passed away though, so I'm working my butt off to get the funds before his sleazy family comes looking to be repaid."

The color drains from Braxton's face. "His family? You're working yourself into the ground because you're scared of his family?"

I nod but feel my face pinch at his tone. "He used to tell us about them. They all sounded horrible, except for his grandson and adopted grandkids. But not all of us have unlimited resources, so I needed to get the repayment sorted before the rich freaking..." I snap my lips shut as soon as the words leave my mouth. "I'm sorry. I didn't..."

He looks down at the floor. "You're stressed, and I get it. But I'm not sure how you'll take this next bit of information."

"He's Ace's grandson," Pops shouts down the stairs. "He owns forty percent of the inn. Now get up here so we can talk about it."

I don't remember standing or balling my hands into fists. Braxton jumps down from the dryer, but I hold up a hand, palm facing him, and shake my head once. It's another thirty seconds before I can gather enough strength to walk up the stairs, and all my control to walk past my grandfather without bursting into tears.

He sold part of the inn? Maisie's Hideaway Inn?

Braxton's footsteps follow me the entire way, but he whispers something to Pops on his way by, and that's what sets me off.

I slam both hands into the swinging kitchen door and take up residence behind the island.

"You should have told her."

"I was protecting her."

"She's an adult, Pops. She..."

"She doesn't need two well-meaning idiots talking about her either." As soon as I say it, their words muffle into hushed whispers—they could be a barrel of snakes behind that door for all the shushing sounds. I drop my forehead to the cool countertop and count backward from one hundred.

The kitchen door swings open, but I don't lift my head.

"No. Nope," I say with my nose squished against the granite. "I need a few minutes to myself. Do not even think about coming in here right now."

The door swings shut again without a word, so I know it was Braxton. Pops wouldn't have been able to stay quiet.

What does Pops mean, Braxton owns forty percent of the Hideaway? He sold it? How could he do that to me?

I close my eyes when my chest beats to that uncomfortable rhythm I used to associate with anxiety, but now think it might be Braxton.

Okay, think, Madison. He owns forty percent, that means we still own sixty. Oh, God. What will he do with his share?

Is that why he's here? Will he try to make me sell?

Sickness swirls in my stomach and acid burns the back

of my throat when tears threaten. Is this why he was getting so close to me?

No. I mentally chastise myself. Braxton isn't like that. Maybe he doesn't even want the inn. Maybe he'll let me repay the loan and he'll give me back my property. That's it! It makes the most sense anyway. He doesn't want to run an inn in Georgia, right?

"Madison?"

"Braxton," I hiss without lifting my head. "Care to explain why my grandfather sold my legacy to you, a stranger we've only known for a hot minute?"

"He likes me?"

"The boy will be good for you, Madi."

The groan that escapes my throat is equal parts angry and sad with a little confusion laced in.

"And he didn't sell it to me, he sold it to Ace, who I guess willed it to me. Um."

I lift my face off the counter. A bead of sweat has formed on his forehead, and his shifty gaze is scanning the exits. I stand upright as my defenses prickle.

"Also, um, Mitchell is my middle name. I'm sorry I deceived you. I'm Braxton Mitchell Reyes. I was named after Ace. But I only said it was Mitchell for privacy reasons. It wasn't to hurt anyone, I promise."

Guilt fills every inch of his expression, but I can't garner an ounce of sympathy when everything I've been working for was just pulled out from under my feet.

Instead, I ignore his comments and plead my case to Pops.

"And what happens when 'the boy' heads back to his real life? What happens to Grams' inn then, Pops?"

"Nothing. If I go home—"

"If?" It comes out slightly shrill as I spin on him so

quickly, hair falls from my messy bun. "What do you mean, if?"

"When I go home, nothing will change for you. I'm here for six months, to be the good Ace wanted to see in the world, but I'm only a silent partner in the inn, and I'll gift it all back to you at the end of the contract."

"The contract?" My voice is pitched so high, I'll be surprised if all the dogs in town don't show up soon.

Braxton shifts his weight from foot to foot. "I haven't seen it yet, but according to Pops, it'll be three or four years."

My eyeballs strain against my skull, and I scoff. Then scoff again while attempting to locate my words.

"I honestly don't know what the heck is going on here, Braxton. So you're not here because you want to be. You have to be here?" I clench my jaw, then inhale deeply through my nose so I can speak at a more acceptable decibel.

"Yes, no. I mean, yes, Ace told me to come, but I truly do love it here. I wouldn't lie about that, Madison."

But lying about your name is okay? Deep breath, Madi. Deep breath and think.

"Braxton, people don't just float into town, drop small cities' worth of cash, and then walk away. I don't get this, I don't get you, and I really don't understand why you, Pops, of all people, would agree to this. Not after everything with Sam and..."

"Lord of the Turds," Pops says with as much glee as he can muster. "It's easy, Mads. I trust him because Ace trusted him. It's not the same as how I trusted Turdknocker and Sam. No, I trusted them because I was trying to be supportive like Grams always was. I trust the boy because Ace had a good soul. He proved that the first time I met him, and I'll believe in the boy because of the love Ace had for him."

"That's so super clear, Pops, considering you never told me how you even knew Ace. He just showed up here one day and you two acted as though you were long-lost brothers, so thank you for that flowery speech about trust." My eye roll is epic even by snarky standards. "I love this place with my whole heart." I hate how my sadness bleeds into my words.

"Listen, Madison, please." Why does Braxton have to use the tone that reminds me of silky smooth chocolate? "I'm a businessman, but I've never felt connected to anything...not until I found this place. I like that your friends check in on you and run interference for you. I appreciate that Cian tried to rip my head off for being on the roof earlier—"

Pops whistles an ear-piercing tune, and Braxton shuts his mouth.

Tapping my forehead with my pointer finger, I take a moment to collect my thoughts that are running in a million different directions.

"Wait a minute." When I spin to face Pops, he immediately looks anywhere and everywhere but at me. "Why was he on the roof? Why were you on the roof?"

"Assessing damage." The old man I love so much nods once. He will forever be an insolent toddler when backed into a corner.

"Do you have any idea what to look for?" I ask.

"Ah," Braxton scratches his chest and I have my answer. "No, but Cian does, and he's going to help."

"Mads?" Clover calls from the front of the house.

"In here," Pops says.

"This isn't over just because Clover's here."

"Agreed." Braxton nods his head. "Let's table it for now,

go to the fundraiser tonight, get Grey and Sage settled in the morning, then we'll draw up some standard contracts and go from there."

"Contracts for what?" Clover asks, entering the kitchen.

"Pops sold part of the inn to Braxton, well, Braxton's grandfather, and now Braxton is going to bring a lawyer into it."

"Whoa, that's not what I said." Braxton keeps his tone gentle, which irritates me even more. "The contracts are to protect you, Madison, not me. You don't have to believe me, but you'll see."

"It's kind of shitty that you've been here this long and didn't say anything about owning part of the inn." Though I hear the bite in Clover's tone, no one else does. To them, she probably sounds as gentle as ever.

"I, ah." Braxton turns to Pops. "I didn't know until about half an hour ago."

And I believe him. While he's handling this news better than I am, he still seems surprised.

Wait... "Oh my God, Pops. That means you've been a little devil running Braxton all over town when you must have known who he was this entire time."

He merely waves her away with a flick of his wrist. "Boy, we got some work to do before you drive the girls to the fundraiser. Madi, don't forget those brownies." Then he grabs Braxton's shirtsleeve and drags him toward the foyer.

Braxton's gaze finds mine, and he mouths the words *I'm sorry* on his way out the door.

"Ah, what the heck just happened here?" Clover stares at me, and then the slowly swinging door.

I try to swallow but it hurts. Getting a throat full of burrs down would be easier. "Clov." My chin wobbles. "I think I just lost part of the inn."

"But to Braxton." She says it so casually I wonder if she actually heard what I said. "Hot, sometimes grumpy, Santa Claus-playing Braxton."

Okay, hot, yes. Grumpy, maybe sometimes. But Santa?

"What are you talking about?"

"Oh, come on. It's no secret he's the one going around doing good deeds all over Georgia. He signed the check for the STEM program over in Hopevale, and everyone in a fifty-mile radius knew about it within minutes," she says dreamily.

"He did?"

Clover nods so happily that the ponytail on top of her head flops around, resembling a cowboy on top of a bucking bronco.

"But he asked to keep it a secret," she whispers. She blushes, and I know for sure that she's finding all kinds of ways to turn this into her next thriller novel.

"And they did that so well." Eye rolling has become a new habit of mine.

"Why do you think he's doing it all anonymously?" She follows me into the pantry.

I quickly run through everything Ace ever told me about his grandson while I pull down dishes and the ingredients for Pops' brownies.

"His grandfather was Ace." I pretend I'm searching for something and don't turn around, but her gasp speaks volumes.

"No. Way."

I spin at the sound of Savvy's voice.

"I just saw Braxton on my way in. Do I need to hurt someone?"

"No." It's all I can manage before Clover trips over

herself retelling Savvy how and why Braxton now owns part of my inn.

"Shit." Savvy chews on her hangnail, then flops onto a stool at the island. "Elle's on her way over. She had to ditch Cian first. Braxton is really Ace's grandson?"

"Yeah." Ace spent time with her while he was here too. He helped her create her entire business plan. "At least we know he's a good guy."

"But why so secretive?" Clover asks.

Savvy and I make eye contact before I say, "Because he doesn't trust very easily."

"His family hasn't been good to him," Savvy says.

I lean against the sink for support. "And now we're partners."

"Pops is a menace," Savvy says with a laugh.

My grandfather is the definition of the word menace.

And now I have to figure out how to get my inn back.

17

BRAXTON

"I've decided I can't really be mad at you." Madison smirks after sucking down her cocktail in less than three minutes. "But what do you think our grandfathers' plan was?"

The lights strung through the rafters of the old barn cast an ethereal glow around her face—she's an angel.

"You can be mad at me, sunshine."

Her lips twitch—the light catching on her sparkly lip gloss calling me home.

Those damn lips haunt my dreams.

She shrugs, backs her body into the bar between Elle and me, then rests her elbows on the shiny wooden surface. When she tips her head up toward the ceiling to look at me, I find moments that make a life worth living hidden in every expression she attempts to keep to herself.

"No, I can't. It's no more your fault than it is mine."

"Want another cranberry juice, Mads?" Moose calls from behind the bar.

"Cranberry juice?" I lift one brow in her direction.

Madison places her hand flat on my chest. The contact

scorches through my button-down shirt straight to my skin. It's a branding and a warning all in one. She stares up at me with bright blue eyes that destroy all my walls to see the naked truth behind them.

She's intoxicatingly beautiful.

"Contrary to what you may think, I'm not a big drinker." A sexy pink flush crawls across her cheeks as she speaks. "The Firefly was a lot for me." I watch the color bloom down her throat and into the neckline of her shirt.

When she tilts her head, I know she's caught me, so I mentally remove the cobwebs and attempt to behave as though I'm a grown man with a little restraint.

"Jesus." I run a hand through my hair. "That feels like a lifetime ago."

"Regretting your stay already?" Her voice wobbles, betraying a hint of vulnerability that makes me want to hold her all night long.

Every night.

Lowering my lips to her ear, I inhale her light citrus scent and allow my breath to caress her bare neck. "I may end up with a lot of regrets in my lifetime, sunshine. But it will never be spending time with you." She shivers, and heat radiates down my spine.

"Never?" The fairy lights above reflect on her beautiful face, and I soften my features. The very last thing she needs is a Neanderthal crowding her space.

"Never," I vow, then take a step back.

"Easy there, big guy. The auction's about to begin," Elle says, cutting in. She places a hand on her ginormous belly and motions toward her husband. "You can head up with Cian."

"The feck he can. I'm not part of the deal," Cian grumbles as he approaches the group.

Elle glares at him, then wobbles off her stool to stand with one hand on her hip and one pointing at her husband's chest. "Yes, you are."

"Ah, come on, Tink. I'm not eligible anymore."

I mouth the word *Tink* to Madison, and she giggles. It's such a delicate sound, I almost lose it in the loud bass reverberating through the floorboards.

Goddamn, how can I be so affected by simple sounds?

She reaches up on her tiptoes, and I bend to meet her. When her lips reach my ear, a fissure of electricity runs through my body at the contact.

I've been a live wire my entire life, and she's the grounding I've been searching for.

My hands immediately fall to her hips—to keep her steady. "They broke up once senior year of high school around Halloween. Elle showed up to the football party dressed as a slutty Tinker Bell." She pulls back an inch to make sure I heard her. My face is screwed up into a permanent smile when she's this close, and her eyes sparkle in return. "I'm not saying the costume did it, but he didn't leave her side again for about three years."

"Smart man."

She lowers back to flat feet, her body rubbing against mine as she does.

"This year, the event is for Patty." Elle has both hands on her hips now. "That last hurricane ruined her paddocks, and she didn't have flood insurance. So march your ass up there, wave at the ladies, and pick a song."

"Ah, what's happening?" I ask, trying to gauge the situation, but no one seems too keen on giving me answers.

Cian snaps his gaze in my direction. "Aye, no one told you what the fundraiser was, did they?"

I look to Madison, hoping for a save, but she smiles sweetly and crosses her arms.

"That would be a no," I grumble while lifting my hands from Madison's hips. I instantly feel hollow, and I'm not sure what to do with that information.

"All the eligible men are getting auctioned off," Elle says.

Now I'm paying attention.

"Auctioned off for what, exactly?"

Madison's gaze turns downright sinister. "Three of the winners get a night at the inn, and those are just the runners-up prizes."

"A night. At the inn. With whoever wins the bid?"

Madison bites her bottom lip until it turns white, then nods, twisting the toe of her shoe into the floor behind her while staring up at me through heavy-lidded lashes.

"You're telling me we have to sleep at the inn with someone?" Without my consent, my voice turns downright feral. "That's not happening, sunshine. Not unless you're planning to bid, so someone had better start explaining right the fuck now."

When everyone around us sniggers, I square my shoulders, bend at the waist, and bring Madison eye to eye with me. "That can't even be legal. It's prostitution. What do the other winners get?"

Her grin splits her face in two.

"Only the bidders get rooms, ya bubbletwat. Ya have dinner, say goodnight and go on yer merry way. You don't even have to stay at the inn if you don't want to," Cian barks.

Stepping into Madison's space until she backs up to the bar, I bracket her in with my arms and feel my lips tilting up on one side. "Is this why you're not mad at me?"

She tips one delicate shoulder up. "Maybe."

"Oh, you sweet, misinformed troublemaker."

"Hey," she huffs.

Reaching into my pocket, I pull out my wallet, and remove a credit card. "Sweetheart, I've got enough on my plate, so there's no way I'm spending a night with anyone else."

I run my credit card along the column of her neck and across her collarbone, then watch as her throat bobs while she swallows. I'd give my left nut to lick the pulse point that's running a marathon beneath her skin.

Instead, I try desperately not to stare at the buttons undone on her flannel shirt that show a hint of cleavage or the way a sliver of her stomach peeks out where she's tied the front into a knot as I slide my credit card into the breast pocket of her shirt.

"I'm trying to keep a low profile here, sunshine." When she opens her mouth to argue, I lower my voice and go with the truth. "I don't want to be taken advantage of, not here. I want people to get to know me for me, not for what my grandfather built. Can you help me do that?"

She stares into my eyes, back and forth as though she's reading all my secrets. "You know you're not really doing a very good job of staying incognito. It's only a matter of time before everyone figures out who you are."

"You already know who I am," I counter.

"Do I? Because your social media presence doesn't give anything away."

That information cracks my heart wide open for her. "Have you been googling me, Madison?"

"Of course we have," Savvy interrupts, bursting our bubble. "And something's not adding up."

Lowering my hands to my sides, I attempt to keep the annoyance from my tone at being interrupted.

"You won't find much about me online," I say smoothly.

"My family didn't appreciate any reminders of me. Probably because I was my grandfather's favorite. But they all fought to give me privacy—my parents for purely selfish reasons, my grandfather to give me some semblance of a normal childhood. But anything else you want to know, you ask me."

"Let's go." Cian curses. "Time to get this over with."

Madison steps forward, and I put my finger through her belt loop as though it's the most natural place for it to be, and I gently tug her toward me. "Do not allow anyone to outbid you. I don't care how much it costs."

Savvy smirks, then pushes between me and Madison, pulling my card from Madison's left breast pocket. "This round is on Brax." She laughs, and I clench my jaw until it aches but allow Cian to drag me toward the front of the barn where a makeshift stage has been set up.

We stand in a semicircle awaiting instructions, and it takes all my self-control not to stare at Madison. It isn't until I'm handed a karaoke book that I feel a glare on me. Scanning the crowd, I see why a second later.

Harry stands across from me with pure hatred coating his expression.

"Fuck me. Does he ever take a hint?" I mutter.

Cian follows my line of sight and grunts. "No. But he will. Pick your song."

"I'm sorry. What now?" I feel a little cartoonish as I say it, and judging by the crinkle at the corner of his eyes, it's not too far off from what he sees as I attempt to shove the book into his hands.

"Your song," he rumbles, pushing the book back to me. "We sing and dance and make a fecking fool of ourselves while they bid on us."

"What do the women have to do?" I glance into the

crowd again. The ratio of men to women is certainly skewed higher on the male side.

"Don't worry. The ladies go next."

This gives me pause. Suddenly it feels like a much better idea for only me to be auctioned off.

"Really? You're okay with that?"

He scans me with a dangerous gleam in his expression. "You're asking the wrong questions, Brax."

My skin is starting to sweat, and I think I should've sat tonight out. I could've just stayed home and waited for Greyson, but he didn't think they'd get here until early morning since they had to make a stop in New York first.

"Oh, yeah? What should I be asking?"

"What we get when we win." Cian's voice booms over the crowd of people milling about, and I know the instant Harry hears because his face turns volcanic.

Without taking my gaze off Madison's ex, I ask, "Okay, I'll bite. What do we get?"

Cian's chest puffs up three sizes as he crosses his massive arms and widens his stance as though he's preparing to be attacked. Absentmindedly, I mimic the big guy's stance.

"Well," he says, glaring in the direction of our current mutual enemy. "Madison has brought in the highest bid for three years running, so there's a good chance she'll be in the top two winners again tonight."

"And..."

"And no one dares bid on Elle."

"Cian! What do I win?"

"Ya each get a weekend getaway to the mountains. It's one of Madison's favorite spots. And I happen to know that there's only one bedroom available in the cabin right now due to construction."

Jealousy heats my blood, and the rushing in my ears

drowns out the noise of the party. There's not a chance in hell I'll allow another man to win Madison. "How do you know that?" I ask through clenched teeth.

The giant winks at me. "'Cause it's my cabin."

"You mother—"

"Take it easy. You really think anyone can outbid ya?"

"I..."

"Pick your song, mate. You've got a girl to win."

Spinning in place, I try to locate Madison and am pleased to find her watching me. She's picking at something on her wrist with her head angled toward Elle as though she's listening, but her eyes are the siren song that makes my pulse race.

"Turd alert," Cian says on a fake cough.

The scent of cheap whiskey burns my nose hairs, but I don't take my gaze off Madison. The worry line is back between her brows, and it makes me irrationally angry that he has this effect on her.

"She's not yours," Harry slurs in my general vicinity.

I smile brightly at Madison, hoping my body language emits a calm demeanor because inside I'm boiling over. No one should be able to cause this much pain. I nod toward Madison. The gesture has her sucking in a large gulp of air that lifts her chest.

She chews on the inside of her cheek, but Elle and Savvy keep her in place. I guess their meddling isn't always such a pain in the ass.

"Last I heard," I say without raising my voice, "Madison's her own woman. She doesn't need either of us making decisions for her." Turning my back on him, I trust Cian to support me.

It nearly knocks the air from my lungs. I haven't trusted this blindly since I was a child, yet here I am with Cian.

"I've got you," Cian mutters quietly enough that only I can hear. "Go give them your song. I got your back and the girls in my sight."

Does he have any idea how big of a step this is for me? If he does, he doesn't make a big deal about it, and that more than anything hits me with the force of a sack of bricks to the side of my head.

"Thanks," I say, then head over to the DJ, already knowing what song I'll sing. Madison is going to hate it, and I can't wait.

18

MADISON

The problem with this fundraiser is that you have no idea what order the auction will go in. People get called up in groups, but Braxton hasn't been called yet.

Cian was in the first batch, and Elle let ninety-year-old Ada Bowman win. He wasn't happy about Elle refusing to bid, but when Ada let out a little whoop of happiness, he caved. Ada's been lonely since her dog died, and no one was going to begrudge her of this, even if it means Cian will likely be replacing light bulbs and fixing shutters while she talks his ear off the entire time.

"Why won't you tell me what group you're in?"

"What would be the fun in that?" Even Braxton's words are wrapped in joy. It's annoying in the most unfortunately cute way.

"You'll see how fun it is when I let Bethany win." I nod toward the woman in front of us. She's a little aggressive with her flirting, and he cringes as the scene plays out.

"You wouldn't." Even his mock outrage is charming. "I thought we had a deal, sunshine? You don't want to go back on your word with me."

A cold chill runs down my spine. Does he mean tonight? Or with the inn?

Dang it. I hate that Harry's turned me into such an untrusting shrew. Brax doesn't even sound menacing, so why am I immediately searching for a way to make him the bad guy? Savvy would have a lot of thoughts on this, I'm sure.

"I..."

"I'm talking about tonight, Madison. If I could gift you back my portion of the inn right now, I would. I'm not looking to take it from you, if that's what just put those shadows in your eyes."

God, I must be an open book now. How the heck does he always know what I'm thinking?

I pluck at the elastic on my wrist, then drop both arms to my side—I don't replace pain anymore. Not since Harry's actions had me nervously picking at my wrist until my skin bled.

"Madison—"

"Can group F please come to the stage?"

"Fuck. We'll circle back to this. Do not allow anyone to outbid you, Madison." He turns to leave, then says, "Please," in the most gentle, pure tone that knocks down my walls faster than a wrecking ball.

"Fine," I manage to say. "I won't let anyone out bid me."

His gaze blazes, and I have to look away or be incinerated by a desire I'm not sure I should act on.

Braxton Reyes nods, and I swear every woman in the room nods back.

This is getting messy.

Savvy hooks her arm through mine. "Good Lord, girl. That man wants to lick, suck, and devour every inch of you."

"Uh-huh." Well, he certainly makes me stupid.

"Do you guys see how everyone in the room looks at him?" Clover asks, clutching my other arm. "Do you think it's because he's so hot or because he's rich?"

"It'd better be because he's hot." A deep, angry voice reverberates through my bones.

In slow-motion, we all turn to see a scowling but also hot as hell man glaring at us.

"Ah, that's G-Greyson," Clover stutters, then slips around to the other side of Savvy and away from the scary-looking *GQ* model. They're physical opposites, but still, Greyson has a familiarity about him I can't pinpoint. Unlike Braxton's darker hair and eyes, Greyson has blond hair and pale-blue eyes that chill the air. He carries himself with foreboding darkness, something Braxton couldn't pull off if he tried.

The three of us take a step back as one.

"If I find out that anyone here is using him or hurts him in any way, I will burn this fucking town to the ground. And I don't make threats I don't intend to keep."

He bellies up to the bar and orders a double bourbon with Savvy right behind him. She's too quick for me to catch, and the next thing I know, they're nose to nose. Savvy is close to six feet tall, but Greyson towers over her.

"You do not get to come in here and issue threats or promises, you jackass. Madison's put up with enough shit, and if you're about to cause more, you can get your ass right back on a plane and go home."

His brow furrows, obviously not used to someone speaking to him that way. "Madison?"

Both Savvy and Clover look to me in confusion.

"Madi." Clover's voice wavers as she points to me.

Shock registers for less than a second before every expression is wiped from his face. He stares me down while lifting his glass to his lips. "Well now, you're not old."

Pressing three fingers into my temple, I try to work out what he's talking about. "Why would I be old?"

The man smirks, and even though it feels a little condescending, I get the distinct impression there's loving humor hidden in it too.

"It would appear my best friend has been holding out on me."

Savvy puffs up her chest, ready to say something so snarky it could shatter Greyson's glass, but I place a hand on her forearm, and she relents. These two already mix about as well as oil and water, and the last thing I need is a perpetual fight between my best friend and Braxton's.

"Holding out on what?" I ask, but the music seems to get louder, and every hair on the back of my neck stands on end.

Slowly I turn toward the stage, and out of my periphery, I see that Savvy and Greyson do the same.

"What the hell is he doing?" Greyson asks with an uncomfortable laugh.

I can't peel my gaze away from Braxton. Time stops, and the entire room tunnels until all I can see is him singing 'Stargazing.' And not singing it off-key as the rest of us do, but singing it well.

Really well.

In a room full of people, his voice twists and turns straight to my heart. When he blinks, it's slow, and I grab ahold of Clover's arm for support.

"It would appear that Happiness is good for him," Greyson says, standing at my side. Is it shock or wonder in his tone? I'm not sure because I can't tear my gaze away from the hottest man I've ever seen singing a song that we danced to at sunrise.

And I feel every word, every emotion, every plea he

pours out deep in my bones. He's asking me not to hurt him. To allow him into my life and to trust him while my pulse beats erratically, violently throughout my body.

Because I do want to trust him. I want...

"Two hundred dollars," Bethany shouts while standing on her chair.

"He isn't even finished singing yet, Bethany. You're being so rude," I shout, which makes Braxton's smile eat up his entire face.

"Two fifty," someone shouts from the other side of the barn.

"What the heck is happening here?" My hands are on my hips, and I'm tapping an angry foot exactly as my gram used to do to Pops.

Oh my God. Maybe I am an old lady.

Braxton holds the last note longer than necessary, and everyone in the room cheers. Freaking cheers—standing ovation cheers!

"Who knew he could sing?" Savvy laughs next to me.

"He's good at everything he does." I peer up at Greyson. "Apparently, he trusts you enough to let you see that. He hasn't had that opportunity often."

"Two seventy-five," someone else shouts, and now I'm getting angry. Cian went for forty-five dollars. Forty-five.

"Three hundred," Jessa shouts next to her mom, who is trying desperately to get her to put her arms down.

"Jessa," I scold. "You're sixteen. You're not even old enough to bid."

"I'll bid for her." Bethany sticks out her tongue at me, and my jaw drops. Everyone has lost their dang minds. "Three hundred."

"Bethany. You don't have an extra three hundred dollars lying around."

"No, but I've got a credit card, and a night with him would be worth it."

Anger boils over in my gut. "It's dinner, Bethany. D-I-N-N-E-R. Dinner."

She waggles her brows in my direction. "We'll see."

"Three twenty-five," Betty from the diner says, holding up a stack of ones that's probably her tip money for the month.

"This is getting out of control," Clover whispers in my ear.

Turning in place, I shoot eyeball flames at those who are bidding, but my jaw drops to my chest when I find everyone in the room staring at me with amusement sparkling in their ridiculously happy eyes.

"Three fifty."

"Was that Moose? Did freaking Moose just bid on Braxton?"

"Three seventy-five." That was one hundred percent my grandfather.

When I turn back to Braxton, he's drinking me in, and when our gazes connect, he simply raises a brow.

Oh crap. I'm supposed to enter this insanity. But four hundred dollars? Seriously?

"Is he worth four hundred dollars?" I mumble. "That seems excessive."

"Madi," Clover screeches while Savvy hides behind me laughing—I can feel her body shaking against mine, the traitor. Where the heck is Elle? She's the only sensible one, and that's saying something since her hormones are all on a different roller coaster with this pregnancy.

Braxton offers a crooked smile that has a scuffle breaking out on my left. Bethany is going head-to-head with Jane from the library. They're counting through a stack of pooled money, then Bethany jumps up and down in place. "Five hundred."

"Do something." Clover pokes me in the side.

"What? What do you want me to do? Five hundred dollars is freaking unreasonable."

"It's for charity," Savvy reminds me.

"Five twenty-five." This comes from a new bidder I can't see.

I'm starting to sweat, and flapping my hands under my pits so I don't end up with a sweat stain. Then I remember that Braxton is watching, and I almost die when he throws his head back and laughs.

"Take a stand, Madi. Do something," Clover hisses.

"Take a stand? What?"

"Claim him before someone else does!" Savvy nudges me again, and I stumble forward a step.

Braxton mouths, *Bid, sunshine*, and just as someone yells, "Five fifty," I stomp toward the stage shouting, "One thousand. One freaking thousand. That's it. I won. Call it off."

Moose bangs a gavel and says, "Going once."

"Moose," I admonish. "You're holding the gavel. You're not allowed to bid, and I heard you do it."

The old man winks and points me toward the stage as if I hadn't just spoken.

I don't bother walking up the steps. I get to the edge of the stage and point to the floor as though I'm scolding a dog.

And Braxton hasn't stopped laughing. He jumps down and stands before me.

"You won."

I cross my arms over my chest. "The entire town has lost their minds."

"You won me." He inches closer so the toes of our shoes are touching.

Is everyone staring at us? Why is it suddenly so quiet in here?

"You own me now, sunshine. What will you do with me?"

Oh my God. Everyone is totally listening in. You could hear a pin drop in here. Or maybe it's just that the blood rushing through my ears has drowned out all the other conversations that should be happening.

"Um..."

"Kiss him."

I'm going to kill Savvy.

"Don't touch her," Harry slurs somewhere behind me.

Maybe it's Savvy's encouragement, Harry refusing to move on, or the way Braxton immediately tugs me into the protection of his arms when he hears my ex, but whatever it is, I hope I don't regret it.

Because the next thing I know, I'm clawing at his shirt, tugging him down, and kissing him. Again. For the second time in less than forty-eight hours, I'm kissing this man, and instantly my sex throbs as though it's been deprived of attention its entire life.

But this time, he doesn't hold back. The instant our lips make contact, he takes full control of my mouth.

If we weren't in front of a crowd of hooting and hollering neighbors right now, I think I'd probably be rubbing myself all over him like a cat in heat. And when his tongue parts the seam of my lips and demands entry, I fall into him, head, lips, and heart.

This kiss is not PG. He does things in my mouth that I feel on every private nerve ending I possess until I'm light-headed and gasping, yet he still doesn't pull away.

His lips are firm and soft, with a hint of Cheerwine on

his tongue, which makes my heart thunder. You don't get more Southern than Cheerwine.

He parts our lips, just a millimeter separating us as he commands my body, and when I suck in air, he dives back in. I'm flying from this kiss, higher than any drug could take me. Is this what it means when they talk about lightning strikes and butterflies? If so, I've been struck down and came back to life as a whole kaleidoscope of monarchs.

The music finally brings the world into focus, and when I find shining eyes in varying shades of happy, my entire body goes up in flames, and I hide my face against him.

"I cannot believe I just made out with you in front of half the town." I moan into his chest.

"Totally worth it." He sounds distracted though, and when I peer up at him, I find his attention over my head.

That's when I remember Harry.

"Let's go get a drink." Braxton tucks me protectively under his arm. I should tell him that Harry wouldn't hurt me here with everyone we know in attendance. I don't think it's in him. His specialty is in the wounds no one can see, but I don't get the chance because Braxton stops short right in front of Greyson and Savvy, who are nearly chest to chest and angry as hell.

I've never seen Savvy this worked up, not even when she was attempting to knee Harry in the balls—any of the times.

Clover stands off to the side with Elle, pulling her cardigan closer to her body. It's what she does when she's nervous.

"Greyson?" Brax says his name, but Greyson is in a verbal sparring match with Savvy.

"He's the best man I've ever known. I would, and I did, give up everything for him. That's what brothers do. That's what I'll always do. So don't go throwing around accusations that have no basis in reality because you, you could never understand what it's like to be me."

"I..." Savvy's mouth opens and closes. I don't think I've ever seen her flustered before either. Not even when she flat-out told her sexual health professor that he didn't know a woman's G-spot from her butthole.

"Grey?" Braxton repeats, this time stepping between our two friends.

Greyson blinks rapidly, as though Braxton is out of focus, and then he tips his glass back until he's drained its contents.

"It's been a shit day, Brax. I just came to let you know we arrived early, and I brought Mercutio with me because he said he missed his ride."

"Mercutio?" Braxton appears thoroughly confused.

"Pops," I say.

"Like Romeo and Juliet?" Braxton asks.

"Yeah, he really lives up to the name too."

"I refuse to call someone I just met Pops," Greyson says stiffly.

"Wait, Pops' real name is Mercutio?" Braxton asks.

"Pops is what he prefers to be called," I tell Greyson with a hint of annoyance. First, he yells at my best friend, who's looking a little ashen, and then he disrespects my grandfather. Who does he think he is?

"Stand down, sunshine. He didn't mean anything by it. Greyson's just a little...formal." Then Braxton turns to Greyson. "I can't believe he told you his name. I've been asking every day since I arrived."

"Yeah, well, I'm not as friendly as you."

"Apparently," Savvy mutters.

Greyson cuts a glare her way that's so cold I shiver. Without taking his gaze off Savvy, he says, "I can't deal with this." Then he turns to me, and for the first time since he walked in, I see a hint of the warmth he must reserve for his family. "Thank you, truly, for opening rooms for us. My nephew—" He sighs with the weight of the world on his breath. "I appreciate it."

It's been such a whirlwind since he arrived, I'm not sure how to answer.

"I'll come with you," Braxton says. But then he peers around the room, and I feel his muscles bunch. "I don't want to leave you here with him though. I don't trust him."

My heart thumps against my chest, and that similar sensation from earlier washes over me.

"It's okay, I'll come too. I wasn't expecting them until morning, and I'm sure Pops' welcome wasn't exactly professional."

"What about the auction?" Elle asks. I hadn't even noticed that she and Cian had moved closer.

"I was the only one who was ever going to win her. I'll pay for both our bids on our way out," Braxton says, engulfing my hand in his.

Even though the concept of him winning me is not at all politically correct, there's something about it that excites me.

I'm not sure I've ever felt cherished before. Loved, yes. Hated, yes. But cherished? That's a whole new level for me.

"Is that okay with you?" he asks, and I melt for him completely. He takes charge but remembers to ask me what I want.

I'm a goner.

19

BRAXTON

We arrive at the house to find Sage in the kitchen. He freezes with a fork in the air halfway to his mouth.

"Oh, please, keep eating," Madison says. "I'm sorry I wasn't here when you checked in. My grandfather means well, but he's not exactly the best host."

He swallows with an audible gulp, then lowers the forkful of pie and reaches out a hand. "I'm Sage. Thank you for..." He waves a hand around the room. "This."

"It's my pleasure. I'm Madi. Can I make you something to eat? A sandwich? Some pasta, maybe?"

"No, thank you, though. I just needed some sugar, you know, eat my weight in feelings."

"I've been there before. I totally get it. How about..." Madison glides through the kitchen and opens the freezer. "Some vanilla ice cream to go with that peach pie?"

"God, yes," Sage blurts, then promptly snaps his mouth closed.

"You're my kind of kid." Madison's breezy demeanor has Sage instantly relaxing.

I cross the room and wrap my arms around Sage. "I'm

sorry, bud." Hugging him now is so much different than when he was little, but when his body sags into mine, it feels the same—it's my job to protect him.

He's always been able to make me feel ten feet tall, and I'm pissed my family could put him through this shit.

"It's not your fault, Uncle Brax. I'm fine. Well, being handcuffed and having my face pressed into the gravel while someone took photos of me wasn't great, but I'm fine now."

Rage makes my skin burn. I glance down when Madison places a hand on my forearm and find that my fists are clenched so hard, I'm trembling.

My family clocks her movements too. Sage lifts his brows but appears happy. Grey...well, Grey doesn't trust anyone.

"Maybe we should talk about this another time." Grey not-so-subtly nods toward Madison, and I try not to get too angry with him. He doesn't know what I'm feeling. I'm not even sure I fully understand it yet.

"It's okay," I say. "Ace trusted her and Pops." Madison turns her pale-blue gaze my way. "And I trust them too."

Grey grumbles something unintelligible and goes back to pacing.

"It's okay. Maybe you should talk with your family alone."

I take her hand in mine, momentarily struck by how tiny and fragile hers is in my palm. "Madison, we're filling your inn. You should be aware of what's going on."

She shrugs free and runs her fingers around the light-brown hair elastic she always has on her wrist as tension fills the room.

"I'm Sage," my nephew repeats, stepping forward, taking up much more space than normal, and holds out a hand to

Madison. "Don't worry about Uncle Grey, he's still learning how to express himself without being a total douchebag."

Leave it to this kid to break the tension. God, I love him.

Madison laughs nervously while she gazes between him and Grey, but Sage and I burst out laughing.

"The kid doesn't lie." I barely get the words out through my snorting fit of laughter.

"I'm not a douchebag," Grey mumbles. His hands are stiffly in his pockets, and he's so rigid you'd think he's made of stone. It makes us laugh even harder.

Sage crosses the room to pat his shoulder. "Not to anyone in this room, but out there?" He points in the general direction of the front door. "You are a single-man douche brigade of epic proportions."

Grey swats his hand away. Sage treats him as though he's the child sometimes just to mess with him, and I'll admit, it usually loosens him up.

"I'm cautious and protective." Grey isn't exactly glaring at Madison, but he's definitely not giving off any warm-and-fuzzy vibes either.

"Greyson? Or Grey? I don't know what to call you. Braxton says both. But if it puts your mind at ease, I'm not here to hurt anyone, or Braxton wouldn't have brought you here. And." She twists her fingers together so tightly I'm afraid she'll break one. "I've been hurt, ruined actually, by people who were supposed to love me, so I understand being cautious, and I promise that you're in a safe space."

Her face twists with a wicked gleam. "Just be careful of Pops. Before you know it, he'll have talked you into climbing up onto a roof to assess damage you have no clue about."

Grey's gaze darts between me and Madison before his ever-present scowl finally relaxes. "He got you on the roof?"

I nod, unable to hide my grin.

"Whoa, Uncle Brax. That's…"

"Stupid," Grey fills in.

"My grandfather has a giant heart, but he's trouble. Harmless, mostly, but trouble always."

"He created a blob in the oven when we were trying to make breakfast, and I almost had to buy a new one because I was an accomplice."

"Shut up." Sage chuckles. It's good to see after the forty-eight hours he's had.

"You wouldn't believe the shit that old man has gotten me involved in since I've been here."

"You look…" Sage steps closer and inspects my face. He took some test to find out that he's a number one empath, and he thinks that gives him magical powers to read people, and unfortunately, he's not usually wrong. "Happy," he finally says after an eternity.

Greyson makes a sound of annoyance, and he spins on him next.

"What, Uncle Grey? He does. Just look at him. Maybe a little time here would do you some good too, you curmudgeon. You act as if you're a ninety-year-old man, and you literally just turned thirty." Sage is seventeen going on forty.

Greyson has never gotten along with many people, but he is a natural leader. It's why his teammates hated him but he led them to the championship every year.

Maybe Sage is right and Happiness will be good for him too.

"Okay, why don't we go into the family room and sit down so you can tell me what happened?" I suggest.

"Before or after you sang your heart out on stage?" Greyson's facial expression doesn't change, but I see the mischief in the twitch of his cheek. He knows he just opened a whole can of shit.

"Shut. *Up.*" How Sage manages to turn two syllables into four every time he says that is truly impressive. "Like, in front of people?"

"In front of a barn full of people who were bidding on him."

Sage holds up both hands to create a T in front of his face. "Time out. We have to sit for this. Mads, is it okay if we bring this pie in there?"

Mads I mouth, and he shyly drops his chin to his chest and offers a shoulder shrug in return. For a kid who has always shied away from people, he's instantly comfortable around Madison.

"Oh my gosh, yes. Yes, please. But only if you grab a fork for me." She's so warm and welcoming. I think Sage is half in love already.

Greyson's body deflates. Not a lot, but the stick up his ass has moved an inch. Madison and Pops will have him won over before the end of the week.

Sage grabs forks and napkins, Madison picks up the pie and hands me some water bottles, then we all pile into the family room.

Madison and Sage squeeze together on the loveseat, probably to give Grey a wide berth, and I perch on the edge of Pops' recliner while Grey paces the length of the room.

I know Madison will have a million questions from the conversations she's about to hear, but I asked her to stay for a reason—I want her to be part of my world. I haven't done more than kiss this woman, and I'm already envisioning myself packing up my entire life so I don't have to leave her side.

Grey will say I'm out of my mind, but I can't help thinking that Ace truly did send me here to find happiness.

Did he know happiness would come in the form of Madison?

"Okay." Time to stop prolonging the inevitable. Plus Sage looks as though he's about to pass out, despite making googly eyes at Madison.

The heavy eyeliner he normally hides behind is nowhere to be found, and for the first time in years, I see the lost little boy inside him. He's always had an old soul, but being arrested on my father's order has obviously shaken him.

"What do we think my father was hoping to gain from this?"

"It wasn't just Sage," Grey says, still pacing.

"What do you mean?"

"Archie had some trouble in Maine."

"Archie is my older brother," I explain to Madison. This isn't what I was expecting, but whatever Alistair did, I'm sure it was horrible. "What kind of trouble?"

"Someone announced that he had a DUI, and the farm he's working on is owned by a woman whose husband was killed by a drunk driver."

"When did he get a DUI?" How the hell did they manage to keep that quiet?

Greyson's dark, thunderous expression says it all. But he answers anyway, "He didn't. Someone spread lies yesterday on the town's Facebook page."

"I hate social media," Madison mutters, and I notice she's snapping that elastic against her skin now.

Before I can move to her, Sage reaches over and cups her fingers with his own. "Same, girl. Same."

There's not a soul alive that can tell me this, right here, with all of us together isn't right. I feel it in my bones.

Greyson's mind is working. Not only does he know and

retain every bit of information that could ever benefit us, he also has the uncanny ability to guess my father's actions before he makes them.

Something tells me he wasn't expecting this though—a hunch that's quickly confirmed.

"This is not the route I expected him to take," he spits out in frustration.

"It's not your fault you couldn't predict the actions of an unpredictable asshole." I say the words even as I see them fly over his head. He believes this is his failure.

He rolls his lucky coin through his fingers, over and over again, the motion almost soothing. "I was convinced he'd come after you."

Madison makes an uncomfortable noise, and Sage inches closer with a shrug. "We all grew up in this mess. It's a lot to take in for a newbie." He comforts Madison while Grey continues to pace and roll his coin.

Greyson is in his own world right now, where he's running probabilities and scenarios as though he's a freaking computer program.

He stops short and finally appears to see the room for the first time. "There's no way Alistair isn't behind this. If he went after Sage and your brother, that means he's willing to take down everyone in your family."

"What would that get him though? There's no way Ace didn't set up his will specifically to keep him from getting anything—especially if the rest of us don't accomplish his goals."

The coin goes around and around.

"He must be so sure of his success in New Mexico that he's willing to sabotage everyone else. He's always been shortsighted."

"So that means he'll do something to you too?" Madison

tucks her feet beneath her on the loveseat, making herself even smaller.

"He'll try," Grey says flatly. At least he isn't snapping at her anymore.

"We'll protect him," Madison says with a forcefulness that surprises me.

Grey snorts, and Sage chucks a throw pillow at his head.

"You're going to protect him how?" Grey tilts his head as though he's studying an exotic animal instead of an incredibly kind and beautiful woman.

"Does he know where you are?" The corners of her eyes tighten, and fear has her voice pitching higher.

Fear for me, I realize. She may not be willing to admit it yet, but she cares for me.

"No, sunshine," I keep my voice calm. "I messed up and said I was in Georgia, but not what town."

"And I left my plane in New York. We chartered a smaller plane to get us here." Grey finally takes a seat on the sofa—but I know him. He's cataloging every movement, every gesture between Madison and me.

"You have your own plane?" she blurts, then wildly waves her hands in front of her. "Sorry, that was, I've just never, wow."

This time Grey's lips twitch at the corner. It isn't a smile per se, but it's close.

"Okay, good then." Madison stands and claps her hands together. "Well—" She bursts out laughing. Was this all too much for her?

Slowly I approach her, and when I place a hand on the small of her back, she stands upright.

"Don't you get it?" She can't control her laughter. She's the fresh air after spending too long in a city.

"No, sweetheart. I don't get it. What's so funny?"

Behind her, Grey flashes Sage an *I don't know* hand gesture.

"We're going" —giggle—"to hide you" —giggle—"at the Hideaway Inn."

Okay, so she might be a little punch-drunk, but she does have a point.

Grey leans forward and steeples his fingers. "She's not wrong. Your father knows you have investments outside of Omni-Reyes. He's never going to come looking for you in some run-down inn."

"Hey," Madison warns.

He holds up both hands. "Sorry, that was rude, and I apologize. It's been a long fucking few days."

She turns to face him. "You're forgiven. But you'll also find your happy in Happiness. You just wait and see."

A bark of laughter escapes Grey. "I don't mean to offend you, Madison, but—"

"Madi," I say. Grey is a brother to me, but him calling her Madison makes me twitch.

The mirth in his expression grows.

"Madi. I don't mean to offend, but I'm already happy. Joyful even. Can't you tell? I'm fine just as I am." He holds his arms out wide, as if to prove a point, but he still comes across stiff, and yeah, maybe a little douchey.

She doesn't let it faze her though. "Right. Well, you'll see. Just wait until Pops coerces you into digging up old pipes."

"That will never happen." He shudders, crossing his foot over his knee, exposing his very expensive shoes.

"If we're hiding out at the Hideaway, we'll need to get the two of you some new clothes," I tell them.

"Ooh, shopping." Sage instantly perks up.

"At Walmart," I amend. "You can't be walking around town in one-thousand-dollar shoes."

"Who paid a thousand bucks for shoes?" Pops asks as he enters the house. The auction must be over.

Pops has been more lively since we've started going on our outings. I only hope that doesn't mean he'll up the stakes on our handiwork.

"Uncle Grey did." Sage rats him out and points a finger in his direction.

"Well if that isn't the biggest waste of money I've ever heard. Are you an idiot, Greyson?"

Grey sits up taller. "No, sir."

I almost laugh. It took a lot of willpower to add that sir in his statement.

"Do you need someone to put you on a budget?" Pops is really going at it.

"I manage hundreds of millions of dollars. I know how to budget, Mercutio."

"Now don't you go spreadin' that name around nowhere." Pops scratches his head. "I don't even know how you got me to spill it."

"I'm good at what I do." Grey's words are what I imagine an eye roll to sound like.

"Uh-oh, Pops. Have you met your match and finally found someone you can't talk into doing your bidding?" Madison teases, and I fall a little in love with her cheekiness.

"Don't you go spreading rumors, young lady. Now why are we talking about shoes?"

"They need to go shopping tomorrow to get some stuff to blend in better," I say.

"Good." Pops nods with his hands in his front pockets. "We'll add it to our list for tomorrow, boy. Now, I hear it's been a hell of a few days for you. Let's get everyone to bed, and we'll regroup in the morning."

"Am I being sent to bed by your grandfather?" Grey asks Madison in dismay.

"I'll let you in on a little secret," she says, moving closer to Grey. "If my grandfather has anything to do with it, he'll not only help you find your happy, he'll also have you married with a white picket fence before you even know what hit you. Sometimes it's just easier to do what he says."

As far as I know, Grey has no plans to settle down. His belief in love was shattered a long time ago. He says the only pieces he has left are for me, Sage, and Ace.

When he walks up the stairs with Pops shouting after him about breakfast, I can't help but hope there's a little magic in this town after all.

20

———

MADISON

It's been a couple of days since Grey and Sage arrived, but it hasn't been as hard as I thought it would be. At least not with Sage. Greyson Reyes, on the other hand, is more mercurial than Mr. Darcy.

"Hey." Braxton groans as he walks into the kitchen.

Crap. I was hoping to sneak out of the house without waking anyone up, but I should know better by now. He's as in tune to me as I am to him. I swear I wake up every time he rolls over, and we're not even in the same room.

"Why are you up so early?" He shuffles around me and starts the coffee before I have a chance to.

"Ah, I was going to get some things done at the Chug before anyone came in, but I was planning to be back before anyone woke up to make breakfast."

He frowns, then squints at the clock on the microwave. "It's five forty-five in the morning, Madison. What the hell do you have to do this early?"

"It's not that early," I say. "Grey already left for a run."

"That's because he's a robot."

"That's not nice," I mutter.

"No, but he would know I was only teasing. Grey has always run in the middle of the night when he can't sleep. It's two forty-five in California. He hasn't adjusted to the time change yet."

Grey isn't the only one having trouble sleeping. Two kisses with Braxton and he's consumed my dreams ever since. I'm having actual sex dreams that wake me up sweaty and needy, and I don't ever remember that happening before, not even as a horny teenager. Every one of my dreams stars the man before me wearing a pair of low-riding gym shorts and a T-shirt so soft-looking I want to sleep in it.

He opens the fridge and pulls out my creamer, then takes my favorite mug down from the cabinet all the while I watch him. He knows all my little habits, my likes and dislikes, and I've never even mentioned them.

"You're staring."

Probably drooling as well. This is why I'm running away this morning. I need a few moments not surrounded by testosterone to get my head on straight. "Sorry. I just have some admin tasks to catch up on."

He hands me my mug and nods. "Anything I can help with?"

"Nope," I say too cheerily, and he narrows his gaze.

"You sure?"

"Yup. You have fun with your boys today. Pops is taking you all to the diner for lunch, right? Then coming into the Chug?"

"Yeah," he says grumpily, then reaches over his head to stretch. "We can't do anything else in the basement until a plumber can get here, and Sage is bored out of his mind."

I wince, and he immediately corrects himself.

"It's not you or the inn, he just finished his entire college semester's worth of work before they got here. He's too smart for either of us to keep up with anymore."

"Have you thought about encouraging him to enroll in more classes or at least harder ones?"

Braxton nods, his eyes softening as he stares at me. "Grey and I talked about it a few months ago. UCLA will probably happen next year—we just didn't want to push him before he was ready socially. He finished high school at fourteen, and it was pretty brutal for him."

"I can imagine. He's a good kid though. I really like him."

He stalks closer, so slowly I don't even notice until he's inches from me. "He likes you too."

A smile starts somewhere deep in my soul before finding its way to my lips.

"And he isn't the only one. I like you too."

"Is that so?" Who the heck flirts before 6:00 a.m.? Me, apparently.

He doesn't answer with words, but when he leans in, slow enough for me to step away if I want to, I know what he's saying with his movements. When his lips touch down on mine, it's as though he sucks all the anxiety straight from my body.

How is he such a good kisser?

His palms cradle the back of my head as he slants his lips over mine over and over again before delving in with his tongue. He commands my body with a single kiss, and when I feel him grow long against my stomach, I whimper.

I'm seconds from dropping to the floor and begging when the kitchen door swings open as though God himself blew it off its hinges.

"Oh, fuck. Sorry," Grey grumbles. I can't see him over

Braxton, but I hear his tennis shoes squeaking against the wood floor. He must be spinning in a circle.

Braxton smirks against my lips before pulling away. "Morning, Grey."

"Morning," Grey mutters back.

When Braxton finally steps to the side, I find Grey with his head buried in his phone and pointedly not looking anywhere near my direction.

"Right," I chirp too happily. "I'll be back."

I scoot from the room before either of them can say anything. Making out with Braxton makes me feel more alive than anything else I've done in as long as I can remember.

Here's to hoping it doesn't bite me in the backside when I'm not expecting it.

"Come on, you dumb thing. Just push over one more inch so I can get to the ones in the back." I groan while attempting to slide another bin from storage. Either I'm getting older or we're storing more crap for the Cozy Cup Festival than ever before.

"Can I help?"

My hands freeze on the bright blue bin, and I swallow hard. Holding my breath, I stand slowly and turn. It's always a toss-up on which version of Harry I'll get, and standing alone in the Chug's storage shed is not where I want to be stuck with the drunk version of him.

"Just offering help, Mads." He stands ten feet outside of the shed with his hands raised but his head bowed.

This is sober, ashamed Harry, and my lungs kick back into gear.

"What are you doing here, Harry?" I ask flatly. When he's like this, I don't hate him, I don't fear him, and I'm not even sad for our shared past. At this point, when he's not drunk and antagonistic, I only feel indifference—for a man I once thought I loved but who no longer exists.

"I was walking by and saw the light on. Knew you'd be getting ready for the Cozy Cup, so came over to see if you needed any help. It used to be my favorite time of year."

My heart pinches because every good memory I have of the Cup once involved him.

"And I wanted to..."

"To what, Harry? Apologize again? Don't you ever just get tired of this cycle?"

He walks to the bin I was struggling with, lifts it, checks the label, then moves it to the back of the shed.

"Thanks," I say, suddenly exhausted, and it's only eight.

"I just...I don't know how to get back to what we had," he says quietly, the weight of his actions clearly much heavier in the sober hours of the morning.

"Harry, you know that's never going to happen."

"Because of Braxton?" Hurt and anger make his words choppy, but I'm done worrying about how I make him feel.

"Because of you. Because of you, Harry. We will never be a couple again. You destroyed every ounce of trust I've ever possessed, and you did it twice."

He nods, and then because he spent so many years doing this with me, lifts the bins he knows I'll need and places them in the wagon I have outside.

"Do you think... Do you think we'll ever be able to be friends?" he asks, tucking his hands deep into his pockets.

I don't even know this person anymore.

"I don't think that will be possible." My words sound strong even if the piece of my heart held for human decency scolds me. "But life doesn't have to be this hard for you either."

He shakes his head because he knows what's coming—we've had this conversation so many times, he probably has it memorized.

"Sometimes you mess up life so horrifically, there is no other life to be had." He's staring at a point far beyond me, and I shake my head.

"You still have people that care for you. Your dad loves you. Coach B. is obviously still holding out hope that you'll get your life straightened out."

He snorts as though he doesn't believe me.

"He wouldn't let you help with the team if he didn't have some kind of fondness for you, Harry. But you have to stop drinking. All it does is hurt you and those who love you."

"Have you seen how everyone in town looks at me, Madi?"

"I have," I say, my voice rising with my frustration. "But you know why. You know why they look at you that way. You know what you've done to hurt not only me but so many people who loved you in this town, and you've never once apologized. You've never once taken accountability." I bite my tongue before I say more because I feel the anger taking over.

"Mads." His voice wobbles back to shame. "If you can't forgive me, how the hell do you expect anyone else to? What's the fucking point?"

"The point? The point?" I'm nearly shouting and don't care. "The point is you don't have to be his horrible version of yourself, Harry."

"I told you I would try to be better, for you I would try."

Old emotions cling to my throat. "That's the problem, Harry. You can't try for me, or for your dad, or anyone else.

You'll never change if you don't do it for yourself. It's a choice you have to make for yourself."

"It's not that easy," he shouts.

I take a step back, an icy chill making me shiver. "I never said it was easy. I said it was a choice. Every time you pick up that bottle, it's a choice. Just like every time you picked up a football instead of calling to tell me you'd be late was a choice. When you chose to cheat on me, it was a choice. When you chose to tell lies about me in order to save yourself, that was a choice too. Until you start making the right choices, life will feel like an endless pit of misery."

"If you know all of this, then why won't you help me?" he cries. He's volatile and shaky as the high of his alcohol abuse wears off.

He won't last long before he opens another beer. I've learned the signs well.

"It's not my job anymore, Harry. All I've done the entire time I've known you is give, give, and give some more, until I didn't even recognize who I'd turned into. All I did was try to help you, don't you see that? I don't have anything left for you anymore."

"But you have time for that rich asshole."

"Don't do that, Harry," I say, defeated that once again I thought we might make some progress with this conversation. "Don't even try to compare my life now to what it was when I was with you. Braxton has never once asked anything of me. Not once."

"Mads, I'm sorry. That's not what—"

"Just stop drinking, Harry. And yes, I'm aware that it's an addiction, but there are people and places that will help you get sober, but you have to make that choice. Don't you see everything you're losing? Everything you're missing out on by drinking your fears away?"

"I didn't come here to fight with you, Madi."

"Then why did you come? It's exhausting to fear you one moment and—"

"You fear me?" He chokes out the words as though they shock him.

"Are you serious right now?"

He can't be this oblivious.

"Why do you fear me?"

"Harry, you were inches away from punching me in the face when you attacked Braxton. If he hadn't pushed me behind him, you would have broken my nose, or worse."

He turns green before me and shakes his head in denial. "No. That's not— I would never hurt you, Madi."

My sad, disgusted chuckle hits the air like an atomic bomb. "Hurting me is the only thing you've ever done well between us, Harry, and every time you pick up a bottle, every time you verbally or physically attack me or someone I care about, you continue to hurt me."

"That's..." He steps back, clutching his chest as if he's winded. "I don't want to hurt you."

The way his emotions fly from anger to humiliation and back again gives me whiplash. It's the reminder I need to put more space between us.

"And yet, here you are, doing it again. You have no idea of the monster alcohol turns you into. But I won't allow you to continue hurting me either. I know that somewhere, deep, deep inside of you is a good man. Or the bones of someone who once tried to be a good man. I hope that someday, you find him again."

"Madi..."

"I hope you find the boy who would rescue stray dogs. The teenager who snuck supplies down to the local food bank when you thought no one was looking. The man who once promised me the world and made me believe him. I hope you find that guy, Harry, because he had the potential to be pretty great." I see the hope flicker in his eyes. "But not for me. We're done, and though I appreciate the thought, I think I should take it from here."

I point toward the shed, then slowly walk away.

"I— I'm sorry, Madi." His voice breaks, but putting him together means tearing myself apart to fix his holes, and I'm not that person anymore.

"I know you believe that, Harry. And someday, I hope your actions will prove it."

Locking the shed, I grab the handle of the wagon and walk to the back door of the Chug. Adrenaline buzzes through me, a dizzying combination of anxiety and pride at having that conversation. I've always put myself last so everyone around me could be first, and maybe it's time to start correcting that character flaw.

Heading up to the second floor of the Chug, I sit at the desk where I do most of my admin work when I need to be away from everyone. I slowly open the bottom drawer. The offer for syndication sits right where I left it.

I read it six more times, knowing this is the route forward for me and a career I love so much, but still unable to pull the trigger. There's something in the legal jargon that isn't sitting right with me, and if I'm going to do this, the offer will have to be perfect.

Or is that an excuse I'm still using because I feel like a fraud? A matchmaker with no match.

Stuffing the file back in the drawer, I pull my laptop out of my bag and get to work on something I should have done a long time ago, my business plan for *The Matchmaker Manual.*

I know deep in my bones that this is where my heart

belongs, and I'm so freaking good at it. It's time to stop making excuses, and start preparing for my future, even if that future means only owning a part of the Hideaway for a while.

What does Braxton's future look like? And how will I feel when it no longer includes me?

21

BRAXTON

"Why are we doing this?" Greyson asks from the passenger side of my truck.

Somehow, he got shotgun, while Pops is in the middle and Sage is squished into the back seat. I saw Pops out messing with Grey's rental car earlier—I know that's why it wouldn't start. I'll have to speak to Pops about that.

"You've got to see the town." Pops sounds annoyed, and I wonder if it's because Grey outmaneuvered him to the passenger seat today. "First stop is the diner 'cause I'm starving."

Grey's stomach growls so loudly we all hear it, so he doesn't bother arguing even though I can see in his shoulders that he was about to.

These two figured out immediately how to push each other's buttons, so it's anyone's guess how it'll play out.

"It's a busy place," Sage says, his head resting on the seat in front of him between Pops and Grey.

"It's Betty's famous meatloaf today, that's why we needed to get here early." Pops huffs. "If I missed out on my meatloaf because you were dicking around with your wiffee meeting, heads are gonna roll, you hear me? Heads will roll."

"What the fuck is wiffee? And I wasn't dicking around with anything. I had a $14 million deal on the table, Mercutio. What the hell is it you think I do anyway?"

"Not making meatloaf, I know that."

I finally find a parking spot, and Grey jumps out of the truck before I've even put it in park. He stands outside, rolling his shoulders. I shouldn't laugh at my best friend for being so out of his element, but I do.

"Come on," I say, following him out. "How about you two put a pin in your little war and let's go eat?"

"He started it." Pops pouts.

Grey stares at me with a wide, bewildered gaze. "Is he for real? What kind of—"

"Careful there, Uncle Grey. We don't want the town thinking you're some kind of rich asshole or anything."

Grey snaps his mouth closed, buttons his suit jacket, because I can't get him to wear anything we bought at Walmart, walks into Betty's Diner, and stops with one foot inside when every head in the place turns to stare at him.

"Not so big in your britches now, are ya, kid?" Pops shimmies under Grey's arm and enters to a chorus of *hello* and *how ya been, Pops?*

"Breathe, Grey. He's just messing with you." I chuckle and walk past him too.

"If my head explodes from being in Happiness fucking Georgia for too long, I will haunt you by singing every NSYNC song ever recorded," Grey hisses to the back of my head.

"Promise?" I say, waggling my brows to get a rise out of him.

He reaches into his pocket and retrieves his lucky coin. It rolls through his fingers and back again.

"Betty said we can have the booth in the back," Pops says smugly, and in all fairness, it is the best seat in the house. "Even your big bucks couldn't get you that."

He saunters past us, stopping to chat at each table he passes. By the time he makes it to the table, we're already seated.

"That's my seat." Pops scowls at Grey, who makes a point of looking behind him and between his legs.

"I don't see your name on it, old man." I don't think Grey even acted like a child when he was a child, so this is a new side of him, and it's a lot of fun to see.

"This is war, Greyson. You're going down."

Grey picks up all his cutlery and like a spoiled child, licks it all, places it back on the table, then gets out and allows Pops to slide into the booth.

Sage and I stare at him with matching expressions of shock.

"What the hell was that?" Sage asks before I can.

"It was the most un-Greyson Reyes thing I've ever seen you do," I say.

"If you boys start a food fight in here, you'll be cleaning my floors with your tongues," Betty says as she drops some menus on the table.

That snaps Grey out of whatever childish hole Pops managed to drag him into, while Pops stares at the side of his head, hooting with laughter.

"How's it feel, kid?"

Grey slowly turns toward Pops. "How's what feel?"

"Getting that stick outta your ass and having a little fun."

Sage and I wait for Grey's reaction. I honestly have no idea what he'll do.

"You're quite possibly the most immature man I've ever met." Grey stares at Pops with a look of...astonishment?

"Why, thank you. You're forgiven for being an unbearable asshole."

Grey's right eyebrow twitches as he stares at me, silently begging me to tell him this is all one giant joke, but all I can do is chuckle and shrug.

"Welcome to Happiness, Greyson."

Pops picks up every item in the condiment tray and shakes it to make sure he has enough for whatever he's going to order, but when he gets to the ketchup, all hell breaks loose. He shakes it, listens to it, then shakes it again.

"We're going to need more of this," he says. "See?" He opens the top so Greyson can see whatever Pops thinks is inside and ketchup sprays all over Greyson's white button-down.

"It looks like someone stabbed you." Sage laughs so hard he snorts, and Grey's face turns as red as the ketchup on his shirt.

"Well now, that was an accident," Pops says with humor lacing his tone. He attempts to wipe it off, but Grey simply sighs and removes Pops' hand.

"I've got it."

Pops shrugs and goes back to checking the packets of sugar. When he's satisfied, he sits with his hands folded on the table, literally twiddling his thumbs.

"Hey, Pops." A man in his mid-forties steps up to our table. "Thanks for volunteering at the animal shelter last month with Savvy. We really appreciated the extra hands for the adoption event."

He and Pops share stories for a few moments, but I didn't miss the way Grey stiffened at the mention of Savvy's name.

When the guy leaves, I lean in to the table. "What's going on with you and Savvy?" I whisper.

"Him and Sav?" Pops says at full volume. "No way. She'd eat him alive."

"Excuse me?" Grey crosses his arms over his chest, only partially covering the ketchup splatter.

"Well, I saw you two bickering at the fundraiser the night you arrived. She doesn't back down, that one, but she's got a real soft center, and she'll tear you apart before you ever get close to it."

"Savvy has a soft center?" I ask. "She always seems so—"

"Argumentative?" Grey interrupts.

"Now you watch it, kid. Savvy's a good egg who's already been scrambled up by a bunch of sack suckers. The last thing she needs is another ball sack jerking her around."

"Why must you be so...phallic?" Grey stares at Pops as if he's an alien here to abduct him.

"Aw, Pops."

I lift my gaze to find Savvy walking up the aisle. Grey heard her too, and his entire body turns to stone. He doesn't generally shut down completely, so the fact that Savvy has gotten to him this way is extremely interesting.

"Savvy. We were just talking about you." The mischievous glimmer returns to Pops' expression. "Join us." He slides all the way to the wall, managing to tug an unsuspecting Grey with him.

Sage and I both watch with silent laughter making our lips twitch as the mask she was wearing slips momentarily, before she feigns indifference and perches on the very edge of the seat, as far away from Grey as she can get.

"So Sage, how are you settling in?"

"Great. I'm having the best time of my life." If he flashes her any more teeth, his face will split in two.

"That's really good to hear." She sounds so genuine, but Grey still glares at her as though she's about to shoot poison from her tongue. "Small towns can take a little getting used to, but I really do hope you like it here. It was...life-changing for me when I landed here."

Some of the ice in Grey's eyes melts at her tone.

"So, what do you have planned for the rest of the day?" she asks.

"Pops wants to take Uncle Grey to Bitter Creek, then he's going to show us the library before we have to get back so the uncles can do some work."

"That sounds...really boring for you." She laughs.

Does Grey realize he's angled his body closer to hers?

"You have no idea." Sage smirks conspiratorially. His words instantly have Grey back on edge.

"Do you not like it here? We can head home now if you want."

"Uncle Grey." Sage groans. "That's not what I said, and we're not running home just because you're uncomfortable."

Savvy turns a questioning expression his way. That's when they both realize how close their faces are, and their necks snap back at the same time.

"I'm not uncomfortable," Grey grouses. "I just have a lot of work to do."

"And on that note, I've got to head over to the Chug to record my next episode." Savvy stands, and Grey's gaze follows much too slowly. "Have a good day," she says to everyone, but never makes eye contact with my best friend.

Grey's phone pings, and Pops groans loudly.

"Shit," Grey curses. His brow furrows as he speed-reads across the screen. Then he turns it toward me, and my tension headache returns.

The headline reads "Spoiled Montgomery Princess

Throws Hissy Fit in Montana Kindergarten Classroom." Below it is a picture of Anastasia looking more pissed off than I've ever seen her. But the interesting thing about the photo is how she appears to be attempting to shield the child she's with from the photographers.

I've never known my sister to protect anyone but herself.

"Ah, Pops. We're going to have to get lunch to go today. I'm sorry," I say.

For all the trouble Pops causes, he's always the first to have the backs of those he cares about. He proves it when he starts shoving on Grey's arm.

"Get moving, kid. Sage and I can grab lunch for you two. Moose will drive us home."

Grey looks between Sage and Pops. I know every thought running through his head, but he eventually slides out of the booth. At least on some level, he trusts Pops enough to leave our nephew with him.

"Lunch, and straight back to the Hideaway."

Pops gives me the shooing motion he usually saves for Madison.

"I mean it, Pops. No stops today. Finish up here and come straight home. Nowhere else, no pit stops, no quick conversations, okay?"

Sage chuckles when Pops salutes me, but I know damn well that man had his fingers crossed behind his back.

"Sage," I say with a parental tone I rarely use with him.

"Don't worry. I'll be the adult here."

Pops crosses his arms, but at least I can trust one of them.

IT'S ALMOST MIDNIGHT BEFORE I HEAR MADISON COME HOME. At some point, she'd snuck in to put a casserole in the oven while we were on the third floor cleaning out furniture, but she was gone again before I saw her.

"Hey," I say, when she reaches the top of the stairs.

"Holy crap, Braxton." She clutches her hands to her heart and shakes her head. "You scared the bejeezus out of me. What are you doing lurking in the hallway?"

The bathroom door opens, and Sage jumps back a step. "Jesus, Uncle Brax. What the hell, you scared the shit out of me."

"See?" Madison says, lightly pounding on her chest.

"Why are you both standing in the hallway?" Sage asks.

"I just got home and found Braxton hiding in the shadows." Her face is partially covered in darkness, but not enough that I don't see the corners of her lips curl up.

"I heard her come home, so I was just checking on her. What are you doing up?"

Sage shrugs and squeezes past me in the hallway. "I just finished a movie. I was brushing my teeth, if you must know. Stalking is still frowned upon."

"Go to bed," I grumble.

Madison and I are silent until he's shut himself away in his room.

"You waiting up for me?" she finally asks while leaning casually against the wall. Is she teasing me?

Closing the distance between us, I answer truthfully. "Yes. Grey and I work long hours, but you're making us look like slackers."

She tucks a loose piece of hair behind her ear, breaking eye contact with me. "I had a lot to do, and Clover asked me to brainstorm a villain with her this afternoon. It kind of threw off my day."

I lean against the same wall she's resting her head on. "You couldn't have done it another time?"

"I'd told Blissy I couldn't go to lunch with her, so I was already stuck at the Chug anyway," she says.

Grey's light flickers to life under his door. When the hell did everyone turn into night owls? Taking Madison by the hand, I lead her back down the stairs and into the kitchen.

She's either too tired to question me or she likes being as close to me as I do her.

"There," I say when I usher her to the island stool. "Have you eaten?"

She frowns, glances at the clock, then yawns as I turn on the dim light over the sink.

"I'll take that as a no. You tell me about your day, and I'll make you a grilled cheese."

"No, Braxton. You don't have to do that. I'm fine, really."

Opening the refrigerator door, I ignore her and pull out the sharp white cheddar slices I bought earlier. "I know I don't have to, sunshine. I want to." Placing the cheese on the island, I lean over it so I'm in her personal space. "It's okay to let someone else be the caretaker every once in a while."

Reaching out, I pull her head forward, press a gentle kiss to her forehead, and my entire being syncs with her cadence.

I step back before she can say anything and reach for the bread and butter, then bend down to grab a frying pan.

"So tell me, why couldn't Clover wait until tomorrow?"

"I—I didn't think about it," she says. "Plus, I like helping. Brainstorming with her feeds a creative need I get sometimes."

"I get that, I do. But by helping, how far did it push the tasks you had planned to do back?"

"Not that long," she mutters.

"Ballpark?" I ask while generously buttering two pieces of bread.

"It's not that big of a deal."

I lift my brows in my most skeptical expression.

"Fine, I don't know. Maybe three hours."

"Three hours? So, you could have been home by nine instead of midnight?"

"I didn't know I had a curfew." She crosses her arms over her chest. It's so much like Pops, I can almost picture her as that unruly kid her parents tried to squash. "Plus, it wasn't just that. After I helped Clover, Coach B. had some last-minute additions I had to work into the schedule, and then Savvy popped in to record a couple of podcasts, so I had coffee with her."

"Mm-hmm."

"What?" she snaps.

Placing the buttered side of bread in the pan, I top it with cheese and the second slice of bread. It sizzles while I grab a spatula.

"Do you ever say no?"

"Of course I do." She sounds as though she's trying to convince me, or maybe herself.

Flipping her sandwich, I reach for a plate. As soon as both sides are golden brown, I cut it in half diagonally, set it in front of her, and grab a grapefruit seltzer water from the fridge. After popping the top, I slide that over to her too, but she's watching me with an expression I can't read.

"Why are you staring at me like that?" I ask.

"How do you just know?"

"Know what?" Sitting next to her, I nudge her plate a little closer.

"What I like. How I take my coffee, what kind of seltzer I prefer, even my favorite kind of cheese."

I glance around the kitchen, waiting for a shoe to drop.

"I'm living in your home, Madison. Why wouldn't I know those things?"

"I've known Cian since I was a teenager, and he doesn't know those things."

I inch closer to her, angling my legs so one knee rests behind her. I'm as close as I can get with us both sitting on stools.

"I pay attention." My voice is low, just for her ears. "I enjoy getting to know all of your likes and dislikes. Is that so bad?"

She hasn't reached for her sandwich, so I pick up a slice and hold it to her mouth.

"Are you—"

I slip the crusty corner of grilled cheese past her lips, and she moans while biting down. Her stomach growls then, and she removes the sandwich from my hands to take another bite.

"You didn't eat." I see it in her eyes.

"It was kind of a crappy day," she says through a mouthful. Her impeccable manners are being pushed aside as she surrenders to her hunger.

Reaching into the fruit bowl at the end of the island, I snag a banana in case the sandwich isn't enough.

"How come?"

She makes a noncommittal noise while picking up the second half of her grilled cheese.

"Because you didn't tell anyone no or ask them to make an appointment? Your time is valuable, sunshine. You can't always put yourself last. It's not healthy."

"No, it's not that."

"Then what?"

"Ugh." She groans. "I ran into Harry today while I was pulling items from the storage shed."

"You...ran into Harry in the shed?" My hand clenches under the island. If he's harassing her, I will do whatever it takes to get him to back off. "Are you okay?"

"It was fine," she says, polishing off the last piece of bread. "Sober Harry is just...sad." Her shoulders slump forward as another yawn escapes.

I don't know what to say, so I hold up the banana in offering.

She reaches for it, but I pull it out of her grasp at the last moment and begin to peel it for her.

"Why is he sad?" I ask while focusing extra hard on the banana.

Her body deflates beside me. "When he's sober is when he feels the shame and guilt of what he's done. It's like seeing tiny flickers of who he once was but knowing it will be snuffed out again with his next drink. And today I might have been a little too mean to him when I told him we'll never have a chance again. I know it sent him right back to the bar, but I don't know what else to say to him. He doesn't have to be who he's become, but I don't think he's strong enough to handle the weight of his conscience either."

"Being honest isn't mean, sunshine. It's protecting yourself. It's putting up boundaries. You're not responsible for his happiness, his sobriety, or his decisions."

"I know. I do. And most of the time I hate him for everything he's done. But there are times, like today, when all I feel is sadness for what he's done to me and what he continues to do to himself."

Holding the open banana away from her body, I spin her and pull her into me. We sit with my body wrapped around hers, her back to my front.

When she leans her head back to look at me, I offer her the fruit. She hesitates for only a second before taking a bite.

I was not thinking about how sexy feeding her a fucking banana would be, so focusing on her words becomes nearly impossible.

She swallows, then looks up at me with pure sunshine in her expression.

"Are you okay with how everything went with him today?" My tone is rougher than I'd like, but jealousy coated in fear for her safety is rearing its ugly head and I can't seem to rein it in.

"I am." She's still leaning her head on my shoulder. "It finally felt like goodbye."

Relief flickers like hot embers across my skin. Pressing my lips to her cheek, I whisper, "Take a bite." I pull back just enough so I can aim the banana for her mouth, and fuck me, my cock twitches in my pants.

She stills in front of me, not even chewing, then pushes back on her stool an inch. I have to stifle a groan when her ass nestles into my thickening length.

I'm breathing through my nose, attempting to control my reactions as she finishes the banana, but the second she swallows the last bite, I pounce, spinning her again and claiming her lips as though they belong to me.

Our teeth clash, and our tongues swirl with untamed desire. I nip at her bottom lip, and she moans so loudly pre-cum leaks into my boxers.

Noise from above is the only thing that holds me back. As much as I want this woman, she's exhausted, and I won't risk someone walking in on us, so after a few more moments, I pull away, pressing my forehead to hers.

"You're dangerous, Madison Ryan. So fucking dangerous."

"Me? Why?"

"Because you might be the only person on the planet who can make me lose control."

Her eyes light up as though it's a compliment, and my chuckle is dark as it escapes my chest. "Come on, you're tired. Let's get you to bed before Pops waltzes in here looking for a party."

The mention of her grandfather has her eyes popping wide. Her chest is still heaving, and it takes all my willpower not to tear her shirt wide open.

"Bedtime, sunshine," I say, standing from my stool and offering her a hand.

She rises silently, and when she places her palm in mine, entwining our fingers on the way up the stairs, I finally admit to myself that everything is about to change.

22

MADISON

Sage is already in the kitchen when I come downstairs at the crack of dawn. I haven't seen much of him over the past week. He's mostly kept to himself, but I can tell he's bored out of his mind.

"Hey, Sage. Oh my Lord. What's that smell?"

He looks up from whatever he's watching in the oven and waggles his fingers at me. "I heard about Uncle Braxton's disastrous attempt at a soufflé. You've been so…" He turns back to the oven. "You've just been really good to us, and you're working so much, so I thought I'd do something I know neither of my uncles can do. I cooked you breakfast."

"You made a soufflé? Sage, it's five in the morning. What time did you get up?"

He shrugs, and it's so strange to see. He's the size of a man but with the fragility of a child.

"I've been having trouble sleeping."

"Is it the room? What can I change? How can I help?"

He angles his face toward me with a soft but sad expression. "You've done everything perfectly, Miss take-care-of-everyone-else-and-forget-about-yourself."

I don't appreciate being called out by a teenager, even if he is right.

"Then what's keeping you up?"

He turns the oven off and cracks the door a quarter of an inch, then joins me at the island.

"Honestly?"

I flash my best "duh" face, and he laughs.

"Okay, I'm bored, like so bored my eyeballs hurt. And that's not your fault, so shut down all the things running through your mind about how you'll entertain me. It's just that, I graduated high school at fourteen. I've been taking classes at community college because I wasn't ready for anything else, and my uncles and Ace supported that.

"But coming here means I don't get to go to campus, and I don't really know what to do with myself because I finished all the coursework weeks ago. Now Pops and Grey have come to some sort of truce, so I don't even have their trolling each other to keep me entertained."

Wow. When he shares, he really opens up. I already thought I liked this kid, but now I know I could love him.

"Well Mr. Smarty-pants, that sounds one hundred percent reasonable. Do you want to take classes while you're here? Happiness U is a great university, and I know some of the professors."

"I appreciate it, but it's already November. I wouldn't be able to start until January, and Uncle Brax only has to be here until the end of March, so I don't know what we'll do after that."

My stomach cramps as I force down my gag reflex. Somehow, I keep forgetting that Braxton is temporary.

"Mm-hmm. I forgot." My voice cracks the silence louder than a bullfrog in the dead of night. "Have you ever had a job before?"

He traces a shape in the island granite.

"There's no judgment in that question, Sage. I never had a job until I was older. Not because I was lazy, but because I spent every waking hour playing field hockey so I could get a scholarship to college. That was my job. There are lots of reasons kids don't have jobs until college or after."

"I bet you were great at field hockey."

The compliment is so unexpected, I don't know how to respond.

"You got that scholarship, right?"

I nod and bite my tongue to keep the tears at bay. I hate myself in this moment. It's been years. I'm over this.

"Hey, I'm sorry—"

"No, it's okay," I sniffle. "Really. I did get my scholarship. But some stuff happened that caused a real mess my freshman year, so the university I was attending asked me to leave the team, without my scholarship."

"What?" His indignation on my behalf is charming. "How can they do that?"

"It's a long story for another time. Now let's discuss you coming to work with me today."

"Oh my God. Are you serious? Yes, yes, please, yes." He clasps his hands together in front of his face, flashing puppy dog eyes he must have learned from Braxton.

His enthusiasm has my tears drying and laughter escaping my lips.

"We have to ask your uncles first."

"Ugh. Then let's go to Brax first. I love them both, but Uncle Grey can be a real hard-ass."

"It's because he loves you," Braxton says with sleep still in his sexy voice.

We both turn toward Braxton, standing in the doorway.

His hair's a mess, and his sleep pants hang low on his hips. When he runs a hand down his chest to scratch his belly, I feel my internal body temperature skyrocket.

He doesn't usually walk around shirtless, and try as I might, I can't look away. The man is all lean muscle that pulls taut as he stretches over his head, causing his pants to slip just the tiniest bit more.

That's too much to handle, so I focus on making some coffee.

"What are you doing up?" I ask without facing him.

"I was hungry, and I heard you close your door. I was afraid you were trying to sneak out early again today." His words shift my hair, and I nearly jump out of my skin when he presses that naked chest into my back, reaches over me and pulls down the coffee mug he uses every day.

It has a picture of twelve-year-old me on it with a chipped tooth I got in a field hockey game.

Peering over my shoulder, I study him as he scans the mug, and when he lifts his gaze to mine, I return to my duty. What was I doing? Coffee, right.

"Um, would it be okay if Sage came to work with me today at the Chug? He's kind of bored, and I thought it might be good for him to meet some folks."

He lifts a chunk of my hair and pulls it back over my shoulder before leaning in, apparently not at all embarrassed to be this close to me in front of his nephew.

"I think that sounds like a great idea."

"But will Uncle Grey?" Sage asks.

"Will Uncle Grey what?" the man in question repeats.

I gasp and slip beside Braxton instead of in front of him.

"I want to go to work with Madi at the Chug today."

"Why are you all up so early? If I wasn't working, you

couldn't drag me out at this hour." I say before Grey can answer.

"I get up to work out at four every morning," Grey says, studying my face.

I hadn't even noticed that he walked in wearing gym shorts and nothing else, but once you see it, it's kind of hard to forget.

"Did you guys all win the gene pool lottery or something?" I mutter.

"Hardly." Grey snorts. He's relaxed since he's been here. A little, anyway. I'm not sure he knows what relaxing truly means though. "Brax seemed to really enjoy being at the Chug, so I don't see any reason you can't go. See? I'm not always an ogre."

It's self-deprecating, but there's no mistaking the love he has for his nephew.

"Not always." Sage smirks. "But most of the time. I'm going to shower. What time are we leaving, Madi?"

"In about an hour? Does that work? Clover, Savvy, and I are all recording today, so we're trying to get it done before too many customers arrive."

"Recording?" Grey asks, taking the mug of coffee that Braxton hands him.

"Yeah, my best friends and I all run fairly successful podcasts out of the Chug."

"And Savvy is one of those friends?" Grey mutters.

Things have been nonstop since they moved in, and I haven't had the time to properly grill Savvy on what went down at the fundraiser between her and Grey, but I need to rectify that soon. Today probably won't work since I'll have Sage in tow.

"Yes, actually. Her podcast *Can We Talk About That?* is consistently in the top three of her genre."

"Which is?" Grey asks without glancing up from his coffee mug.

"She's a sex therapist," Sage blurts. "I've been listening to her show for years."

"You what?" Braxton is the first to jump in, but Grey is right behind him.

"Is that appropriate for teenagers?" Grey asks with fire in his tone.

Staunch loyalty flares in me, and I stick a hand on my hip. Admittedly I take a little bit of strength from Braxton's hand on my lower back, but mostly, my indignation is for my friend. "Listen up, it is not Savvy's fault if you didn't have parental controls set on his devices. She has a well-respected show, and she's helped a lot of people. She's saved so many relationships too, so don't go placing blame where it doesn't belong."

"That's not—"

"Yes, it is, Uncle Grey. And she's right," Sage interrupts while moving toward the door. He pauses just inside the threshold. "Out of curiosity, what's Clover's called?"

"*Flirting with Fear*," I say with pride. "She writes best-selling thrillers but scares the crap out of herself while doing it."

Sage allows the door to close, but I hear his laughter all the way up the stairs.

"I'm protective of him," Grey says quietly.

"We both are," Braxton continues, "but Madison wouldn't take him somewhere he'd be treated poorly."

"Why would he be treated poorly?" I ask.

This time, Grey lifts his head and sears me with his gaze. "His birth was famous for all the wrong reasons, and where we live, it followed him. He's also way smarter than either of us, so he's never fit in well with his peers because he didn't know how to interact with kids his own age and the kids in classes with him were several years older."

"That might've been our fault. We were kids helping raise a kid, but we did the best we could." Braxton's expression is full of concern.

"He's a good kid," I say gently. "And sure, mean kids exist everywhere, but I can assure you, that won't happen at the Chug. That space is mine, and I've worked hard to keep it with the theme of our town."

Grey scrutinizes me for long seconds, then he blinks and nods. "Thank you. It'll be good for him to get out."

"Anytime. Sage made breakfast—it's in the oven. I'm going to get ready for the day. I'll see you boys later."

I make it to the stairs before hands at my waist pull me to a stop.

Braxton slowly turns me. Standing two steps above him brings us eye to eye. He doesn't speak, and I attempt not to breathe, morning breath and all. But when he leans in, thoughts of toothpaste slip my mind. His lips are gentle but demanding against my own, and my body releases tension when he cradles my face.

The kiss is far too short for my liking, but when he rests his forehead against mine, it feels more intimate than the kiss.

"Thank you for being so understanding. It's been a long time since we've let anyone into our lives. It won't be easy for them—we haven't had much luck with trusting people."

"Me either, but I meant what I said. Sage is a good kid— I'd never let anyone hurt him."

He nods and swipes my nose with the side of his. "I know."

"Ah, thank you," I say when he steps back.

He tilts his head as though he's confused. "For what?"

"The kiss?" My face flames with embarrassment.

His eyes light up brighter than the stars. "No, sunshine, thank you, because I'd very much enjoy doing it again. And again."

I reach for the elastic around my wrist and have to settle for squeezing it when I remember I left the elastic on my nightstand. "Is that a good idea though? With everything going on and you leaving in March. It seems as though maybe we're setting ourselves up for...for something not great."

He stares at me full of kindness and a hope I haven't experienced in years. "I don't know what the future holds, but I do know Ace wanted me to be happy, and I am for the first time in a very long time. That's not something I can just give up on."

I bite my lip because it's neither a declaration nor an explanation of what we're doing.

"Right," I manage because what the heck do I say? "I'm going to get ready."

"I want to take you on a date. A real date."

I miss the next stair and fall to my knees.

"Jesus," he says, taking two stairs at a time to check my kneecaps. "It's just a date, sunshine. I don't need you on your knees for me...yet."

My chin literally unhinges as every piece of my brain short-circuits.

Is Braxton Reyes a dirty talker?

"What happened? You okay, Mads?" Pops asks, deflating our moment like a sad clown balloon.

"Yup. Just tripped. I'm taking Sage to work with me today. You, ah, stay out of trouble, okay?" I hop up and take the remaining stairs two at a time.

Air. I need air.

I don't need you on your knees for me...yet.

Ovaries exploding, nipples pebbling, thighs clenching.

My libido is all in for a date with Braxton. But can my battered heart handle it?

23

———

BRAXTON

Pops' feet keep our porch swing swaying in a gentle rhythm while Grey inspects the shutters I leaned against the railing last night. It's still warm out, but the cloying stickiness is gone.

"You're not afraid of heights too, are ya, kid?"

Grey lifts a scornful-looking brow at Pops. "No. I'm not afraid of heights. But please remind me when I agreed to hang these for you?"

Pops kicks out his heels and clasps his hands behind his head. "It was yesterday afternoon, before I asked if you've ever plucked a turkey for Thanksgiving and after I asked if you loved working at Omni-Reyes or if you were doing it out of duty to Ace."

Grey scoffs. "Right. You do enjoy tossing out those invasive-as-fuck questions, don't you?"

"Life's too short not to be doing what you love."

"Brax, come down here and hand me these things so I can get back to work."

I wink at Pops, then help Grey move all the shutters. He's only at it for about fifteen minutes when Sage and Madison walk outside. I hope he didn't make her late. I heard them whispering upstairs so I gave them privacy, but she had planned to leave an hour ago.

"What happened to your eyes?" Pops bluntly asks Sage. The poor kid shuffles his feet on the porch.

"Pops," I say, as Grey growls, "What the fuck?" and Madison stands behind Sage, whipping her finger back and forth across her throat to tell him to cut it out.

Pops ignores us all.

"I thought it would be better to try and fit in today." Sage tugs on his earlobe, something he hasn't done in years.

"Why?" Pops asks before I can intervene. Grey is stomping down the ladder, but I hold up a hand to stop him. In the time I've spent with him, Pops has never done anything malicious, and I'm choosing to trust him with Sage now.

Look at me trusting again.

"It's a small town, and I didn't want to embarrass Madi."

"What?" Madison gasps. "You would never embarrass me."

"Let me ask you this, Sage." Pops calls him by his name, and I'm still *boy*. Go figure. "Do you wear all that black crayon stuff to *hide* who you are, or do you wear it because it feels like *who* you are?"

Grey, who had been marching across the lawn toward the porch, stops short at Pops' question.

Sage tilts his head and stares at the floorboards below him, but we all give him time. I'll count to ten, and then if he doesn't answer, I'll cut in and give him an out. But this is probably something we should've asked him a long time ago.

When I glance over at Grey, I'm guessing he agrees by

the frown on his face. He's the only man I know with fifty shades of frown, but this is the one meant for himself.

I reach number nine, when Sage finally opens his mouth. "People always thought I was weird. It felt safer to give them the version they thought I was than show them the real me and risk getting hurt."

Grey's heavy footsteps land on the stairs next to me, and the railing rattles a little when he clutches it. He looks as shaken up as I feel.

"Sage, I—I didn't know that." My throat feels thick and uncomfortable.

Sage shrugs. "I don't think I did either." His brows are still pinched together when he looks back at Pops.

"Now let me ask you this," Pops says, putting his swing into motion again. "Did you leave it off today because you were afraid of embarrassing Madi or because you wanted to see if people would accept you for you?"

Jesus. When did Pops turn into a shrink?

"I don't know," Sage admits. "But it is exhausting hiding all the time though."

"There ya have it, Sage. Be you, and don't ever hide. If you want to wear crayons, you wear crayons and hold your head high. If you want to dye your hair blue and call your-self a peacock, then you do that too. The world is alive with color, as it should be. It would be a damn shame if we were all shades of the same color, don't you think?"

"What the hell just happened?" Grey whispers.

"Yeah, I—I agree," Sage says. Then he walks over, bends down, and hugs the old man tight.

He's always been an affectionate kid, something neither of us were used to and were probably not great at giving, but for him, we tried.

Pops wraps his old wrinkly arms around him and

squeezes him back. He whispers something I can't hear, and when Sage pulls back from the hug, he's as content as I've ever seen him.

Somehow in the last five minutes, Pops has managed to break down walls we didn't know existed.

"Well, fuck me," Grey mutters the second he gets a look at Sage.

The change in his posture is immediate. Whatever Pops said to him had more of an impact than anything either of us has probably ever said to him.

When Pops finds us staring at him in varying degrees of disbelief, he chuckles. "What's got y'all tongue-tied? I've got a rainbow flag out there so folks of all flavors know they're welcome here. We don't discriminate, and I think kids should be who they're meant to be."

"This is not the South I thought we were getting involved with," Grey says to my back.

"Nope, this here is Happiness, Georgia. The Heart of Joy lives in Happiness, didn't y'all see the sign on your way into town?" He chuckles to himself, then whistles to the sky as though he didn't just rip open our world and heal it in the same damn sentence.

When I finally turn to Madison, her face is shining with emotion. "He may get into trouble more than his fair share, but he loves, and he loves hard."

"Nothing is more valuable than love from someone who cares. I've been telling her that since she was knee-high," Pops agrees.

Grey clears his throat, then tugs at the collar of his button-down—yes, he's still dressed for the office even climbing ladders. He's never been great with his emotions, but by the pale shade of his face, I'm guessing this has more than quadrupled his limit for the day.

"I'm going to finish hanging these shutters so I can get back to work. Have fun with Madi, Sage. Call if you need anything."

"Two weeks, Grey," Madison calls to his back. His shoulders lift infinitesimally.

"Two weeks what?" he asks, not quite turning around.

"It took two weeks for Pops to rope you in. I told you it would happen, it always does." She laughs, but she's not laughing at Grey, or even this situation. I think she's laughing because she's finally accepted that Pops gets what Pops wants, and right now, he wants me and Grey doing manual labor.

"It's not my fault. The old man talks me in circles until my head's spinning." Grey does the most un-Grey thing then —he smiles at Pops. "You would've made a great lawyer."

Pops shoos him toward the ladder. "Nah, too much school. The words never did work right for me."

"Pops is dyslexic," Madison explains.

"I didn't know that." It feels like something I should've known.

The old man simply rocks his head side to side. "We all have obstacles that test us. That was one of mine. Now get to work. Daylight's running short."

"It's eight in the morning," I remind him.

"Lots to do, my boy. Lots to do."

Madison giggles, and my chest dances to the sound. I watch as she and Sage pile into her car and back out of the driveway.

It's then that my chest pinches as though someone's squeezing my heart in their fist.

I peer up at Grey on the ladder. "Have we sheltered him too much?"

He's nodding his head. Does he have the same fears that

I do? Did we unknowingly install our hang-ups on our nephew in the name of keeping him safe?

"Give him time," Pops says. "He's still got a long time to find himself."

"He's the real-life version of Bert from Mary Poppins," Grey says, hitching his thumb in Pops' direction.

It was Sage's favorite story for three years straight—*Mary Poppins and the Match-Man.*

And he's not wrong.

Perhaps Madison isn't the only matchmaker in Happiness.

"WHY THE HELL DO I HAVE TO SIT IN THE MIDDLE?" GREY grumbles as he faces off with Pops at the passenger side door of my truck.

"Because I said, and I'm not too old to whoop your ass. Now get in the truck," Pops says sternly.

"Whoop my ass?" Grey scratches the side of his head. It takes a lot to stump him, but Pops is proving to be a worthy opponent.

"I said what I said. The sooner you learn you won't get your way acting a fool, the happier you'll be here in Happiness."

Grey leans down into the truck to stare at me with wild eyes. "Why is it every time I talk to him it's one giant mind fuck?"

I shrug and start the engine. "He's had a lot of years to perfect it. Just get in. I want to check on Sage."

He curses under his breath but slides in. "Are you fucking kidding me? I have to straddle this thing?"

"It's a gearshift," Pops says, following him inside.

"I know what it is."

I glance down at Grey's legs and burst out laughing. He's practically resting his chin on his knees in here.

"Just go," he barks. "How the fuck does a brand-new car just die in the driveway?"

He had a new Mercedes delivered a few days ago, but when Pops starts whistling, I think I know why it wouldn't start, and I keep forgetting to talk to him about it, even if it is funny to see Grey this way.

Reaching over his legs, I put the truck in reverse.

He pinches the bridge of his nose. "Fuck me and my life."

"Don't be such a crybaby." Pops pats his knee and chuckles. "Ace said you needed to loosen up. You just haven't found anyone who can go toe-to-toe with you yet. But you will."

"No. I won't. How long until we get there?"

"Ten minutes," I say.

Grey presses his lips together into a thin line, and Pops whistles a melody I can't place. When I give Grey a sideways glance, his eyes are closed, and I think he's praying for patience.

Just one big happy family.

By the time I pull into the Chug, Grey has moved on to the breathing exercises Ace made us learn as teenagers.

"Look at that. Busy place today," Pops muses.

"Get. Out."

Grey hasn't even opened his eyes yet, so I elbow him in the side. "You need to relax, okay? This place is...different. You'll see."

"What the boy said." Pops opens the door and slowly exits the truck.

"I have a billion-dollar company to run. I don't have time

to." He scans the building in front of us. "Seriously Braxton, I want to be in and out of here in five minutes. We can leave Sage if he's having fun, and we'll snatch him out of there if even one person is looking at him funny."

I bite my cheek to keep from laughing and lie to my best friend. "Fine. Let's go."

There's no chance in hell we'll be out of here in one hour, let alone five minutes, but lying to him is the only way to get him to move.

Exiting the truck, I head straight for the front door, knowing that he'll follow, then I roll my neck from side to side on the way because there's no telling what kind of chaos we'll find in here today. Pops stands waiting for us at the top of the stairs.

"What are you doing?" Grey asks.

"There's a lot of people here today," I explain, "so when you place your order, you'll be choosing sides. It's coffee or tea, and there's enemies on either side."

"I don't have time for riddles, Brax."

"The town is divided. You'll see."

"Is this what people do in small-town America? They fight over caffeinated drinks?"

"It's much more than that, kid. You'll learn." Pops opens the door and ushers us inside.

I've never seen this place so packed. The sign in the quiet room says *book club in progress*. There's a crowd around the sound booth, but I can't see who's inside. Madison's friends sit in the center of it all, and taking up the entire right side of the space is the offense for the football team.

And Sage is sitting right in the middle of them, pointing at something on a screen. His face is animated and energized. He looks as though he's having fun—real fun with people his own age.

"What's going on over there?" Grey mutters but makes no move toward Sage.

I don't either. We just stand and watch, completely lost to the moment and unaware of anything but Sage.

"Ethan is a good kid," I say.

"The MacBook kid?" Grey asks.

"Yeah, he's sitting to the right of Sage."

Applause draws our attention back to the sound booth. Madison is in the doorway, shaking hands with some, hugging others, and she takes pictures with them all.

She's a small-town celebrity.

"What's going on over there?" Grey asks. He hasn't moved an inch, but his gaze tracks everything.

"I'm not sure."

"Hey, boys," Blissy says, stepping between us.

"Hey, Blissy. What's Madison doing?" I ask.

"Oh, that girl. She's the sweetest. About four times a year she hosts a live show, and people come from all over Georgia for a chance to pick her brain."

"Pick her brain about what?" Grey asks before I can.

"Have you listened to her show?" she asks.

His only response is to frown harder.

"Well, she's the matchmaker." She looks at him expectantly. "You know, from *The Matchmaker Manual*?" When he continues to stare at her, she huffs as though he offended her. "First she gets you to fall in love with yourself, and then she helps you determine what type of partner you'd be the most compatible with. She's poured her heart and soul into it since she was knee-high. How have you never listened to her? She has near a hundred percent success rate."

"Why not a hundred?" I ask.

"I'll give you one guess." The disgust in her tone tells me everything.

"Harry," I grumble.

"You got it. Now, what can I get ya boys?"

When Grey doesn't answer, I order for the both of us. "I'll have a coffee, black, and a tea with sugar, please."

She cackles, startling Grey where he stands. "Still haven't picked a side, huh? No problem. You still have some time before the Cozy Cup Festival, that's when it gets cutthroat around here."

I start to ask more about the Cozy Cup when I catch sight of Madison walking in our direction and practically glowing, but it's the confidence she exudes that has me looking a little bit closer.

Whatever went on here today is what she should be doing every day. This is her calling.

"Hey," she says. Her cheeks are flushed as though she's still on an adrenaline high.

"Hey. What's all this?" I ask.

"Oh, nothing. Just a little thing I do for listeners a few times a year. I actually forgot about it today. I've never done that before. Did you see Sage?" She's obviously deflecting, but it's something I'll make sure we come back to.

"We did. What's going on over there?"

Grey is made of stone. He hasn't moved, but I can tell he's absorbing every inch of this place by the way his gaze darts around the room.

She grabs both of our sleeves and drags us over to the check-in desk where it's only the slightest bit quieter.

"Sage was helping me move stuff around the room to accommodate the crowd, and the boys were in here watching game film. Their kicker broke their leg, and the backup and their prospect for next year committed to our biggest rival."

She looks from me to Grey to make sure we're following

because even though the buzz is dying down, it's still louder than she normally allows.

"Anyway, from what I could tell, they were studying their footwork because someone on the O-line will have to fill in for the rest of the season. Sage stepped in to offer a suggestion, and they've been over there for almost two hours now."

The group of boys erupts in laughter that has Blissy ringing a bell, and instantly the entire room falls back into the relative silence of a coworking space.

At that moment, Sage lifts his head and finds us watching him, and it's as though he grows up right before our eyes. When Grey tugs on his collar, I know he feels it too. Sage has been holding himself back, for us.

He points in our direction, then slowly rises and comes to meet us.

24

MADISON

As Sage draws nearer, Grey and Braxton's expressions morph into ones of...I don't know. Guilt? There's emotion there that doesn't make any sense to me, but the shift was instantaneous in them both.

"Hi." Sage bounces to a stop right in front of us.

"Hey." Grey's voice is rough, as though his throat is closing on him.

Braxton scrubs a hand through his hair before he finally smiles. "Looks like you were having fun over there."

"Yeah, I—I was. And they were wondering if I could go over to the field with them and show them some kicking techniques."

Braxton and Grey exchange a panicked expression. It's how I imagine dads look when deciding if their daughter is old enough to date.

They both try to speak, but gibberish comes out. Surely Sage had playdates when he was younger—this isn't much different. Well, okay, it is. Some of these guys are giants and old enough to drink, but they also know the town would kick their butts up and down the field if they ever got a seventeen-year-old into trouble.

"I can make sure Ethan keeps a close eye on him and drives him back to the Hideaway when they're done. Ethan is truly a very good young man."

"Yeah," Braxton says.

"Right, yeah. Okay. That seems..." Grey trails off.

"Guys," I snap my fingers to get them out of whatever funk they're in. "It's a university football field, and it's three in the afternoon. There will be staff and grounds crew all over that stadium."

"So is it okay if I go?" The hope in Sage's voice makes my heart ache for him. Do his uncles have any idea how lonely he's been?

"Sure," Braxton says, and before he's even finished, Sage is pulling his long, dirty-blond hair into a ponytail.

"Great. I'll be home for dinner. Can—can the guys come? I mean, if they want to?"

Braxton turns to me with so many questions written on his face, as if he's lost and needs directions.

"It's fine with me. Your uncles will have to buy pizza because I can cook for an army, but not on such short notice."

As soon as money comes into the conversation, Grey appears to snap out of it. "Done. Text me how many are coming, and I'll take care of it." Then he spins in place and gets in line at Blissy's.

"Is he okay?" Sage asks, but I was asking myself the same thing.

"He'll be fine," Braxton says. "I think maybe we're just realizing that some of our choices may not have been in your best interest over the years."

"That's stupid," Sage says, tugging on his ear. "You did

the best you could, and that was pretty great. I know that you know that, and I'm fine."

"I know. I won't hug you because I don't want to embarrass you in front of the guys, but I do need to have a conversation with them."

Sage wears the expression you'd expect of a seventeen-year-old at that statement, so I insert myself once again.

"I'll go with him. Come on, guys."

I walk toward the table that's littered with play sheets and notes. "Hey, guys, this is Braxton, one of Sage's uncles."

"Hi, Mr. Braxton," they say in unison. It's almost cultish and it makes me chuckle. Coach B. has taught them well!

"Sage was a great soccer player. I hear you'd like his help?" Braxton asks.

"Yes, sir," Ethan says, standing.

"And you know that he won't be eighteen for another few months?"

Ethan nods. "Yes, sir." The military precision of Coach B. is unmatched.

"Okay, Ethan. I'm trusting you."

"If anything happens to him, I will destroy you and your families," Grey growls over my head.

"Grey," I gasp, spinning and pushing him back a step with a hand to his chest. "You can't threaten people here."

He stares every player in the eye. "Watch me."

Ethan, who is over six foot four and probably two hundred and thirty pounds, swallows loudly.

Even Braxton seems taken aback. "Um, have fun. I'll see you at home."

Sage nods, spares one worried expression Grey's way, then turns back to the team. "I'm ready."

Braxton and I back out of the way as the group files out of the Chug.

"And wear your seatbelt," Grey shouts into the quietly buzzing space.

"What's that about?" I ask, unsure if I actually want the answer.

"We've been sort of protective of Sage." Braxton's back to rubbing that spot on his chest.

"I can see that. But you can't smother him, you know? He's growing up."

He nods but doesn't answer.

"Hey, Madi," Rose, the church coordinator, says. "I have you and Pops signed up for the Thanksgiving feast. Will he be serving as well?"

I completely forgot that Thanksgiving was coming up. "Oh, yes," I spare a quick glance in Braxton's direction. He's listening, but I'm not convinced he's paying attention. "Well, I'll be serving. Pops will be, well, Pops."

The older woman blushes. "Yes, and we wouldn't want him any other way, now would we, dear?"

Ugh. Gag. Gross. Rose was friends with my grandmother, but that has never stopped her from flirting.

"I'll see you on Thanksgiving. Have a good day," I say, actively dismissing her.

"What's happening on Thanksgiving?" Okay, so he was paying attention.

"It's a lot of work to make Thanksgiving dinner for only me and Pops, so we volunteer at the church, cooking and serving meals to those in need."

He stares at me as if I confuse him. "What about your friends? You don't spend it with them?"

I shake my head. "Sometimes Clover will join us at the church, but she didn't grow up with holidays, and any kind of organized religion makes her jumpy, so she really only goes to be with me, otherwise she likes to spend the day scaring herself silly with horror movies."

Those lines between his brows could rival Grey's. Speaking of Grey, I glance around the room and find him having an animated whisper-yell conversation with Savvy at the sound booth.

What the heck is wrong with those two?

Spinning back to Braxton, I suddenly understand his earlier confusion. "Oh, don't worry. I'll still make y'all a Thanksgiving dinner. That's no problem."

His nose crinkles. "You just y'all'd me."

"Huh?"

"You just said y'all. I think a little Southern sweetness has seeped into your bones, Miss Madison."

Why does that fluster me so much?

"But we don't exactly have a traditional Thanksgiving either."

"What do you do?" I ask.

His eyes soften, and the right side of his upper lip tilts up. "We order enough Mexican food to feed a family of ten, then gorge ourselves all day long while watching football. Well, that's if we weren't playing football."

"Mexican food, huh?" I cross my arms over my chest, drawing his gaze to my neckline.

He licks his lips, and I take a step forward.

"It sounds like we'll have a full house tonight." The worry creeps back into his features. "Do you think any of them will actually come? What college kid wants to hang out with a seventeen-year-old?"

"I do think so, yes," I say with conviction. "Those boys take their Friday night lights seriously, and they truly believe Sage can help. But also, I think a lot of those boys are only a year older than Sage. It's a young team, and from what I could tell, they were really having fun with him."

"He was...different," he admits. "With them."

"Kids do that when they're around their peers, I think. It's not necessarily a bad thing."

"I think you're right. It was just such a shock."

We're close enough to touch, but I don't reach out even though everything in my body is screaming at me to make a connection. "Doesn't he have any friends?" I ask to keep from throwing myself at him again.

Braxton drops his gaze to the floor, hiding his features from me. "He graduated high school so early, it's been difficult."

"I get that. Let's see how tonight plays out, huh?"

"And tomorrow, I'm taking you for that date."

That elicits heat to rise high in my cheeks. It's as though just the thought of a date with Braxton presses on all my pleasure buttons.

"Is that so?"

"Fact, Miss Madison. Now let's go grab Grey before Savvy knees him in the balls. Do you know what they're arguing about?"

"I have no idea. She said she only met him that night at the fundraiser, but I've never seen two people more at odds than them. He's fire, and she's the gasoline."

Braxton sighs heavily, then takes my hand for everyone in the room to see.

"Let's go keep our best friends from killing each other, and then go spy on Sage."

"What?" I laugh. "We're not going to spy on him."

"Oh, but we are. And you're going to help us."

I roll my eyes but allow him to tug me across the room.

Sometimes it's better to go with the flow than trying to walk upstream.

"WHERE THE HELL DID YOU FIND BINOCULARS?" GREY whispers to my left.

We're belly-down underneath the bleachers of the student section, trying to get close enough to see and hear what the boys are doing.

"If we get caught, I'm blaming the both of you," I whisper. "And I grabbed these from Moose's truck before we left. He always has an extra set."

"Do I even want to know?" Grey sighs.

"So, you're a thief, are you?" Braxton teases.

"I prefer habitual borrower, if you will. I'll give these back tomorrow."

"What are they saying?" Grey cuts right to the chase.

I lift up onto my elbows and peer over the top of the bottom bleacher. "I'm not a professional lip reader, but I'm proficient. It looks, well..."

"What? What is it?" Grey has no chill, so he also lifts onto his elbows, and when he finds Sage, he tilts his head like a dog about to get a treat.

"Fine, I'll look myself." Braxton mutters, pressing up next to me. Then he too peeks out through the metal bench.

Sage has a whistle around his neck and is standing next to Coach B. as the offensive line takes turns kicking a field goal.

"Don't they have a special teams coach for this?" Grey whispers.

"They did," I say. "But he went to our rivals over in Cheshire County."

"And that's how they lost next year's recruit. He followed the coach," Braxton guesses.

"Oh, yeah. And we play them in two weeks, so everyone in town will be fired up. They're already putting up signs everywhere."

"That's what all the *You Got Burned* signs are for?" Braxton asks.

"Yup. Wait until you see mine."

He stares at me as if for the first time. "I think I like this competitive side."

"Shh," Grey hisses. "They're coming this way. Get down."

All three of us fall face-first into the dirt.

"Practices are closed."

"Oh, crap," I whisper. "That's Coach B."

"We got some spies, Coach?" I can't place that voice, but then one voice melds into many and I know we're caught.

"Is it County?"

"Or maybe Kennesaw," someone else says.

"Show yourselves." That's Trevon's voice. At least he'll show us some mercy.

I blow out a harsh breath, then army-crawl backward until I can stand, and the guys follow me out. By the time we walk to the end of the bleachers, the entire team is standing there ready to kick our butts.

"Madison? What in the Sam Hill are you doing under there?" Coach B. bellows.

The three of us walk with our heads bowed.

"For fuck's sake," Coach mutters.

All three of us snap our heads up to find Sage brimming with glee from ear to freaking ear.

"Coach, you know Madi. These are my uncles I was telling you about."

Coach narrows his gaze. First at Braxton, then at Grey.

I'm shocked when Coach B. takes a step away from Grey because I've never seen that man back down from anything.

"Did you know this boy can kick a forty-yard field goal and make it nine times out of ten?"

"Professional players average at the thirty-five," Grey snaps. He really needs to work on his tone.

"I know. And he's here kicking forty-yarders in tennis shoes while my O-line can't hit the broad side of a barn."

"Let him walk on," someone in the back yells.

Grey and Braxton look at each other in shock.

"Excuse me?" Grey doesn't raise his voice, but he commands these players—maybe better than Coach B.

"He's already enrolled in community college, right? He hasn't officially dropped?" In all my years living in Happiness, I've never seen Coach B. rattled. But he is now.

"What's your point?" Poor Grey. His jaw is going to crack if he doesn't loosen up.

Braxton shifts so he stands between me and Grey, probably in case he has to hold back the angry bear.

"We have co-ops here at the university with a lot of community colleges. And it's football in the South—the school will make it happen."

"I'm sorry," Braxton says, holding up a hand. "What are you saying?"

"I want Sage enrolled at Happiness University, and I want him on my team."

I've been in this stadium hundreds of times, and never, not once, has silence been this loud.

BRAXTON

"Do you want to talk about it?" I ask, entering the room that Grey's using as an office.

"Nothing to talk about." He keeps his gaze firmly on the screen in front of him.

"Don't do that, Grey. We've been a team for over twenty years—that doesn't stop now."

Shutting the door behind me, I cross the room and sit in the small chair set up in front of his desk as though he'd actually have meetings in here. But I know two things to be true about Greyson—he's as loyal as they come, and he loves his routine.

"Did we fuck him up?" he blurts without looking at me.

The truth is, I've been asking myself the same question. Not because he dresses differently, or even because he sometimes wears eyeliner as a mask. But because we've always treated him as an equal.

"We were twelve when she died, Grey." He throws his pen across the room. "When he killed her."

"When he killed her," I agree. Once Violet began to show during her pregnancy, their father kept her locked in her room so no one would find out. *Image above all else* was his motto.

We used to sit outside her door and talk to her. My grandfather tried to get her removed from the home multiple times, but no one would believe us—even with all the wealth and connections my grandfather had, Mr. Wells had more.

That's when we learned that money can't buy everything.

We later found out that she had something called preeclampsia and went into labor early while we were at school. When we got home, we couldn't get the door down in time. Grey and I delivered Sage with the help of 911 while the ambulance was on the way, but Violet passed away en route to the hospital, and she would never tell us who the father was.

She was seventeen—the same age as Sage.

"We were kids playing house, Grey. Sure, we had nannies and Ace who supervised sometimes, but we were very clear from the beginning that Sage was our responsibility—we owed it to Vi. We did the best we could, and we've loved him every day of his life. We gave him the best of us at every step."

"He's seventeen." He coughs to hide his emotion.

"He is, and we all handled that birthday differently, but we're here, and he's been taking college classes for three years. He's going to be eighteen soon."

"He really wants this." Grey finally looks at me, and all the pain he's carrying shows in his expression. The guilt, the misplaced shame, the fear.

"I think so. He's never really asked us for anything, so that right there is telling."

"I know, but he spent all of eight hours with them. And

he's not conditioned. He's never even played a contact sport with guys that size."

"Greyson. You know kickers don't get tackled that often."

"But they do sometimes."

"They do...sometimes, and we can work with him. All those boys who showed up for dinner, they promised to work with him too."

After Coach B. pulled us out from the bleachers, which has circulated town more than once, two things became abundantly clear: they want Sage on the team, and Sage is ready to go to college.

"What happens when we leave, though? What's he going to do? Stay here with Pops?"

"He's at that age where most kids are going off to college anyway, and there are worse people he could count on while he's away."

I knew Grey would have a hard time letting go, but I didn't realize it would be this bad, so I don't tell him that this place feels like home for me too. The last thing I ever want my best friend to think or feel is that we're moving on without him.

He is and always will be my family.

"Is the way they're getting him enrolled partway through a semester even legal? What happens if we let him go and then he ends up getting removed from the school and the team?" He's grasping at straws, and by the deepening of his frown, he knows it.

"I have someone in Mr. Coop's firm looking into it."

"Why is this so hard?"

"Because letting him go, even when it's the right thing to do, is a reminder of who we've lost."

"Fuck me." He points an angry finger my way. "You need

to get the fuck away from Pops. You're sounding too much like him."

"He did say happiness is found here."

"Fucking happiness." He reclines in his office chair and stretches his arms over his head. "Life is changing, Brax."

"I know that's hard for you, but not all change is bad."

After Violet's death, he did everything in his power to keep things regulated, easy, safe. Sometimes I think that's why he gravitated toward football too—it was the only time he let his emotions loose.

He leans forward and places his forearms on his desk. "You really like Madi, don't you? I've never seen you this way before."

"I do, and I've never felt this way. Please, just give them a chance. Let them in, and let them see the person who held my head up and out of the toilet when I had Covid and was vomiting for days. The kid who kicked Larry Johnson's ass for pantsing me in PE class. The man who's stood by my side when I didn't know who to lean on."

"Who the fuck am I going to be if I'm not Sage's uncle?"

"You're a moron." I chuckle. "We'll always be his uncles, he'll always need his guardians, he just won't always need us holding his hand and protecting him. Jesus, Grey. The kid is nearing six foot four."

Finally, he laughs, and something unclenches in my stomach. My friend has been hiding behind spreadsheets and to-do lists for so long I'm afraid he won't be able to find his way out.

"But he's a scrawny thing. He'll break something if he gets tackled. He gets that from you," Grey deadpans.

"Not a chance. I'm one solid rock of muscle, my friend— what the kids call a snack."

He picks up a pad of paper and tosses it at my head.

"Nobody is saying we have to go home, Grey. If Sage is happy here—"

"And you're happy here," he interrupts.

"And if I'm happy here, don't you think it's worth a shot to see if we all could be happy here?"

"I am happy," he snarls, and I pointedly lift my brows. "I'll try. I have missed football."

"I know," I say sadly. "I wish you hadn't given that up for me."

Every scout in the country had picked Grey as the number one draft pick, but he skipped the draft that year to stand by my side at Omni-Reyes. We'd just received Ace's MS diagnosis, and my father started burning down innocent people's lives, so we walked away from football, college, everything, and we did it together, but I know it was harder for him than it was for me.

"It wasn't for you," he mutters. "Well, not only you. Whatever, it wasn't a choice. Family always comes first."

"Which is why I already turned in Sage's health forms."

"Asshole. You were that confident you could talk me into this?"

"No, I was that confident that you loved Sage enough to let him try."

He nods and wakes up his screen by aggressively shoving his mouse around. "I have work to do. Have fun on your date."

I stand to go. "You know, Madison has a lot of friends."

The sound that Grey emits is part disgust and part horror. "I've met her friends. I'll pass."

"Care to tell me what's going on between you and Savvy?"

"Who?"

"You know who. The tall brunette. What did she do to piss you off so badly?"

"Nothing. She made assumptions she shouldn't have. I don't care if she's pissed or angry. I really have no feelings toward her at all."

"I want Madison to be my girlfriend." My voice cracks as though I'm fifteen again.

Slowly, he lifts his head. "You've never had a girlfriend." He digs in his pocket and produces a coin.

"Neither have you," I throw back.

"At least I've gone on actual dates." He leans back in his chair and really studies me. "Are you asking for permission or for advice?"

"I— I don't know. It's just, it's a big step."

"Another change," he says, rolling the coin through his fingers. "You want a girlfriend, and Sage wants to join a football team."

It's almost as though saying it out loud makes him process it in a different way because his face relaxes as he mutters it again, this time to himself.

"Maybe change is what we need, Grey."

The line forms between his brows, but he doesn't disagree with me. "Maybe. Send Sage up on your way out, please. Maybe I'll take him out to dinner."

"What do you think about me and Madison?"

"I think it doesn't matter what anyone else thinks, Brax. This is something you have to do on your own. But if you want my opinion, I think she makes you happy. Now go before you're late. And send Sage up. I'm starving."

"Don't forget Pops."

"Oh, I would never," he says sarcastically.

I chuckle and enter the hallway as Madison exits her room. She stops short when she finds me.

I stalk her slowly, even though heat rolls through my veins faster than a Bugatti.

"You look beautiful," I whisper when I'm close enough that her light citrusy scent creates a Pavlovian response.

She juts a hip out to the side as she leans against the wall. "You haven't even looked at my outfit."

She's right. I fall into her cerulean-blue eyes every time she graces me with a glimpse.

"I don't need to." Lifting my hand, I rub one of her curls between my thumb and forefinger. It's so damn soft. "You always look beautiful."

"Charmer." She's shaking her head while staring up at me through long, thick lashes.

"I want to kiss you." The words mix with a rumble of desire in my chest.

"Yes. I mean, okay."

I love that I fluster her when I'm this close. "But I'm not going to, not yet."

"What?" She frowns. "Why not?"

"Because I'm taking you on a proper date, and a gentleman wouldn't kiss you until you've gotten to know him better. Are you ready to go?"

"You're really weird. We're basically living together. Oh, God. Not *living together*, living together. I mean you're staying in an inn that I live in. I think I've gotten to know you pretty well over the last couple of months."

Leaning in so we're sharing breath, I grin wide and carefree, then press my cheek against hers. "You want me to kiss you."

Her chest hitches, and heat warms my neck when she exhales.

"That's a dumb question." She shivers, and I love the feel of it against my skin.

"It wasn't a question, sunshine. You want me to kiss you, and I will, but I'm going to make you work for it."

She swallows, and I feel it everywhere.

I press my lips to her cheek and hold them there a beat longer than necessary before pulling away.

Madison's pupils have dilated, and her chest heaves. She's fucking perfect.

She stares up at me with her lips slightly parted, and I almost give in. I've never wanted anything as badly as I want to pin her to the wall and run my fingers and tongue over every inch of her body.

My dick agrees and twitches in my pants. It's my sign to back away, but even space won't be enough to ease the ache of wanting her.

"I'll see you in a few minutes," I say and step past her so I don't do what every molecule in my body is screaming at me to do.

"Wait," she calls after me, but I'm already halfway down the stairs. "Where are you going?"

"You'll see," I say without turning back.

Pops is sitting in his recliner in his favorite position— feet up, hands clasped behind his head, wearing a smile that probably matches my own.

And then he starts whistling.

Sage walks out of the kitchen with a slice of pizza that's bigger than his entire head.

"Hey, Grey wants to talk to you about dinner, he's upstairs."

Sage gives me a two-finger salute, crams half the pizza in his mouth, and walks up the stairs.

Teenagers.

"You too, Pops. Grey will be down in a bit to take you out, so you better behave."

"Pfft. I always do," he says while rolling his feet back and forth on the footrest. "I'm looking forward to going."

"I think Grey is too. I'll see you in a minute."

He nods, and I go out the front door.

Cian really came through for me today. After we finished pulling wallpaper from the third floor that looked as though it hadn't been used in a hundred years, he ran out to pick up flowers for me. They should be in my truck.

Opening the driver's side door, I find them beautifully wrapped and resting on a giant box of extra-small condoms.

There's no way I'm carrying these into the house, but if I leave them in the truck, Madison might see them, and that's not going to happen.

Picking them up, I spin in a circle, but the only thing I can find is the mailbox, so I jog over to it and shove them inside.

Do not forget to get them out before Pops does. That's the last thing I need.

Then, with the flowers in my hand, I walk up the front steps and ring the doorbell.

"Mads, that's for you." I hear Pops shout.

When I lean to the left, I find him waving at me through the window with both hands.

He is a loveable menace.

The door swings open, and Madison stands under the glow of the hallway light. I take her in as though it's the first time seeing her, and maybe it is, because what I see tonight is my future.

She bites her bottom lip and tilts her head as if she's thinking.

I pull the flowers from behind my back and hand them to her.

"Blue looks stunning on you, sunshine. It is definitely

your color." She's wearing a cornflower-blue form-fitting sweater dress that she's paired with ankle boots. Her jewelry is minimal, something so opposite of the women I've grown up around, and it makes me want her even more.

The small gold cross she wears highlights the slight dip in the neckline of her dress and matches the gold bracelets that jingle on her left wrist.

"I mean, you really are gorgeous."

The dimples on each side of her cheeks deepen, and she swings the door wide so I can enter.

Pops stands to the side holding a shotgun, and I about shit my pants.

"What the hell, Pops? What are you doing with a gun?"

His cheeks twitch as if he's holding back laughter. "Just what are your intentions with my granddaughter, young man?"

Young man? He didn't call me boy, or Braxton. It hits me then. He's playing a part—he's giving us both something we never had, and a wall of gratitude wells up inside me, even if I wish he'd put the fucking gun away.

"Her last beau never picked her up, never held the door. That jackass even made her pay. That no-good son of a trucker's hat with no cap—"

"Ah, Pops."

He peers over his shoulder at Madison.

"You're getting a little off-topic," she reminds him.

"Whoa. What the hell's this?" Grey asks from the stairs, attempting and failing to keep Sage behind him.

Pops points to me with the end of the shotgun. "I'm finding out what his intentions are with my granddaughter." He finishes his sentence with a sharp nod of his head, as though that's the end of the discussion.

"Oh, this is going to be good." Sage plants his ass on the stairs to watch.

"This is something I'd like to see too." Grey plops down on a stair just in front of Sage.

"Pops. Don't be ridiculous." Madi reaches for the door, but I take her hand in mine and turn toward her grandfather with her behind me.

He shrugs, pulls the trigger and a little flag shoots out that says *Pop!!!*

"You've got to be fucking kidding me." Grey chuckles. Sage sits just behind him with his chin in both hands, howling in laughter.

"Jesus, Pops." I rub my chest as though he shot me while everyone else laughs at my expense.

Whatever. Pops wants this, and I'm willing to play along.

"My intentions, sir, are to treat Madison with respect, get to know her when she isn't everyone's right hand, and then bring her home safely because I am a perfect gentleman."

Grey chokes and makes a rolling motion with his hand as if to continue, but his shoulders shake with laughter.

So what if perfect gentleman isn't exactly what I'd call my encounters with other women? Madison isn't other women.

She's mine.

As soon as I think it, I know it's true. I also know that I'll do whatever necessary to make it my reality.

"Fine. Fine," Pops says, tossing the toy gun onto the sofa. Then he makes an *I'm watching you* gesture with his fingers. "I've got eyes everywhere. Remember that."

Then he literally doubles over laughing. With one hand on his thigh, he slaps the other on his knee. "Go, have fun," he says in between fits of laughter.

Madison tugs on my arm and leads me back to the front

door. I'm not even sure when I started moving closer to the slightly unhinged man with a toy gun.

"Bye," she calls over her shoulder. Once I'm on the porch, she pulls the door shut with a loud snap. "Sorry.

"He does enjoy keeping things interesting." I laugh, and her shoulders relax. "Ready?"

"You didn't tell me where we're going."

Placing my palm on the small of her back, I guide her down the stairs and to my truck. "It's a surprise."

"Then you should know, I don't handle surprises very well."

"If you hate it, then we'll leave. Tonight is all about you."

I follow her into the truck, and my chest puffs up with pride when she slides to the middle seat. I may even strut as I round the hood and get in.

My hand skims her knee, and I gently squeeze it before turning the ignition. "I like you here."

"I like being here," she says softly. "Are you sure you don't want to tell me where we're going?"

"And ruin the surprise? Not a chance, sunshine. Not a chance."

26

MADISON

"You're taking me to Envy's Edge?" I ask, more confused than anything. "I'm not really dressed to sit out and watch the stars."

He peers over at me, drinking me in, and my entire body comes alive with pins and needles. "Do you trust me?"

Such a loaded question.

"Sure." I aim for casual, but when I shrug, my shoulders refuse to unlock from my ears. "As much as I can trust anyone I've only known for a couple of months."

I'm protecting my heart, but the truth is, I think I trust him as much as my best friends, and that has never happened before.

"Not anyone," he clarifies before taking the final turn that will lead us to the top of Envy's Edge. "Me. Trust me, Madison."

His tone is low and sultry and so dang velvety—the most decadent of chocolates—the forbidden fruit. And when he uses that voice on me, I want nothing more than to please him.

Please. Him. Like, what? Is that really the reaction he provokes in me?

Red flags flash—warning me of what happens when I dive too deep—but it's too late. I'm already in over my head with this man.

"I do trust you." The words barely kiss the air, but when his dimples flash, I know he heard me.

I'm so focused on staring at his profile—the strong jaw and perfectly straight nose—that I don't see what's ahead of us until the glow of the lights illuminate the interior of the truck.

"What's happening?" I ask.

Someone's constructed a fancy white party tent in the spot where we parked last time. Fairy lights twinkle from its ceiling, but I can't see what else is inside it. Sweat starts to trickle in very intimate areas, and it is not at all sexy.

"Tonight is all about you," he repeats, and when I angle my body toward his, he squeezes my knee again. "And I had a little help."

When his words register, I look out into what should be darkness, just as Elle, Savvy, and Cian slip out of the tent.

"Traitors," I hiss in the direction of my friends. "They told you."

"Only after many hundreds of text messages did your friends relent and give me clues as to what your perfect date would be."

"And you made it happen?"

This is not the action of a man who's leaving in a few months, but it's all so confusing because of course he's leaving. He has a life, and a company, and it's all in California.

"I did." He slides out of the truck, then turns to help me down.

It's such a small gesture, but so sweet, and he's not doing

it because Pops told him to. He's doing what he's done since he rolled into town—putting me first.

"Mads," Elle squeals, starts to move, then thinks better of it and waves me closer.

"Are you okay?" I ask.

"She'd be better if she'd let me be the one crawling around in there on my hands and knees. Sweet Mother of Mercy, she's trying to kill me, Mads. She is." Cian always has an accent, but there are certain times when it's so thick I struggle to understand him.

This is one of those times.

"Elle," I scold. "You're about to have a baby. You should've let someone else help."

"I'm the interior decorator, and this was a once-in-a-life-time chance." Elle groans. "I wasn't about to pass it up no matter what *Mr. I'm going to chain you to the bed until you have this kid so you don't hurt yourself* says."

"And what were you doing?"

Savvy kisses my cheek, then whispers, "That's for us to know, and you to find out."

"But..."

"Go," they all say. Cian's the loudest, probably because he wants to get Elle home, and I don't blame him.

A moment later, Cian's headlights blind me momentarily, then they cut through the darkness and are gone.

"He's going to be a really great dad."

"I bet he will be," Braxton says. "He's been very patient with Grey and me, and I promise you, that's no easy feat with what we've been working on."

A gust of air flips up the back of my dress, and I lower my arms to keep it down. It's much colder up here this time of year.

"Welcome to our first official date, Madison Ryan." He holds out his arm. "May I escort you inside?"

"Inside? Inside the tent?"

"Actually, it's called a miniature marquee tent, if you want to be specific, but yes."

"Braxton, what did you do?" I ask, just before he pulls back a heavy-looking flap and I get my first glimpse at what can only be described as magical.

I tentatively enter the space that glows from the fairy lights, and I can't decide where to look first. A small sofa I recognize from the third floor of the inn has been cleaned and is set against the back wall with a table in front of it holding a charcuterie board and two glasses of champagne.

In front of the coffee table is a large freestanding fireplace that must run on gas. It separates the sofa from the intimate dining table that's directly in front of me. It's set with the most beautiful peonies that make the entire space smell divine.

A tear slips free, and I quickly brush it away before turning my attention on Braxton.

"What did you do?" It's amazing that my voice only wobbled a little.

"I'm giving us a first date we'll never forget." He's calm, and his voice is soothing, but I sense him studying every reaction as though he's afraid I'll bolt at any second.

"But how?" I spin in a circle to really take it all in. Large crystal vases of peonies and white flowers I can't name decorate the corners, while the light reflects rainbows from the crystal all over the wide-planked wooden floor.

"Well, I had to get a permit, which meant I had to ask Pops, who took me to see Moose, who introduced me to his brother-in-law, who was able to get me a permit on short notice." He says it with a straight face, but I know he's dying to laugh.

"That sounds about right. Small-town living and all." I shrug playfully, all while trying to keep the well of emotion that's bubbling in my chest from opening a dam I can't control.

He pulls something from his pocket and taps it with his thumb. Cole Swindell plays quietly in the background.

"You said you were going to be my small town."

A freaking dining table at Envy's Edge inside a freaking miniature marquee tent. What is happening in my life?

"That was the song," I tease.

"But I accepted." He tosses what I know now to be a remote onto the dining table, never releasing my gaze as he stands before me. "Dinner won't be here for about an hour and a half."

"Someone else is coming up here?"

"Afraid to be seen with me?"

"What? Of course not. This is just... It's..."

"Worth it, and it's nothing less than you deserve."

"But this is over the top, Braxton. Please tell me you know I don't need all of this. I would've been happy with pub food over at the Firefly."

He walks in a circle around me, then wraps his arms around my shoulders and steps into my space, plastering my back to his front—it's my favorite place to be.

"That's exactly why I did it. You didn't expect anything from me, yet you give so much every day."

"Braxton." I attempt to pull away, but he holds me tighter. Just tight enough that I know he wants me to stay, but not so tight I couldn't get away if I wanted to. "I don't believe in tit for tat. If you did this because you felt you owed it, or Pops somehow guilted you into it..."

His entire body stiffens behind me, and I have my answer.

Dropping my chin to my chest, I allow my lashes to fall. "Pops talked you into this, didn't he?"

I'm expecting him to rush an explanation, to say it's not what it sounds like. What I'm not expecting are his lips on my neck, so when it happens, an indelicate moan slips through mine.

His tongue sneaks out to taste me, and my whole body sings for him. All the wants I never dared speak. All the needs that were never met. All the times I prayed that someone would just see me.

He's every desire I've never allowed.

I didn't think I deserved it.

But when he gently bites down on the tendon in the side of my neck, my knees buckle.

His arm bands around my waist, holding me up and pressing me more firmly into him, and another wanton moan crawls up my throat. His penis is hard, and it throbs through the fabric of our clothing.

If my butt were any form of actual measurement, I'd say he's big—really big, and so dang thick.

"I'm trying to be a gentleman here, sunshine. So if you have any doubt that I want to be anywhere other than here with you, think again. I wake up craving your voice. I go to bed replaying every single interaction I was lucky enough to have with you."

"But that doesn't mean you want—"

"What I want is you. All of you. Your mind, your heart, everything."

My hips roll, pressing me against his groin. My self-awareness has taken a dive off the deep end and has no intention of returning.

"Do you know I dream about being inside your tight little pussy every night while you sleep one wall away from me?"

"Oh, God."

Harry is my only other sexual partner, and he only ever grunted while rutting into me. This is...this is some next-level intimacy I've only ever read about.

"Pops didn't make any of this happen. I did because I wanted to. I want to be here, with you. I want you, just as you are." He steps forward, pushing my right leg to move with his because he doesn't release me. I'm a rag doll moving at his whim, and it's the most erotic thing I've ever experienced.

"Tell me, sunshine." He walks us around the table to the sofa, somehow turning on the fireplace as we go by. "Do you ever just...let go?"

An open-mouth kiss lands on that spot between my neck and shoulder, eliciting a rush of goosebumps to erupt down my arms.

Oh, crap. What was his question?

"Or hand over the reins?"

Right, letting go. Well, right now, I'm not having any trouble letting go of my words.

His teeth nip my earlobe as my shins touch the sofa.

"Do you ever let anyone take care of you?" His words are murmured against my skin. The heat of his breath, mingling with the damp trail his tongue leaves, is turning my insides to jelly.

With strength I appreciate and grace I wish I had, he lifts me with the arm banded at my waist and manages to maneuver us in one fell swoop so he's sitting on the sofa and I'm straddling him.

"O-oh." I whimper as he settles me over him with his large, callused hands on my thighs.

My dress has ridden up high on my legs to allow the spread of my knees, and now I'm acutely aware of his penis pressing against my core.

Cupping my face with the gentlest of touches, he asks, "Is this okay?"

"Wow." I glance down at where our bodies meet. "This is...this is way more intimate than at the dining table."

"And why I'm asking if this is okay. I don't have an agenda here, Madison. But I also desperately want you to know how much I want you, how much I value and treasure you. I don't do things I don't want to do. Period. Ever. Not anymore."

My body responds to his words with a nudge of my hips against the zipper of his jeans. His gaze narrows. It darkens and demands so deliciously I do it again because I want to see my carnal needs reflected in him.

His long fingers press into my hip bones. Strong. Commanding. Marking. He jerks me forward while lifting his hips. We meet at our most intimate spots, and stars dance behind my eyes.

"Tell me you understand."

"Understand what?" I gasp when he rocks me again, but this time he keeps up the motion. Back and forth, he drags me over his thickness, painfully, agonizingly slowly. God, it feels so good. So, so good.

"That I'm here, with you, because I want to be."

"Yes," I gasp when he thrusts up again. I don't think dry humping has ever been this sexy.

"Do you feel how hard my cock is, Madison?" He holds me still, but my body desperately wants to gyrate, to move, to feel.

"I feel it."

"Do you know that I only get this hard for you?"

My eyes roll, from his words but also the sensations that have my clit throbbing.

He sits forward and presses his lips right up against my ear. "I love when you roll your eyes in everyday life, sweetheart, it shows how strong you are. But if you roll your eyes in this situation again, I will spank you until you come."

My core convulses as if it's thrilled by the prospect of a grown freaking man tossing me over his lap, pulling down my panties, and spanking me to orgasm.

The first sparks of my release have panic worming its way into my mind.

Oh, God. I do like that idea.

His fingers squeeze into my sides one at a time, halting my movements, and I nearly cry out from the unfairness of it all.

"Your entire body shuddered at the idea of me spanking you." He growls. "Do you enjoy that?" He's gruff, and it takes me a moment to recognize the jealousy in his tone.

It does something messy to my heart. It's all kinds of dumb to get excited by someone being jealous, but when it's him and me, it's the best sensation in the world.

"I—I don't know." My voice sounds foreign. I'm not sure I'm even speaking English anymore.

"You don't know?" His habit of repeating my words is extremely annoying right now.

"Sex has never been all that...exciting before."

He pulls back to stare at me, and the fire in his expression scorches my soul.

"What do you mean, exciting?"

Oh Lord, please don't make me say it. "Can't we just

keep..." I attempt to move my hips, but he grips me harder, keeping me exactly where he wants me.

"My dirty talk turns you on, sunshine, but I want to hear your voice. I want to hear you. What do you mean it wasn't exciting?"

I've googled this before, so I know you can't actually die of embarrassment, but I'm one hundred percent sure I'm about to be the first case in the history of sex.

"Please," I whimper.

He moves me achingly slowly, the friction more of a tease than building toward a release now.

"I'll keep you moving as long as you keep talking."

"Evil," I moan. But heck yes, I'll talk because I want this more than the Moravian sugar cake sitting on the corner of the coffee table.

I want him.

"Talk," he commands, and the words bubble and burst in my head.

"I've only been with—with..."

"Him," he growls.

"Yes. And...and he wasn't really into—"

He slams his hips up, giving me a moment of friction that steals my words.

"Into what, sweetheart? Keep talking." One hand holds my neck from behind, his entire forearm pressing into my spine, while the other on my hip keeps the pace torturously slow.

"Foreplay. Positions. I don't know," I blurt in a rush. "It was always just missionary. He wasn't adventurous. At least not with me."

He bites down on my shoulder with that admission while simultaneously licking it better, and I drop my forehead to his chest.

"Madison." Lifting my head is akin to staring directly at the sun, but I do it, and he blinds me with the compassion and need dancing in his irises. "I very much want to be adventurous with you." He doesn't break eye contact, and it makes his words much more intense. "I want to find out your body's likes and your most secret fantasies. I want to explore and dive and fall into every inch of your body searching for your release."

He finally blinks, and I swallow hard.

"And then I want to do it all over again." A bead of sweat forms at his hairline, but it's the only indication that he's as sensitized to this situation as I am. "But if you're not ready for that, in general or with me, we can drink those glasses of champagne and go back to the plan."

"This wasn't the plan?" I sound disappointed, and his dimples make an appearance.

Our bodies move against each other, needy and so freaking good.

"It honestly was not, but plans can always be changed. You're in control here."

Biting my lip, I count to five, mostly so I don't pass out but also because I want to make sure I'm making this decision while I'm fully in control of my faculties.

Then I smile, and his chest stops moving—he's literally holding his breath—for me.

"I'm ready."

He moves my hips faster.

"Ready for what, sweetheart? Remember, I want to hear your words. I'm listening. I'll always listen."

His penis twitches in his pants, and my lashes drop to my cheeks. It's the only way to focus.

"I'm ready to be adventurous. With you. I want that with you."

The sound he emits at my declaration is more animal than human, and it makes me think he's hanging on by a thread too.

Suddenly both of his hands are cupping my face, holding it only inches from his own.

"This is not exactly a private area, and this is not how I envisioned our first time." His voice strains, and gravel roughens every word.

"You've thought about it?" The question tumbles from my lips as if I don't quite believe him.

"Fuck me, sunshine. You have no idea how much I've thought about this, but as I said, we are technically in public."

Again, my body shudders, and that darkness flashes amber and gold again—he felt it.

"That excites you."

How does he read me so completely?

"You excite me." It's not a lie. I'm scared he could talk me into just about anything and I'd barely put up a fight.

He slides me down his thighs, losing the friction my body is begging for.

"What are you doing?" Holy crap, was that me? I sound almost hysterical.

"We need a moment to cool down and think about this. I don't want you making a decision you'll regret later."

Is this guy for real? I'm literally on top of him, ready to strip naked and give him the piece of myself I hold onto most tightly, and he stops it? He stops us?

"I'm not turning you down, Madison." His voice cuts through whatever Cole is singing in the background. "I'm simply asking you to be sure." His Adam's apple bobs. Is he nervous? "I can't handle being someone you regret."

The tension that filled my core relaxes into something

much more meaningful. His words are what make this an easy decision, one I know I'll never regret.

"I won't regret you, Braxton. I want this, here, with you, away from the inn and our responsibilities. I want this to be about you and me."

He slides me forward, and I moan in relief.

"It will always be about you and me. There's simply no other way."

27

BRAXTON

Something snapped in me the second I had her in my lap.

It was an awakening and understanding that everything in my life has been done for the benefit of someone else. I've never taken something I wanted outside of my duty to my family. I've never even stopped to think about what I want outside of the Reyes name, the Montgomerys immoral compass, or what Grey, Sage, and I needed in the moment.

But Madison Ryan is who I want, who I need, and who I'll uproot my entire family for.

I wait for her to give me her final consent. Her cheeks are rosy, and I loved openly following that flush as it crept down toward her breasts without restraint.

I bet her nipples are aching, and I can't wait to give them all my attention.

"Please," she whimpers. I press my cheek to hers, inhaling deeply before allowing my hands to roam her beautiful body.

"Madison."

"Hmm," she murmurs as my finger draws a circle around her nipple through the cotton of her dress.

"Will you be my girlfriend?" Fuck me. That's not how I intended to ask her. Why the hell did I just spit it out that way, and now of all times? Jesus, I'm losing it. "Never mind. I'm pushing too fast, it's—"

Her silent laughter bounces her body against mine, and my cock deflates a bit. Being laughed at has that effect on a man.

How did I lose control of my mouth so stupidly?

"Why are you laughing?" I'm defensive, and my tone has her sitting up straighter and searching my face, while hers is crinkling in all the right places to tell me she's happy.

"We're about to have sex, and you stopped to ask if I'd be your girlfriend. It's the very last thing I expected." There's honesty in her expression, but there's still laughter in her voice.

"It's important. I'm not looking for a quick fuck here, sunshine. I want to date you, get to know you, and yes, I really want to fuck you, but I'll take the blue balls if that means I do this the right way with you."

Utter disbelief—that's what her expression says now. Fucking disbelief.

"You say that as if you're planning on staying," she says so quietly I read her lips to make sure I heard her correctly.

"I—I..." I fumble for words. "The truth is, I don't know what the future holds, but here, with you, I feel at home. I don't only want to explore your body, Madison. I want to explore your mind, our connection, this town. Can we just take this one step at a time?"

"Starting with me becoming your girlfriend?" The dimple on her right cheek attempts to make an appearance.

"Yes, starting with you becoming my girlfriend."

"I don't think people actually say boyfriend or girlfriend anymore. They say dating."

"No."

She blinks twice.

"No, because dating implies that there may be other people involved, and that is not happening."

The shimmering of her eyes would knock me to my ass if I weren't already sitting.

"Then I guess I'm your girlfriend."

Very slowly, I kiss the corner of her mouth, but not on the lips. I said I was going to make her work for this kiss, and I intend to do just that.

"Say it again." My hands continue to knead and squeeze the soft flesh of her breasts.

"I'm your girlfriend." She gasps when I pinch her nipples. "I'm your girlfriend, and I want to have sex with you right now."

I chuckle into her neck.

"Telling me what you want makes me so fucking hard. Give me more."

"Oh, please, Braxton. Please—I— When you talk so filthy, when you tell me what to do. It makes me feel...sexy and—and wanted."

Her admission locks a chain around my soul and tosses away the key.

Moving as one, I flip us so her back is flat on the sofa. "I didn't plan this very well. This fucking sofa is tiny."

"It's a loveseat," she says.

I glide my palms up her smooth legs around to the outside of her thighs and lift her dress as I go. I'm watching her closely for any sign that she doesn't want this, but she only bites her bottom lip until it turns white, so I climb higher.

"Then I suppose we should make love on it."

Her neck works to swallow, but her back arches when I reach the apex of her thighs.

"Oh, crap." Her hands come down to hold mine through the dress that's dangerously close to showing me heaven. "Ah, I wasn't expecting this, so I'm, how do you say this? Oh God, this is embarrassing. I didn't. I mean I haven't. I forgot to—"

"Are you trying to tell me you're au naturel down here?" I run my thumbs up the center of her panties and grind my teeth when I find them soaking wet.

"Mm-hmm." She nods frantically, and I groan into her open thighs.

"Sweetheart, I'll take you any way you want to give yourself to me."

Her little button nose scrunches up.

"Trust me, a little hair will not deter me."

She lies back down and flops an arm over her face. To prove my point, I press harder into her panties until my thumb enters her a nominal amount.

"Okay. Yes. Yes, go."

I keep my head lowered because she wouldn't appreciate the smirk on my face. Hooking my fingers into the waistband of her panties, I slide them down her legs.

She's wet. So fucking wet.

"Is that for me?"

She peeks out from under her arm, so I swipe my index finger through her folds. It comes away glistening.

"Is this for me?" I repeat, this time showing her how wet my finger is.

"You're dirty."

I stick the digit in my mouth and suck it clean.

"I can be a good man and a dirty one, but you're the only one who gets to meet dirty me." Kneeling between her legs is a bitch. My feet hang off the edge of the sofa, but I'll make it work. For her, I'll make everything work.

The first swipe of my tongue across her slit has me growling like a bear—a hungry bear.

Her hips lift off the sofa, so I pin them down with one hand while separating her pussy lips with the other, then I tilt my head from left to right. The hair where she shaves is only starting to come back. It grates against my skin and oddly makes my cock so fucking hard, more pre-cum stains my boxers.

It doesn't take long for me to learn her rhythm. She moans every time I flick her clit, and writhes when I dip my tongue in as deep as I can go. But it's when I pinch that bundle of nerves that I get the first ripples of her orgasm. She plucks her nipple with her thumb and forefinger, and I growl my approval into her flesh—it's so fucking sexy.

She's going to come too quickly, but when I peek up at her and desperation clouds her vision, I give in and tongue fuck her until she's begging me to stop and go and stop again.

Her legs tremble around my ears when I slip a finger into her, and she makes a garbled sound of ecstasy when my middle finger joins the first. Scissoring them, I open her for a third, then bite down on her sensitive nub, and she convulses around me.

It's an orgasm that infiltrates her entire body with quaking spasms while she oscillates between "Oh God, more" and "I can't."

Her hands fist in my hair, and I release her clit from my teeth, but my fingers keep working her. "Are you ready to work for that kiss?"

Her eyes are wide and glassy. Her mouth hangs open and she shakes her head no, then yes, then no again.

"You're going to give me another orgasm, and then I plan to fuck you so hard, you'll need me to carry you home."

Madison's legs quiver at my words, and she wraps them more tightly around my head.

"You're not really going to work all that hard, are you, baby?" I massage her clit and fuck her with my tongue. "You're going to give it to me, and I'm going to love it," I say into her pussy.

She screams loudly enough to wake the dead, and I silently hope no one is lurking around outside. That's a sound for my ears only.

I hold her still as she thrashes against me, her orgasm leaking all over my face. I drink her in. She's sweet like strawberry ice cream, and I can't get enough.

When something too close to a sob falls from her lips, I gently ease away from her pussy, pressing one last gentle kiss to her clit before crawling up her body.

She's gasping for air, and I watch it all as she comes back to earth. Those beautiful blue eyes are hazy as she blinks up at me with a slow, satisfied smile.

"I didn't know I could come from oral," she says in a dreamy state. But her words make me irrationally irate. Her fucking ex never appreciated her. I won't make that same mistake.

Lowering my hips, I press into her just to watch her lashes snap open.

"Was it too much, or are you ready for more?"

"There's more?" She looks so innocent that I almost feel guilty for the things I want to do to her.

Almost never won the girl though.

"Oh." I rut my pants-covered dick into her. "There's so much more. The question is, do you want it?" I'm grinding into her again—a fucking teenager, needing a release before I explode.

"I want it. I want it," she chants while running her hands down my chest to fumble with the button of my jeans. "You're wearing too many clothes."

I quickly scan my watch. There's no way I want the caterers to show up at the wrong time, but we still have forty-five minutes. My girl responded to my tongue like a motherfucking champion.

Rolling off her, I lift the dress over her head and place it on the dining chair, then unbutton my shirt as I'm walking back.

It's only a few steps, but she's already pressing her thighs together.

I shuck my shirt, and my shoes come next, followed by my pants and boxers.

"Holy shit," she curses. Have I ever heard her curse before? "You're veiny."

I stare down at my dick and wrap a hand around it. "I've never thought about that before, but I suppose you're right."

"And big. You're like the model for every romance novel ever written. You even have that weird V thing going on that I always read about."

Throwing my head back, I laugh. It's a full belly laugh, but my hand on my cock grips harder because I'm so close I'm willing to fuck my own hand. What would she think of that?

"Is this where you tell me you don't think it will fit?"

Her jaw comes unhinged, which might be useful another time, but not tonight.

"What?" I smirk. "Violet read a lot when we were kids. Grey and I got a very early introduction to romance novels that way."

"You're unlike anyone I've ever met before, but no. I know you're going to fit, and I'm ready. I'm so ready. Please don't make me wait."

I've never been a particularly kinky guy, but the way she begs makes me want to explore every single kink with her that I can dream up.

My right knee falls to the sofa, and I nudge her legs apart while slowly stroking my shaft. Her gaze follows my hand. When she licks her lips, I'm done for.

Dropping my cock, I use both hands to spread her wide before remembering a condom.

"Fuck. A condom."

"Thank you, Savvy." She giggles.

"Um, excuse me?"

"When she hugged me, she slipped a bunch of condoms into my jacket pocket."

I will never say a bad word about that woman ever. Moving with superhuman speed, I find her jacket tossed over the back of the chair and have the condom on before I'm back between her legs.

We don't speak as I move my hips and allow my cock to part her for me, the tip brushing against her clit with every pass.

"Please," she whimpers again, and this time, I don't hold back.

Entering her in one thrust is not an option. She's fucking tighter than I thought, and I don't want to hurt her. Slowly, I roll in and out, allowing her cum to lubricate my cock until finally, finally, I bottom out.

"Are you okay?" I ask through gritted teeth. Her small hands are braced on my forearms, her nails digging into my skin.

"Yes. Just..."

"What is it?" I ask against her lips. They instantly open for me, and my tongue sweeps the inside of her mouth. She's every treasure lost at sea, and I hold the map. "What do you need?" I ask, holding myself still inside of her, loving the heat and the way she grips me tighter than even my own fist.

"You said you were going to fuck me. I want that. I really want that."

The word *fuck* falling from her lips is such a turn-on, my hips lift and slam into her before I fully register what she's said.

"What about making love?"

"No." She moans as I pick up the pace. "This. This. I want this." Her words fall from her lips in staccato pants each time I pull out, and I'm hypnotized by the way her tits bounce when I slam back home.

"You like it a little rough, a little dirty."

She averts her gaze, so I lower my mouth to her ear, loving the reaction I get when my breath tickles her neck. "I'll let you in on a secret." She finally looks back at me, and her pussy clenches as I speak. "With you, I love it a whole lot dirty, and I'll go as hard as you want me to."

She nods, so I slide my hands under her ass, hooking my arms around her thighs and pulling her into me as I thrust.

The slapping of skin on skin, her sounds of pleasure, and my grunts of pure bliss mingle into a song I want to remember forever.

"I need you to come for me again. I want to feel you come on my cock."

I don't even get the words out before she explodes around me, clenching so hard my vision blurs before I fill her with my release.

I collapse on top of her, and she wraps her limbs around me as if she'll never let go.

And truthfully, I hope she never does.

28

———————

MADISON

"THREE TIMES?" CLOVER WHISPER-YELLS. SAVVY IS LEANING over me on my other side practically salivating.

This isn't a conversation I wanted to have at a college football game, but Clover was running late because she had to finish writing a letter to Valen, freaking Valen, who responds with excerpts of sonnets none of us understand, and since Savvy always drives, they both arrived just before kickoff.

We haven't had any other time to get together this week because Braxton and Pops have now roped Grey into their renovation projects and I've had to rush home for two minor injuries—both involving a nail gun. It got to the point that Blissy told me to just stay home Thursday and Friday to make sure no one lost a finger.

"Yes," I whisper back. The three of us have our heads together while the game and the crowd roar around us, but Braxton and Grey finally made a beer run that gave us a moment to catch up.

"Was it good?" Savvy asks.

"Better than good. I think my head exploded a couple of

times, and I left my body at least once. Why didn't you tell me sex could be—"

"Bow chicka bow wow," Savvy sings.

"Oh God," I mutter, dropping my face into my hands when Mr. and Mrs. Cross turn around in front of us. "Sorry. Ignore her. She's been cooped up in the house all week."

Mrs. Cross winks at me, and I officially wish for death by embarrassment.

"I mean, it's pretty romantic." Clover always has a dreamy quality to her tone, but now she has hearts in her eyeballs too. "I don't even know if he slept the night before. We were getting texts all night long with suggestions and questions and credit card numbers. By the way, you should tell him to never, ever do that again. Who just hands over a credit card number via text message?"

"Someone who's never had to worry about money, that's who." Savvy leans back in her seat and crosses her arms.

"Hey," Grey says, then holds a beer out to Clover.

Now Savvy's sudden attitude shift makes sense.

Just as Clover's reaching for it, Sunny, the team's giant smiling sunray mascot, bumps into Braxton with one of his outstretched sunbeams. It causes him to trip over our bags on the ground and fall into Grey, who still has a beer in each hand. When Grey lurches forward, beer spills from both cups and lands all over Savvy.

Braxton stands behind him, holding three beers while staring at the mess as if it's his fault.

Why couldn't this just be a normal outing?

Savvy stands slowly while Braxton steps in front of Grey, apologizing profusely.

"It's fine," she says, holding her pale yellow cropped sweatshirt away from her body.

"For fuck's sake," Grey says. "Take these." He hands

what's left of the beer to Clover, then wraps his giant fingers around Savvy's slender wrist and drags her behind him.

"Hey," she says, attempting to swat his hand away with her remaining free limb. "What are you doing?"

They're already three stairs up and away from us before he turns to her.

"The game is about to start, and I'm not going to miss it because everyone is scrambling to get you dry. Let's go."

Her wide gaze seeks mine, but all I have to offer is a shrug. I have no idea what the guy is up to.

Braxton places the beers in the cup holders, pulls out a giant wad of napkins from his back pocket, and begins wiping down the seats. "I'm so sorry," he says for the hundredth time.

"It was an accident," Clover says. "She wasn't mad. We've all done it."

He nods in thanks to my friend, drops the wet napkins to the ground, and takes a seat next to me.

"She's got to be a little pissed." He nudges my arm off the armrest, slips his arm underneath mine, clasps our hands, then places them in his lap. "I'll buy her a new outfit."

The band begins, and Clover startles in her seat with both arms shooting into the air, sending the popcorn she was holding in every direction.

Since these are our season ticket seats, everyone around us is used to her and simply brushes the popcorn away.

"See, we're all a little messy." I cuddle into his arm. I'm so at peace it makes me nervous for what's to come, but I'm determined to focus on the good today. Tomorrow is a worry for future me.

He chuckles and kisses the top of my head. A collective chorus of "Aw" breaks out around us, and Clover elbows me in the side, then points to the jumbo screen where we've caught the attention of the kiss camera.

What did I ever do to deserve being put on display when things are finally going right?

"It's a pretty big step." Braxton's mouth is at my ear. "What do you say, sunshine? Can I show them you're mine?"

I swore I would never belong to anyone ever again, but this man has a way of getting me to break every promise I've ever made to myself.

"Kiss, kiss, kiss" is the new chant around the stadium. A quick glance up tells me the camera is still on us.

"Does that mean you're mine too?"

"Well, you are my girlfriend, and I'm your boyfriend, so yeah. That's exactly what it means. But do you want all of them to know?"

He's slowly moving toward me. A hand in my hair. Turning my face. He's giving the crowd what they want while giving me the time to decide.

"Show them."

The instant the words leave my mouth, his lips crash into mine. By the noise around the stadium, you would think we'd just won the Happiness Cup.

When he pulls away, my body follows him, and my lungs burn with the need for oxygen.

"You literally suck the life from me when you kiss me that way. You're like a vampire kisser, or a—"

He kisses me again, but there's no applause this time—the camera has moved on.

This one is gentler, softer, loving. Then he holds my head with one hand so he can speak directly into my ear.

"The first kiss was a fucking kiss. This one was a love-making kiss. See the difference?"

I've officially turned into a live version bobblehead, and I'm so thankful I'm not on the jumbotron right now.

The coin flip is in our favor, and he squeezes my hand as they kick the ball to our opponent. The energy of this stadium is intoxicating, and for a few minutes, I get to pretend that we're a normal couple, living a simple life of college football and home renovations.

Truly, it's been my goal since I was a child—stability—and for the first time I remember, it feels as if it might be within reach.

The euphoria filling my mind is cleared quickly by Savvy's cutting voice.

"I didn't ask you to come with me." Her voice is so cold it could freeze hell with one syllable.

Clover has shifted seats to sit on Braxton's other side, so when Savvy enters the row, she's beside me and Grey takes the only one left—right next to her.

"Should we put a buffer between those two?" I ask Clover by leaning over Braxton's lap.

She lifts up in her seat to stare at them over our heads. When she sits back down, she shakes her head. "Nah, let them work it out."

"Good luck with that," Braxton huffs. "This is a side of Grey I've never seen."

I frown at Clover but sit back in my seat and watch them out of the corner of my eye. It's silent for all of thirty seconds.

"You hardly missed anything," Savvy says dismissively, then crosses her legs in the opposite direction of Grey, angling her body into my space.

"Half a quarter. It took you half a quarter to pick a goddamn sweatshirt." Grey grumbles. "And Sage is on the field."

"He's not playing," she snaps back.

They engage in some sort of glaring contest, but Savvy glances away first. I don't blame her. The blue fire that burns behind his eyes is kind of terrifying. But my best friend isn't one to back down from a challenge either, so this will be loads of fun today.

"Ignore them," Braxton whispers, tucking me into his side.

"I didn't get to see Sage before he left this morning. Was he nervous?" I ask.

Braxton shrugs one shoulder. "I don't think so. This kid did half a semester's worth of work in a week, so I don't think he's had time to be nervous. We're pretty sure he won't be active until next season anyway. Today is about getting a feel for the field and playing in front of this type of crowd. Plus, we're going to have to work him out pretty aggressively so he's ready to take these kinds of hits."

"He looks great in his jersey. Oh!" I bounce in my seat. "We all have to get jerseys with his name and number on the back."

He stares down at me, and if I weren't such a chicken, I'd allow myself to believe he's staring at me with love.

"He's releasing too soon," Grey shouts, which startles Clover again, but this time it's her Sour Patch Kids that go flying.

We learned early on not to get her anything wet or sticky at the games, and she takes large, intermittent gulps of her beer when she thinks it's safe—injury timeouts are her jam.

Grey jumps up. "He's releasing too fucking soon," he shouts again.

We're close enough to the field that if any of the coaches were paying attention, they'd probably hear him and want to kick him out of the stadium.

"Why the hell can't anyone see that? Who are the clowns coaching these kids?"

"Ah, so I take it he's competitive?" I murmur into Braxton's side.

"Football was his outlet growing up. He loves the game, but this is the first time I've seen him getting into it since he quit."

"What the hell?" Grey pulls on the ends of his hair. The man's going to give himself a heart attack before this game is over.

"If you know so much, why don't you march your ass right down there and have it out with the coaches?" Savvy taunts.

"Oh, shit," Braxton mutters.

Here comes another fiery standoff between the two of them.

"You don't think I know what I'm talking about?" The rumble in his voice rivals everyone in the stands stomping on the floor.

"I don't care if you do. That's not the point. You're sitting here complaining like an ex-pro reliving his glory days. If you know better than the coaches, do something about it."

"Savvy," I warn. "You know he can't just march onto the field."

"Fuck," Braxton curses.

Grey is on his feet again, but he's not looking at me or Braxton. No, he's still throwing that blue fire Savvy's way. And if I could see her expression, I know it would match his.

Grey leans into Savvy's space. She and I recline in reaction to the volcano of a man.

"Don't ever underestimate me, sweetheart."

The next thing I know, he's gone, and Savvy and I exhale as if we share lungs.

"He's going through...something," Braxton says with unease coating every word.

"'Through something'? You don't say." Savvy is all snark and acid today. "At least he's gone. Now can we watch some football please?"

I nod but keep an eye on her. She shakes out her hands like she's releasing tension, but I know she's not afraid of him. I have no idea what emotion he's pulling from her, and I'm not sure she does either.

"I'll speak to him," Braxton says on my other side. "Now, can we talk about something fun, like Thanksgiving?"

Clover snorts next to him, and even Savvy leans forward to glare at him.

"Fun?" He has to be joking.

"Yeah. Why not?"

"You forget that I'm volunteering at the church that day, and then Sunshine U's rival is playing that night."

He smirks as though I missed the joke. "Sounds fun to me. Grey and Sage will help too. What do you ladies have going on? How about we volunteer with Madison, then Grey and I will make dinner for everyone and we can watch the game on TV."

"You're going to make dinner?" Yup, I sound horrified because I am.

"I can follow a recipe when I don't have a seventy-year-old helper. Where is he today, anyway?"

"Scorekeeper's booth," Clover says with a mouthful of candy.

Braxton looks to me for explanation.

"He used to be the spotter for the announcer. You know, he'd watch jersey numbers and tell the announcer, but his eyesight is going, and they don't have the heart to kick him out, so he sits up there chatting everyone's ear off. It's a highlight for him."

Braxton's laughter fills me with such joy. "I should've guessed. I thought I heard his laugh over the sound system before the national anthem."

"Yup. That's—"

"How the hell did he get down there?" Savvy interrupts and points at.the field.

Grey marches across the turf as though he owns the place, and goes nose to nose with Coach B. From here, it appears that they're both shouting at each other.

"Gross," Clover says. "They're going to get spittle in each other's mouths if they keep shouting at each other that way."

It goes on for two full minutes with them both waving wildly, then just as quickly as it started, it stops, and Grey points to Ethan, then practically drags him to the medical tent.

"What's he doing?"

Braxton is relaxed and smiling, not at all bothered that his best friend just got into it with a college football coach.

"He's taking him into the medical tent. It's the only enclosed space on the field. It'll allow him to make adjustments to Ethan's arm without prying eyes on him."

"They've been in there a long time," I say after the other team gets a second down.

"He'll take every second available. Trust me, he knows the play clock, and he hears what's going on in the field. He'll get the kid out there when he's needed."

True to his word, three plays later, our defense intercepts the ball, and Ethan comes barreling out of the tent, while Grey saunters to the sidelines.

No one knows what to make of him, so they give him

wide berth as he stands there, rolling up the sleeves of his crisp white dress shirt.

"Does he know it's Saturday?"

"He always dresses that way unless he's working out," Braxton says.

The teams line up, and on the very first play, Ethan throws a forty-yard touchdown.

The jumbotron camera zooms in on Grey, but he's staring into the crowd, directly at Savvy, then he salutes her and walks off the field.

"Okay." I'm a little disoriented from that display.

"So, Thanksgiving will be fun, huh?" Braxton practically bounces in his seat as though he's never been happier and shoves a handful of popcorn into his mouth.

And that...

My thought is cut off when I spot Harry standing where the field meets the railing that leads to the spectator seating. His face is a mottled red, but that's nothing to the hatred I find in his expression.

Braxton's arm around me squeezes tighter, but I don't dare to look away from my ex. I've seen Harry this shade of angry before—when his body is one tense muscle that rattles violently to contain it.

"Ignore him," Braxton says with a kiss to the side of my head. Savvy squeezes my right hand in hers. I hadn't even felt her grip it.

I wish I could ignore him. I wish I could remove him from my life. But the reality is, I know deep in my bones that Harry will never let me go.

The first time I walked away from him, he ruined my life.

What will happen now that he's witness to me moving on?

29

BRAXTON

"Hey, Pops, guess what?" Sage asks, walking into the room with a large duffle bag slung over his shoulder. Today he's wearing his eyeliner again, and secretly I'm relieved. I don't want him changing himself to fit in.

If the people in his world can't accept him, then we're living in the wrong environment. He said the 'guys on the team' don't care, and so far, that seems to be the truth.

Kids are truly more tolerant in some ways than they were when I was young, but choosing a path that's different than the majority will never come without friction.

"What the hell's all over you?" he asks, pointing to me, Grey, and Cian.

We've just come down from the attic and are covered in dust and cobwebs. This place is a modern-day money pit from hell.

"What's that?" Pops responds to Sage's first question before any of us can answer his second. Pops is reclining in his chair again, as happy as I've ever seen him—I think he enjoys having a full house.

Sage spares a quick glance my way with mischief in his

gaze while inching closer to the front door. "Uncle Brax's been sleeping in Madi's room every night this week."

I take a step in his direction. I truly want to throttle my nephew, but he escapes out the front door, howling with laughter.

"That so?" Pops says, pressing the button to sit his recliner up.

"I guess we'll talk budget after practice," Grey says, backing up to follow Sage out the front door.

"I'm staying right here for this one," Cian chuckles.

"Did you think about Coach B.'s offer?" I ask Grey, attempting to divert Pops' attention.

"Grey." Pops leans forward in his chair. Maybe it actually worked. "You'll take the coaching job, least for the rest of the season. It'll be good for you, and you can keep an eye on our kid there—ya know, make sure no Harry Turds give him any trouble."

"Fuck," Grey curses. "I hadn't thought of that."

"Mm-hmm." Then Pops turns a stern glare my way. "And you. You been sleeping with my grandbaby?"

"Good luck," Grey calls over his shoulder. "That's for leaving that present on my desk." I try not to laugh as he shuffles out of the house, slamming the door on his way by. I guess he didn't find the box of extra-small condoms to be as funny as I did.

"Well, Pops. She is my girlfriend."

"That so? I don't remember you asking my permission."

Cian snorts but makes no move to save me.

"I thought I only had to ask permission for marriage."

"Well, what the hell you got a girlfriend for if you're not looking to marry her? Don't go fucking around with my grandbaby, boy. I don't care how friendly I was with your granddad, she's my priority."

"I'm not," I say with hands raised. I've never seen this fiery protective side of Pops before, but I knew it was in there.

"So you are lookin' to marry her then."

"I, well, we've only been dating for a week, Pops." Tugging on my collar, I have the urge to blow cool air down my shirt.

"When did you know you were going to marry Elle?"

Cian stands up straighter, suddenly not looking so pleased with his decision to stay for this conversation.

"You know how that went down, Pops." Cian's face flushes. At least I'm not the only one in the hot seat.

"When did ya know?"

Cian curses out the side of his mouth before looking right at me and saying, "I knew I'd marry her on our second date, but I was young and an idiot."

"I married Madi's grandma after three dates. You know when it's right. So I'm asking ya, is it right?"

I'm having a hard time swallowing, and it's hot as balls in here. Sweat gathers at the base of my neck, making me itchy. "I mean, it feels right." I scan the room, searching for a tissue and wondering if I can crack a window without being suspicious about it. "But I've never had a girlfriend before. We're taking it slow, I guess."

"And sleeping in her room is taking it slow?" Cian's smirk makes his eyes squinty, but I'm past being intimidated by him. The guy is as soft as a teddy bear.

I practically hiss in his direction. "You're supposed to be on my side here."

"Nah," he says flippantly. "We're all team Madi in this town."

"Good," I say. "She deserves to have everyone on her

side. But I think she wants to take things slow too. We're just...getting to know each other."

"By sleepin' in her room," Pops muses. At least his lips are starting to curl at the corners. "Well, are you giving the hatch a cover?"

This is one of those moments in my life when I feel the need to search for hidden cameras. "Ah, what?"

Cian chokes on a laugh.

"Rolling on the overalls." Pops is fucking with me. I can see it in his ruddy cheeks, but I have no clue what he's talking about. "Outfitting the old chap."

Heat spreads through my body as he directs weird rapid-fire words my way.

"Donning the safety suit." Cian howls.

"Suiting up the rooster." Pops' entire body is bouncing with each word.

"Loading the cannon cover."

My gaze jumps between these two fools when it hits me —they are fucking with me.

"Yes, I'm sheathing the sword," I growl.

"Dressing the pickle." Cian clutches his stomach at his own idiocy, and Pops finally breaks into a belly laugh.

"Securing...the...sausage...wrapper." Pops wheezes between each word.

I cross my arms over my chest, attempting to keep a straight face, but laughter is freaking contagious—especially his.

"Are you done?" I ask Cian because I'm fairly certain Pops could go on for days.

"Getting a glove for the love shove." Cian falls into a chair, swiping at tears on his cheeks.

"The love shove!" Pops cackles.

"Getting the goalie ready." I honestly didn't know Cian had this in him. "Okay, okay, stop. I can't breathe."

"Stop?" I ask, incredulously. "You're the one keeping it going."

The two of them blubber incoherent words with tear tracks staining their faces. It's quite the sight to see, but I can't get over the fact that Pops is asking me if I'm having safe sex—at thirty years old.

"Okay. I think we're good," Cian says when he's semi-composed.

"I'm so glad." The sarcasm in my tone does nothing to keep them in check.

"Well, boy. Are ya?" Jesus. He actually wants me to answer him.

"Yes, Pops. I'm using a condom. I always use a condom. Is that what you wanted to hear?"

"I should shoot you right in the ass for having sex in my house."

My jaw drops to the floor.

"But seein' as this ain't my house anymore, there's not much I can do 'bout it now, can I? But I'm watchin' you."

"I would expect nothing less," I say truthfully.

"Now don't go telling Madi I asked 'bout none of that. That's her business, not mine to go messing around in."

I'm fully dumbfounded. "Madi's sex life is her business, but my sex life is up for interrogation?"

"Damn straight, skippy. You ever tried to interrogate Madison?" The old man shivers with a shit-eating grin. "You're much easier to rile up."

Pinching the bridge of my nose, I pray for patience because dealing with Pops requires all the tolerance in the world.

"Can we get back to the inn now?" I ask. "We need to

insulate the attic and probably gut at least the entire third floor. Is that where we stand now?"

Cian nods. "Structurally, we're sound, but technically we still need the report from the engineer before we continue. Cosmetically, if you want to do it right, I think you need to gut the entire place and start over. Update the electrical and the HVAC, all of it."

"Right. Okay, but we can keep true to the original design in most cases, right? Madison loves this place the way it is. I want it to be safe, but I don't want to take away all the charm that makes it hers."

"That's probably a question for someone like Elle. Not Elle because her due date is quickly approaching, but you can work with an interior designer to keep the elements you want."

"Not me? Are you out of your damn mind?" Elle scolds from the front door. I hadn't heard her come in, but I can tell immediately that something's off.

She's gripping the doorframe so tightly her knuckles are white, and she's a little ashen. Did she walk over here? They're literally next door, but it's a hike through the field that connects the two properties.

"No one will be working in here but me, so stop trying to push me out, Cian."

He rushes to her side. "What's wrong?"

"Nothing, damn it. I have a bowling ball on my bladder. How does that sound to you?"

Pops, Cian, and I all grimace.

"Braxton." She says my name with the vehemence of a curse. "Don't you dare hire any other decorator. This job is mine. I've known Madi since we were nine years old. I know every dent and bump in this house because most of the time, I was the one getting into trouble with her, and I love this place as much as anyone."

I hold up both hands. "That's fine, Elle. The jobs yours."

"Good," she huffs. "And you," she says in a deep, guttural voice that's more demon than woman. "If I hear you trying to put me out of business again, you'll walk around with blue balls for a year. A year." She groans, and her knees tremble.

"Um, Elle? Are you in labor?" I ask.

"No, I'm not. It's too early, she's not due yet. And I think I'd know, and I'm not ready. I'm not ready. There's too much shit to do, and—"

We all glance down at the puddle that splashes to the floor beneath her.

"Holy shit. Your water broke." Cian spins in a circle with one hand on his head, so I move to Elle's side in case she falls over. "We practiced for this. I'm ready, you're ready. The bag is ready. Oh my God. The bag is at home. Did you bring the bag, Elle? Did you?"

"Yeah, Cian. I waddled my fat ass over here with a bowling ball trying to push out of a pea-sized hole with my delivery bag slung over my shoulder. No, I didn't bring the damn bag," she shouts. Her eyes fly open and stare me down while she grips my hand in a crushing hold.

"Contraction," I say. "Breathe, Elle. Breathe through it."

"You fucking breathe through a pinhole, you fucker," she says through clenched teeth.

"Hospital," Cian says, running out the front door.

"He's lost his mind," Pops says with a chuckle.

"Cian O'Brien, get your big ass back in here and help me," Elle shouts.

There's a clatter on the porch that sounds like him falling up the stairs, and then he's back in the doorway with both hands in his hair and sweat staining the front of his T-shirt.

"I'm going to be a da—a dad."

"Cian, if you don't get me to the hospital in time for an epidural, you'll be known as sperm donor for the rest of your life. I will teach this giant-headed baby to call you sperm donor. I swear it."

Flashbacks of Violet make my stomach heave. "Let's go," I demand. "Cian, pick her up and put her in my truck. I'll drive."

He doesn't bat an eye at following my directions.

Pops' hand lands on my forearm as I'm digging in my pocket for the keys. "It's different this time, Braxton. Elle has had prenatal care, and they're ready for this."

He knows about Grey's sister. It shouldn't shock me, but it does. I nod in response because my throat is itchy and I think I might throw up.

Thank God Grey wasn't here. I have no idea how he would react, but my gut says it wouldn't be good.

"I'll call Madi, you get them to the hospital." Pops nudges me toward the door, and I move on autopilot.

Elle will be fine.

She has to be.

She has to be because I can't go through this again—ever.

"Braxton?"

Madi rushes through the door with Pops in a wheelchair.

"What happened to him?"

She glances down at Pops, then back to me. "Nothing. I can move faster if I'm pushing him."

"She got in trouble for running twice," Pops tattles, but by the glint in his eye, I'd say he loved every minute of it.

"Is she okay?"

I nod, then shrug. The truth is, I don't know.

"I think so. Her doctor was ready for her when we got here, but I haven't heard anything since she and Cian got whisked away."

"Right. Okay, that's normal," she says, but her tone suggests her mind is elsewhere.

"Mads?" Savvy and Clover barrel into the waiting room, with Sage and Grey on their heels.

"We were finishing practice when Coach B. said Elle went into labor," Sage says quietly. "Savvy was teaching a class, and we found her in the parking lot trying to unlock her car."

"She couldn't drive that way," Grey grumbles. "So we picked up Clover on the way." His jaw is tight, and tension has him coiled up tighter than a rattlesnake.

The only pregnancy we've ever experienced ended in trauma neither of us ever truly recovered from.

"Are you okay?" I ask.

He nods sharply. "I spoke to your mom earlier. You need to call her."

The subject change gives me whiplash. Why would I call my mother, and now of all times?

"I fact-checked what she's saying, but the call is yours." My best friend's voice is cold, robotic, and I don't know how to help him.

This is not a situation I ever thought about, so I doubt he did either, but I know it's bringing up painful memories that are never far away.

Madison is sitting along the back wall with her best friends on either side, and Grey hands me his phone.

"It's time-sensitive, so you should go make the call now."

"What did she want?" I ask.

"There aren't enough beds or sleeping bags at the shelter, and it's so cold outside they'll freeze to death if they don't have a roof over their heads. She's asking you to help locate a larger space with more accommodations."

"That's...okay. We should do that, right?"

"Yes," Sage says. "We'll stay with Madi." He understands our pain and has his own, but there's excitement on his face too.

"Are you okay?" I ask him.

"Yes. They're having a baby. It's amazing. Think they'll let me babysit?"

Grey turns to him, confusion clear in his expression, but he quickly schools it. Sage has always been his priority. He'll bury whatever he needs to in order to support him. And if that means pretending to be happy about a new baby entering the fold, he'll do it.

I just don't know how long he can keep everything locked away like this.

"I'll just tell Madison," I say, squeezing both of their shoulders, then walking toward the three excited but nervous friends.

"I have to make a phone call. I'll be right back. Do you guys need anything?"

Madison looks surprised, but then she tilts her head, looks from me to Grey, and frowns.

"We're good. I just have to make a phone call," I tell her.

"Okay. We don't need anything." She opens her mouth to say more, but I lean down and kiss her before she can.

"I'll be right back."

"She'll be fine." Savvy looks to me with a little bit of wonder in her eyes. "Labor can take hours and hours. We'll be right here."

Hours? Really? Sage was born so quickly, I never stopped to ask if it was normal. Nothing about his birth was normal.

My head is a cloudy mess as I exit the hospital and find a bench to sit on, and an image of Madison with a large round belly nearly knocks me onto it.

I don't want kids. Do I? Does Madison? Is it too early for those kinds of thoughts?

What if she does want babies? Could I handle her being pregnant?

Grey's phone vibrates in my hand, and my mother's name flashes on the screen. Pushing everything to the back of my mind, I answer her call.

30

MADISON

It's after one in the morning before I make it home from the Chug, so I'm not expecting anyone to be up. But as soon as I open the door, Braxton sits upright on the sofa. His hair is sleep mussed, and he has lines on the side of his face from the pillow he was using.

"Hey." His voice is gruff, tired—he's been this way since we left the hospital a few days ago.

"What are you doing down here?"

"It's late." He looks at the clock on the wall. "I didn't mean to fall asleep. If you weren't home by eleven, I was going to head down to the Chug to wait for you."

Dropping my bag by the front door, I feel my shoulders relax as he crosses the room. "I'm a big girl, Braxton. I've been doing this a long time."

"I thought you were going to cut back since I rented all those rooms."

How do I tell him I'm planning for the future—a future I'm not certain he'll be around for?

"Tell me what you're thinking," he pleads. His hands

wrap around me and tug me into his chest. He smells of home, and safety, and all the things I shouldn't want from a man.

"Right now, I have a buffer," I admit. "But what happens in March? What happens next summer or next year? You never know what the future holds, I know that better than anyone, so I have to prepare for a time when I don't have..."

The truth is, ever since I held Elle's beautiful baby girl, Keela, in my arms, my own future has felt more fragile than I expected.

"When you don't have what?" He runs his hand in soothing motions up and down my spine.

You. When I don't have you. I wish I could say that. I wish I could tell him every fear in my head, but my fears have been used against me before, and I vowed to never put myself in that position again.

"When I don't have that buffer," I say instead.

He doesn't respond with words. But he takes me by the hand and leads me up the stairs and into my room. When he flips on the light, it takes a moment to adjust to the brightness, but when I blink the room into focus, my heart pinches. It's not only my room anymore—it's ours.

His sweatshirt is draped over the back of my chair, and the dress shoes he arrived in are lined up next to all the heels I hardly ever wear. There's an indent I know smells of him on the pillow on his side of the bed, and a laundry basket that contains both of our clothes.

Braxton shuts the door, then spins us so my back is to it. One hand cups my face as he kisses the side of my neck.

"Explain your buffer to me, sunshine."

It's hard to think when his lips and tongue dance across the pulse in my neck.

"We, ah, we don't know what the future holds."

His fingers work the buttons on the front of my blouse. "You see, to me, that sounds an awful lot like you're worried about what happens when my time is up here."

A giant boulder settles in my throat, and my stomach turns with unease.

When I don't answer, he bends his knees, putting his face in line with mine so all I can see is him.

He slides my shirt down my arms and tosses it into the laundry basket, then goes to work unbuttoning my jeans.

"The problem with that," he says, kissing a line down my center until he's on his knees. "Is that there are too many variables for me to tell you exactly what the future holds. I have to hear the reading of Ace's will, figure out what to do with my family, and how that all unfolds is anyone's guess."

He leans back on his heels and stares up at me. "But the one thing I can tell you is I have no plans to leave you behind. However things play out, I will find a way to make us work. I can't guarantee I'll be a good lifetime partner. I've never had a good example of it, but I can promise you I'll try. I can promise you that I feel more strongly for you than I've ever felt before. I'm falling in love with you, Madison, and that's not something I ever expected, so I'll need you to be patient with me."

"You're falling in love with me?" I stammer, disbelief making my voice wobbly and weak.

He holds his arms out wide. "Look at me. I think I might already be there."

Wait. Does that mean he loves me?

"You are?"

He nods, then continues to drag my jeans down my legs, lifting one foot at a time to remove them.

"I want to be your full-time buffer, Madison. But we have some obstacles to get through first."

"Like your mom?"

He told me the morning after Keela's birth that his mother called to ask for money. But the shocking thing was she wasn't asking for herself. She was asking for the women's shelter, and Grey corroborated that the account info she sent for the wire transfer was sent directly to the director and anything extra would be used for a Thanksgiving Day meal.

He nods against my legs. "She did a good deed, but I'm not sure that erases a lifetime of selfishness."

His hair tickles my thigh, so I run my fingers through it, massaging his scalp as I do, and he groans against my skin.

"I'm scared." As soon as I say it, regret slams into me. Harry ruined parts of me I haven't been able to heal—my confidence is one of them.

He lifts up onto his knees, and it puts his head right at my breasts.

"Of us?" he asks while emotion dampens my lashes.

Biting my lip, I nod, and a tear slips free. "Sorry, I'm just tired," I say, wiping away the errant liquid I hadn't wanted him to see.

He places a gentle kiss between my breasts but never breaks eye contact.

"I'm not going to leave you, Madison." Another kiss, a few inches higher as he lifts himself to his feet. "And I'm not going to hurt you." His lips land on my collarbone and he sucks hard enough to leave a mark.

"But your life is in California." Why am I arguing this? Am I really that much of a glutton for punishment?

Braxton's lips hover over mine. His breath is hot against

my skin, and his tongue darts out to lick at my mouth until I release my bottom lip from my teeth.

"But my heart is here." My head swims with his words.

His heart is here, with me. Emotions flood me, so many I can't grab hold of just one.

"No matter where life takes us, my heart will be wherever you are. I don't know how that works, or what we have to do, but I know in my soul that it's true."

I have no chance of stopping the tears now. I want to believe him. I want to believe in him, but there's a piece of me that holds back.

Will the trauma of my past always keep me from fully moving forward?

"I—I want to believe that. So much I want to believe you—in you."

"I know you do," he says, then kisses along my jaw from one side of my head to the other. "And I'm going to show you that you can, no matter how long that takes."

A choked sob gurgles in my throat, and before I can say anything, he lifts me in his arms and carries me to our bed.

Laying me down gently, he pulls back and removes his clothes. He doesn't bother turning off the light, so I see every hard line and sharp edge of his body, and his long, throbbing penis that bobs against his belly when he releases it from the confines of his underwear.

When he walks to the dresser and removes a box of condoms from the top drawer that he stashed there last week, my pussy clenches. That's something that never happened before him, and no matter how many times Braxton and I have sex, my longing for him only intensifies.

I lift up to my elbows as he walks back to the bed. Is there anything sexier than watching this man roll on a condom? It's not anything I've ever thought about before, but now I dream about it.

He's a fantasy come to life.

"No matter how many times I kiss you, I always want more." His whisper barely reaches my ears. "Do you have any idea how beautiful you are? Or how hard you make me? I never seem to get enough of you."

Braxton stands at the side of the bed fisting his hard penis with a condom wrapper in his other hand. When he brings it to his teeth to rip it open, I sit up and wrap my hand around his.

The groan that rumbles in his chest is all the encouragement I need.

Flopping onto my belly, I lick his tip. His hands fist in my hair, and I moan as he slides into my mouth.

Giving head has never been particularly enjoyable, but my panties are soaked at a simple taste of this man.

"Fuck, baby."

Stiffening my tongue, I drag it up the underside of his shaft as he pulls out and his thigh muscles clench beneath my hand—I want to make him come undone. Holding myself up with one arm, I use the other hand to grab the back of his leg and pull him to me until he reaches the back of my throat.

I fight the reflex to gag, breathe through my nose, and swallow him down.

"Jesus Christ." He grunts, holding the back of my head, pressing me into his groin, and I love every second of it. When he pulls out, he stares down at me with wide eyes and a sexual hunger that makes me feel powerful.

"You want me to fuck your face, beautiful?"

I nod shyly, trying to avoid looking directly at him, but he grabs my throat, not too roughly, but enough to keep my head up and focused on him, and I love it much more than I ever anticipated.

He blinks as if he's in awe, and that wave of power rushes straight to my core.

"You dirty, dirty girl. Open wide and keep your tongue out."

I do as he instructs, and he slips back down my throat. My insides are trembling. I'm so turned on my hips grind against the mattress, seeking relief I know will only come from him.

He moves in and out of my mouth quickly as drool drips from my chin. He gathers it and wipes it on the bed, then he reaches for the back of my bra and unhooks it with one hand.

Braxton slides his fingers down my spine and dips into the back of my panties. I nearly cry out when he dips a finger inside me, rolls it around to catch my wetness, and uses it to lube up my back entrance.

I slide forward to escape the pressure of his finger on my back hole, and it pushes his penis further down my throat.

His finger breaches my entrance, and I moan so gutturally around him that he hisses his pleasure before freeing himself from my mouth, but his finger never relents as he stretches me.

It's sensation overload. I wasn't expecting that to feel as good as it does. Oh, God. I might come from this alone.

"Has anyone had you here?" He slides his finger in deeper with the question.

"No." I exhale harshly and drop my forehead to the mattress.

"Does it feel good?" he asks, leaning his whole body over the top of mine and shoving my panties down. Imagining his gaze on his finger, I whimper into the mattress. It's all too much, but it still has me clenching around his finger as I push back against him.

I can't form words, but I don't have to—he feels how my body responds to him.

"You love it, and someday we'll explore this more, but right now, I want to feel your tight, wet pussy squirt all over my cock."

His dirty freaking mouth. My core spasms as he flips me onto my back and kisses me hard before retrieving the condom.

I don't want tonight to be gentle. I'm already on an emotional wire from his confession earlier. I can't take any more sweetness without dissolving into a puddle of emotions, so I lift to my hands and knees, then crawl backward until my feet hit the edge of the bed.

He grips my hips with the passion of a lover but the gentleness of a soulmate, and I gasp.

"You want it this way tonight?" he grits out. Is he angry?

"Yes," I moan when his tip glides through my wetness.

"You're hiding from me." He slips a hand around my hip to tap on my clit. It causes him to lean over me, his mouth at my ear. "But you should know, fucking this way is no less intimate, baby. If anything, it can be more so."

His penis enters me with one thrust, and it takes all my willpower not to scream out and wake everyone in this house.

I'm panting as my body gets used to the intrusion, but it's as though he's everywhere at once. In a move I can't comprehend, he lifts my upper body from the bed, holds my back to his front with a hand splayed over my collarbone, and his fingers trace along the column of my neck.

He squeezes, just once, and it heightens every sense.

"You see," he whispers into my ear. "All this does is allow me deeper, closer to you, feeling every reaction."

His hips piston in and out of me. With one hand holding me upright, he uses his other to strum across my swollen clit. I'm not going to last long.

He controls my body in this position, and I'm helpless to do anything but receive the pleasure only he can wring from me.

"Did I scare you when I said I've fallen in love with you?" he pants. The slap of our bodies colliding fills the air around us.

My core clenches, on the verge of an orgasm, and all I can offer is incoherent whispers that tumble from my lips like lava from a volcano—hot, deadly, and yielding to no one.

He bends his knees, then thrusts up while pulling me down onto him. We grunt in unison.

"I'm falling for you, Madison Ryan." His movements become as erratic as his fingers pinching and rubbing my clit. "And it's not because you make me come so hard I pass out, or because of what you do for me."

"Oh God. I'm going to—"

His fingers stop, and I whimper in response.

"Not yet. You can come after you listen." He's buried so deep inside me I feel him everywhere. "I'm falling for you because of who you are. Because of this giant heart you keep guarded behind layers of hurt. One day, I'll peel back all those layers, set fire to them, and see the pure love you hold beneath, because I love all of you." He grinds into me as if he can't help but move. "It may have taken me a while to realize what it was you brought out in me, but now that I know, I won't let it go unless you ask me to. Do you understand what I'm saying?"

Holy crap. Does he seriously expect an answer right now? My core is spasming around him. I'm so close to an orgasm that my body erupts in goosebumps and a sheen of perspiration. I can't hang over this edge much longer.

"Please," I cry. "Please make me come."

He chuckles darkly against my ear. "I'll always do as you ask, but I need you to answer me first."

Braxton doesn't play fair. He uses one long finger to trace my pussy up and down but never gives me the friction I desperately need.

"God you're so fucking perfect." He twitches inside me, and I shiver. "See how perfect we are together? Feel how we fit together? Your body is my playground, and I'll worship it as my altar. Is that what you want?"

"Yes. Yes. Yes," I chant. I'm saying yes to all of it and more. I have been holding back from him, but for what? "I don't want to hold back anymore." The admission comes from someplace deep in my chest. It barely registers as my own voice, but he takes me at my word and his body commands mine.

I come so hard, I lose control of myself. He cups a hand over my mouth to muffle my cries, and it makes me come harder.

The quivers in my body go on for what feels like eternity, and one orgasm swells into two as he falls on top of me, rutting into me from behind, my body pressing hard into the mattress, and he sticks his thumb in my mouth.

And then that thumb is entering my other hole, working in tandem with his penis, and I come so violently when this orgasm hits, I shake the bed.

I can't breathe, I can't think, I just feel as wave after wave of pleasure rolls through me.

He comes with a muted roar that vibrates through his

body and into mine, and then he collapses next to me, curling my body into his as we come down from this high in tandem.

It's when I take a deep, shuddering inhale that I know we might have a problem.

"Oh fuck," he says. When he nudges my body forward a few inches, I know he sees his cum slipping out of my entrance. "The condom broke."

31

———

BRAXTON

"It's fine. I'm fine. We're totally fine," Madison says in the shower. It's the third one she's taken since last night, so I know everything is not fine.

I got up this morning and drove an hour away to buy Plan B, only to remember that today is Thanksgiving and the twenty-four-hour pharmacy is running on limited hours. What if someone needed insulin or an EpiPen?

"Tomorrow is fine. It will be fine." She's still muttering to herself as steam billows out over the shower curtain.

She's spiraling and is anything but fine, so I strip down and step into the scalding water behind her.

"You can't burn my sperm away, sweetheart." I reach around her to adjust the temperature.

Her shoulders droop, and she hiccups. Fuck me, she's crying.

Spinning her to face me, she attempts to avert her gaze, but I see the tears mixing with the shower spray, and it guts me. I nearly crumple to the floor and beg for forgiveness even though we both know it was an accident.

Still, I blame fucking Pops for jinxing us with his talk about safe sex.

"The pharmacy in Hopevale opens at noon," I tell her. "I'll go as soon as it opens."

She drops her forehead to my chest. "They don't sell Plan B there. It's a family-owned pharmacy, and they refuse to sell it."

What kind of backward bullshit is that?

"I'll go back to the twenty-four-hour one tonight. They're open from two to eight."

"It's not that I don't want to be a mother." Her voice is so low the running water almost drowns it out. "But my mother isn't winning any parenting awards anytime soon. What if I'm bad at it?"

Now is not the time to tell her that the thought of being a father terrifies me to my very bones. But there's something about Madison questioning her own ability that twists the knife in my chest a little harder. She'd be an amazing mom.

"You could never be bad at it. You're too full of love." It's the truth, even if it confuses everything I thought I wanted after raising Sage.

But if we find out that she's pregnant, it's ultimately her decision, and I'll support her no matter what she decides.

She inhales deeply three times, then stands upright with a too-bright smile. "I'm sure it's fine." There's that fucking word again. Fine. It's a bullet to the nuts every time she says it. "I just had my period not that long ago." Her words gain strength, but the sadness in her expression tells a different story. "Women ovulate before their periods. It's totally going to be fine." Her smile turns the sunbeam down a few notches until it almost resembles her real one.

"No matter what happens, Madison, I am here for you,

for us." My gaze draws down to her stomach. Could my baby be inside her right now? The thought makes my mind spiral.

She turns away quickly. "Don't look at me like that."

"Like what?" I reach around her again to turn off the water. She was hiding in here, but it's time to face the day.

"Like the idea of me being pregnant terrifies you."

"I wouldn't be human if it didn't scare me at least a little. But let's not borrow trouble. There's no use in worrying about something that might not even be."

Wrapping a towel around her, I turn to retrieve one for myself.

"What if I don't want to take Plan B?" she whispers, but the words detonate explosions inside my body.

I take my time wrapping a towel around my waist before turning back to her. She's biting her bottom lip again, and I can practically feel the fear rolling off her.

What if she doesn't take it? I don't fucking know. Think, Braxton. Don't say something stupid—something you will definitely regret.

"If you don't want to take it, then we'll figure out all the right steps to keep you safe. I'm here to support you whatever you decide," I say with a confidence I don't feel. "You just have to tell me what you want, and I'll do whatever I can."

"I'm not saying I won't take it, it's just not something I ever thought I'd do." Tears stream down her face, and I know without her saying it that she feels alone, even though I'm right beside her. It cuts deeper than I would've expected.

Pulling her into my arms, I hold her tight. "Whatever you decide, I'll be by your side."

"But what do you want?" She sobs into my chest, and I drop my chin to the top of her head.

"I honestly don't know, sweetheart." It's the truth, but it makes her cry harder, and I feel like an asshole.

A sharp knock on the door has us both standing a little taller.

"Brax?" Grey calls through the door. "I've got an errand to run. I'll be back in a couple of hours, so I'll meet you guys at the church. The turkey is prepped and ready to go in the oven."

"Okay." It comes out crackly, so I clear my throat. "See you there."

He doesn't answer, so I know he's already gone.

"We'll get through this, okay? I promise you. I'm not going anywhere."

My mind is running a hundred different scenarios, but Madison needs me, and it makes my decision easy.

I want what she wants.

Whatever that ends up being.

***

GREY ENDED UP TAKING MUCH LONGER THAN HE EXPECTED, though I still have no idea where he ran off to. It left Sage and me to cook Thanksgiving dinner for everyone when we returned from serving lunch at the church. Luckily, everyone pitched in, so when he finally walks through the door at six o'clock, we're just sitting down to eat.

Madison sits to my right. Sage sits on my left with Pops at the head of the table. Then it's Clover and Savvy, and Grey heads up the other end.

"Nice of you to join us," Savvy says with a cluck of her tongue.

"Missed me, did you?" His voice is full of ice.

Clover sits across from us, staring at Madison's face, and when I look down, she's mouthing *I'm fine* to her friend.

She's put on a great show all day, but the tension around her is a force field keeping me at bay, and I hate it.

We all hold hands as Pops says a relatively normal grace, but when we break apart, I keep Madison's hand in mine under the table. She looks up at me with a watery gaze, and I wish I knew what the right thing to say was.

Since words aren't enough, I lean in and kiss her cheek at the same time as I squeeze her hand.

Thankfully, Sage and Pops keep the conversation flowing. They talk about everything and nothing, but I don't think Madison hears any of it. She smiles at all the right times and answers direct questions, but she's lost to her fears where I can't reach her.

After all the plates have been passed around, I sit back in my chair, taking in my surroundings in a different way—a new way—a family way.

Friends laugh and talk. Savvy and Grey bicker on one end of the table, while Clover and Sage debate who will win the Sunshine Bowl next season.

This is family. My skin prickles as though I'm being watched, and when I scan the room, I meet Grey's gaze. He seems a little lost. Is he experiencing this the same way I am?

When the forks are set down, the conversation keeps going around and around, but Madison stands with her plate in her hands, causing everyone to look up at her.

"Um, I'll just start clearing the table, for, ah, dessert," she says, not really looking at anyone.

Grey stands so suddenly that his chair scrapes against the floor. "I'll help you."

Savvy frowns, and I start to rise too, but Grey holds out a

hand. "Stay," he says. "I'll help. I missed the rest, and Madi can show me what to do."

I nod, even as a sense of unease makes my neck prickle. I'm hating myself a little that two of the most important people in my life are struggling, and I have no idea how to help them.

Madison and I decided I'd leave right after dessert, when everyone's in a food coma and too tired to question me. She must've decided to take the medication that would terminate a pregnancy before it had a chance to start.

My knuckles dig into my chest. There's an unbearable ache there, and it feels like a loss, but that's ridiculous. I can't mourn something that never happened, something I don't even know for sure that I wanted.

But as she stands to go with Grey following closely behind, I know it is.

I wanted that baby.

I want a family, my family, all of them, and I want it all with Madison.

***

"ARE YOU OKAY?" MADISON ASKS, CLOSING THE BEDROOM door behind her.

I'd made an excuse of needing to pick up a prescription my doctor called in, and only Grey knew I was lying, but he didn't call me on it as I made my way upstairs to get my keys.

"Yeah, I'm fine. Are you okay?"

She scans my face, and I know she's reading all the mixed emotions in my expression, but I can't shut her out—and I don't want to.

Madison nods, then pulls the desk drawer open and

holds up a package that clearly says Plan B, and my fist digs into my chest again.

"Where—"

"Grey heard us at some point last night, or probably me crying this morning. He drove all over today to find this. He gave it to me in the kitchen after dinner."

Fucking Grey. I should've known. Solving problems is his only love language.

"I'm sorry if he overstepped..."

She places a hand over mine, and I follow her to sit on the edge of the bed.

"He did it because he loves you and kind of tolerates me." She looks up at me with a smile that's so sad my heart cracks in two. "His words, not mine. He also said he thinks you'd make a really great dad."

My throat closes, but it's for the best. I can't influence her —it has to be her decision.

"He loves you." She squeezes my hand, but I can't tear my gaze away from the package in her hand.

"We're family." I guess it's explanation enough because she nods.

We sit in silence for a long moment. And just when I'm about to ask her what she's thinking, Sage knocks on the door.

"Uncle Brax? Braxton?" His knocking is incessant and so unlike him, I stand abruptly while Madison shoves the box under her pillow.

Opening the door, I find Sage shifting from foot to foot and Grey taking the stairs two at a time, and my gut sinks.

Somehow, I know they're going to deliver bad news.

"What's wrong?"

Madison places a hand in the center of my back, and I immediately tuck her under my arm.

"Well, I've been doing something I shouldn't," Sage says. He's squirrely and won't look directly at me.

"What is it, Sage?" Madison's always so gentle with him.

"I've been kind of cyberstalking his family." Madison stiffens in my arms. "You know, to make sure they're not trying to do something shitty to you."

"We talked about that, Sage." I focus on him instead of what he's found when the bad feeling rotting in my gut intensifies.

"Tell him," Grey says. His hands are in his pockets, which means this is serious. He always hides his fists when he can't compose himself.

"Okay, so your dad not only spread lies about Archie. He's also trying to get the school that Anastasia is working at shut down, but he's blaming her for it, and as far as I can tell, she's actually invested in the kids there. And she's been staying with a single dad whose kid goes to the school. That was shocking, but a completely other story. And now there was a fire on the farm where Archie is, and he's been arrested for arson, but we both know that's not his style. Plus, rumor around that small town in Maine is that he's getting cozy with the widow and the kid."

"What are you saying?" I ask.

"It all points back to Alistair Montgomery. At least the money trail does."

Madison sways on her feet, and I want to kill my father for an entirely different reason. She's got so much on her mind already, the last thing she needs is to hear about a narcissist on a war path.

"M—Montgomery?" she stutters. I flash a worried glance at Grey, who nods toward the bed, so I guide her into the room and sit with her in my lap.

"That's my father," I tell her. "He's always been evil, but I had no idea he'd go to these lengths."

Her body trembles, and I look at Grey as if he can help, but he shrugs and looks as panicked as I feel.

"It's okay, though," Sage says. "I hacked into his personal computer so we can stop him before he comes here."

"Here?" Madison scrambles to get free of my hold.

"Fuck. This is too much. Can I meet you guys downstairs in a few minutes?"

Sage stares at Madison with confusion and sadness.

"Yes," Grey says, taking Sage by the arm.

"I'm sorry, Madi. I didn't mean to upset you." The worry in Sage's voice makes my anger hit new levels.

I'm so fucking tired of my own father ruining every good thing in my life.

"You didn't," she manages to console him just before Grey shuts the door.

"Madison, talk to me."

Her chin is trembling, and I think I can actually hear her teeth chatter. "No, sorry. I'm fine. Really. It's all just, it's a lot." She reaches under her pillow and pulls out the box—it's the final dagger to my heart that only just learned to beat. "Honestly, go do what you have to do. It sounds serious, and I'd like to be alone for a bit anyway." She waves the box in the air, and the pit in my stomach expands painfully.

"Right. Yeah. I'll come back up as soon as I can, okay?"

"Actually, I—I think I should be alone tonight." She stares at the floor as the world crashes down around us.

"Are you sure?" I choke out. "Madison, I meant it when I said I'm here for you, okay?"

"I know. I'm... It's been a long day. I'm tired. I'll see you in the morning, all right?"

I nod even though she doesn't see it.

"Can I at least hug you before I go?"

She nods, but she's shivering, and I know she's crying before I touch her.

"It's okay. We will be okay." My words do nothing to console her. And when I leave her room that night, it's with the awful fear that once morning comes, nothing will be the same.

32

MADISON

"You know they're coming back," Sage says. He's been following me around the inn all day. He's worse than a dog with a bone.

It's only been a week since Braxton and Grey returned to California to sort out whatever messes his father caused, though my heart says it's been much longer than that.

He calls multiple times a day, but I don't know how to tell him that it was his father who helped ruin my life. The fact that they can't locate him is what keeps the fear flowing through my bloodstream faster than cyanide.

"Madi," Savvy calls from somewhere in the house. "We know you're here, and we came with boxes, but you're also not getting rid of us, so show yourself now."

"Please," Clover adds. "Elle is on FaceTime too."

"Ugh," I groan, then immediately the guilt hits because I haven't been to see Elle or her baby all week and she's having a horribly difficult time getting around.

Her birthing story scared the hell out of me. Why didn't anyone ever tell us that you could potentially tear from belly button to butthole? I might be exaggerating, slightly, but still, it feels like something we should know.

"What did you expect? You've been avoiding them all week too." Sage tsks. I do love the kid, but sometimes I want to tell him to mind his own dang business.

"I'm not avoiding anyone. Your uncle dropped a bomb that we have to move into a rental house so he can get three crews in here to gut the place. And he never even consulted me."

Sage shrugs as if it's no big deal. "He wanted it done as quickly as possible."

I swallow a spiky ball of emotion that cuts with jagged edges of glass going down. Does he want it done quickly for us, or is he just trying to get the hell out of here as fast as he can?

He hasn't asked me specifically if I took the pill, but he reminds me every day that he supports me.

Why hasn't he asked? *Why haven't I offered up the information?*

"There you are," Savvy says. "You know, he hired movers to pack up all this stuff and put it in storage for you." She drops the flat boxes in her hands to the floor.

"Say hi to Elle." Clover shoves the phone in my face.

"Just because I can't be there helping doesn't mean I'm not helping." Elle holds up a piece of paper that has tears welling quickly. "It's the kitchen. And it will look exactly like this by the time we're done."

She's kept everything that made that room feel reminiscent of my grandmother, and it's overwhelming. All of this is overwhelming.

"Sage," Pops calls from downstairs. "Come help me."

Sage looks from me to the door. He's been my shadow since his uncles left, and I can't tell if it's because he's worried about me or them, but I give him a reassuring nod, and he hustles out of the room.

Savvy shuts and locks the door behind him. "Spill it," she demands.

I don't want to lie to my friends, but I don't know how to share all of this either.

"Mads, don't make me come over there," Elle says.

"You're not going anywhere, woman. You've got stitches holding your hoo-ha together," Cian growls from somewhere behind the camera.

"Out," she demands. Cian drops his face into view and gives me a scolding glare.

"Listen to what she says, Madi. I mean it. She's not getting out of this bed."

I nod, then crumple to the ground.

"Aw, feck, Mads. Do I gotta kill him? I was just getting used to the fecker."

I laugh, and snot forms at the tip of my nose. "No," I say, wiping it away with my sleeve. "He's fine."

"Uh-huh. Fine. I know what that means. I'm married, remember?" He kisses Elle's forehead, takes the baby, and exits the frame.

"Spill, Madi. What's going on?" Elle uses her best mom voice on me, and I crack.

I tell them about the broken condom and about the Plan B. But it's explaining that it was Braxton's father that published all those lies about me that stuns the room to silence.

It's Savvy who pulls herself together first. "Okay, I need to repeat this out loud because it's not computing in my head. When Harry Balls drove drunk into that tree and shattered his collarbone in three places, then told everyone that you were driving when you weren't even in the state." She stands and paces the room, not unlike her archenemy Grey. "You're telling me that the person he fed those lies to in an attempt to save himself, his scholarship, and his football career was Braxton's dad?"

I nod. The tears are coming so fast I can't keep my face wiped dry.

"And it's his dad who owns the Whisperloop that was doing those shitty exposés blaming all the college girl-friends for the professional football players' bad decisions."

I nod again.

"The same man who got sued by you and fourteen other young women?"

"I think we're all on the same page here, Sav." Clover approaches me as you would a caged animal, and I cry harder.

"Oh my God," Elle murmurs. "Do you think that's how Pops met Ace? He did start coming around after the trial ended."

"He was always so worried about you." Savvy's still pacing, and it's making me dizzy. "That also explains why Pops would allow him to come here. He must have been keeping an eye on you. Pops even said Montgomery's father-in-law gave a character statement condemning him—Ace befriended Pops at the trial."

Suddenly it all makes sense. Why Ace was so willing to help Pops with the inn. Why Ace sent Braxton here. It's all some way of easing their guilty consciences.

"Do you think Braxton knew?" Clover's words carry a hint of anger that I wasn't expecting, but I'm so lost in the question I don't give her tone much thought.

"I—I don't know. I don't know anything anymore."

"Are you sure about this?" The sadness in Pops' expression rips my wounds wide open, but I'm too hurt and betrayed to trust any of my instincts right now.

If Pops kept this from me, I know he thought he was doing what's right, but my trust in everyone is hanging on by a thread, and I need to sort through my feelings before I address any of it. And I can't do that here, where everyone is watching my every move as though I'm some fragile doll.

Moving into Clover's guestroom, even temporarily, will give me time to think, and maybe to grieve something that may not have been real.

"I'm sure." My voice wavers, and I blink back tears. "You and Sage will be fine here in the rental until they get back. I just need some time to think is all."

He searches my face, but eventually relents. It's good because I can't back down—I won't. Not this time. Not when I don't know who to trust or what my truth is anymore.

Somewhere along the way, I lost myself in little boxes made by other people. It's time I found myself and my voice again.

"He won't like it," Pops warns. "I don't either."

"My vote is also a big fat nay," Sage says from his slumped position on the porch steps.

"No one has to like it, but they do have to respect it. I just need time."

"I get it." Pops sullenly crosses his arms over his chest. "I wish you'd just tell me why. I can't fix what I don't know is broken."

My smile feels dim, but I plaster it on anyway. "This isn't for you to fix, Pops. I love you. It's not as if I'm skipping town. I simply need some time to sort through what's on my mind."

"Promise you'll come home." His voice cracks, and it's

almost enough to make me put my needs aside, but that's what I've been doing my entire life. I can't do that anymore. Not if I want to have a future, or any kind of life worth living.

"I promise," I say to appease him. "Regardless of what happens, you're my grandfather, and I'll always be here for you."

His frown deepens, and it's mixed with pain I'm only now coming to understand.

"I'm still working at the Chug," Sage says, as if I'd take that away from him.

"Good. I'm glad."

"They're coming home tomorrow, you know." Sage, for once, sounds his age, but I know it's fear that's making him snarky. "Are we not supposed to tell Uncle Braxton where you are?"

"No, Sage. I'd never ask you to lie for me."

His face lights up with devilish intent that tugs on the strings of every emotion I'm attempting to sort through. "But we don't have to make it easy for him either. Whatever he did, I know he'll fix it though. You know that, right?"

"I know he'll try. I'll see you guys soon. Sage, don't let Pops cook anything. Pops, don't corrupt Sage."

They both stare at me with matching expressions of confusion and sadness, but for my own sanity, I close my eyes and count to ten, and when I open them, I walk away.

"Sweetie," Clover says through my closed door. Well, it's her door. I've confiscated her guest room.

I hear it creak open, and I bury my face under the pillows. I have no idea what time it is because I knocked the clock to the floor two days ago, or was it three days ago?

The edge of the bed dips, then she pulls the pillow away and brushes my dirty hair off my face.

"He's sitting in his truck in the driveway."

I don't ask who. I know it's Braxton. He's been here every day this week.

"You have to talk to him eventually. Savvy said he's losing his mind with worry, and you're not returning anyone's phone calls."

It's true. The second I fell into this room, memories swam up from the darkness, trying to drown me. It doesn't help that since the moment I met Braxton, he's felt like my one true match.

I've gone years avoiding the feelings from long ago. I'd gotten to a place of numbness, and then as soon as Braxton entered my life, making me feel and live and laugh, the pain of betrayal came crashing back too.

I guess that's the risk of allowing love in—pain finds a way in too.

Is it fair to blame him? No. But it was his father who pushed me into a depression so deep the only way to survive was to shut out everything that hurt me, and I have nowhere else to push that blame at the moment.

"Madison," he bellows from downstairs. I sit upright and glare at Clover. She never, ever leaves her door unlocked. She's too scared of everything that moves to do it, so when I hear his voice getting closer, I know she unlocked it for him.

"Sorry," she says sheepishly while backing up to the door. "You need to talk to him. The guy hasn't slept since he got home."

I frown. I wasn't expecting him to make himself sick. When I said I needed space, it was so I could figure myself out.

A quick glance at my four-day-old pajamas makes me wince. I haven't been adulting very well.

"I know you're in there. And I know you needed space. But you have to talk to me, sweetheart. I have no idea what I did wrong, but fuck, I'll do whatever it takes to make it right. Is it because I left?" His voice fades before coming close again. "We talked about that. I thought we were on the same page." He sounds...broken, and my stomach tightens. "We've given Ace's attorney all the information he'll need that ties Alistair to the fire in Maine. We should have a case against him by the time he turns up."

"Just talk to him, Mads. Maybe he didn't know either, but you won't know until you talk to him."

"But what if this was all a game, some way to make up for the mistakes of his father? What if all he wants is Ace's company and he can't get it without making up for what happened to me?"

"What if what he wants is you? Talk to him." There's a command in her tone we almost never hear. "He's here, and he wants to talk to you—do you know what a gift that is? Ask him whatever you need to know, but for fuck's sake, talk to him."

Shock has me gaping at my best friend. She's never this assertive.

"Madison." He bangs on the bedroom door, and I give Clover silent permission to open it.

When she does, light filters in, blinding me. I've lived with the shades closed for too many days to count.

Finally, my eyes adjust, and Braxton fills the doorway. Exhaustion shows in every tight muscle on his face. He looks as pained as I feel.

"Sunshine." He says it reverently, sweetly, as though he feared he'd never say it again.

He enters the room, closes the door behind him, and cracks the blinds open so he can see without turning on the overhead light. Then he falls to his knees beside the bed.

"Talk to me. What happened? Is it because I rented the house without talking to you? Is it because I left? I've been running through every worst-case scenario, and each one is worse than the last, but it's the not knowing that's slowly killing me."

I'm exhausted. I've been in bed for days, but sleep has eluded me, and now, with him in arms reach, I know why—I need him.

"I didn't take the pill," I blurt, then snap my lips shut, but once it's out in the open, there's no taking it back, and the emotions I've been blocking exit in a rush of words and explanations that I'm not even sure make sense.

"And it was your dad who sent camera crews here for weeks and weeks. They camped out on the sidewalk outside of our house. My field hockey team in Charleston asked me not to return because I was a distraction and a danger to the other girls. Then I lost my scholarship because I wasn't on the team anymore, and the cameras kept coming. They flashed every time we opened the door. They shouted horrible things to me and all my neighbors. They told lies and would talk in circles until even I wasn't sure what the truth was anymore.

"I begged Montgomery Media to leave me alone, and they laughed in my face. Our stories were getting clicks, and I was famous for a bunch of lies. No one wanted to hear that I wasn't even in town when Harry crashed his car. He made himself a victim, and his lies kept spiraling, saying I tried to trap him into marriage and—"

Braxton stops my tirade with a firm kiss that makes me sob harder, but it also halts my word vomit from continuing.

"When was the last time you slept?"

I frown and stare at him. Is he freaking serious right now? I tell him that his dad's scheming and lies almost broke me, and he asks if I've slept.

"Did you hear me?" I ask instead. "About the pill or your dad and Harry. Any of it?"

"I heard you," he says, kicking off his tennis shoes. "When was the last time you slept?" he asks again.

My mouth opens and closes as he uses two hands to slide my body to the middle of the bed, then climbs in beside me.

"Madison," he says, pulling me down and into his arms.

"Ah, sleep has been hard." The words are garbled through a yawn.

"That's what I thought." He kisses the back of my head, but my lashes are already growing heavy. "We'll talk after you've had some sleep."

I'd love to argue. I should argue, but my mind is already slipping into unconsciousness.

I blink, wanting to explain, but the room is cloaked in darkness.

"Hi," he whispers.

"How long have I been asleep?"

He lifts his arm from my belly and his watch illuminates with the time. "About twelve hours."

Alarmed, I attempt to sit up, but he holds me to him— my head resting over the comforting beat of his heart.

"Twelve hours? I've been asleep for twelve hours? Have you been here the whole time?"

"Clover brought me some water and aspirin a few hours ago, but you'd need a team of Navy SEALs to get me out of this room while you were passed out."

"I'm sorry, you should have—"

"Madison," he interrupts, his voice sharp, carrying an edge of fear. "The last time I left you alone in a bedroom, you disappeared from my life. If you think I would risk that happening a second time, you've lost your damn mind. I belong wherever you are. If that's not what you want, I'll go, but I'll never be far away, not until we've worked out all this shit."

"But—"

"Damn it, Madison. I told you I loved you. Do you think that's a throwaway phrase for me? Do you think I'd say that if I didn't feel every ounce of emotion that those three little words carry?"

"You're angry."

He has a right to be, doesn't he? But so do I. The fears of what he knew or didn't know bubble to the surface, reminding me to protect what's left of my broken soul.

His long exhale blows the hair around the back of my head. "I'm not angry. I'm terrified that I've lost you and I don't even know why. I deserve to know, don't I?"

The muscles in his forearms flex. They're a steel band around my middle, so I feel his sharp intake of air.

"You were one of the fifteen," he says. "You brought the class action suit against Montgomery Media and donated all the winnings to an anti-bullying nonprofit."

I nod, but it's a monumental task that instantly zaps my energy.

"Ace was at the trial to ensure you all won your case, so you think I knew what my father did." Sadness bleeds from his words.

"I don't know what to think." My voice is raw and thick.

His arm falls away, and he stares up at the ceiling. I hate that I instantly feel untethered and lost.

"And you didn't trust me enough to ask. I noticed that

you didn't say I love you in return, but I thought you at least trusted me."

"I did. I do. I—"

"You don't, Madison, or we wouldn't be here in your best friend's guest room."

My pulse races, and blood whooshes in my ears. I suck in a deep breath, then another, but I don't feel like I'm getting any oxygen.

The light on the nightstand flickers to life.

"Breathe. Deep breaths, in and out slowly." Braxton cradles my cheeks in his large, callused hands. He blocks out everything so all I can focus on is his face—his breathing—his voice.

In this moment, we share air as if we're one, because that's how he makes me feel. I feel whole when I'm with him, and I feel loved.

"Why didn't you take the pill?" He doesn't release my face, and I know why. He wants honesty. He deserves honesty.

"I—I don't know. I just couldn't do it. If we made a baby, I—"

"Will you keep it?" His voice cracks, and he clears his throat. "If you're pregnant, will you keep it?"

What kind of question is that? "Of course I'll keep it."

He releases the tension that was crinkling the corner of his eyes, even as his gaze darts back and forth, reading between the lines I've drawn.

"I didn't know."

I slow blink. Didn't know what?

"About my father. I didn't know. I mean, I did know—"

I try to pull away, my stomach churning with bile.

"No, listen. I knew after the fact what he had done, but not that it was you specifically. You and those other girls are the reason Grey and I left school to work at Omni-Reyes our senior year. We knew we had to stop him and that Ace wouldn't be around forever. We learned as much as we could in a short amount of time so he could retire and handle his bad days in private. But the number one motivator for me was to be in a position to stop Montgomery Media from ever harassing people that way again."

Tears fall down my face and over his hands that still hold me tight.

"What he did to you and the others, that wasn't okay. Ace didn't know it was happening until it was too late."

"That's why he sent you here? To make it right?"

His expression darkens, and I feel as though I've lost him somehow.

"I don't know why he sent me here, but I know why I'm here, in this room with you. I know why I chose to sit outside this house for the last three days, driving myself mad worrying I'd never get a chance to fight for you. I'm here, with you, because it's where I want to be."

"For how long though?"

This is what it all boils down to—my fear that he'll leave me at the end of this.

"Sweetheart." His voice cracks again, and you can't fake the pain clouding his face. "I'm here for as long as you'll have me. Where we'll live, and how we'll do it? Those are all details we'll figure out as we go. I just want you."

A new fear bubbles in my chest. "And, what if...what if I'm pregnant?"

"If you're pregnant, I'll learn how to build the best damn crib I can find."

My stomach plummets even as a small bubble of hope builds in the back of my mind. "You're not scared?" How can he not be scared?

"Oh, baby, I'm fucking terrified. I'd never thought about having kids of my own until that condom broke. But I also know that I love you, and if we're meant to have a baby, I'll love him or her because they're a piece of us."

Relief hits me hard, and exhaustion makes me weepy.

"I was so afraid you'd be mad. I—I don't know if I want to be a mom, and I didn't know if this was real. It was all just so much—"

"So much that you felt as though you had to hide," he finishes for me.

I nod, but I don't allow the shame to creep in. I was doing the best I could, and I'm not going to apologize for that anymore.

"But also, the more I've thought about it." Anxiety rattles my ribcage. "The more I realize Pops must've known. He was at the trial every day. That must be where he met Ace."

"I'm sure it was. Ace went every day to ensure Alistair didn't win. There wasn't much else he could do because Alistair owned Montgomery Media until the day Ace passed away."

I nod while thoughts fly through my mind. "I couldn't go, I was terrified of the cameras. And I couldn't stomach seeing your father, knowing it had all been a sick experiment for him to see if he could manipulate the world on his whim. He exploited young women—girls who were barely out of high school, and whose only crime was loving someone who may or may not play professional sports."

"That's how he targeted all of you. I never read the details, but I know that much. It's why we shut down all our offices on the East Coast during the trial—Ace refused to inflict more pain, even unintentionally."

When he stares at me, it's as though he's staring straight into my soul. "He will never do this to anyone else. I promise you that. Grey and I were already cutting him out of Omni-Reyes, and we're shutting down Montgomery Media, but he will pay for what he's done to you."

I don't have a response for that, so I stay silent.

"Come home, please. Let me take care of you. I need you close so I can protect you whenever he comes after me. I can't have you here on your own."

"How do you know he's coming?" A shiver works its way through my body.

His sigh could knock over the entire house. "Because he's already gone after everyone else, and because I hold all the cards now. Also, because Grey and I control all the finances, so he has nothing to lose."

"Braxton, I don't know if I can go through that again."

"I won't ask you to. But please come home while Grey and I come up with a plan. I haven't slept in days, and as much as I love Clover for taking care of you, this full-size bed isn't going to cut it."

He points to where his feet hang off the end of the bed, and a snort escapes, followed by laughter that feels so good I could cry, again.

"Is that a yes?" he asks.

"Yes. I'll come home."

"Thank, fuck. Let's go." He lifts me from the bed as if I weigh nothing.

"Right now?"

"Ah," he glances around the room. "Is there a reason we shouldn't go right now?"

"I'll have to talk to Pops."

"You have to talk to him anyway, sweetheart. The old guy has a broken spirit. He's barely left the sofa since you left," he says, gently placing me on my feet.

Guilt is a sneaky little jerk sometimes, but even if he did

lie to me, I know deep in my bones it's because he thought it was best for me.

"Okay. I should tell Clover though," I say, slipping my feet into a pair of UGGs.

"Heard ya. Love ya," Clover calls from behind the door.

"Clover," I say, wrenching open the door. She and Savvy had their ears pressed to it, and neither one of them has an ounce of shame over being caught.

"We had to make sure he was treating you right," Clover says in a huff.

"We were ready to bust in there if you needed us," Savvy adds. "But happy to see it all worked out. I'm going home. I'll see y'all tomorrow."

She sashays down the hallway. Clover shrugs and follows us to the front door where she envelops me in a giant hug. "Love you."

"Love you too," I say. "Thank you. For everything."

"Always." Then she hugs Braxton too. "Do not let anything happen to her."

"I swear on my life," he says.

"Ew, don't do that." She makes the sign of the cross, then scratches at the air. "I don't know why I did that. I'm not Catholic, but I don't know how to ward off bad juju, so take it back."

He chuckles, but takes it back, then leads me outside, where we wait for Clover to engage all three locks, and then he takes us home to our rental, knowing another shoe will drop, but this time we'll attempt to catch it together.

33

———

BRAXTON

Cinnamon fills the air as Blissy walks around the room holding warm cookies under everyone's noses. It's one week before Christmas, and the Chug is as busy as I've ever seen it.

"Why are there so many fucking people here?" Grey grumbles, echoing my thoughts.

"Christmas is as big around here as anything." Blissy drops a cookie and a napkin onto Grey's desk. "But this is the first week folks are allowed to plan their booths for the Cozy Cup Festival."

"The what now?" Sage asks, handing Grey his third cup of coffee in the last two hours.

"Maybe you should cool it with the coffee." Grey's eye twitches at my comment. "How the hell do you sleep with this much caffeine in your system this late in the day?"

"Don't worry about it."

"I'm slipping him some decaf when he isn't looking," Sage whispers.

Grey's long pointer finger shoots out in Sage's direction. "Don't do it."

Sage grins but winks at me, and I know he's one hundred percent messing with Grey's caffeine intake. He also loves working here. He's become a social butterfly in town, and everyone genuinely seems to care about him.

"Now, tell me all about this Cozy Cup Festival." Sage leans in and rubs his hands together as if he's about to get the best gossip known to man.

"It takes place after New Year's, but we spend the week after Christmas getting ready, and every business in town has a booth. We mix them up, so all the tea drinkers aren't on one side of the park and coffee drinkers on the other. It started as a way to bring people together, but it's turned cutthroat in recent years. Everyone's divided these days," Blissy laments and Grey goes back to working on his computer. "Maybe you boys'll be the ones to bring everyone together again."

"Us?" I ask, pointing to me and Grey.

"Yeah, you," she says with a scoff. "What other boys am I talking to?"

"I don't own a business here," Grey complains.

"No, but this one does," she says, pointing to me. "And it's all-hands-on-deck for this event, so you're in it to win it, Greyson. It'll be good for ya anyway. Rumor 'round town says you're the neighborhood grinch, and no one likes a grinch."

"I'm the grinch?" Grey actually sounds offended. "I've hardly talked to anyone. How can I be the grinch?"

She shrugs. "Well, it's not hard next to this one here." Again, she points to me.

"I have a name, Blissy."

"Yeah, it's Santa Claus. Don't think I didn't hear about the donation made to that church you were serving food at with Madi. You have to stop handing out checks with your name on them if you don't want to be identified."

She clucks her tongue and walks away as if I'm the neighborhood idiot.

"Just how many donations have you made this week?" Greyson asks in a low voice.

I roll my eyes, but because he's probably already checked the account, I say, "I made another to the shelter and the school where my mother and sister are. I paid to rebuild the barn that burned down in Maine. I made one to the theater group in town—they're trying to restore the old theater on Main Street. That was just good business."

"And?" he says with a smirk. He knows me too damn well.

"And I filled the bin at the fire station with new toys, bought a hundred turkeys to be delivered by the food bank, plucked all the wishes from the wishing tree at town hall and bought everything on them, and went to the superintendent of schools who found a list of kids who might not have Santa visit and I bought a bunch of shit for their parents to dole out however they saw fit. You happy now?"

"I am." He sits back with a smug expression. "Are you?"

"You know I am."

"It shows."

"Good."

"I'm not trying to fight with you, Braxton. You look happy, and I'm happy for you, but we have a little problem."

He has my full attention. "What's that?"

"Your dad hasn't shown up at the elder care facility for almost a week. Mr. Coop called this morning to let me know."

"Fuck me. He's coming for us, isn't he?"

Grey doesn't have to answer me. We both know it's a

certainty. The only unknown is when he'll arrive and what kind of bomb he'll drop on us.

The front door opens, and I glance over to see Madison standing in the doorway, sadness filling her expression.

She shakes her head, just once, and my stomach hollows out—she's not pregnant.

"Shit," Grey curses beside me.

He's the only other person who knew we were waiting for...something.

I'm not prepared for the wave of sadness that washes over me. Am I mourning a child that never existed?

"You fell in love with the idea of the baby, Brax. By the looks of her, she did too. Go, get her out of here, and I'll look into Alistair, then start researching this...festival."

I barely register his words as I stand and walk toward her. My legs are heavy—weighed down by regret and an aching sense of nothingness.

Grey's right. I wanted there to be a baby.

"Are you okay?" I whisper when she tucks her face into my chest.

"I don't know. How can I be relieved and sad at the same time? It doesn't make sense."

"It does though. To me, it does." She tilts her head up to search my face, and I know the instant she finds the same warring emotions in my expression. Her lips fall into a frown, and she nods.

"It was too soon anyway." She's trying to talk away her feelings, so I don't push, but she needs to understand that they're valid too. Whatever she's feeling is valid.

"It doesn't make it hurt less though. Someday..." I can't get the rest of my words out.

"Someday," she agrees.

Together, we stand in an embrace, surrounded by people but lost to our own world.

"I love you." I mentally count seconds every time I say those words.

She nods but doesn't pull away. "I love you too."

Her declaration knocks the air from my lungs. I'm still replaying it when a voice I don't care to ever hear cuts into my joy.

"Isn't that sweet," Harry snarls. "You know, I figured out who you are."

Greyson steps to my side and takes Madison from my arms. Today is not the day for her to fight her own battles.

As soon as I know he has her out of harm's way, I turn to this asshole, fully aware that everyone in the Chug is watching.

"Couldn't have been too hard to figure out, since I never hid who I was."

"And you're okay with that, Mads? You love someone whose family put you on blast for months on end?"

I step into his space, anger boiling in my veins. "Alistair may have been the one to print it, but he was publishing your lies, your betrayal. As far as I can tell, you're the only shit stain in the building, and I'll be damned if I allow you to disrespect my fiancée in any way."

"Oh, shit," Sage mutters. "You're kind of supposed to ask her before you publicly claim her."

"Fiancée? You're going to marry this fucker? Do you even know who his family is? They'll ruin you, Mads. You don't belong in that world."

I take a step to the left, blocking his view of Madison.

"And what? You think she deserves you? All you've done is hurt her. If anything, I'm the one who doesn't fit in her world, not the other way around. But the difference between you and me, Harry, is that I'll give up my whole fucking world just to spin in her orbit while you only try to drag her down to make yourself feel better. You're not a man, Harry. You're a fucking sleazeball who never deserved her."

"Hell yeah," Blissy shouts, and people around us clap and cheer. It's fucking weird. It's like we're in some shitty reality television show, but I don't care how much mud I have to sling. His will never touch Madison.

"You have no idea what I'm capable of," he hisses, the stench of cheap whiskey and cigarettes clinging to his breath.

"I'm sure we'll find out. Now I'm going to ask you to leave, and if you ever set foot in here again, we'll get a restraining order against you."

"Madi," he bellows. "You don't want to do this. You don't want to choose his side."

"Go to hell, Harry." She doesn't shout it, there's no venom in it. Her tone is flat, indifferent, and I know first-hand how much harder apathy hits. "I'm done listening to your sob stories. I'm done being your punching bag. I'm just done with you."

"You'll regret this," he shouts, pointing to everyone in the room.

The door opens behind him, and Cian stands there, his face turning red. "The one time I bring my girls out, and this is what I gotta deal with?"

Harry turns toward Cian's voice. At least he has the good sense to shuffle back a step.

"Out. Harry. Now." Elle stands behind Cian, holding the baby, and just the flash of Pepto-Bismol pink makes my chest squeeze.

When I turn to check on Madison, she's gone. Grey

points toward the office, and I don't waste one more second on the oxygen thief.

Madison is my priority.

She'll always be my priority.

I find her in the closet, of all places. She's rearranging paper and boxes only to put them right back where they started.

"Madison," I say from the doorway. She doesn't turn around.

"I'm fine. I'll be out in a minute, I'm looking for... something."

I enter the room and softly close the door, then meet her at the closet. Wrapping my arms around her from behind, I trap her arms at her sides and hold her.

"I'm not jealous of Elle," she says shakily.

"I know."

"It just caught me off guard."

"I know that too."

"How can I feel so happy for someone else but also so sad for something I'm not even sure I wanted?"

"I don't know, but I get it. I do. I had that instant ache in my chest when I saw the flash of pink, but my sadness doesn't distract from my happiness for them. It's just life, sweetheart."

"Yeah." She turns in my arms and rests her cheek on my chest.

I've never felt more content than I do standing in this closet, holding her close.

After a long moment, she pulls away. "I need to go see Elle and Keela. Will you come with me?"

My chest expands three sizes. "I'd love to."

Together, we go in search of her best friend and find her at a table next to Grey. He's holding Keela in his arms with an odd expression on his face. I haven't seen him hold any child except for Sage, and we were kids ourselves when he was that little.

There's a strange rightness to seeing an adult Grey holding a small pink bundle. When he sees me staring, he stands up, and you'd think Cian was about to combust by the way he lurched forward as if he thought Grey would drop her.

Grey scoffs at the big guy. "It's not my first rodeo." Then he hands her to me, but he never takes his eyes off the baby.

"You okay?" I ask him, then lower the baby so Madison can see her.

The expression on Grey's face has my shoulders tensing up—he's made a decision about something.

"Fine. We'll move here, and move the company here, and then I'm going to get one of those."

"Ah, excuse me?" Madison asks. "You're going to get what?"

I'm too stunned to speak.

"A baby."

"They don't exactly come made to order." Cian stands guard as though he believes Grey might take his little girl and run.

And truthfully, right now, I'm not entirely sure he won't.

"Can you take her?" I ask Madison, then gently shift Keela into her arms.

Once she's settled, I return to Grey, but his expression hasn't changed.

"What do you mean? How are you going to get a baby? And why are you going to get a baby?"

"It's time," he says without any further explanation.

"Time for what? You understand why we're a little taken aback here, right?"

"You're happy here. Sage is happy here. I'll get a baby and be happy here too."

"That's a little backward. How about a wife, or Jesus, I don't know, a girlfriend first?"

"I don't need one."

Cian chokes on a laugh. "Actually, ya do, mate."

Grey is clearly frustrated with this conversation, and he pinches the bridge of his nose. It's the equivalent of someone counting out loud for patience.

"I realize I need a woman to actually carry a baby, but you can pay people to do that these days. I simply need to find a carrier."

"Oh my God." Savvy slaps her forehead so loud it draws all of our attention. "Please don't ever call a woman's body a carrier again."

Grey shrugs. "I'm getting myself a baby. Maybe a girl this time." He closes his laptop. "I know what to do for the Cozy Cup Festival. We'll get on it tonight."

We all stand dumbstruck as he packs up his stuff and waltzes out the door. He has an actual spring in his step too.

"Well, that was—"

"Fecking weird." Cian's watching the door too, but I can't refute his statement. It was fucking weird.

"I think he's feeling a little lost with all the changes lately." Even as I say it, I know it's more than that.

"A baby isn't going to fix that," Savvy says. Is that concern I hear in her tone?

"She's beautiful," Madison whispers, drawing me back to her.

And when I take her in, holding that small baby girl, I see my future.

"Why did he say you're moving your company here?" Cian asks. "Is that for real?"

I nod. "I brought it up to him after Sage said he wanted to join the football team."

"He has a real hard time letting go, huh?" It's concern in his tone, not judgment, and it's all I need to hear to know that Grey is going to find his way in this town too because he'll have a support system we've never had before.

"It's hard not to get baby fever after holding her," Madison murmurs while snuggling the tiny little girl.

"Someday." That one word carries the weight of a promise.

Madison lifts her shining gaze to mine. "Someday," she says, a happy smile lighting her face.

Ace may have sent me here to make a difference, but perhaps I misunderstood the assignment. Maybe the difference wasn't for the town.

Maybe the difference was for me.

34

MADISON

When I pull into the Hideaway's driveway, I'm nearly blinded. The lights that cover the outside could rival *National Lampoon's Christmas Vacation*. I've never seen so many decorations on one property before and the inn hasn't ever been so...bright.

Apparently, Braxton was too ambitious, and the reno is going to take much longer than he anticipated, so I'm not sure why he asked me to meet him here.

"What the hell has he done?"

Cian walks around the side of the house, holding a bunch of extension cords, so I jump out of the car to greet him.

"Hey, Cian. Ah, what's going on?"

"Ask your boyfriend. He's pushier than six-year-olds at an Easter egg hunt."

"I thought he didn't celebrate Christmas." A gust of wind has me pulling my cardigan more tightly around me.

"No, we always celebrated for Sage's sake, even when it was hard," Grey says, coming from the opposite direction. He and Sage are pushing a giant sleigh outfitted with lights.

"Like this?" My voice pitches higher than normal.

"When I was old enough to understand it." Sage is wearing a Christmas sweater that actually jingles. "But the uncles always hired someone else to do it. Uncle Brax insisted we do it ourselves this year."

I spin in a circle. "But...where is he?"

Grey laughs. It's such a foreign sound it startles me, which is sad because he has a nice laugh—friendly, happy, kind, and completely at odds with the attitude he presents to the world.

"He and Pops are working on the inside," Sage says. The kid is bouncing on his toes.

"Guys, Christmas is tomorrow. You're doing all this work for one day?"

"Talk to your boyfriend," Cian says again, then leans down to plug something into the extension cord. "I think he truly believes he's Santa Claus."

"What the hell is that?" I don't think my voice can go any higher.

"A twenty-foot snowman." Grey chuckles.

Is he drunk? He must be drunk.

Sage runs up the porch steps, opens the door, and shouts, "She's here."

The interior of the inn falls dark a second later.

"Come on," Sage says, waving wildly in my direction.

"Humor him." Grey stuns me with a magnificent smile.

Not knowing what else to do, I allow Sage to lead me inside. Once he has me where he wants me, he counts to three.

Before I can adjust to the darkness, I'm blinded once again.

Christmas lights are everywhere I look. But it's the ten-foot Murray cypress tree in the corner that has my heart stutter-stepping on my lungs. The scent of pine and cinnamon carries my imagination to what I always dreamed the holiday could be once I moved in with Pops and Grams. And even then, it was never like this.

Stockings hang on the mantel that's decorated with snowman nutcrackers and snow globes that light up and spin glitter all around. Each stocking is embroidered with one of our names in gold lettering. There's one for everyone, even Keela.

I peer down the hall. Every inch of the place has been decorated.

"How? Where did you get all this stuff?"

"Amazon," Pops calls proudly. I move through the space and find him in the dining room that's now open to the den.

"Oh my God. It's all done."

The intricate crown molding looks brand new. The floors are so shiny they reflect all the colored lights.

"Not all done." Braxton stands in the doorway. "The first floor is done, but the furniture Elle picked out won't be here for a couple of weeks."

The den is packed full of camping mattresses and sleeping bags. A quick count tells me there's nine of them, and a twin cot is pushed up against one wall.

"What's going on here?"

"We're making new memories," Braxton says.

"It was all his idea." Elle walks in the door, wearing Keela, with Clover following behind, carrying a bunch of bags.

My lungs feel tight, and my chest flutters as though it's about to have a panic attack. "What do you mean? What's happening here?"

"Everyone you care about is here, Madison." The warmth in Braxton's tone makes my heartbeat feel heavy against my chest. "Everyone who loves you wants to start a new tradition, create new memories, here with you."

"We're all sleeping here? Over there?"

"That's right," Cian grumbles. "Instead of sleeping in my king-sized bed, we're going to cram onto thin little mattresses and wake you all up every two hours when Keela cries."

Elle swats him in the gut.

He grunts. "And we're so happy to do it."

"But why?" My chin wobbles, but I have no hope of controlling it.

"Because from here on out, holidays will mean more than what we've lost." Braxton watches from across the room, and I feel his gaze tracking every inhale I take. "They'll be a celebration of life and love. Ace wanted me to find happiness in Happiness, Georgia. And I'm going to spend every day making sure those I love experience it too."

"Aw, mate. Ya love us. How sweet," Cian teases. "Where's the eggnog?"

It's as if that one question puts the party in motion. People move all around me while I'm still trying to catch up.

Elle and Clover set up some sort of folding crib in the den while Grey hands out mugs of eggnog and spiked cider —he's definitely been imbibing in his creations for some time. Sage finishes hanging the garland that Pops was working on, and I can hear Savvy banging around in the kitchen, so I finally snap out of it and go to help her.

The kitchen...

"What happened in here?"

It's brand new and so much better than I could have imagined, but every available surface is covered in pans, tinfoil-covered items, and mixing bowls. There's so much stuff I can't imagine there's even one kitchen item not in use at the moment.

Savvy stands upright with a guilty expression lining her beautiful face. Her hair is falling out of its braid, and her cheeks are flushed.

As I stare at her, her gaze keeps darting from me to something over my shoulder, and when I turn, I find Grey smirking in our direction over a mug of cider.

"Oh my—"

"Don't say it." Savvy practically jumps over the counter to shush me. "I got stuck cooking with him all day. That's it."

"That's it? Savvy, your leggings are inside out. And your hair is…"

"Fine. Fine. I don't want to talk about it. Help me get the ham out of the oven."

"Ham?"

"Yeah, Braxton decided we'd have ham on Christmas Eve and turkey with a crown lamb thing on Christmas. That's all him though. I'm not cut out for this shit."

"But why?"

The kitchen is an absolute disaster. It's as messy as my mind right now.

Christmas music begins to play softly from the ceiling.

"He put in surround sound. Isn't that cool?" Savvy is obviously desperate to keep the topic of conversation off herself.

It's just as well—I don't have room for anything else in my head at the moment.

She wraps me in a crushing hug. "This is for all of us, hon. I don't know if one person in this house has ever had…" She pulls away and waves around the room. "This. A house full of love. He's trying to give it to us all."

"Braxton."

"Yeah. He's head over heels for you."

"He is?" I'm still in a state of shock.

"Yep, so snap out of it and enjoy this gift." She physically shakes me to get my attention.

"You're right. Sorry. It's just…"

"A lot. I get it."

"Yeah. What didn't you and Grey get up to in here?"

Her face pales.

"I mean food-wise, you pervert, though I hope whatever else you got up to wasn't near any food. I love you, but that's disgusting."

She laughs uncomfortably but doesn't confirm or deny anything.

"Savvy," I hiss.

"We didn't. I didn't. The food is safe," she rambles, then turns toward the oven. As soon as she opens the door, nostalgia wafts around me.

"It's Maisie's recipe. Pops found it in a box of kitchen stuff," she explains. The scent of maple syrup makes my mouth water. "Can you mash the taters? The recipe calls for four sticks of butter. Four. I'm going to gain a hundred pounds before New Year's."

"It's how Pops likes them," I say, finally getting on board with the night.

Savvy was right. This is a gift. It might be the most meaningful gift I've ever been given, and Braxton knew me well enough to know that this was exactly what I needed.

I am truly and completely in love with that man.

<hr>

"I can't believe they got the fireplace to work," I muse,

staring into the crackling fire. "We've used the gas insert for years now."

I'm sitting between Braxton's legs on one of the camping cushions, and everyone I love is in a semicircle around the expanded fireplace. It's truly a work of art. The stonework goes all the way to the ceiling, and the hearth is made of stacked stone.

I couldn't have dreamed something so perfect.

"One of the first things they did after fixing all structural elements was rebuild the fireplace. If you go upstairs, you can see it's still exposed but fully functional," Cian says. He stands next to the fire, swaying side to side with Keela in his arms.

"It's really beautiful," I tell Braxton and nuzzle my cheek against the arm he has draped across my shoulders.

"That was all Elle. She had a very clear vision for this place."

"Not me," Elle says. "I just knew what would make my girl happy."

Braxton leans into me and presses his lips to my ear. "And what *my* girl wants, my girl gets."

I pinch his arm.

"Ouch. What was that for?"

"I'm not convinced I haven't dreamed this whole thing up."

He chuckles, and the sound rolls down my back like a gentle caress. "Sweetheart, you're supposed to pinch yourself."

I smirk. "Next time."

We fall into silence, listening to the conversations happening all around us. They're loud, and happy, and all mine.

"This might be my favorite memory," I murmur, not really expecting anyone to answer.

But I should know better when Braxton is around. Something deep in my gut tells me he'll always hear me.

"I hope this is only the first in a long line of happy memories, sunshine."

Settling back into his chest, I exhale the sadness that has followed me for years. But this time, when I turn to kiss Braxton, something on the wall catches my attention. Actually, it's two somethings that steal all the air from my lungs.

I stand silently and step closer to the wall. I feel Braxton's heat at my back, but he doesn't say anything. He allows me the time to work through the feelings assaulting me.

"It's, that's me and—and Elle, before I moved here. A different photo used to hang here," I say.

"Pops told me. I thought maybe one of someone who loved you would be a better memory than the one of your parents."

We're sitting on a swing Pops had hung from the tree out front. We're staring at each other, our heads thrown back in laughter—we were only seven or eight here. It makes my heart so happy even as a tear slips down my cheek.

"It's perfect. Really, it's perfect." I stare at it for a long moment, my finger tracing the memory, then move to the one next to it.

The girl is a younger female version of Grey.

"That's Violet," he says.

"She's beautiful. And she looked so happy. I love that you did this."

He pulls my back into his front and kisses the top of my head. "I want our lives to meld together, Madison. And I thought that maybe the first step was linking our trauma in a way that brought happy memories instead of sad. Violet loved to laugh, and your friends were here for you when you felt like you couldn't. She would have loved you, and them."

"This is all... I don't know what to say, Braxton. I'm standing here, staring at a picture of my childhood before my parents threw me away and not sobbing. I don't know that this has ever happened before."

I spin in his hold and link my arms around his neck. He has to bend down a few inches for me to clasp my hands together, but he does it on instinct.

"The inn, you, all of it. How do I even thank you for this?"

His smile is lazy, and love shines in his amber gaze. "I have a few ideas, but you'll have to wait until tomorrow. And honestly, you already have. You made me want to live for love, not just live to exist. That's more than I can ever return."

"Get over here, you lovebirds," Grey calls cheerily.

"Is he drunk?"

Braxton chuckles. "I think so. But he's happy, so I'm not going to stop him."

I look across the room. Grey is more relaxed than I've ever seen him. "How do we get him to live that way all the time without copious amounts of alcohol?"

"Time. We just have to give him time. I think Happiness will change him too, but he has to be ready for it."

Grey presses a button on a remote in his hand, and a large screen descends from the ceiling.

"It's for TV," Braxton explains. "There's a tiny projector in the wall over there." He points to a wall as we walk back to our mats.

"Best Christmas movie of all time?" Grey asks the room.

The guys all say *Die Hard*, while the women say *It's a Wonderful Life*.

"Girls win." Savvy crosses the room to take the remote that Grey holds out of reach. "There are more of us, so we choose."

He leans into her and whispers something that has her straightening, but she still demands the remote with an open palm. When Grey stands upright, he's wearing a smirk I think is going to cause us a ton of trouble in the near future.

"*It's a Wonderful Life* it is," Grey says jovially, then swaggers to his spot on the floor.

Swaggers.

Savvy huffs as she searches for an open mat, but the only one available is the one next to Grey.

Grey pats the spot next to him, and Cian chuckles. "Good Lord. It's going to be a long night."

As if on cue, Keela lets out an ear-piercing shriek, and he hands her off to Elle, who wraps a blanket around one shoulder and begins to nurse.

Braxton and I settle into our spots on the floor, and moments later, he's snoring.

He really is trying to give me a wonderful life, and I might be at a place in my life to finally accept it.

BRAXTON

"Fuck," I hiss, clutching my side.

"Shh."

Who the hell is shushing me? Rolling over onto my back, I almost scream when I find Cian peering down at me.

"Jesus, man. Did you kick me?"

He shrugs. "My arms are full," he whispers.

Sitting up, I realize it's still the middle of the night and everyone in the room is sleeping.

"You said you had something to do before everyone wakes up," he says.

"Right, thanks."

As quietly as I can, I slip away from Madison. We unzipped our sleeping bags and made a bed out of them, so after I stand, I take care to tuck her back in.

"You okay?" I ask.

He nods. "She likes the lights." Cian is staring at his daughter in a way that only a dad can.

I pat him on the shoulder and tiptoe through the house, then as quietly as I can, I start pulling presents out from the closet and filling the stockings.

"You're shitting me," Cian mutters. I hadn't realized he followed me over here.

I grin at him. "Santa has to come."

"Keela too? Mate, she can't even hold a pacifier on her own."

"Everyone," I whisper. "Now go away before you wake everyone up."

"Too late," Elle says, coming closer, then stopping to kiss Keela's cheek. "You're not the only Santa in town though." From behind the tree, she carefully drags out a large garbage bag full of gifts.

"I like your style, Elle O'Brien."

"Same, Braxton, same."

We work side by side with Cian supervising, and an hour later, all the gifts are laid out and arranged by Elle to create a picture-perfect scene.

"Thank you," she whispers when we're walking back to where everyone sleeps. "For including us all. It means a lot to us to see her this happy."

I'm choked up by her words, so I simply nod, then sneak back under the blankets next to Madison.

She is my home.

THE GIFTS THAT TOOK ME FOR-FUCKING-EVER TO WRAP ARE spread all throughout the room with wrapping paper in every shade littering the floor.

Clover walks around with a garbage bag, collecting the trash, while Cian and Grey roll up the mats to make way for the folding table and chairs we borrowed from town hall.

"Today was perfect, thank you." Madison lifts up to her tiptoes, and I lean over to meet her lips.

She's so damn sweet.

"I'm going to help Savvy in the kitchen." She tries to pull away, but I catch her by the hand.

"Give me five minutes?"

She arches a brow. "For what?"

"Not that," I laugh. "Five minutes is not nearly enough time for that. Come outside with me."

"Five minutes, that's it. It's not fair to leave Savvy with all the work."

"Don't worry about Savvy. Grey is heading in there next to work on the lamb, and the turkey's already in the oven."

"Grey is what I'm worried about," she mutters. And I don't blame her.

Grey has lost his damn mind—especially around Savvy. He announced this morning that he's started the search for a surrogate. As soon as this holiday is over, I need to talk some sense into him.

"Five minutes." I take her hand, grabbing a folded blanket by the door, and we slip outside. It's in the low sixties, but the breeze causes a chill as I lead her to the new porch swing.

Once we're seated and the blanket's tucked around her, nerves settle in. My palms are sweaty, and I'm fidgeting as though I've been rolling around in poison oak.

"Are you okay?" she asks.

"Yeah, I, I love you, Madison. So damn much it scares me."

"I know you do." Her shoulders relax, and she settles into the swing. "And I love you too. It's not as easy for me to say it sometimes, but I feel it. I hope you know that."

"I do. And I know we've only known each other for a few months, but—"

"Braxton." Her tone is cautious, and her gaze darts from me to the front door.

Shit, is it too soon?

"Fuck, I'm nervous," I admit as she picks at the hair elastic on her wrist.

"At the Chug, I told Harry that you were my fiancée."

She frowns. "You did?"

I nod. "Maybe you didn't hear me. There was a lot going on that day."

"You told him in front of everyone?"

"Yeah. It just happened."

She laughs, and my jitters fade away. Her laughter will always bring me joy. "Well, that explains why everyone's been congratulating me. I thought they were talking about the inn."

"Nope, it was probably because of me."

With a smile that outshines the sun, she pats my knee in a reassuring gesture. "Don't worry about it, Braxton. Is that why you're so nervous? It's not a big deal. We can explain to Blissy what happened. She'll get a laugh out of it, and the whole town will know by lunchtime."

That's not what I want. Doesn't she know that?

Damn it. My skin feels too tight for my body.

"Braxton?" Her tone is concerned.

I have no idea what's going on with my face because I've lost all control of my features.

"What if we don't?" I blurt.

"Ah..." She searches the porch, presumably for answers as to why I'm acting as though I stole Santa's sack. "What if we don't what?"

"Tell Blissy. What if we don't tell Blissy that it was a mistake?"

"I'm sorry. You're not making any sense. What are you saying?"

It's now or never. Reaching into the pocket of my hoodie, I pull out a small box. It's empty inside, but it's the thought that counts, right? I hold it out to her in my open palm.

She stares at it with her mouth wide open.

"It's empty, don't worry."

Now she frowns, blinking furiously.

"No, I mean temporarily it's empty. Pops gave me your grandma's ring, and I want to merge her ring with one I buy for you, but I didn't want to mess with her ring unless you said it was okay. It's okay with Pops, but is it okay with you?"

"You talked to Pops?"

I nod, a tiny amount of confidence returning. "About ten minutes ago. I was afraid if I did it any sooner, he'd blab it to everyone."

"I don't really know what you're asking here." She frowns. "You haven't really asked anything, so I'm not sure what to say?"

And the insecurity is back. "Shit. I'm messing this all up. I'm really nervous. I've never done this before."

"You're not someone who gets nervous, Braxton. Ever."

"Well, I've never asked anyone to marry me before either."

Dimples show on both of her cheeks. "Is that what you're doing here?"

I run through our conversation at warp speed in my mind. Thank God I didn't do this in front of everyone. I'd never, ever hear the end of it.

Dropping to the floor, I take her hand in mine. "Yes. I'm doing a spectacular job of screwing it all up, but I'm asking you, Madison Ryan, if you'll be my wife."

Tears spill down her cheeks, and I hate how they make

me feel. I don't ever want to see this woman cry—not if I can help it.

"Y—yes," she splutters, then throws herself at me, and we tumble to the floor just as Cian steps onto the porch.

"Crickey, mates. Seriously? I gotta get more wood for the fire, and you're out here fooling around?"

I hold up the empty jewelry box, and he beams like a proud papa.

"They got engaged for real this time," he yells into the house.

It causes a mass exodus, and she explains three times why she isn't wearing a ring. I need to make that a priority. I had no idea people would be asking to see it already.

The day evolves into one giant celebration, and as carolers knock on the door, one of Madison's friends or Madison herself tells anyone who will listen that she's engaged.

It fills me with joy to see her this happy.

"You did good, Uncle Brax," Sage says at my side. "But what are we going to do with that one?" He points to Grey, who's in the corner scrolling on his phone.

"What's he doing?"

"What do you think?"

"Is he serious?"

"He's on some website. He seriously needs an intervention." Sage throws his hands into the air for emphasis.

"Or a fucking dog. I'll be right back." Leaving Sage in the foyer, I march over to Grey and swipe his phone from his hands.

Sure enough, he's scrolling through surrogates. "Put this on pause for now, will ya? Let's get through the will and everything before you make any monumental life decisions."

"Oh," he sasses. "Like you did? Getting engaged is a pretty monumental step, if you ask me."

I hold his phone in the air. "But this is... This requires more thought. Today, focus on the people who are already in your life, for me, please?"

He purses his lips, but agrees, so I tuck his phone into my pocket.

"Hey." He jumps to his feet.

"No devices. You need to cool off, Greyson. I'm serious."

He mutters one curse after another but stalks off toward the kitchen, and relief settles over me—at least for now.

The rest of the day and night is spent indulging in the happiness of the people around us. It's a luxury money couldn't buy, and it's one I'll never take for granted.

"THIS IS HOW HAPPINESS SPENDS THE DAY AFTER NEW Year's?" I ask.

Madison grins up at me, and the bitterness I had about freezing my balls off at the park floats away.

"Yes. At 8:00 p.m., everyone can start taping off their booths. Tomorrow, construction starts." She's downright giddy.

When I glance around the park, I realize the giddiness appears to be contagious. She's wearing gloves, so I can't see her ring, but the bulge on her ring finger tells me it's there.

Not only did I mess up the proposal, but I didn't even give her the ring properly. The jeweler on Main Street saw her walking by the shop tonight and pulled her into the store because it was ready. The man did everything I asked in record time. Surrounding her grandmother's diamond is a circle of yellow diamonds, and when the light hits it, it shines like the sun. It's everything I wanted it to be, but I was probably the last one to see the damn thing.

Nothing has been conventional about our engagement, but then again, neither was our courtship.

"Now will you tell me what your idea is for the booth? I've never not been involved in the planning, you know, and it's killing me."

"Yes, but how many audiobooks and podcasts did you get caught up on while I was doing this?" I hold up a three-ring binder containing a rudimentary sketch and all the steps we need to take to win this thing.

"Oh, no. No, no, no," she cries when we reach our designated spot.

And then I see what's upset her. To our left is a sign that says *Blinky's*.

"What the hell? Who would've done this?" Anger mingles with a protective side that comes out whenever Madison is involved.

She drops her head to her hands. "It's a lottery, and it's done in front of the town council so no one can cheat. Once your spot is chosen, it can't be changed."

"Real sorry 'bout this, Madi," Moose says, walking up beside us. "I tried to change it, but Old Man Cracken is a stickler for the rules."

"Is that his name? Cracken?" I ask.

"Yup. He's a real ornery son of a bitch too."

"It's okay, Moose." The excitement she carried only a moment ago is burned out, and her shining expression has dimmed. "Thanks for trying."

"Always, Madi," he says before moving on to the next spot.

"I met Harry's dad," I whisper. "He seemed like a good guy. Hopefully he'll be here to keep him in line."

Madison moves her head as if she agrees, but her thoughts are somewhere else.

"Hey, he isn't going to ruin this for us. Put him out of your head. I'll be right by your side, and so will Pops and Grey. We've got this, remember?"

She flexes her hands and forces a tight smile. "You're right. Come sit and show me."

There are two folding chairs and a small folding table on each booth's platform, so I sit down at ours and open the binder.

A bevy of emotions flit across her features as she turns the pages.

I'm starting to sweat.

"You did...all of this?" She points to the binder. "You had beans and leaves flown in from all over the world to...to try and unite the town...with a drink?"

"Yeah. Why are you looking at me that way? Did I miss something with the planning?"

She closes her eyes and rubs small circles into her temples with her pointer fingers. It's a slow movement that causes a newfound anxiety to spike.

"No," she says. "I'm in shock. No one has ever done anything like this for me, Braxton. First the inn, the donations that pop up everywhere, and now this. You know that even if you didn't do all those things, I would have still fallen for you, right? It's not about money or what you can give me. It's that you thought to do them in the first place. No one has ever cared this much."

"Oh my God. You scared the shit out of me, Madison. I thought you were breaking up with me or something."

She laughs. "I didn't know you were so insecure."

"I never have been, not until you. I care so much that losing you would physically destroy me."

"I love you. We need to discuss boundaries and your tendency to go extremely overboard, but I love you. Let's get going on this thing, huh? Then we can go check out the competition." She pulls a roll of masking tape from the large bag she's carrying and hands me a measuring tape.

"You measure, I'll follow along with the tape. Construction begins tomorrow."

"I'm at your beck and call, my dear."

"That does sound good." She stands suddenly, a question forming on her expression. "Wait, did you actually try this...this Dirty Matcha? Is it any good?"

"Oh, sweetheart. Have you ever known me to do anything half-assed? Grey and I have been working since Christmas on the recipe. We finally perfected it last night."

"Is that why he's been bouncing around so much? He's on a caffeine high?"

"Yup. It was better than him focusing his attention on a surrogate. I had to give him something else to obsess over while our company is shut down for the holiday."

She snorts a laugh. "That's true. I don't think he's actually given up on it though. He was in the Chug yesterday on baby websites."

"He's grasping at this baby idea because he feels as though he's losing me and Sage. I don't know how to get through his thick skull that he isn't losing us, he's just gaining all of you."

"You're a good friend, Mr. Reyes." She wraps her arms around me and hugs me tight.

"And you're a fabulous fiancée, future Mrs. Reyes."

"I love how that sounds."

"Mm-hmm. Me too. Let's hurry up and get this done so I can get you home and naked."

"Are you always thinking about sex?" She bends over to unroll the tape, and I groan.

"With you, always. In every position, and every—"

"Braxton," she gasps.

"You asked, sweetheart. And I'll always tell you the truth."

No matter what, that's a promise I'll keep forever.

36

MADISON

"I'm going to kill him," Braxton seethes.

We're standing side by side in the park, staring down at what should be the outline of our booth. Instead, someone, likely named Harry, rearranged all the tape to say, 'fuck you.'

"Braxton, it's fine." I pull the tape from the platform the town council insists we build on so we don't kill the grass. "We don't really need the tape anyway. It's more ceremonial than anything."

"He's going to fuck with our booth every step of the way."

Sadly, he's right.

"I know. But I've been ignoring him for years, I'm not going to stop now. He's throwing a tantrum because he didn't get his way."

"He's not going to get away with it. We're winning this entire damn thing."

His vehemence makes me laugh. "Did you ever think you'd get so worked up over a festival celebrating caffeine?"

"I'm serious," he grumbles.

"Serious about what?" Grey asks, joining us at our booth. Sage and Pops walk behind him with their heads together. Those two could be serious trouble if they join forces.

"We need to set up a neighborhood watch or something so fuckface turdroaster doesn't mess with our station again."

"Braxton." I laugh. "This isn't the Olympics. We're not vying for gold. The prize is a freaking silver cup that is half teacup and half coffee mug. It's so ugly, people fight over which side belongs to coffee and which side belongs to tea."

"It's the principle behind it. I did my research, and I know this event is about community, not the caffeine drink of choice. It's about bringing people together, celebrating each other, and simply having a good fucking day with our neighbors." His voice is raised with anger and passion, and I kind of melt a little because he's mine.

He chose me.

A slow, annoying clap draws closer, and the chatter around the park drops to a low whisper as people pause to watch.

Grey and Pops turn at the same time, giving us a straight view between them to the man casually strolling our way with danger in his grave expression.

Cian, who is six booths away from us, follows the man. Close enough to lunge for him, but far enough away to be respectful. So it's not only me weirded out by this stranger.

The closer he gets, the more my body begins to tremble as nineteen-year-old me claws her way to the surface.

"What are you doing here?" Braxton asks, pulling me behind him—he really needs to stop doing that. But he must feel my arms vibrating beneath my skin because he spins around to check on me. "I'm right here. He's not your monster anymore. Okay? Trust me."

I don't know what's happening to my body, but I can't respond. He curses, then turns his back on me while still holding me close with one hand.

"That's cute," his father snarls. "You know, she's ruined a man once before. Are you going for a double play, Madison?"

"Don't," Braxton warns.

"We're here," Savvy whispers to my left. Clover closes in on my right, and I lean on them both for support.

Braxton must sense them at my sides because he releases me and steps toward his father.

"I don't want to be this meek version of myself anymore," I whisper to my best friends. "This isn't me, and he doesn't have any right to take that power from me. Not anymore."

Savvy nods as if she's proud of me, but Clover looks terrified while attempting to be supportive.

"What do you need?" Savvy asks.

"Nothing. I know you're here for me. I know I have support. But dang, it's scary facing your fears."

"You've got this," Clover says with false bravado. I appreciate her trying, but confrontation isn't in her DNA.

I bounce on my toes a little. It must be useful because fighters and boxers do it. Are they the same thing? Whatever, it gets the blood pumping, and I don't care if everyone thinks I'm going to freak out—I know I'm not. Brushing the hair from my face, I focus on what's happening in front of me, then take a small step, and another, and another until I'm close enough to press into Braxton's side.

He flinches until he realizes it's me, and whatever he finds on my face has determination growing on his.

"You've done enough damage, Alistair," Braxton warns. "Not only to us, but to the kids you say you love and to your wife. You're not going to do that shit to me or my fiancée."

"Sweet. Really, that speech is sickeningly sweet. But you don't get to cut me from my own company, take everything I've worked for, and leave me with nothing." His body is twitchy, almost as if he's on something, and that makes him dangerous, but his gaze is clear even if it is ice cold, so I know its rage making his body react this way. That might make him even more dangerous.

Cian stands nearby, but the older man barely spares him a second glance.

"I owe you nothing," Braxton says.

How the heck is he remaining calm? I'm ready to charge this jerk. I'll be a bulldog who hasn't eaten in days. Glancing down, I almost laugh when I realize I'm still bouncing on my toes. I guess I really am ready to fight my battles.

His dad steps forward, and I can't control the way my body flinches. He sees it too because the evil gleam in his expression turns downright vicious.

Clenching my teeth until my jaw aches, I square my shoulders and glare right back.

Grey leans into Braxton's side. "Mr. Coop's team doesn't have a case against him yet." Braxton nods but never takes his gaze off Alistair Montgomery.

He's dressed in a suit that was probably made just for him. Everything about him screams dirty money in a way that makes good people run and hide. There's nothing about him that's welcoming or kind. From his too-narrow eyes to his turned-up nose and shiny gold watch with too many diamonds, he radiates arrogance constructed on the backs of others.

"It was such a shame, what happened to you." He tuts. "Had I known how this would end up..." He flicks his wrist as if I'm a gnat he can't get rid of. "Well, maybe this time around will end better for me." His laugh is sinister.

"Are you threatening her?" Braxton steps into his father's space. He towers over the older man, and I can't find a single resemblance between them.

"I wouldn't have to if you'd only be reasonable." Alistair leans around his son to peer at me. "It's never easy, is it, Madison? Those fifteen minutes of fame you never asked for. Just imagine what will happen when the world finds out you're marrying the son of a Montgomery. The very Montgomery you say harmed you terribly." He spits with so much venom I'm stunned into silence.

"Walk the fuck away, and don't come back. If you think what I've done so far is unjust, you wait until you see what I do next." I've never heard Braxton sound this way. He's as dangerous as his father, but protective and caring.

"Leave," Cian rumbles low in his chest. "Now, or I will escort you out."

Alistair finally takes in my giant friend, but ignorance gives him a false sense of confidence.

"You have five days to hand back control of Montgomery Media, Braxton. Or I'll make sure the world knows the truth."

"Go for it, old man. I have nothing to hide."

Alistair makes a point of looking from Braxton to Grey before turning to me. "Are you sure about that?"

"Out," Cian says, taking hold of Alistair's elbow.

"Get your hands off me. I have lawyers who will take everything you love should you touch me again."

"Yeah? And how are you going to pay for them?" Braxton taunts.

"You'd better run, little girl." The old man's tone sends a chill down my spine, but I don't back down.

"I was a child when you sent those reporters after me, spewing lies and hate. I'm not that little girl anymore, you overinflated egotistical piece of shit." Holy crap. Did I just say that?

The stunned expression on Cian's face tells me that yes, yes, I did say it, and I smile just as manically as the monster before me.

"You hurt innocent girls." I take a step forward, but Braxton grabs me by the belt and holds me back. "And they were girls, Alistair. Young girls, not yet women, that you exploited for a fabricated exposé that got you nothing in the end. But I'm all grown up now, and this time I won't run, no matter what you throw at us."

"That's where you're wrong," he seethes. "I got millions of clicks and ad revenue from your face alone. Imagine what a few, shall we say, racy photos would do for me now?"

"That's enough," Braxton roars, but I hold up a hand to stop him. This is my battle today, and it's one that I can win.

"Racy?" I scoff. "The closest I get to being racy is wearing a bikini. So, if that's what gets your rocks off, go for it, you old pervert. I'm not ashamed of my body."

Standing up for myself against the worst person I've ever dealt with is both terrifying and invigorating.

"Bikini or birthday suit. It's all the same thing, isn't it?"

God, he's so slimy.

"I've never once taken a nude photo, you idiot. Cian, get him out of here."

Cian grabs him more forcefully this time, not giving a crap about his threats. But as he's pulling him away from us, Alistair digs in his heels to glare into my eyes.

"Are you sure about that, Madison? You don't have to be the photographer for them to exist."

Braxton loses it then, and the next thing I know, he's dragging Alistair out by one arm and Cian has the other. The man's feet don't even touch the ground.

I stand strong until Braxton returns, and then the adrenaline flees my body faster than a failing dam.

"I'll see what I can find out," Grey whispers. I barely hear him, but he's talking to Braxton anyway, so I tune him out.

"Everyone's staring," I mumble.

Their gazes feel like an attack by a million tiny needles up and down my body.

"They're worried about you, Mads." Clover and Savvy step in front of me, blocking me from view, and that's when the tremors start. They're not noticeable from the outside, but my insides riot violently.

"What do you want to do?" Braxton wraps his arm around my shoulder, easing my internal war.

"What's he going to do to you?"

"Me? I don't care about that."

Pressing up onto my toes, I kiss him, hard. "I do. I care. There are no naked photos of me, and if he even tried to photoshop something, I've got enough birthmarks and freckles to prove it's not me."

He frowns, and the hard lines along his face show me how troubled he is.

"He won't hurt you. I'll do everything I can to make sure he never even says your name again."

"I trust you." I trust him more than I've ever trusted anyone.

"What do you think he'll do in five days?" Clover asks.

"I don't know," he mutters. "But Grey will look into it. If there's something to find, he'll find it. And when he does, I'll end my father in the ways that matter most to him—social standing and financial power."

"What do we do in the meantime?" Savvy asks. They were witness to my breakdown when Harry turned my world upside down, and I see the fear in her expression now.

"I'll be okay, Sav. I'm not the same girl I used to be. I'm stronger, and I have all of you." I point to all my favorite townspeople, who are making no effort to hide the fact that they're eavesdropping.

It's then that I realize Pops has been quiet this entire time, and I find him standing with Sage.

"Pops? Are you okay?"

"Fine," he says, and I lift my brows in surprise. That's it? That's all he's going to say?

"Are you sure?" Braxton asks.

"Yes. Gonna go find Grey and see if he needs some help. Sage will take me."

He walks out of the park before I can ask any more questions.

"That was weird." Braxton places both hands on his hips and watches my grandfather walk away. "Should I go after him?"

"No," I say. "Let's—let's get started on our booth. If we get behind, we'll never catch up."

"Are you sure?" The concern on his face would be endearing if the reason for it wasn't such a viable threat.

"I'm sure. We all have a lot to do."

"We'll just be over at the Chug booth helping Blissy," Savvy says. "If you need anything, and I mean anything, you shout our names, and I'll put these track and field legs to good use."

"Same," Clover says. "But without the athletic ability."

Clover is so deadpan, it's hard to tell when she's joking if you don't know how to read the signs, but I do, and I laugh. It eases the tension that's hanging in the air, and eventually everyone gets back to work.

But I know that the looming threat hanging over our heads is about to change something. Maybe everything, and I don't think there's any way to stop it.

37

BRAXTON

"You know, I've never used a sewing machine before, but I'm pretty sure they have new ones that don't require my foot to move the needle."

"Look around, Braxton. They're all in use. This is the only one available, but you're doing great." Madison doesn't look up from the sign she's painting. Originally that had been my job, until she realized I couldn't paint a straight line and the lettering I was working on was better suited for a haunted house.

The Chug is packed full of people, all ribbing each other with good-natured competition. The atmosphere is light and fun even if everyone in the damn place does keep shooting worried expressions Madison's way.

Once we finished the framework at the park, I thought we'd be done for the day, but these people are no joke. When ours was finished, we helped at the Chug, then the Huckabees booth before finishing the Firefly's.

For a competition that's so cutthroat with trash talk, the competitors were all quick to help their neighbor.

Then with hot cocoa—the widely acknowledged neutral beverage—in our hands, we all walked over to the Chug for the second part of the night. The outfits. Not our outfits, but outfits for our booths. I've truly never seen anything like it.

"Just finish what you can," Madison says breathlessly. "We only have ten more minutes tonight before I have to lock up. We can't start again until noon tomorrow."

"Noon? Don't people work?"

"Business owners take time off throughout this week to prep for the competition." Madison holds a paintbrush in both hands as she explains. "Originally, it was a way for the business owners to relax and chat about how the holiday season went for everyone. But as time went on, the competition got a little..."

"Intense," Blissy shouts from across the room.

"Yeah, intense." Madison agrees, then starts painting again. "We had to put some rules in place a few years ago so everyone had a fair chance."

"So, it's cutthroat but fair?" I ask.

"Yup." She doesn't look up this time. "Hurry. Five more minutes."

The threats from my father haven't left my mind, but being here with her and all these people helps me internalize it without losing my fucking shit.

I don't want to worry Madison more than necessary, but my father has never made an empty threat. He's planning something, and it's up to me to figure out what before he can implement it.

"Time," Marty calls out, and everyone calmly puts down their work.

"Great job everyone." Madison rises from the floor, looking around at everyone's handiwork. "I'll lock this place up, and we'll be ready to go again at noon tomorrow. No one, not even me, will be allowed back in here before then, so make sure you take all your personal belongings with you."

The excitement of the event is only dimmed by exhaustion. People's cheeks are rosy, expressions filled with happiness while ideas are shared as we all file outside.

"Ready, Chief?" Madison asks Pops' old friend.

"Ready. Got me a new one this year too." He jingles a heavy chain, and when I peer down at Madison, I see she has one too.

She laughs when she finds me staring at her. "We chain the doors with two different padlocks, so everyone knows that no one entered before they're supposed to."

"That's right," Chief says, adding his lock to the chain she just wrapped around the door handles. "Had a problem a few years ago with an accountant we won't name, *Jonah*, but since then, Mads here has taken extra precautions, and we all appreciate her for it."

I'm starting to understand that Madison is much more than the town sweetheart, she's the pulse of the town.

"All set, folks." She tugs on the chains, and when nothing happens, people disperse to their cars. "Ready?"

The way she stares at me—as if I hold the key to all her happiness—incites feelings so intense I'm not sure my body is strong enough to contain them. She's honest, and loyal, and she's all mine.

"Ready."

"How much longer until the inn is done?" she asks as we climb into the truck. She still sits in the middle, and it makes me love this truck even more.

"They made some good progress on the second floor today. The general contractor said they should be done in about a month, but if we want to move back in, we can when they finish the second floor next week. Moose said we can stay at his rental for as long as we need to though."

"That's what's the most shocking," she says, laying her head on my shoulder. "Moose never rents that place to anyone. I don't know how you sweet-talked him into it, but you must be much smoother than I gave you credit for."

"Why doesn't he rent it?"

Madison shrugs and nuzzles into my side. "He built it for him and his wife, but she passed away before he was finished. He doesn't want to live there without her, so he only stays there when his kids and grandkids come to visit."

"That's really sad. I had no idea."

"We all thought he'd sell it, but he goes up there to putter around sometimes. He says it makes him feel close to Lilly."

I turn left onto the home's long driveway, and dread settles heavily in my stomach when we pull up to the house and all the lights are on.

Madison doesn't say anything as I put the truck in park, or when we walk up the steps, or even when we enter the home and find Grey has commandeered the great room with Pops and Sage each working at his side.

The scents of Christmas linger in the air. The joy that pine trees and cinnamon evoke are at complete odds with the concern on everyone's faces.

"What's going on?" I hesitantly ask, taking Madison's coat and hanging it on the hook.

Sage comes at me with a large cotton swab. "Open," he says while jabbing it at my mouth.

I have no reason to argue, so I open, and he swishes it all around both cheeks.

When he's finished, he tucks it into a little tube and returns to the table.

"Anyone want to tell me what the hell that was about?"

"Tell him," Grey says, tossing his pen onto the table. He always has one behind his ear when he's nervous, and he plucks that one and chucks it to the table too. I'm guessing his lucky coin will make an appearance any moment now.

"Tell me what?" I search all their faces. It's Pops who appears the most uneasy, so I focus on him.

"Pops, what did you do?" Madison takes the seat next to him.

I'm too on edge to sit, so I stand across from them, waiting for someone to start talking.

"Well," Pops says, ringing his hands together in his lap. "He wasn't sure. And he wanted you boys to decide."

"Decide what?" It's difficult to remain calm when every hair on my body is standing on end and my stomach has that freefall sensation you get when bad news is coming your way.

"It's not bad, exactly," Sage says, staring at a point over my head. If they told him, it can't be too bad, so I start to relax.

"Ace thought that maybe you and Grey were related." Pops speaks so fast, it takes me a moment to register his words.

"Related." I drag out the word as though I don't quite understand its meaning. "Related how?"

It takes him a moment, but when Pops lifts his gaze to mine, I already know.

"He thinks something may have happened between your mother and Grey's father. That's why they named you Reyes and not Montgomery. I think he was going to tell you all of this in the will but, well...you haven't read it yet."

"And you've known this the entire time we've been here?"

"It wasn't my story to tell," Pops argues.

"Pops. You should have said something," Madison says gently.

"I called Mr. Coop," Grey says, interrupting my spiraling thoughts. "He confirmed that there is a letter for the both of us, but he isn't at liberty to say anything until we've met all the stipulations Ace set."

My legs turn to Jell-O, so I finally take a seat across from them.

"Then I called your mother." Grey's tone gives nothing away, but the tightness in his jaw and the way he works his coin through his fingers speaks louder than words.

"What did she say?" I'm not sure my lungs are working properly. My head is a little woozy, and the tension in my neck begins to ache.

"Nothing. I asked her how well she knew my father, and she went silent. Then she told me he was a horrible man and hung up."

"The swab?"

"A DNA test. Uncle Grey and I both took one. Wouldn't it be tight if you were actually my uncle?" Sage is taking this news in a vastly different direction than I am.

"I am your uncle, Sage. Fucking DNA doesn't change that."

He frowns. "I'm sorry. I didn't mean—"

Guilt slaps me in the face. "No, I'm sorry," I say. "But I also mean it. I'm your uncle, regardless of what a Q-tip says." I scrub both hands over my face, using the pressure to center myself. "Ace thought we might be related, but wanted us to decide for ourselves because..."

"Because maybe it opens a can of worms you can't undo," Pops says.

"There are a lot of scenarios here," Grey agrees. "If we're brothers, our parents could've had an affair. Or..." He swallows hard, the alternative too shitty to even say out loud.

"Or it was just a hunch that Ace had that turns out to be false, and my father hated me for reasons we'll never understand. Let's pretend, for the sake of covering all our bases, that our parents did have an affair. It makes sense that they'd want to keep that quiet."

"My father was so caught up on image he allowed it to take my sister from me, so yeah, I believe he would've done anything possible to keep it out of the press." Grey grows agitated and stands so he can pace. "But Alistair has nothing to lose now. Why wouldn't he have already leaked it if it were true?"

Madison reaches across the table with her palm facing up. I place my hand in hers and squeeze, thankful for the contact.

"Okay," I say slowly, gathering my thoughts as I go. "Your father would've done anything, and mine, well, we know he'd do anything for money. But how far would he go? If he's not my father, and knew it, why would he sign the birth certificate? He had everything he ever wanted. He married into money. He had full control of Montgomery Media, at least until he crossed that final line."

"He did." Grey scratches his head, then meets my gaze. "But what if he took money for something that wasn't exactly legal, or to cover up something?"

Do we look alike? Our coloring is different, but the rest of our features could definitely pass as a relation.

"Wait." I rub at my temples as a memory fights its way to the surface. "Didn't Ace say he didn't give Alistair any funding for the Whisperloop after the initial start-up money because he thought gossip columns were trashy?"

He nods as the pieces fall into place in my mind.

"Yeah." Grey's already rushing to his computer. "And that start-up money would've only carried him so far."

"Do we have access to the financial records for Montgomery Media from thirty years ago?"

"It'll take some digging, but if it's there, I'll find it."

"Find what?" Madison asks.

Grey lifts his face from the computer screen, and the second we connect, I know it's true.

"We're searching for evidence that Alistair took a big payout from Darren Wells before or shortly after I was born," I say. "And if there was a payout, there would be some kind of contract or paper trail."

"That would explain why he hates you so much," Sage mutters.

"It would," I agree while searching my memory for any clues that make this true. It's all there—the disdain from Alistair, the indifference from my mother. I don't even resemble my siblings, I look...like a dark-haired version of Grey.

"Let's say this is all true. What would he do with this information now?" Madison asks.

"Revenge," Grey and I say in unison.

"He has nothing to lose," I say gently. "Grey's father is in prison, and Alistair's already turned on my mother and siblings in a bid to save himself."

"And this would..." Grey pauses mid-sentence, and when he turns to Madison, I see concern in his features—he cares about her because I care about her. "This would kick up a media frenzy we haven't seen in years. A scandal between the Wells and Reyes/Montgomery families would be front-page news, and not only on Alistair's Whisperloop site. This kind of scandal would make every late-night talk show, every morning news broadcast. It would be everywhere."

"But...why?" Her voice cracks, and I stand to take the chair next to her.

"If my father invested in Whisperloop so that Alistair would falsify the birth certificate and raise Brax as his own, that sounds an awful lot like selling a baby, and—"

"That's illegal and unethical," she mutters.

"Right." Grey's fingers fly over his keyboard. "And Alistair is too arrogant to think we'd ever find proof. He's so sure of himself, he'd do it just to ruin Omni-Reyes."

I snap my attention to Grey, and when the room remains silent, he lifts his head.

"Customer satisfaction is down." He rolls his coin through his fingers at a pace I've never seen. "I didn't tell you because I didn't want you to worry. But Ace was the face of honest, reliable news—people trusted him. With the story Alistair put out about you running from responsibility, and me being born a Wells, we're losing customers on every platform. The Reyes name has always been associated with good, while Wells is quite literally equated with the devil. If this got out, it's a hit our reputation might not recover from."

A hit to the head with a baseball bat would hurt less than this. Could Alistair really ruin everything my family has built with lies?

"So how do you stop him?" Madison is wringing her hands in her lap.

Grey meets my gaze over her head. We know the truth, and we can't keep it from her—it will only make it worse when the inevitable happens.

I hold her hand with both of mine and spin her in her chair, so I bracket her thighs with my own.

"We don't, Madison. We can't. We have to get ahead of the story, it's how these things work."

"You're going to do what, exactly? Tell the world that you might be siblings? Won't that result in the same outcome?" Her fear is etched into every syllable, and each one cuts me to my core.

"It will. I'm sorry. If there were any other way…"

"We'll be ready for it though," Grey says. "It won't be an attack on you like it was before. We'll hire security, and we'll do everything we can to mitigate the damage."

"He said five days, Braxton. Five days is the festival. Is he going to do something to the festival?"

I can't answer that because I don't know.

"We'll have to get ahead of it before then, Madi. We won't let him ruin your festival." Grey's fingers fly over his keyboard.

"It's not my festival, Greyson Reyes." Madison stomps her foot under the table. "It's ours. All of ours. That means you too. You have to stop separating yourself from the people who love you."

"Yeah, Uncle Grey." Sage smirks but has the good sense to jump out of Grey's reach.

"Fine. It's our festival. We take care of what's ours, Madi. But it isn't going to be easy. I meant what I said. This will be a shit show."

My girl squares her shoulders, looks him dead in the eyes, and says, "What can I do to help?"

"It depends," Grey says, and I already know where he's going with this. "How good of an actress are you?"

She spins back to me so fast her hair whips the side of my head.

"Actress?" She tilts her head adorably. "I mean, I did play the old oak tree when I was in the first grade."

So fucking sweet.

"You'll have to do better than that, sunshine. We have to make the entire town believe us."

"Believe what?" Her gaze jumps from me to Grey.

"That you've broken up," Grey says. "Because if this deposit for twenty million dollars is what I think it is, Braxton and I are half-brothers."

38

MADISON

"I don't think I can lie to them, Braxton. Everyone else, yes, I'll do whatever it takes, but these girls know me too well, and I'm—I'm going to need them when you're gone."

I don't have to pretend. These tears are real.

After Grey found the deposit from the day after Braxton was born, they put a plan into motion. First, they called Mr. Coop and told him this was something they had to do, and if it nulled them from Ace's will, they'd deal with the repercussions.

Then everything happened in a whirlwind of activity, and all I know right now is that Braxton and I are breaking up today, he's going back to California for a press release, and I have to sit here twiddling my thumbs and pretending I'm heartbroken.

"I know, baby," he says. I haven't been far from his side since we walked in the door last night, not that any of us got more than a couple of hours of sleep. "It will be hard for me too, but with me in California, the media frenzy will never make it to Happiness or your doorstep. We're trying to keep this as far away from you as possible."

I know they are, but it doesn't make it any less painful.

By the looks of Grey, who's still in his suit from yesterday, he hasn't even been to bed.

"If you tell them," Grey says from his perch at the island, "they have to play the part of pissed-off friends. There can be no slip-ups, Madi. Alistair will be searching for any weak links."

"I trust them. I do, I trust them with my life. And if something happens in Happiness, I'll need them."

Grey peers down at his coffee, and Braxton tugs on the back of his neck. "I trust them too," he says. "How quickly can they get here so Grey can prep them? He has more experience with the media than I do."

Running my fingers under the elastic around my wrist, I stare at his right ear because I can't look him in the eyes.

"They're on their way, aren't they?" he asks, but he doesn't sound mad. If anything, he sounds relieved. "I'm glad you'll have their support."

"It's probably not a bad idea to have Cian in on it too. At least we know he'll protect her if anything happens." Grey's voice doesn't carry the same edge to it today, and that worries me more than anything else.

"Protect her from what?" Savvy's voice is loud and echoes off the high ceilings.

"Calm down, Rocky." Grey smirks and I know he does it to irritate her.

In the hopes of keeping those two separated, I jump up from my chair and rush to my friends. I reach Elle first, and she hugs me so hard she squeezes the air from my lungs.

Cian enters the kitchen, muttering about knocking, and sets the infant car seat on the floor.

"What's going on?" Clover asks. She's even more fidgety than normal—it happens when her fears are in control.

"Braxton and I have to break up," I blurt. The chorus of curse words and threats that erupt around me make my head spin. "Hold on," I shout to be heard over my friends defending my honor. "Let us explain."

I turn to Braxton, who wraps his arms around my shoulders and rests his chin on my head.

"I'm confused," Savvy mutters. "What the hell is going on?"

I study each of their faces as Braxton and Grey take turns explaining what's about to happen and what we'll need from each of them. The expressions range from distrust to anger to fear, but not one of them walks away.

"For fuck's sake," Cian says when they've finished. "This is some right shite you've got here. You pulling Sage from school?"

"No," Braxton says. "I spoke to Trevon this morning. There's an extra room in the football house since their last kicker went home when he broke his leg. He'll stay there with undercover security. We'll also have security on Madison and Pops, but they'll only be able to do so much."

Savvy's still cursing in hushed tones, but she's listening, and that's all I can ask.

"We're hoping that by going back to California, the media won't even have a reason to come here. But if Alistair brings the fight to Happiness in a petty ploy he'll never win, we need you all on Madison's side." Braxton squeezes my shoulder more tightly, and I know he's struggling to let go as much as I am.

"We're always on her side." Savvy flops down into one of the dining chairs and exhales loudly. "I did not have this on my bingo card today."

"None of us did," I assure her. "But I need you all. I'm

stronger than I was, but when I think about all the possible scenarios...I'm scared."

"Fuck." Braxton's body goes rigid behind me. I know my words cause him pain—we've already had this conversation, but I will always be truthful with him.

"I'm scared, but I'm doing this. Will you help us?"

Clover barrels forward for a hug and nearly knocks both Braxton and me over. "Always." Her voice wavers, but she's pushing through her own fears to help me, and I love her dearly for it.

"Okay, tell me again what you need us to do," Savvy demands.

Grey walks them all through the plan one more time, then we pile into our vehicles and head to the Chug.

MY HANDS TREMBLE AS I PUT THE KEY IN THE LOCK. IT'S taken me twice as long as it took Chief, but as soon as I have the chain off, Braxton storms past me.

It's just pretend. It's just pretend, I silently chant.

"That was a dick move," Savvy says, a little too loudly.

When I turn around, I see all the concerned faces staring at me. I shrug and open the door. "Let's get started," I say flatly. The concern grows deeper as friends pass by. They've mistaken my nerves for sadness, but I'll take it.

I wasn't prepared for how crappy this would feel.

Pops is the last to enter, and he walks by with a reassuring squeeze to my shoulder. The door shuts behind me with a loud clap. This place has always been my sanctuary, and I pray I'm not about to jinx it with all this phony bad juju.

Braxton is at our workspace, grumbling loudly and tossing scraps of fabric around. He's much better at pretending than I am. I actually believe he's upset.

"Braxton," I can't keep the concern from my tone.

"What?" he snaps, causing more than a few heads to turn.

It's pretend.

There's a flash of regret hiding in his expression before he masks it with disgust.

"I told you I'd have to go back and forth. I can't just move my company here for—for you." His voice drips with disdain, and I struggle to remain calm.

"I said I understood." My voice is much quieter than his, and while it feeds into the scene we're playing, it's also because my stomach is revolting.

"Do you though? This has all been fun and games, but I'm the CEO of a billion-dollar company, Madison. Do you know how much time and effort that takes?"

"Hey," Cian says curtly. "What the hell's gotten into you?"

"Stay out of this, Cian. This is between Madison and me."

"Yeah, well you're airing it out for the entire town to hear."

"Fuck off," Braxton hisses. "I have real-world problems going on. Real work and real employees that count on me. I can't live in her little fairy-tale world forever."

I suck in a gasp. It hurts. It hurts so much, and he won't even look at me.

It doesn't feel like pretend anymore.

"I didn't ask you to give up anything for me," I say shakily.

"Didn't you though?" That cold glare turns on me. "Maybe not with words, but you don't want to be in front of the media."

"Hey, now," Pops cuts in. "That's going too far."

"You won't come to California for events. You won't even try to fit into my world, Madison. How the fuck is this supposed to work if I'm the only one bending here?"

I'm hyperventilating. This feels too real.

"I don't belong in California, Braxton."

"And I don't belong here," he says through clenched teeth. "What is it you think will happen, Madi?"

He's never called me Madi before, and a sob breaks free.

"What else could you possibly want from me? And tell me the truth for once, not what you think I want to hear, and not what you think everyone expects you to say. What do you want from me? I've given you everything you need, everything you could possibly want. I'm fixing the inn. I'm giving you more time with your beloved podcast. I've paid off debts and given you a financial cushion."

"I—I never asked for any of that." Pain and fear are two sides of the same coin. How did we veer off into something that feels too real not to be true?

"You didn't have to ask, Madi. I had to do it."

Oh, God. He had to do it. Do what? Fix the inn? Spend time with me? All my initial fears of his true reason for spending time with me roar to the surface.

"Then—then what happens?" Tears fall from my eyes. Real tears.

He looks at me as if he wants to hold me, like he wants to make this better, but then he lowers his head and presses into that spot on his chest. "We don't. I'm heading back to California tonight and—and maybe we should put the brakes on before you get hurt."

"Too late." The words blend with a sob. His shoulders tense, but he won't look at me.

It's too hard to remember that this is pretend. I just want him to hug me, hold me, and tell me everything will be okay.

But he doesn't. Of courses he doesn't. That's not the plan, and we have to stick to the plan.

"You're just like the rest of your family, you know that?" His face pales at my accusation. "You're no better than any of them, you just have more money to throw around in people's faces, thinking it will solve all your problems. Well, news flash, *Brax*." My voice breaks, and I take a step back to give myself more space from him. "I never wanted any of your money or what it could buy. I only wanted you, and look at me now." I point to my tear-stained face. "This is what your money does. Are you proud of yourself?"

Real anguish dims his expression before he lowers his lashes and stares at the floor. "I'm sorry to hear that," he mutters. "Goodbye, Madison."

His footsteps echo on the floor because no one else is making a sound.

"I'm going to fecking kill you," Cian growls.

Braxton doesn't say a word. The next sound I hear is the door slamming shut, and my soul breaks in half.

I sit in his spot at the sewing machine, thankful now that it faces a wall, and moments later, Clover, Savvy, and Elle are at my side.

"It wasn't real," Clover whispers. "But you both could have won an award for that performance. I think he just broke everyone's hearts."

Half sob, half laugh escapes me, but we get to work on the booth without saying another word. Soon, the town will start gossiping, feeling sorry for the girl who had her heart shattered so publicly again, but for now, they give me space and time to regroup.

If I have any chance of getting through this festival and the mess that's about to swirl around faster than a tornado, I need to have my head on right.

"We've got you," Elle says, sitting on the floor with a paintbrush in hand. "We've always got you."

It happens on Thursday.

Clover and I stayed home while my friends and neighbors finished the booth for the Chug and the inn. They thought it was because I was too upset to see anyone, but in reality, it was so I could stay home and watch Braxton's press conference on TV.

And he was right. Within hours, their faces were plastered on every website. They showed up in my social media feed so often I had to unplug from them all.

By Friday morning, it was all anyone was talking about, even in our little town—maybe especially in our tiny town because now they all know who he is—and not one person has said another nice word about him since he left town.

At least not to me. While I appreciate that they have my back, it hurts to hear them talk about Braxton that way.

"Are you doing okay?" he asks. I answered his FaceTime call on my iPad, so his face was life-size—that's how pathetic I am these days.

"I'm fine. I hate lying to everyone, but they'll come around. Have you slept at all though?"

"I haven't," he admits. "Since we got the DNA results back, things have gotten messy, but as long as nothing falls back on you, we'll be able to handle it."

"Savvy and Elle have been strolling through town a few times a day, and they haven't seen anyone who looks suspicious."

"Good. That's good. I didn't think this would be so hard. I hate being so far away from you."

"It hasn't been a walk in the park for me either. I'm worried I'm too attached to you."

His eyes glow like a cat's at night. "You can never be too attached."

"We'll see what you think when you come home and I glue myself to your side."

"I can't wait."

We're quiet for a few moments, staring at each other, memorizing every eyelash and crease. It's just not the same as having him in the house with me.

"How is Grey handling the news?"

He runs his hand through his hair. It makes it all messy and so dang sexy. It's probably a little too long, but it makes things feel less out of control knowing I haven't missed something even as mundane as a haircut.

"He seems fine. My mother refuses to talk about it though, so I think that's making it harder for him. His mother was the complete opposite of his father—she was kind and gentle, at least from what I remember of her. She died when we were eight, and with his father still in jail for Violet's death...it's just hard not having answers."

My heart hurts for them both. "What about you? Does it change anything for you?"

He thinks for a moment, but he's shaking his head long before he answers. "No, Grey has always been my brother. It doesn't change anything for us, but he did go through his father's files."

My stomach plummets. "That doesn't sound good."

Braxton tugs on the ends of his hair. "It's not. He found proof that his father paid off Alistair to take the baby. Basically, it proves that Alistair took money to raise me as his own. The problem is that because my mother won't talk, we have no idea how involved she was with this. We haven't found anything implicating her, so that's good, I guess, but if Alistair pushes us, we will use it to take him down."

"But you're worried because it seems as though she's actually been trying to make some changes with the shelter she's working at."

He nods. "She wasn't a good mother to me, but maybe now I might understand it a little better."

"I'm so sorry. I can't imagine how hard that is. I miss you." It slips out. I don't want to be a stage-four clinger, but it's so hard to go from seeing him every day to only talking once a day.

His shoulders relax for the first time today. "I miss you too. But it's one in the morning there, so I'm going to let you go back to sleep. We'll figure this all out soon, I promise."

"I believe you."

He smiles in that way that curls his lips on the right side. It's something I only ever see him use for me, and my tears grow hot.

"I love you. I love you so much." My voice catches, and I mentally berate myself. My sadness isn't going to make things any easier for him.

"I love you too, sunshine. I'll be home soon."

"Okay."

"Bye, baby."

"Bye." I hang up before I can ask him to forget everything and just come home so we can deal with it together. I know that won't work. He has a company to think about, with thousands of employees. And that's only the surface stuff I know about.

There's so much I still don't know.

Sleep eludes me, and I end up tossing and turning all night. I'm up before the sun and forcing Pops out of bed at seven.

"The festival doesn't start until tomorrow, Mads. Why the hell you got me up so early?"

"I don't know. I—I have a lot of energy and anxiety today. You know that feeling you get before something bad happens?"

He nods solemnly.

"Okay, well, I have that feeling now. So I think we should head over to the inn and just poke around. If nothing else, it will give me something to do. I can't keep sitting here waiting for my life to happen. Braxton is out doing...stuff. I can do stuff too. He doesn't have to deal with this on his own."

"It is his mess to handle." He looks at me with pity, and I hate it.

"It's ours, Pops. I may not be wearing the ring right now, but the promise is still there. It's our life."

His eyes twinkle. "Well, what are ya waiting for then? Let's go see what kind of damage they've done to the Hideaway."

"I can't win with you, Pops." I want to laugh, but it's stuck, almost as if my fear is holding every other emotion hostage.

"Nope. Your gram couldn't either. I'm too hot to handle, she used to say."

"You're hot something, that's for sure. Thank you, Pops, for always having my back."

"Don't go gettin' all mushy on me now. I'm family, and that's what family does. If we've got a battle on our hands, I can't be blabbering on with you about my feelins."

A chuckle is ripped from me even though it's painful. "I got you, Pops."

"Ditto, kid."

39

____

BRAXTON

"Braxton, get out here," Grey shouts up the stairs, and I know instantly that something is very, very wrong.

Jumping out of the shower, I wrap a towel around my waist and run down the stairs. Water drips everywhere I step, but I don't care.

"In here," he shouts again. I follow his voice to the theater room, and my entire world falls out below me.

There, on the screen, is Madison's beautiful face, frozen in fear on her own front porch, holding the very same toy shotgun Pops used on me.

"What the hell is this?"

Grey rewinds the segment and then presses play. Alistair Montgomery stands at the foot of the inn's porch giving a press conference.

"I'm heartbroken to find out my son isn't mine biologically. It's even more devastating to me that after raising him as my own, protecting him from the life of celebrity, he's chosen to completely wipe me from his life. Sadly, he's even gone so far as to remove me from my own company. I'm not even allowed in the building."

Grey pauses the television on Alistair's fake sad expression.

"Is he fucking kidding me? He saved me? He ridiculed me. He left me for Ace to raise." The anger rising inside me happens so fast, my fists vibrate at my sides.

"He's the master of manipulation, Brax. He thinks this will force your hand. You better sit down. It gets worse."

"Worse?" Then I remember he'd paused on Madison holding the shotgun.

I drop like dead weight into the sofa, and he starts the broadcast again. Within seconds, Madison stands on her porch, glaring at the cameras.

"Ah, here's my son's fiancée now."

"You're a liar," she hisses. The camera visibly backs away from her, then zooms in for a close-up of her face.

She's beautiful in her determination.

Pops walks down the stairs, removes the microphone from the podium, a fucking podium, and throws it in the bushes.

"You didn't raise Braxton," Madison spits. "You took a bribe from Darren Wells to raise Braxton as your own because you were both too worried about perception to care about an innocent child."

Oh, shit.

"Is that what he told you?" Alistair chuckles, but for once, he appears uncomfortable.

"This is who you're going to listen to?" She's speaking directly to the cameras now. I have no idea how many are there, but I'm guessing a lot. "A man who created a phony documentary on student-athletes he thought would make it to the pro level? Did you know he lied and fabricated every piece of that story so he could follow pretty teenage girls around and harass them?"

"I followed no one, get your facts straight, little girl." Alistair doesn't have the microphone anymore, but there's no mistaking his words even if he isn't on camera.

"No, you just hired the reporters and paid them exorbitant amounts of money to harass me and fourteen others until we lost control and lashed out. That's the footage you used, not the truth of any single story." Alistair stands in front of the cameras, attempting to block her from view, but they move around him, and they're faster than he is. "And I'll tell you a little secret, you pompous jerk, my ex was never going pro. He barely made the team. I was the athlete. I was the star player, and you turned me into some kind of pinup girl who ruined careers. I ruined nothing. You did. My ex did. And you know what happened after we sued you?"

"Let's get back to the matter at hand." Alistair raises his voice, apparently trying to speak over Madison, but she raises her voice too, and it's her story they want to hear.

"She really does look good on camera," Grey says, causing me to scowl, but I can't tear my gaze away from the screen.

Has she ever looked stronger? Sexier? "She's beautiful."

"It was your father-in-law who came to look after us." She's no longer yelling to be heard. They must have moved a microphone closer to her. "He showed up here every other month for two years to make sure I was okay, and I'm pretty sure he did it with all of us."

"Oh, stop complaining. You roped in an entitled billionaire because of it, didn't you? What happened, did you trap him with a pregnancy?"

I shoot to my feet. "Oh, fuck no. No. No. No. Get the plane ready. We're heading back to Georgia right now. I'm going to kill that fucker."

"Shit." Something in Grey's tone has me looking back at the screen.

Madison has stepped closer to Alistair, aiming the toy gun at him that he obviously has no idea is fake.

"G—get her away from me. I told you something wasn't right with her."

"If I lose control, it's you who pushed me to it. Braxton merely reclaimed what was his, well, now his and Greyson's, I suppose. I don't know why Ace didn't toss you out sooner, but I promise you, Braxton will clean up the trash, and if you ever step foot on my property again, I will shoot you."

"She threatened me, did you hear her? She's threatening me on live television." Alistair's face is so red it shines brightly on the screen, and sweat drips down his forehead.

"Why did you do it? Why did you take the twenty million to raise Braxton as your own if you were only going to abuse and mistreat him?"

The camera spins to Alistair, but it's as though he isn't even aware of them anymore. He glares at Madison as if she's the only person in the world, and he looks like he might actually attack her.

He steps into her space. The cameramen are farther away now, but they zoom in on her so only the back of Alistair's head is visible. But the sound comes through as though they're each holding a microphone.

"I didn't abuse him, little girl." His voice is low and menacing. It's obvious he thinks his words will only reach Madison. "I let Ace take care of the mess his daughter created."

"Madison," someone shouts in the background. It sounds a lot like Cian.

"No, but you're the one who took the money. Why?"

"Why? Why?" The camera catches the spittle flying from

his lips. "Because Ace gave me a dying company and expected me to put my own money into it. He expected me to fail, and I refused to give him that satisfaction. But once I was a success, he couldn't take it away from me. That was the deal we made."

"Huh." Why is she waving that damn gun around? Even if it's not real, she must be terrifying everyone.

Cian enters the camera frame, takes one look at the shotgun, and howls with laughter, then takes a seat on the porch steps.

"It must cut so deep then." She smiles brightly, and I can almost feel the camera crews falling in love with her.

"What does? And will you please put that damn gun away before you hurt someone, little girl."

"He just can't help putting people down, can he?" Grey mutters in disgust.

"Funny, that. You keep calling me a little girl, but I'm the one who owns a thriving business, three of them, actually. I'm the one who's going to marry the man who will destroy you for everything you've done. To him, to me, to all the other innocent victims of your sick and twisted fake news."

"So, you are engaged?" someone shouts.

"When's the wedding?"

"How long have you known Braxton?"

"Fucking hell. I'll call the pilot now," Grey says, rushing from the room, his phone already held to his ear.

Madison ignores them all and speaks directly to Alistair. "I'm not the scared, innocent little girl you harassed all those years ago, and you'll never intimidate me again."

"You have no idea who you're messing with," Alistair shouts, crowding her against the railing with the barrel of the fake gun pressing into his chest. "You don't have the balls to pull the trigger."

He steps back when Cian approaches.

"That's where you're wrong." Madison pulls the trigger. It makes a loud popping noise, and Alistair falls to the ground, patting his chest. The instant he sees the little flag that says *POP!!!*, he scrambles to his feet.

"You don't think I have anything? You think I can't still ruin you?" He steps closer and holds up his phone, practically shoving it into her personal space, and whatever is on it drains all color from her face.

"Grey." I don't know if I shout it or whisper it. The blood rushing in my ears makes it impossible to gauge. I don't even blink as I watch her face for any sign of what the hell he's pulled now.

She takes the phone and backs up to the door. Cian glances down at the phone and quickly looks to the sky. I can tell by the way his lips are moving he's cursing the heavens.

Then Madison holds up the phone. Her hand trembles, but she doesn't let it stop her.

"This is who you get your information from? This is the kind of sleazeball you all work for? Someone who would encroach on a private moment between two loving, consenting adults." She waves the phone angrily at the cameras.

"You shouldn't have been having sex on a mountaintop in a public space," Alistair hisses. Lights flash wildly, and it must snap him out of whatever hate-filled spiral he was in because he instantly starts smoothing out his clothing and holding a placating hand out to the cameras.

"A public space that was rented legally with permits for a private event," Madison throws back. "You're all okay taking orders from someone who would record such an intimate, special moment and then weaponize it? You're all okay with revenge porn? Don't you have daughters? Sisters? Mothers? What if this were them? What if one day he decides to do this to you?"

"God damn it," Grey shouts from the doorway.

"Hey, I didn't sign up for revenge porn. I thought this was a story about the renegade billionaire," one cameraman says as another joins him. "I'm out. This is too messed up, even for me. I'm not getting sued for him."

"That's nonsense. I didn't record that," Alistair blusters, waving at the camera crews.

"No, I know you didn't." Madison once again raises her voice to be heard above all others. "I can tell by the shoes and the finger that keeps covering the lens that it's a wretched excuse for a human, otherwise known as my ex. The same one you paid to tell lies when I was nineteen. Tell me, Alistair, how much did you pay him for this?" She throws the phone on the ground and smashes it with her heel.

Over and over again, she uses all her weight to destroy the phone until Cian pulls her off.

"I didn't fight back last time, Alistair. I was young and too terrified to even leave my house, so I allowed my grandfather to be my proxy. But make no mistake. I'm not that little girl anymore. I will fight back with everything at my disposal if you come near me or my family again." She starts to turn, then stops. "And to make myself very fucking clear, Braxton is my family. Greyson and Sage are my family, so think very carefully before you come attacking us again."

"She cursed again." Grey sounds shocked and a little bit proud, and he isn't the only one.

The camera crews start shouting new questions about our relationship at her. She answers a few, then my phone rings, and I wonder how long the time-lapse was between what I just saw and real time.

"Madison?" I answer in a rush. "Are you okay?"

"Ah, yeah." She drags out both words as if they're a complete sentence. "But I think I just made a very big mistake."

"I saw, sweetheart. I saw, and you were magnificent. Where are you now?"

"But I told them all that we're getting married." Her voice trembles, and I regret ever leaving her alone.

"We are getting married."

"But we had a plan."

"And plans change. Where are you?"

"I'm at the inn. There's a lot of people outside. More than the last time I went through this."

"I'm so sorry. Grey and I are heading home. We'll figure out how to handle everything from the air."

"No." Her tone makes my stomach lurch. "I mean, yes, I want you home, but I'm okay. Don't come home for me. I can handle this, I promise. Please, just take care of whatever you have to do to shut down Montgomery Media for good. When you come home, I want it to be forever."

"Baby."

"I mean it, Braxton. I've already faced my monster, now it's time for you to do it as well. I have a support system here. They won't allow anything to happen to me, and I can take care of myself."

That reminds me about her security. "Where the hell was your security team?"

"Don't get mad," she says.

"Madison, I'm way beyond mad."

"Okay, well don't blame them then. I told them to go

help Blissy at the park because I wasn't going to leave the inn."

"Madison," I groan. "They're not carpenters, they're very highly trained personal security."

"And they made Blissy very happy today. Cian and Pops have everyone on the way over here to make a plan, and Savvy is picking up Sage to bring him home too. We'll be fine here. You do what you have to do there, then come home. Okay?"

No, that's not okay. I don't want to be away from her for even one more second, but I also know she's right.

"If one more thing happens, I'm coming home."

"Fair."

"Are you sure you're okay?" My heart is still heavy from seeing the fear on her face only moments ago.

"No."

I suck in a painful gasp of air that burns my lungs.

"But I will be. I'm shaken up, but I'm not down. I meant it when I said I'm ready to fight, Braxton. I've allowed my past to determine my present for too long now."

"You're incredible, sunshine. I love you so damn much."

"I love you too. So hurry up and shut down that gossip factory and get home."

"You don't have to ask me twice. I'll see you soon."

"Braxton?"

"Yeah, baby?"

"I love you."

My pulse evens out and the knot in my stomach unties. "I love you too."

She hangs up, and I get to work.

"It's going to cost us a shit ton of money," Grey says.

"But it will feel so good doing it." I smirk at him, and he chuckles.

"This is going to put a lot of people out of work," Carla, the head of HR at Omni-Reyes says. The mumbling in the background is probably Montgomery Media's HR and legal teams.

They're not happy about Carla taking over since Montgomery Media reverted to the Omni-Reyes umbrella, but I couldn't care less.

We've been on this conference call with them for over an hour.

"They're welcome to apply for other positions within Omni-Reyes," I say. "After a thorough vetting to ensure they're not tied to Alistair, they'll be given a fair shot."

"You want everything shut down. Effective immediately." I don't blame her for being shocked, but at least she's finally getting on board.

"Yes. Shut and lock the doors. Take down all websites and stop all publications with an order to be destroyed."

"You're going to do severance packages, but you'll also have to deal with all the subscription cancellations." I can hear Carla frantically typing and almost feel bad.

"Yes, legal, finance, and PR can handle that." I'm beginning to get a headache.

"I don't know how long it will take to shut down the networks," Grey says. He's also on his computer. I've always preferred to take my notes on paper.

"I heard that Thane Wilder once literally pulled the plug on his servers himself when others wouldn't do it. If the greatest technological mind of our time can do that, then so can we."

Grey chuckles but doesn't argue.

"What's your deadline for this?" Carla asks.

I really don't see the issue. Effective immediately means now. "By midnight tomorrow, at the latest." She doesn't say anything for a long moment. "Carla?"

"Yes, sir. I—heard you. But we have to go through the legal teams for both Omni-Reyes and Montgomery Media. That can't be done overnight."

I look to Grey who nods. Fuck, he agrees with her.

"Fine. Just do it as quickly as possible."

"Yes, sir." She sounds slightly relieved, and it pisses me off.

"Thank you," Grey adds. "We'll be available if you need anything."

With that, he ends the call.

"You're so much better at this shit than I am," I say. It's the truth too.

"Funny you should say that because I've been thinking about our future," he says, reclining in his desk chair.

"Is that so?"

A Cheshire-like smile slides across his face.

"How do you feel about an expansion—a new business venture that includes some people in Happiness, Georgia?"

I know exactly where he's going with this, so I hold up my pad of paper to show him my notes. "We'll be following the Reyes men before us—giving the amazing ladies in our lives the platform they need to show the world just how great they really are."

"In your life. Not mine."

I wonder how true his words are though. He may claim Savvy's the enemy, but where there's smoke, there's fire, and those two are more combustible that propane.

Studying him, I nod in agreement to keep the peace. "I like the way you think, brother."

We both stare at each other. I'd meant it in a yo-bro kind of way, but the deeper meaning hits us both now.

"Yeah, that's going to take some getting used to," he mutters.

"But it feels so right, Greyson Reyes. Brother to brother, we're going to shake up this entire industry, aren't we?"

"Feels that way." His tone is bored, but he can't contain his smile.

Laughing, I rub my hands together. "Let's get started then."

He chuckles, but it does feel right. We're on our way to happiness, which is exactly what Ace always wanted.

40

MADISON

"THERE'S AT LEAST A HUNDRED OF THEM," CLOVER SAYS, tugging her cardigan around herself so tightly the threads holding it together are pulled to their limits. "The media vans are parked up and down Main Street."

It's two hours before the Cozy Cup Festival is set to begin, but we've called an emergency meeting at town hall, and dozens of Happiness business owners are sitting on benches, awaiting direction.

"And they're all waiting to get into the festival?" I ask.

Clover, Blissy, Chief, and I are huddled together at the front of the room, attempting to keep this from becoming a disaster.

"Yes, they're lined up around the corner," Blissy blusters. "I had to fight my way through them just to get out of the Chug this morning."

"Okay. That's...not ideal." My mind is running through every possible scenario when Braxton pops into my mind. Not that he's ever been far from my thoughts, but it's his kindness and generosity that unravel an idea in my head. "I think I have a plan," I say, smiling so hard my cheeks ache.

"Well, ya better start telling the folks then. They're getting antsy," Chief grumbles. He's been muttering about security since I called him first thing this morning.

"Go get 'em, girl," Clover says with a little fist pump into the air. Did she spike her tea already? I wouldn't blame her if she did, but it's a little early and we have a long day. "No, I didn't add sambuca to my tea. Yet," she teases.

Some of the tension eases in my shoulders as I take the stairs onto the stage. The noise of the room fades away as people notice me.

"Ah, hey guys. So, first, I'm sorry Braxton and I misled you. And second, I'm sorry about this mess. We were trying to save you all from this happening again."

"Ain't your fault, missy. You just keep doing you," someone calls from the back of the room. It sounds like Old Man Cracken, but I must be mistaken.

"Thanks, I think. So there isn't anything we can do about them being in town. But we can make them pay for being here."

"What do you have in mind?" Moose asks from the third row. He's sitting right next to Pops, who's been prancing around all morning prouder than Pride Peak.

"I'm so glad you asked. Chief, you're good at spotting fake identification, right?"

"Yes, ma'am. And I keep a running log of everyone here in town all the way over to Hopevale." That sounds illegal, but I'm running with it.

"That's wonderful, Chief." My confidence begins to grow, and I feel ten feet tall. "Then my suggestion is to set Chief up at the entrance, and he can charge anyone from out of town—or at least the ones who look as though they don't belong here—meaning they're carrying a camera around their necks or on their shoulders—a $100 entrance fee. We can pool all the money made and reinvest it in next year's festival. We've been needing new platforms."

"The old outlets in the park need replacin' too," someone says.

"And the string lights."

I hold up my hand to stop the suggestions before they spin out of control.

"We'll pool the money and put it in the festival bank account. Then we can place a vote before next year and divvy the funds that way."

"We should charge them per cup too," Blissy says to a chorus of support.

"Since we don't normally charge a fee, we have to be very careful that we're not charging a local. So if you have any questions, it's best to ask them for their ID. What does everyone want to charge them?"

"They're going to be fightin' for your line, Mads." Pops is positively beaming. "So I say we charge those soul suckers twenty bucks a cup. If they don't like it, they can get out of the line."

Again, everyone nods their heads in agreement. I don't think this town has ever agreed this readily on anything the entire time I've lived here.

"Savvy," I call. She's standing in the back of the room because she's had a headache all day. "Do you think you can make some signage quickly for the entrance fee and maybe print some for each booth?"

"Thank God. Yes, I'll go do that now." She doesn't wait for any more direction before she hustles out of the room.

"Again, I'm truly sorry for all this mess. I never wanted to be this kind of burden on you again." My chin wobbles because I feel so dang guilty it makes my stomach hurt.

"Madison Ryan." My name is followed by a loud crack.

Old Man Cracken is at the back of the room and has silenced us all by slamming his wooden walking stick onto the hardwood floor.

"Now you hear me, child. This town was built around caring for our own folks, and you is one of ours, and you always will be. You've brought the happiness back to Happiness with your god-awful sunshiny smile and can-do attitude." If he scowls any harder, his furry eyebrows might touch his nose. "If you think for one second we're going to hold those big hairy dicks against you, you ain't been listening to your own advice."

My mouth drops open in shock while the crowd of neighbors chuckles in their seats.

"Now no more of this apologizing bullshit," he continues. "We've got a festival to get to, and not all of us are as spry as we used to be. And every one of you"—he points his walking stick around the room—"let's go bleed those beasts dry."

An unexpected roar of applause has him scoffing in disgust and stomping as fast as his old legs will take him right out of the building.

"Guess we're going to bleed some big hairy dicks dry." Clover laughs at my side.

"I need to bleach my eyeballs. I'm never going to get the image of old Mr. Cracken saying 'hairy dicks' out of my head."

Clover laughs, links arms with me, and leads me to what is sure to be a festival to remember.

"WE'VE MADE $7500 FROM THE ENTRANCE FEES ALONE," POPS

says, cutting my line and not caring who he pisses off. "You're doin' real good, Madi. I'm proud of you."

"Come on, Pops. Don't make me cry. They're still taking pictures, and the last thing I want to do is wake up to a picture of me ugly crying."

He reaches over the booth and pats my hand. "You could never be ugly, Madi, inside or out. You're a beauty." He leans closer. "How are the hairy dicks treating ya? You need a break?"

Paparazzi will forever be known as hairy dicks around here thanks to Old Man Cracken.

I soften my gaze for my grandfather—he's a little ball of menace and chaos, but so full of love he's bursting at the seams. I wouldn't be who I am without him.

"Nah, Pops. I'm good. In case you haven't noticed the two secret service-looking guys on either side of my booth, they're not letting anyone give me a hard time. Plus, I have the beefed-up Sage back here helping me make the drinks."

"Beefed up," Sage snorts. "I lifted two times—I wouldn't exactly call it beefed up." He chuckles but flashes a wicked smile too. He's not wearing his eyeliner today, and he's dressed head to toe in football swag he got from the team. He's as happy as I've ever seen him.

"Good. Good," Pops says, dragging me back to reality. "I'm goin' to sit with Blissy. She's all up in a tizzy over your Dirty Matcha thingamajig. People are asking her for it, and she ain't got the recipe."

"Aw, poor Blissy. Tell her I'll happily give her our recipe...after the festival."

"Good girl." Pops turns to the crowd of annoyed paparazzi who are surprisingly waiting patiently in line. "You give her any shit, and you're going to deal with me. Got it?"

As soon as he steps out of the way, another camera greets me. I take a deep breath and try not to look constipated as he clicks and clicks and clicks.

"Thanks, Madi. Can you tell me how you met Braxton Reyes?"

"He rolled into town looking for happiness, and he found me." It's my canned response for that question.

The next guy asks, "Will there be a prenup?"

"We haven't been engaged long. We have a lot to work out."

The guy after that is the one who throws me off my game.

"What do you think about Braxton firing everyone at Montgomery Media and taking a suspected $15 to $20 million loss." The guy is more smarmy than the others, and he returns to snapping pictures when he realizes he was the one to put me off balance.

Sage crouches down to get something from under the bar top I'm standing behind. "Remember," he whispers. "If that's true, twenty mil is like a trip to Disney for them. It doesn't hold the same value when you have more zeros behind your name than you can count."

He squeezes my ankle, stands, and returns to his drink station—he's such a great kid. As much as all those zeros make me uncomfortable, he's probably right, so I plaster that plastic smile back on my face.

"I'm sure whatever he did was for the betterment of the world. He and Grey have a vision for their company, and I think it's safe to say that anything or anyone that doesn't meet that vision will be cut loose."

The gross guy chuckles darkly. "Are you speaking for him now?"

"Why wouldn't she?" I jump up and down trying to see

over the heads of photographers because I know that voice. "She is my fiancée, after all."

Braxton's head finally appears, followed by the rest of him, and I'm so happy I nearly collapse right there.

Instead, I duck under the booth, almost knocking over our display, then run and jump into his arms.

"You're home," I say, peppering his handsome face with kisses.

The flash of cameras is blinding and never-ending as he holds me up by my thighs and walks us behind the booth.

"Give us five minutes, and we'll be back to answer all of your questions," he calls over his shoulder just before we disappear from view.

The men and women standing in that line are so greedy for photos, they don't make a peep.

"So that's how you do it?" I say, grinning against his lips.

"I tried to get here earlier. I was worried you'd be overwhelmed or at the very least require some PR coaching before handling those assholes. But once again, you surprise me, Miss Madison."

"Once I decided to use them just like they're using me, it wasn't so bad."

He laughs and gently guides me down his body to my feet.

"Is that why *The Matchmaker Manual* logo is all over the inn's booth?" His voice carries a hint of humor, but it's his eyes that undress me, making my pulse skyrocket.

"Mm-hmm. And I've already gotten 10,000 new subscribers, so it's worth answering a few questions over and over again." Nerves hit me, and I drop my gaze to the ground. "Are you mad that I used the inn to pimp my podcast?"

He uses one long finger to bring my chin up to face him.

"No, sunshine. I think it was brilliant. The inn and the podcast are both yours to do with as you please. And we have a business proposal for you, Savvy, and Clover." He shrugs. "If you're interested, anyway."

"Oh my gosh. Are you serious? What kind of proposal?" Butterflies attack my stomach, and I can't help bouncing a little on my toes.

"Braxton? Mr. Reyes?" the paparazzi shout, and he immediately envelops my hand in his.

"We'll explain it in more detail later, but essentially, we're thinking about starting a broadcast channel, and we're hoping to syndicate your shows while also having you consult on other programming. You'd have full control of your show."

"Mr. Reyes." Dang paparazzi.

"That's—I, that's incredible, Braxton."

"It was both of our ideas, but I'll be getting it off the ground. We decided to pool our resources from Omni-Reyes and his inheritance from the Wells fortune. He's going to run Omni-Reyes with me as a consultant—as long as Ace's will doesn't have any more surprises—and I'm going to run Sunshine Studios while expanding our Daily Deeds nonprofit."

"You get to be a helper." Pride fills my chest. I love this man.

"Yeah, I guess I do." He nods, and his eyes glow with emotion.

"Holy crap, Braxton. You guys figured all this out already?"

"We haven't slept much." He squeezes my hand. "But this makes us both happy. And the best part is, we're going to do it all from Happiness, Georgia. Well, I think Omni-Reyes will open headquarters in Hopevale—they have more industrial space, and from the looks of it, they need a boost in their economy. But we think it will bring people from all over to work and help all the surrounding towns too."

"Mr. Reyes, please." Those dang paparazzi are so stinking pushy.

"Ah, guys?" Sage pokes his head out the back of the booth. "I'm loving all this love, but if you don't get out here soon, things are going to get ugly."

"Coming," Braxton says. He hasn't let go of my hand since I attacked him.

"That's a lot of information to take in. I'm still kind of processing, so if it seems as if I'm not excited, that's why. It all sounds really, really good." I inhale a shuddering breath. "And I'm so happy that you're making Happiness your home."

"Sweetheart," he says, pulling me under his arm and walking us back to the booth. "Wherever you are is home to me. I came here searching for something as elusive as happiness, and I'm staying because I found it in you. Oh, before I forget." He reaches into his pocket. "We stopped at the house before coming here. I believe it's time to put this back on your finger."

He slips the ring he had made onto my ring finger, and I smile. It will always remind me of love and happiness.

I am his sunshine, and he is my happy place.

EPILOGUE I
BRAXTON

Two Months Later

"It's still sitting there?" I mumble to Greyson. Just like the last time we were in Mr. Coop's office together, we're the only ones on time.

But this time, Madison is with me.

"What the heck is that thing?" Her hands are in the air, as though she wants to touch it but doesn't dare.

"That was Ace's final F-U to Alistair. Excuse my language, Ace's words, not mine," Mr. Coop says, and I can tell how much he loved saying that out loud.

"What do you mean?" I ask.

"Well, it's in all your letters, but I can tell you now that he's—"

"In prison?" Grey says.

"Actually, he's in jail, awaiting trial."

Turning my head, I find my half-brother Archie in the doorway, dressed in jeans and a button-down.

It's odd, I don't think I've ever seen him in jeans before. Alistair insisted on suits whenever he left the house.

"Archie," I say mildly. Leaning into Madison's space, I take her hand and hold it in my lap.

I'm honestly not sure where any of the Montgomerys' heads are. Grey has been back in California for about six weeks, but Madison and I arrived this morning.

"Is it true?" Archie asks. His normally antagonistic tone is gone, and his head is bowed. I'm not calling him a changed man, but I'm starting to believe Grey's private investigator's report about how Archie has...shifted might be true.

"Is it true that your father took a bribe to take Braxton as a baby from my father? Or that he hired someone to set your barn on fire?" Grey asks, but he manages to keep his tone neutral. "Because both are true."

"Ah, hi." Anastasia enters the room with a gentle knock on the doorframe. She's back in her designer clothes, but there's at least an inch of dark roots showing in her dyed blond hair, and she's not even attempting to hide it.

Old Ana would wear a giant headband at the first millimeter of dark hair.

"Everything makes a lot more sense now," Archie says. When we all stare at him, he continues. "Why he hated you so much."

"It does." I agree.

Behind Ana, my mother enters, holding the hand of a small girl with sad eyes.

She lights up when she sees my half-sister and runs into the room to wrap herself around Ana's legs.

"This is Piper. Ah..." Ana fidgets with the sleeve of her blouse. "Her dad had to work, and she wanted to see where I grew up."

Someone let her take a child across state lines?

She runs a soothing hand down the little girl's hair, and when I glance up at Ana, she's completely focused on Piper.

"It's nice to meet you, Piper. It's my first time in California too," Madison says gently, and the little girl flashes a toothy grin and a shy wave.

My mother looks as she always has—put together, the perfect wife, except now she has dark shadows under her eyes. Did she even attempt to cover them up?

"Well, now that we're all here, should we get started?" Mr. Coop asks, offering everyone a chair.

Piper climbs into Ana's lap and cuddles into her. Surprisingly, Ana seems comfortable with it.

"As we all know, Alistair is in jail, awaiting trial, and was denied bail because he's a flight risk. He didn't meet any of Ace's stipulations, and therefore he is considered null and void for the remainder of these proceedings."

"Ana, I'm hungry," the little girl whispers.

Without missing a beat, Ana leans down into her oversized Louis Vuitton bag and retrieves a small plastic bowl filled with orange Goldfish crackers. Her attention never left Mr. Coop, as though she's done this a million times.

"Did you know?" I blurt at my mother. She doesn't ask for clarification—she knows what I'm asking. Did she know that Alistair essentially received payment for their silence and raising me.

She shakes her head with her gaze pointed at the floor. "Alistair convinced me to keep the pregnancy, even though you were conceived..." Her gaze draws up to the little girl in Ana's lap. "Even if you were conceived without an ounce of love or care. I thought..." Her chin wobbles, but she doesn't look at me. "The very best thing I could do for you was allow my father to raise you—he gave you the love I couldn't. I'm sorry."

Madison squeezes my hand. Can I really blame my mother for this?

"I'm grateful you allowed Ace to raise me." It's the best I can do, but it's enough for her shoulders to droop in what I assume is relief.

"This thing is really creepy," Archie says, pointing to the giant hourglass. "What does it mean?"

It's an obvious deflection to a lighter topic, but it's needed right now.

"Well, when Alistair created Montgomery Media, he sent Ace an hourglass inscribed with *I'm coming for the top.* He wanted everything Ace had built, but Ace knew Alistair would never have control of his empire. Ace decided twenty years ago that it would be Braxton and Grey to pick up the pieces when he was gone."

"His final f—udge you," I amend, remembering Piper.

"Yes. Now, each of you had a representative checking in on you while you were away," Mr. Coop says, steering us back to the matter at hand.

"What?" Ana sits up straighter.

"Yes. Anastasia, yours was James' sister-in-law, Maggie."

Ana looks down at the little girl in her lap. "I thought she just hated me because—because…it doesn't matter."

"Archie, yours was Clara's aunt. Amara, it sounds as though you had a rocky start with the program director, but you ended on good terms."

"She hated me," my mother mutters.

Madison picks at the elastic on her wrist. "Were they all related to the fifteen in some way?"

"They were," Mr. Coop confirms while gathering papers on his desk. "And I guess you know that your grandfather was keeping tabs on Braxton. Grey's monitor was me, and for what it's worth, Greyson, you fell into that role exactly as

Ace thought you would, with grace and courageous leader-ship." He turns back to Madison. "Ace understood why you all donated your settlement against Montgomery Media to anti-bullying campaigns, but he also wanted to ensure you were all taken care of, and I have instructions to check in with all of you again in a year."

Madison swipes an errant tear from her cheek. "He was a good man."

"He was," Grey says solemnly.

"And I'm happily surprised to announce that you all met the requirements that Ace laid out for you, so your trust funds will be reinstated. However, any further transfers into those accounts must be approved by both Braxton and myself. At the time of my passing, that duty will transfer to Grey."

"Are there any, ah, further stipulations? Do we have to live here or work for Omni-Reyes?" Ana asks, and Archie leans in for the answer.

"If you wish to work for Omni-Reyes, you will be awarded a position that fits your knowledge base, but it is not required, no."

"So if I wanted to go back to Montana, I could?"

"What?" My mother gasps. "You're—you're going back... to live?"

"I am," Ana says firmly. "We need some updated ameni-ties—I'm not totally giving up my lifestyle—but...I've found...love and purpose there with James and Piper."

"I think I've really messed up in Maine, but I would like to go back as well," Archie says. "I'd like to be able to work for Omni-Reyes in some capacity though, if possible. Maybe remotely? Turns out I'm not a very good farmhand."

I nod in acknowledgment. I'm not sure if now is a good time to spill our plans for the future of Omni-Reyes or not.

"And you, Amara? What are your plans?" Mr. Coop asks.

"I'm going to stay involved with the women's shelter, a lot of them actually, but from California. My strengths are not cleaning bathrooms. My strength is fundraising, and I can do a lot of good for those women."

"That sounds like Ace's plan worked then." Mr. Coop stands and hands out more envelopes. "Final ones, I promise, and no more stipulations. These are Ace's final goodbyes."

Mr. Coop offers me one, and I hesitate before I take it. His final goodbye. This makes it real. The sadness and pain hit as though they're brand new, then Madison lays her head on my shoulder, and I slowly open the letter.

Dear Braxton,

If you're getting this version of my letter, it means that my hunch was correct, and you and Grey are brothers. I'm sorry for not telling you myself. I was selfish. As Coop and I started making my final plans, I remembered that upon my passing, Montgomery Media would revert back to your control—Coop always was a sneaky one— thus opening the financials for the first time since Alistair took over.

I knew Grey would look into it as soon as he could, and I knew he'd find what I had suspected—a money trail leading to his father.

I also knew it would create havoc in the lives of everyone I love, and I didn't want that for my final days. As I said, I was selfish, and I'm sorry about that.

Grey peers over my shoulder at my letter with tears in his eyes.

When I glance around the room, I find everyone fighting

emotions they didn't show the last time we were here. Perhaps there's hope for them after all.

"There is also a turn of events I was not anticipating," Mr. Coop says, interrupting the silence. "It appears that Alistair has been embezzling money from Montgomery Media for the last five or six years. A disgruntled employee brought it to my attention yesterday."

He looks almost joyful, but I'm not sure I'm following.

"That means a forensic accounting has been initiated for everything Alistair has ever touched. Including the people he paid for information that may not be, shall we say, ethical."

"Harry," Madison says without a single ounce of emotion.

Mr. Coop nods. "Don't get me wrong, I think Grey's PI should keep looking for that Sam man and the paper trails between him and Harry, but this will certainly shine a light on the dark side of the media."

"That's..." I don't know what to say.

"You reap what you sow," Madison says.

"Th-thank you for this," Archie says, standing abruptly. "If you don't need me for anything else, I have a plane to catch."

"There are papers that I need you to sign," Mr. Coop says. "Then you're free to go. If you'd like to follow me to the conference room, I have them all laid out for each of you."

My siblings and mother walk out of the room. I'm still an afterthought in their lives, but the pain of their rejection no longer stings because I've found my own family, and I'll do everything in my power to keep them safe, happy, and loved.

EPILOGUE II
MADISON

Six Months Later

"If you guys don't hurry the fuck up, I'm going to be late," Grey growls from the bottom of the stairs.

It's his first full day back in almost five months, and the only thing he's unpacked since he bought the house from Moose is a desk. I wrangled everyone to at least get his bedroom set up.

"We're coming," Braxton shouts back. "We told you to go ahead. Weren't you supposed to be there hours ago anyway?" He walks out of the bathroom and meets me at the top of the stairs. Savvy and Clover slip out of a guest room, and we all head downstairs to the perpetually cranky new assistant football coach.

"Yes, I was. And that's why we didn't have to do this shit right now."

I place my hands on my hips and glare at him until he gets uncomfortable. It's my new favorite party trick.

"Fine, I told Coach B. I wouldn't be there until warm-ups

today anyway. I thought I was going to have an important call to take."

"More important than football?" Braxton asks, but I know he's just trying to wind Greyson up, so I elbow him in the gut.

"We got a hit on Sam," Grey mutters.

"A—a hit, like you killed him?" Clover backs away from the grumpy CEO.

"What?" Grey snaps his head up, shock registering in his expression. "No, I don't kill people, Clover. Jesus. What I mean is, my PI found him, and the police took him in." He turns his glare on me, but something shifts in his gaze as he stares. "Harry was with him. They were running another con together at a fifty-plus community in Arizona, but from what I can tell, all the money they stole is gone."

I'm too stunned to speak. Harry disappeared shortly after Alistair was arrested, almost as though he knew his time was coming to an end. But I wasn't expecting this.

"Whatever happens," Braxton says, tugging me into his side, "he did it to himself."

"I know. I just feel bad for his dad."

"Roger was the recipient of a new grant that will allow him to hire some help and not have to work as much," Grey says.

"Greyson," Braxton growls.

His best friend, his brother, simply gives him a two-finger salute and shrugs before walking toward the front door.

"You said you would tell me when you're handing out donations to locals." I'm so mad I cross my arms over my chest so he can't hold my hand.

"And I will," Braxton says. "This didn't come from me,

per se. Discreet Daily Deeds had a makeover, and the guy needed a break."

He leans into my space, shifts the hair off my neck, and whispers, "I'll make it up to you tonight. Over and over again."

His words cause a shiver to work down both arms.

"Let's go, people," Grey commands in his booming voice.

Savvy is the first to move toward the exit, but then she stops short and picks up something from the entryway table.

"W-what are you doing with this?" she asks Greyson. She's holding up some sort of manual.

When it flops back on her hand, I see the title: *Ray of Hope*. Georgia's premier surrogacy agency.

Oh, crap. I thought he gave up on this.

"I told you, I'm getting myself a baby." Somehow in the last ten seconds, Grey and Savvy have drifted so close that they'll touch if they breathe too hard.

"Why this one?" Savvy sounds pissed, and her tense body language shows it.

"Because I only want the best, Savvy. And the best is in that book." He takes a step back, and we all watch in stunned silence as she thrusts the manual into his chest and storms out the door.

"Well, that was weird," Braxton whispers. "Also, what the fuck? I thought we were over the whole *get a baby* thing."

"That's on you. You need to talk him into getting a dog or something."

Grey waves us out the door, and he might be the only resident in Happiness who actually locks the door behind him.

Braxton presses the button on the SUV he purchased for occasions like this. His truck is still my favorite though. We all pile in—Grey and Braxton in the front, and the three of us girls in the back.

"What time did Pops get to the game?" Clover asks, tugging her cardigan closer to her body. She's going to melt in this heat. It may be September, but it's unusually warm today.

"Braxton dropped him off at one," I say. "I'm sure he's driving everyone in the booth nuts already."

"They love him up there," Grey says without turning around. "He's kind of a legend."

"That's for sure." I can only imagine what kind of chaos Pops is creating.

Savvy sits beside me, biting her nails and attempting to kill Grey with eyeball lasers.

So today should be fun.

"Why does Coach B. let him strut around barking orders at everyone?" Savvy is definitely pouting in her seat next to me.

"Because he knows what he's talking about," Braxton answers through a handful of popcorn. "And rumor has it Coach B. is thinking about retiring in a couple of years. He's just been waiting for the right replacement to come along."

"And he thinks it's Grey?" Savvy's voice is pitched so high, I cover the ear she was shouting into.

"Here he comes." Pops' voice is three times louder than the other announcers, and Clover jolts, spilling peanuts everywhere. "That's my boy. Sage Reyes for the field goal attempt."

"Pops, you're not supposed to use the microphones," someone else says, though it's muffled as if he's wrestling the microphone from Pop's hands. The more I think about it, the more I know that's exactly what's happening.

Braxton squeezes my hand tightly. Sage is definitely in better shape than he was at this time last year, but he's still a lot skinnier than the men about to charge him.

"He hasn't missed yet," I remind him.

"No, but he got crushed last week."

"It was an illegal hit. Those don't happen every game."

On the field, Grey rolls his coin through his fingers. Even Savvy is back to biting her nails as we all watch on.

"If he makes this, it's game over," Clover says excitedly. "This would just really stick it to dumb Coach Carlson. He never should've left us last season."

"He won't miss," Braxton mutters.

Sage steps up to the ball, takes his long strides back and two to the side, holds up one hand, and goes for it. The ball sails through the air and hits dead center in between the goalposts just as time runs out.

His team rushes the field while we jump up and down. When I look up at Braxton, his eyes are misty—it's the look of pure, unfiltered love, and when he turns that same expression my way, I know I've found my forever.

BONUS SCENE
BRAXTON

"I understand why you wanted to get married during the Cozy Cup Festival, I do," Grey mutters as we walk through the park in our tuxedos. "But does it all have to be outside? I'm freezing my balls off over here."

"Fair point." Happiness hit a record low temperature today, and no one was prepared for it. "But when did you turn into such a fucking complainer?"

"Since Ray of Hope won't put me in touch with the surrogate I want," he grumbles. "Fuck." He most certainly didn't mean for that to slip out.

"Grey," I say, spinning on him with all the exasperation of an irritated dad. "I thought you were over this."

"No, I just stopped talking about it so everyone would leave me the fuck alone while I got the company moved to Georgia. Now I'm here and I've got plans."

"Jesus Christ."

"What's with the language?" Cian asks, strolling up beside us in his tuxedo as if he enjoys the ball-shriveling cold.

"Grey is still looking for a surrogate." My tone says exactly how I feel about it too.

"Whoa, okay. That's news. News that maybe we can put off until tomorrow?"

"Yes," Grey huffs.

"Fine, but this conversation isn't over."

"Like Madi's conversation about your payments to the inn isn't over?" He smirks, the asshole.

But it does lighten the mood. She's still pissed as hell that I wouldn't accept her refund for any of the days that Grey wasn't here.

"Man, she's taking that fight to the grave." Cian chuckles.

"Where's Elle and Keela?" I ask.

"They're over by one of the booths to keep the baby warm. They'll come over as soon as we're ready to start."

"Pops, I swear to God if we can't get that soot off your suit, Madi will lose her mind." Savvy hisses.

I spin to find them walking our way. Clover is brushing off Pops while he swats her hands away. Savvy is spitting mad with black stuff all over her face.

"What the hell happened?" I ask, rushing to their side, but Grey gets there first.

He lifts her arms one at a time, then spins her like a rag doll.

"What the hell are you doing? Let me go," she protests.

"Are you hurt?" he asks, inspecting every inch of her as if it's his right. But since neither of them will talk about the other, or even to each other most days, I have no idea what's going on.

"It's not me, you numbskull. Pops is the one who started a fire in the Chug booth."

"What?" Grey and I both reach for Pops and inspect him too.

"Your...jacket is smoking," Grey says. His face is turned down in confusion.

Clover swings a rag through the air, swiping at Pops' backside. "He set himself on fire doing something with a wood-burning tool in the booth."

Pops spins away from her. "I was makin' Madi a gift. If Savvy hadn't been barking about being late, I wouldn't have turned away from my piece of wood."

I silently rub my knuckles against my chest. "Are you okay? Is everyone okay?"

"Yeah," Pops mutters.

"We have five minutes before Moose is going to drop off Madi for your first look. We have to get him clean." Savvy doesn't generally panic, yet here she is, about to hyperventilate.

"Him? We need to clean you up too," Grey says, swiping his thumb across her cheek.

Her gasp fills the space like a whale out of water. Then she shakes her head and pushes his hand away.

"I'm not the one doing the first look. Pops has to walk Madi to her spot. He cannot do that covered in soot and smoke—it'll ruin her dress."

Grey holds up his hands in surrender. Also very unlike Grey. Maybe Pops is right and Grey is going through a midlife crisis about twenty years too early.

"Tell us what you want us to do," he says calmly.

Savvy is as flustered by his response as I am.

"Sav?" Clover says gently, and it snaps her out of her momentary brain freeze.

"Fine, here, hold this stuff so Clover and I can get him clean. There's a waterspout for dogs by that tree over there." She shoves everything from a hairbrush to her telephone into Grey's chest.

And the most shocking thing is, he takes it without complaint.

"Pops started a fire on our wedding day."

"It is on-brand for him," Grey says with a chuckle. "I guess just be thankful he didn't burn down the entire festival so the wedding's not ruined."

"Right. That is a bright side, especially coming from the king of darkness over there." Cian laughs, and it shakes his entire body.

"If my phone rings, you have to answer it," Savvy calls over her shoulder. "Moose said he'd call when he's on the corner. The code is 5212 if you need it."

Grey holds up her phone in agreement.

"All kidding aside, I'm really fecking happy I didn't have to kill ya, Braxton. We're happy to have ya...even if you come with this asshole." Cian laughs again, and the tension in my shoulders releases.

"Why am I an asshole again?" Grey mutters.

"Because you're still secretly trying to get a baby instead of putting yourself out there and finding a loving, stable relationship with some nice girl," Sage says, walking up behind Grey.

"You knew about that?" I ask, peering around Grey.

"Sorry, Unc. This one swore me to secrecy, but I totally would've spilled the beans if he went any farther with it."

"Sage," Grey and I sigh.

"What? I'm taking care of you both. No biggie." Sage isn't our little boy anymore, and there are times, like this, that I can understand Grey's desire to do it all over again.

"This might be him. Hold on," Grey says, pushing all Savvy's stuff into Cian's arms, then looks at her phone.

And continues to stare at the screen. One second turns into five, then ten. Is he really so cold that he's shivering over there? His hand holding the phone is vibrating. Maybe we should get him some gloves.

"Grey?"

The phone rings in his hand, and he answers it. "Got it. We'll get him ready." He pockets the phone, but his expression is murderous. "Moose is at the corner."

"Okay. Everyone into their places," Savvy shouts, which is completely unnecessary since we were already moving. "He's as good as he's going to get. Elle, come on."

She walks Pops to the edge of the park, then runs back to us. Grey steps forward to stop her, then takes the pocket square out of his jacket, grabs her by the chin, and spit shines her face clean.

"Stop it. That's disgusting," she hisses.

"Not the first time we've swapped spit, Firefly12."

Savvy's face goes from molten red to ashen gray in seconds flat. "H-how? What?"

He fishes her phone out of her pocket and holds it in the air. "Firefly12 had a message come through while I was holding your phone." I don't think Grey even moves his jaw as he speaks.

This could be a nightmare. Greyson's face says it all, so I step in to shut it down before it escalates. "What the hell is Firefly12, and do we really have to do this right now?" They both stare at me for five long seconds.

Then Grey stiffens, buttons his jacket, and takes a step back. "No. We don't have to do this. Ever."

"Grey—"

"Don't. Speak." His voice is lethal, but just as I'm about to ask *what the fuck?* Elle steps into line next to Clover as Moose pulls up in front of the park in the horse and carriage. Madison sits in the back like a snow queen.

She's the most beautiful person I've ever seen, and the noise, the chaos that surrounds us on the daily, fades away.

I hiccup when emotions overwhelm me, and Grey reaches out to squeeze my arm. "I'm happy for you, brother." He's not all hard edges and anger, he's like a completely different person from a moment ago. In this moment, he's my brother, standing by my side while I marry the love of my life, and I love him for it.

Pops offers Madison an arm, and when she takes it, she scrunches up her nose. When she stops halfway to us, I know she's interrogating him. But Pops is Pops, and his defiance shows when he tips his nose in the air and continues to walk.

"I love that old fool too," I say.

When Pops and Madison reach me, Savvy presses the remote she had hidden in her bouquet, and the shooting stars light up the park. We had to hire a crane to get the special lights high enough in the trees to pass for shooting stars, but the expression on her face makes it all worth it.

"What did you do?" she asks, her face alight with wonder.

"You once asked me to count shooting stars with you. And this is to show you that even when the sky doesn't cooperate and things are dark, I will always find a way to count them with you."

"Braxton." Her chin trembles, so I lean down and gently kiss her lips.

"Savvy might kill me if you cry," I whisper when I pull away.

"He's right," she says, but when I peer over at our friends, I don't find a dry eye in attendance.

"Okay, I've got what I need," the photographer announces. Shit, I'd forgotten he was floating around us this entire time. Scanning the area, I notice that most of the town has found their way to their seats.

Moose steps in front of us, his notebook in hand. "Are you ready?"

I never envisioned being married by a man named Moose, but then again, I never thought I'd wind up at a run-down inn in the middle of Georgia either.

They may have called me the renegade billionaire for much longer than I would've liked, but I'm done running—from life, from work, and from family.

Madison squeezes my hand. "We're ready." The happiness that surrounds her glows brighter than the moon.

"Love brought these two together," Moose begins, but all his remaining words float to the sky because when I look at Madison, nothing else matters—she is my small-town sweetheart, and she's become my whole world.

The ceremony goes by in a blur, and the reception is held in a tent much like the first one I constructed at Envy's Edge, just twenty times the size. Heat lamps surround the tables and sit in corners. Fairy lights dangle from the rafters.

And when our song plays, I know that Madison and I are a dance that will never end.

"They did it," someone yells, interrupting our first dance. "They did it!"

Everyone spins and turns until we find Old Man Cracken in the back of the room, holding up an iPad.

"Cracken, sit down before you ruin my grandbaby's big day." Pops puffs up as though he's about to start a fight, but Grey steps in to intervene.

And then it's Grey who's shouting. "They did do it. Madi, *The Matchmaker Manual* is the number one podcast on Apple right now. Clover's is fifth."

"Don't forget Savvy," Cracken pipes in. "She's number three. Our girls did it."

"Oh, we could never forget Savvy." Grey's voice is like chunks of rough gravel on Savvy's name.

"Ah, what's going on with them now?" Madison asks.

"I honestly don't know. But they're a worry for another day. Tonight is just about you and me."

"Forever," she whispers.

"And ever."

"Fire, fire!"

"Is that...Blissy?" Madison asks. Once again, we separate to look around our reception space. Sure enough, in the back is a small fire with Pops waving his suit jacket over it.

Grey is closer than I am, and he hurdles a chair to get there and extinguish the fire.

"Nothing to see here, folks. Just working on my gift for Madi is all," Pops says merrily.

"No more pyrography, Pops. Ever." Grey uses the tone we only ever used on Sage twice, but Pops gets it more like twice an hour.

"Oh my God." Madison laughs, then places her arms back on my shoulders, and we sway to the music. "He certainly keeps us on our toes."

Pops holds up a half-burnt wooden sign that says *Welcome Ho*.

"I guess after two small fires, we're left with *Welcome Ho* as our wedding gift." I feel lighter than I've felt in years. "You weren't kidding when you said trouble follows him everywhere he goes."

Her laughter is the balm to my soul.

"No, I wasn't." She bites her lip as she peers up at me. "Hopefully our son or daughter won't take after him."

"Right." I laugh. The smile freezes on my face when her expression shifts to nervousness.

We've talked about kids since the...scare. And we agreed it's something we both want to explore someday, but we never said when.

My heart races so fast it's actually hurting my chest. Wait, I need clarification before my heart gets involved again.

"Are you? Are we?"

Tears spill down over her cheeks. "Pregnant," she cries through a watery smile. "Savvy took me in this morning to be sure."

"We're pregnant." I'm stunned. Truly stunned.

"Are you...are you mad?"

My gaze focuses in an instant. "No, Madison. How could I be mad? This is—you're sure?"

She nods while tears continue to stain her face.

"I'm going to be a dad."

"Mm-hmm."

"Oh my God," I say much too loudly. "I'm going to be a dad."

My words echo in the tent just as Clover cuts the music for speeches.

Greyson raises his glass in one hand and a microphone in the other, and there's a strange expression on his face before he wipes it clear. "Well then, it looks like we're going to have a lot to celebrate this year. Cheers to the happy couple, and all the babies that will join us in the new year."

"All the babies?" Madison whispers.

"I am not going to be your surrogate," Savvy hisses. "Not now. Not ever."

"Say that a little louder. I don't think the microphone announced it to everyone yet." Grey's voice is droll, but the spark in his gaze tells me this coming year is going to be more than exciting—it's going to be a lot of new and strange beginnings.

Ace always said there was healing to be done in happiness, and I now realize what it all meant. My healing, Grey's and Sage's healing, will all come when we find our home. Only Ace knew our home was in a small town called Happiness, Georgia.

ACKNOWLEDGMENTS

My family: I wouldn't be here without them. Thank you for putting up with my chaotic mess of sticky notes and loving me when I forget your clothes in the washing machine overnight because I was working through a difficult character arc—it happens more than I'd like to admit.

My publishing family at TWSS: Thank you for your continued support and your patience with my three-year plans that change every year. I appreciate your guidance and friendship so much.

Team Avery: Thank you for being the solid foundation of all things Avery Maxwell. I'll never be able to be a one-woman show, and I appreciate you sticking with me through all my ups and downs.

My support system: Thank you for keeping me grounded, for telling me to get to work, for sending gifs and screenshots of smirking faces, and for always reminding me how much I'm loved. I appreciate you more than you'll ever know.

My author pals—mastermind edition: Thank you for making me feel like I have something to share, even when I show up in my PJs and can't remember what our homework was. The accountability you give me is what keeps me productive.

My readers: My dear readers! Thank you for continuing to show up for me book after book. None of this would be possible without you. From the Luvables in my reader group to the readers who respond to my newsletter week after week, I appreciate you. Your confidence in me as a person and as an author and your unwavering support is what keeps me going. Thank you for being the very best part of authoring.

Nathan Van Coops: Thank you for telling me to drop the mafia thread in this story (what was I thinking?) and for asking me "why" four million times until finally saying, "You're trying to do too much. Simplify it." Whenever you want to start that side hustle, I'll be your first client!

Jessica Snyder and her team at HEA Author Services: Thank you for always pushing me to be a better author. From coaching calls, middle-of-the-night DMs, mastermind meetings, and everything in between, thank you for pushing me, encouraging me, and supporting me in my effort to level up.

Kari March Designs: Kari, you bring my books to life in picture form, and you knock it out of the park every time. Thank you for being so easy to work with and for being the very best at what you do.

Wander Aguiar: Thank you for taking beautiful photos.

Griffin F: Thank you for perfecting that smirk!

ALSO BY AVERY MAXWELL

Standalone Romance:

Without A Hitch

Your Last First Kiss

Falling Into Forever

The Westbrooks Series:

Book 1 - Cross My Heart

Book 2 - The Beat of My Heart

Book 3 - Saving His Heart

Book 4 - Romancing His Heart

Book 5 - One Little Heartbreak - A Westbrook Novella

Book 6 - One Little Mistake

Book 7 - One Little Lie

Book 8 - One Little Kiss

Book 9 - One Little Secret

Single Dad Hotline Series:

Book 1 - Love Notes & Lifelines

Book 2 - Late Nights & Love Lines

Happiness Ever After Series:

Book 1 - The Renegade Billionaire